FUNTIME SUMMER 72

by Les Edwards

CHAPTER 1 - Interviews (March 1972)

["Funtime Su   itles]

The limousine surfed along Oxford Street like ɛ   ier
had been relentless throughout March 1972 ar   t
End this particular morning. A purple Rolls Roʲ
admiration but it glided by largely unnoticed wl   he
storm. Workers and visitors desperately huddled up against shop front windows ror snelter or
bravely continued, getting soaked through as they tried to hop over or wade through ever
widening tea-coloured puddles.

Even a car as smooth running as a Rolls Royce couldn't help but skid slightly as it came to a
halt in the Reserved Parking space outside a plush office block. A frumpy lady in a long
raincoat rushed out from the entrance door, armed with a large umbrella. She tried to avoid
slipping on the wet pavement and act professionally as she trotted up to the vehicle as fast
as she dared. Thankful that she hadn't made a fool of herself, she thrust open the umbrella
branded with the purple colours and logo of the *Funtime* organisation. At the same time, as if
in unison, the chauffeur opened the rear passenger door. Together, they guided their very
important passenger out of the car and directly underneath the umbrella thus avoiding
getting a single drop of rain on his Savile Row suit.

Biddy Rand surveyed the scene from her office window. She sighed as she watched her
secretary, Cynthia, whisk her boss, Sir Albert Burren, into the building. Biddy was resigned
to the fact that Sir Albert would be "borrowing" Cynthia for the whole day, in preparation for
the board meeting at the end of the day.

Sir Albert Burren – the founder and managing director of the *Funtime Holiday Group* – had
called tonight's board meeting a "Readiness Review". The term was officially coined by him
– but more likely to have been suggested by one of his advisors - in response to a rise in
customer complaints from the summer season of 1971. The aim of the "Readiness Review"
was to ensure all the *Funtime* holiday centres were ready to accommodate, feed and
entertain paying holidaymakers for the 1972 summer season from May to September.
Starting promptly at 5pm, the directors would one-by-one have to stand up in front of Sir
Albert and their fellow directors to explain how well they had performed against the targets
they'd been set at the beginning of the year.   It was no coincidence that the initials of this
meeting matched the initials of the limousine Sir Albert was chauffeured around in. His
vision, since the company's inception in 1966, was that *Funtime* holiday resorts would be
recognised as being a 'class above' all others. To back this up, Sir Albert insisted that all
Funtime staff refer to their resorts as holiday centres and the holidaymakers visiting them as
their 'guests'. He believed that this term differentiated the *Funtime* brand from other
companies that ran holiday camps in the UK and called their visitors "campers".

The dark menacing clouds somehow matched Biddy's mood this morning but she was hopeful that the clouds would dissipate and the light shine through before the end of the day, not just meteorologically, but professionally at a personal level. As the *Funtime* Holiday Group's Entertainment Director, her main responsibility was to manage the supply and development of entertainers and sports organisers working across all the sixteen *Funtime* Holiday centres located at seaside resorts around the UK. Their uniforms featured purple blazers with the *Funtime* logo emblazoned on the front pocket and were generally referred to as *Purplecoats*.

Back in January, Biddy had been given the statistics from each *holiday centre* listing the number of *Purplecoats* that had accepted their contracts for the upcoming summer season and, most crucially, the number of additional *Purplecoats* that needed to be hired. Cynthia had totted up the figures and worked out that, on average, Biddy would need to place at least seven new *Purplecoats* per week for the three months to the end of March to cover the shortfall and get contracts out to successful applicants before the season started.

Biddy placed an advert in UK entertainment magazines but by mid-February, the number of successful candidates signed up was way behind schedule. To help get back on track, she placed a simpler advert in city newspapers across the UK and invited a wider range of candidates to be interviewed. More crucially, she decided to forego the usual singing, dancing, acting auditions and sports questions. Instead, she simply went through basic questions with the candidates and took their answers at face value, making notes on the official candidate review forms. She believed herself to be a good judge of character and reasoned that any further training could take place "on the job" with the help of the resort's entertainment manager and experienced colleagues.

The face value strategy worked so well that Biddy steadily caught up with assignments and now she was tantalisingly close to completing her target. She only needed to place two more successful candidates in order to proudly announce the completion of her campaign at the "Readiness Review" meeting that very evening. Cynthia usually accompanied Biddy at these interviews as a note taker and sounding board for Biddy. She would also type up Biddy's comments on the candidate review forms and send them out to the entertainment manager at the resort successful candidates were allocated to. With Cynthia tied up for the day looking after Sir Albert, Biddy would have to manage the interview process on her own.

Biddy had just finished reading through the introduction letters and career details of the four candidates to be interviewed today when her phone started ringing. She picked up the receiver and the voice at the other end said 'Good morning, Ms Rand. Shirley on reception here. Sorry to disturb you but thought you should know that the two candidates scheduled for interviews at 2pm and 3pm have cancelled, however ...' Biddy interrupted Shirley mid-flow and bluntly asked 'Did they give a reason?' Shirley said 'They mentioned that they'd accepted roles in a musical called "Jesus Christ Superstar" that would premier later in the year'. Biddy had pinned her hopes on recruiting these two men as they had plenty of stage experience. Feeling let down, she remarked 'They're mad – West End shows come and go. "Godspell" has had a successful run but there's no guarantee that another musical based on Christian or any other religion will be a hit. Perhaps they'll regret their actions especially if they're playing the role of Judas!' Shirley wasn't sure if she was supposed to laugh so responded with 'Yes, well, the Finance Director heard that the afternoon candidates had cancelled so asked if he could have a private meeting with you at 2pm in his office – can I tell him you're okay with that?' To Biddy, it sounded like she was a naughty schoolgirl being summoned to the headmaster's office but she had to accept the invitation despite having a

FUNTIME SUMMER 72

by Les Edwards

Table of Contents

DEDICATION

This novel is dedicated to my wonderful wife Kath Kaveney for putting up with my endless ramblings, reviews and edits in putting this tome together over more years than I can guess at.

good idea what the meeting was about. She would no doubt have to justify recent expenses or face them being discussed at the board meeting.

Biddy swore under her breath. She had been so confident of successfully reaching her resourcing target that she'd already prepared the acetate for declaring this at the "Readiness Review" meeting. Now that the experienced actors had cancelled their interviews, her only hope was that this morning's two candidates would be good enough to be taken on.

The tea lady brought in hot Earl Grey tea, but, just as she went to place it on Biddy's desk, a blinding bolt of lightning lit the office and caused her to tip the whole cupful over the paperwork. The tea lady tried to mop up the mess but the official candidate review forms were unusable. Biddy was annoyed but could see that the tea lady was distraught so told her not to worry as she would simply make notes on an A4 writing pad instead.

Biddy's first *Purplecoat* candidate of the day was a 20-year-old called Callum Carmichael. As a first impression, Biddy thought that he was almost too well-groomed for an entertainer position. The conservative blue suit he wore would be more appropriate for the financial sector and his raven black hair was neatly cut and unfashionably short. Callum was a little nervous at first, but he was taking the interview very seriously and had a nurturing manner as he gently went through his relevant experience. He'd been working in both the publicity and entertainment industry around the London area as a DJ and event host. Biddy imagined that he would be very comfortable using a microphone while hosting family-oriented entertainment events as well as *Miss Funtime, Most Elegant Grandmother or Knobbly Knees* competitions. Another factor that pleased Biddy was that Callum had thoughtfully picked up a *Funtime* brochure from the reception area. This showed how prepared and keen he was to join the *Funtime* organisation.

Biddy told Callum she was very satisfied with the interview and would send him a job offer letter in the next few days. Callum thanked Biddy as she shook his hand before she let him out through the lobby. She quickly returned to the interview room, grabbed the A4 writing pad and scribbled her thoughts on Callum: "Mature for his age, entertainment hosting experience so should be good for family-oriented activities.' She then tore off the page and placed it with Callum's other details.

The next candidate was Lenny Eglin. He was a totally different character to Callum but not in a good way. His mousy brown curly hair was so long that it merged into his brown suit. Biddy thought he looked very much like one of those *peace and love hippies* she'd seen in the news since the late 1960's. During the interview, Lenny came across like a cockney market barrow boy. Without hesitation, he confidently assured Biddy that he could carry out each and every *Purplecoat* activity she put to him. As a kid, he'd sung at holiday camps that his parents had taken him to, in fact he confessed the host had found it difficult to get him off the stage once he'd started singing 'The Whole World in His Hands.' He also said he could pick out a tune on piano and guitar. Biddy had no time to check if this was simply bravado but Lenny was keen on playing different sports and looked trim and fit so at least he would be suitable for activities like hosting fitness classes, leading rambles and organising games like football, rounders and tennis. Despite some misgivings, reaching her target was uppermost in her mind so Biddy told Lenny she would consider him only on the proviso that he got his hair cut short. Lenny assured her he would do this if she took him on. Biddy promised to be in touch as she led him out of the interview room. As soon as he'd gone, she tore off another blank page and scribbled 'Keen candidate and confident Sports Organiser but a bit of a cocky "Jack the lad" that will need careful management'.

Biddy gathered together all the documentation from her two interviews. To finally complete her recruiting target, she just needed to drop off the files at her secretary's desk ready for them to be typed up and referred to when sending out job offer letters to the final two successful candidates. Her candidate comments would then be forwarded to the Entertainment Manager at the holiday centre they were assigned to.

Biddy glanced at her watch and cursed as she realised that she was late for her meeting with the Financial Director. In her haste, she inadvertently dropped all the candidate details on the floor. Quickly scooping everything up she stuffed them together with the other files but didn't realise she had inserted her candidate comments referring to Lenny being a "Jack the lad Sports Organiser" into Callum's file and her comments on Callum being a "Family-oriented entertainment host" into Lenny's file. This would have a profound impact on how they would be received when they arrived at the same holiday centre six weeks later.

CHAPTER 2 - **Preparations for the Summer season** (30th April)

[Playlist Track: "The Times They Are a-Changin'" - Bob Dylan]

The *Funtime Seaview* holiday centre was picturesquely situated on a hill overlooking the South Devon coast near Brixham. Jason Peters was having lunch in the dining room but was too busy to enjoy the view that the resort was named after. He had a lot on his plate, metaphorically speaking but definitely not physically. The start of the summer season was just a few weeks away and the kitchen was training new chefs in cooking basic meals. Sometimes ingredients were changed or forgotten so the plate in front of him was typically sparse.

Jason was literally a seasoned professional - he started at *Seaview* when it first opened in 1966, consecutively working two summer seasons as a *Purplecoat* entertainer then returning for four more as Entertainments Manager. He was rightfully proud to have repeatedly trained and managed *Purplecoat* entertainment teams to consistently and successfully carry out a host of activities. Thanks mostly to his drive, management and guidance, the *Seaview* holiday centre had gained a reputation as being one of the best run venues on the *Funtime* circuit for holidaymakers and a favourite for performers as well.

Summer holiday seasons in the UK generally began mid-May, however, *Funtime* entertainment managers needed to prepare for each season many weeks beforehand. The holiday season finished around the end of September so Jason would be at the holiday centre for at least six months of the year.

Outside of the season, holiday centre workers would have to seek alternative employment. Even if senior staff had negotiated a retainer from their employer, the figure would be unlikely to sustain them for more than a few months. Like most *Funtime* entertainers, Jason worked out of season as a singer and actor. He performed various theatrical supporting roles in pantomime, farce and more serious plays then filled in work gaps by singing in clubs and hotels. Although never becoming an international or even national star, he was nonetheless a great entertainer. Jason loved to hear the applause of an appreciative audience but managing the entertainment programme at the *Seaview* holiday centre gave him the most satisfaction. Here, he had created and nurtured an environment that allowed him to thrive by emphasising actions that would be criticised elsewhere as too camp. He chuckled to himself when he realised the irony that working at a camp allowed him to be just that - camp.

Unbeknownst to anyone in the *Funtime* organisation, Jason was a member of the UK Gay Liberation Front. With a gay buddy he had attended their first meeting in the basement of the London School of Economics in October 1970. He joined after hearing how the UK GLF would follow the US movement's lead in pushing for gay rights via revolutionary politics. He was desperate to take part in demonstrations and protest marches but realised he risked being recognised by *Funtime* management or holidaymakers watching news coverage on television or from photos in local/national newspapers. The News of The World (or 'News of the screws' as it was colloquially called) was the most popular gossip newspaper of the time and Jason could well imagine how one of their reporters could have broken a scare story with a headline such as 'Manager of family holiday camp flaunts his deviant sexuality.'

In the early 1970's, any scandal or complaint of a sexual nature, no matter how unfair or untrue it was, could have put anyone's position at Funtime untenable, especially someone in a senior position. To avoid this possibility, Jason wore a long purple scarf to cover most of his face while supporting GLF public facing activities. In his professional career, he always tried to keep his 'deviant sexuality' a secret by being nothing less than professional and sexually ambiguous in front of his colleagues and holidaymakers. Despite his attempts at subterfuge, some guessed or knew better but it had never become an issue.

Jason even masterminded a crafty development on the accommodation front. Funtime entertainment managers would regularly meet with their holiday centre's business manager to allocate spare on-site chalets to all the members of the Purplecoat team. In preparation for the 1970 season, Jason met with the Seaview centre's business manager - Eric Arden - and told him he'd found out that a house located just outside the centre's gates had become available. Jason suggested they use company funds to lease the house and make it suitable for all of the Purplecoat team to stay in. One of the benefits discussed was that it would provide a private and dedicated place for the Purplecoats to stay together as a team outside of the Seaview centre's working environment. Crucially, it would distance them physically from the holidaymakers, thus reducing the potential for extracurricular activities and overnight liaisons - there had been plenty of scandalous misdemeanours in the past that had been hushed up in one way or another and neither Jason nor Eric wanted the Seaview to gain a reputation as a veritable knocking shop.

Eric agreed to Jason's suggestion and the house was leased that very month. Jason redesigned the layout to create what became known as 'the purple flat.' Within its conversion, Jason managed to provide for himself a private unit on the first floor with a separate entry via metal stairs at the back of the building. This enabled his male 'friends' to visit him without being seen by colleagues, holidaymakers or reporters.

Jason carried three sets of documents into the empty ballroom and placed them onto different tables all within arm's reach. One set contained a draft sports and entertainment programme and schedule of activities. Another set contained the details of current and incoming *Purplecoats* and the third set was the room layout of the accommodation that the *Purplecoats* would live in. As Jason sat down, he was grateful that the ballroom was ghostly quiet. He recalled busy nights when the season was in full swing. This ballroom was packed with excited holidaymakers dancing, drinking and shouting to be heard over throbbing music or a cabaret act. Now, he needed the utmost peace and quiet to help him concentrate on the work at hand: Formalising plans for the 1972 summer season at the *Funtime Seaview* holiday centre.

The mission of *Funtime* Entertainments Managers was to ensure visiting holidaymakers had the time of their life. Jason looked at his workload and promised himself that the summer season of 1972 would be his best yet. To achieve this would require careful planning, astute management and a strong performance from his team in order to successfully deliver the schedule of activities he had set out.

When *Funtime* holidaymakers first arrived and checked in at Reception, along with their chalet keys they were given a specific number of the dining room table they would be eating at for the duration of their holiday. The table numbers also signified which of two 'planets' the holidaymakers were assigned to: Saturn or Neptune. Whenever they entered a competition, they would earn points for their planet, as well as receive a small cup or medal if they won. The competing planets had their own colour schemes: As Saturn is the Roman god of agriculture it had a green colour scheme. Neptune is the Roman god of the Sea so it had a blue coloured scheme. Holidaymakers could show support for their particular planet by waving pennants stamped with the logo or wearing matching colours on clothes they brought with them or bought in the resort shop. Belonging to and supporting a particular planet promoted competitive excitement and camaraderie.

Jason's sports and entertainment programme for the 1972 summer season was certainly comprehensive. It's schedule of activities filled up every day of the week to satisfy the fittest, most adventurous or fun-loving holidaymaker.

Beauty-related competitions included the Most Elegant Grandmother, Miss *Funtime* for over 16s, Mini Miss for younger girls and Man Of The Week. Jason's favourite competition to host was, unsurprisingly, Topsy Turvy. This was where men dressed as women and women dressed as men so Jason could give full vent to his flamboyant preferences.

Sports-related competitions included Football, Netball, Table Tennis, Snooker, Billiards, Darts, Mini Golf, 3-legged race and tug-of-war.

The 'Junior Club Programme' included swimming instruction, children's television, donkey rides, magic show and a trip to Paignton Zoo.

Other activities included putting, trampolining, swimming, rambling, keep fit, rounders, bingo, coach/boat trips, ballroom dancing, sing-along, wrestling and cabaret shows.

Alternative activities were on standby for switching to if any outdoor activities were rained off. These included cards and board games, indoor cricket/hockey/bowls, films, quizzes, beetle drive, race days and progressive table tennis - where you queue to hit the ball at one end of the table then follow the queue around the table to get another hit at the other end. The winners would be the remaining two players at the table after everyone else had been eliminated.

Household name suppliers were heavily marketed in the programme and Jason had to ensure his team constantly promoted the sponsors during the activities they were linked with, presumably to satisfy a key part of their business contracts with *Funtime*. A major shampoo supplier sponsored *Girl with The Most Beautiful Hair* while a well-known hosiery company sponsored the prizes for *Miss Lovely Legs*. Even the kids were targeted with marketing messages. The winners of the handwriting, drawing and colouring competitions were rewarded with branded pens and pencils while the winners of the *Jack and Jill bucket and spade sandcastle competition* were rewarded with prizes from a night-time hot drink supplier with the slogan 'Yummy, yummy!'

As well as finalising the activities schedule and publishing the programme, Jason had to prepare his team of entertainers and sport organisers. This included accommodating, training and integrating the incoming *rookies* into his *Purplecoat* team. He would rely heavily on help from his experienced *Purplecoat*s and he considered each one in turn:
1. Mike - his serious but reliable second in command
2. Dale - his fun-loving but ambitious Junior Club entertainment manager
3. Jeannette - his steady all-rounder
4. Bill - an ageing eccentric.

Mike was Jason's right-hand man - a burly 40-something who lacked star quality but was an excellent organiser with plenty of experience having worked as a *Funtime Purplecoat* for many years.

Dale, on the other hand, was the most accomplished entertainer within Jason's *Purplecoat* team. Dale came from a family of entertainers - his brother was a famous comedian and his cousin had his own band who played in another *Funtime* holiday centre. Dale could wow an audience delivering jokes or singing and playing the guitar. Unfortunately, but unsurprisingly given his family background, Dale had an ego the size of the universe and clearly expected to be Jason's number two. The trouble was, when push came to shove, Dale was too self-indulgent to be able to compete with Mike's practical and organisational skills.

Jeannette was a 6-foot-tall, 30-something blonde with a long jaw but a soft personality. She was as steady as a rock, reliable and flexible.

Although Bill appeared to be a kindly old-fashioned gentleman, underneath a softly spoken exterior hid a curmudgeonly pessimistic luddite who was past his prime and could no longer carry out the physical activities he once enjoyed. Bill was forced to switch to less energetic duties as a kiddie's uncle even though he was sick to the back of his remaining teeth with working amongst children!

CHAPTER 3 - Senior Purplecoats arrive (1st to 2nd May)

[Playlist Track: *"Yellow Brick Road" - Captain Beefheart*]

At noon on a bright and breezy Mayday, Mike was the first of Jason's experienced *Purplecoat* team to arrive at the purple flat. The taxi driver helped him carry his luggage to the door and looked disgusted when Mike paid the exact fare without any tip and insisted that he gave him a receipt. As pre-arranged with Jason, the front door had been left unlocked and the team's room keys had been hidden under the grill in the kitchen. By mid-afternoon, Mike had handed all the Senior *Purplecoat*s the keys to their allocated rooms. Mike and Bill had their own rooms at the back of the flat, Dale had an upstairs room next door to Jason's suite and Jeannette was in the triple-bedded room for the girls at the side of the flat. They soon settled in for a short rest before they all had to make their way up to the *Seaview* holiday centre for a reunion dinner with Jason.

Mike ensured they were all ready to set off promptly at 6pm by knocking on the ceiling for Dale and the wall for Bill. Jeannette came out of her bedroom door while Mike and Bill were in the hallway and Dale was waiting outside as they shut the front door behind them.

They took the all too familiar walk through the entrance gates and trudged up the steep hill towards the holiday centre. Bill was soon out of breath and said to Mike 'This bloody hill will be the death of me'. Dale strode on ahead with Jeannette. As they reached the summit, he looked back at his flagging colleagues and shouted sarcastically 'Come on, you old gits! You should have got yourselves fit for the new season'. He sniggered and glanced at Jeannette looking for support but she simply smiled and nodded submissively without comment.

Eventually, they all entered the reception area where Jason was waiting for them. He smiled and shook hands with them to welcome their return to the fold before they all went through to the dining room and sat in their usual places at the *Purplecoat* table ready for dinner. The 'old gits' ignored Dale's critical look as they asked the waitress for extra helpings.

One by one, they described the jobs they'd taken while away from the *Seaview*. As they did so, they couldn't help but exaggerate their role and embellish the importance of the work they did.

Jason started with 'I played theatrical roles in and around London and was offered a lucrative contract in a new show but turned it down to return to the centre'. Jason had indeed performed various supporting roles in pantomime, farce and more serious plays but only in provincial theatres, never in established west end theatres. Jason also carefully avoided any mention of his interest and participation in the development of the UK's Gay Liberation Front organisation.

Dale said 'Yeah, well I also continued in the entertainment business, singing and playing in an up-and-coming rock and roll band'. Dale was actually a roadie for his brother's pop band, driving a beat-up Ford Transit van around Essex to each of the band members' homes, carefully loading their instruments and speakers into the van, lugging them through the back doors of village halls and dingy clubs then setting them up on stage as specified by the players. He would have loved to join the band onstage, but never got an opportunity or invite.

Jeannette said 'I worked most of the off-season as a Personal Assistant to a top lawyer in the City of London. The company were very disappointed when I told them I was returning to the *Seaview* rather than continuing my career with them'. She had actually been working for an agency as a temporary clerical assistant at various offices, none of which had offered her permanent work.

Bill simply said 'I carried out a number of roles during the off-season but I don't want to go on about it like you buggers have'. He had actually signed on the dole as soon as he moved back in to his younger brother's flat in London. He managed to find excuses for attending any of the interviews that the employment office had set up for him.

Mike was the only one to tell the whole truth when he said 'I returned to my old job as a line inspector in a components factory. I trained up a university graduate to cover my role while I'm away'. He either didn't want to exaggerate his comparatively mundane role or didn't have the imagination or bravado to make up a better story.

As Jason left the table, he advised everyone to get a good night's sleep and an early breakfast next morning before a 9:30 meeting in the television room as he wanted their input and ideas to prepare for the upcoming summer season.

At 9am the next morning, Jason was sat in the dining room with his senior *Purplecoats*. The 'old gits' once again ignored Dale's critical look as they munched their way through their Full English Breakfast. Jason left the table early to set up for their 9:30 meeting. Mike looked at his watch once he'd emptied his plate. The time had moved on to 9:20 so he suggested they all make a move because Jason 'will want to crack on with the preparations for the summer season'. They all made their way to the television room - a long wooden shack at the back of the main ballroom. Jason had just finished rearranging the chairs into what looked like a magic circle. Once they'd all sat down, Jason played the role of the magician and handed out copies of his draft 1972 programme. Under his leadership, they painstakingly reviewed all of the activities on the schedule. Each *Purplecoat* offered or was coerced into agreeing which tasks they were happy to deliver alone or with a colleague's help. Mike put initials against tasks with confirmed allocations and made notes of activities that needed to change.

Jason and Dale had designed and developed an acrobatic show that they performed each week during the previous season with a *Purplecoat* called Linda. The act had been well received by the holidaymakers as it was quite daring, but it got increasingly dangerous when any or all of them got complacent and had an alcoholic drink or two prior to a performance. Up until their final show of the season they had somehow managed to avoid any mishaps. Just before this last performance, Dale had celebrated nearing the end of the season by downing a few extra drinks so he was well inebriated when they started going through the act. During a dramatic somersault routine that provided an exciting finale, they lost their grip on Linda. Fortunately for everyone involved, especially Linda, she managed to twist her body as she fell backwards from Dale's shoulders on to the stage floor, narrowly avoiding a serious accident. Linda knew Jason and Dale had unnecessarily and stupidly put her health at risk so, at the end of the 1971 season, she confirmed she wouldn't be returning. Jason now had a big decision to make for the 1972 season. Should he and Dale train Jeannette, their only experienced female *Purplecoat*, to go through the same moves, perhaps working out an easier routine? Bearing in mind that Jeannette was taller and heavier than Linda, Jason didn't want to risk an even more serious injury to any or all three of them so he decided to or scrap the act completely.

Taking the acrobatic show off the schedule left a gap in the programme but Jason came up with an idea on how they could fill it. The highlight of the entertainment programme was the weekly *Purplecoats Variety Show*. This show enabled all the team to showcase their talents to the holidaymakers. In previous seasons, the show included a short section that recreated an old-time music hall singalong sequence. For an authentic look, all the *Purplecoats* changed out of their normal evening attire and dressed up in Elizabethan-themed fancy dress. Unfortunately, the changing time between this section and the other parts of the show was limited to just a few minutes of filler music which often caused a problem. The dressing room was situated in the corner of the ballroom. It was handy for the steps up to the stage but had no private areas and limited space to allow all the team to quickly change clothes. Both male and female *Purplecoats* had got used to the entertainer's norm of undressing and changing clothes while squashed together in a cramped room but, when up against the clock, they invariably bumped into the walls or fell over each other in a state of dishevelment. It was a laugh for most of the team but a nightmare for Jason - he was in a state of panic that his team would not make it back onstage in the right clothes at the right time. It was obviously more important for the whole team to be dressed correctly than be ready on time so, if they were late for their cue, the band had to repeat their intro music over and over until they could see the *Purplecoats* emerge from the dressing room and run onto the stage. As much as they tried to cover up for delays and backstage mishaps Jason knew that it was amateurish by his exacting standards. To avoid a repeat of this fiasco, he came up with the idea of taking the old-time singalong sequence out of its slot in the *Purplecoats Variety Show* and creating a separate but more extensive song and dance music hall show for the 1972 *Funtime Seaview* entertainment programme.

Once all the experienced *Purplecoats* had chosen the activities they were happy to carry out, they looked at the activities that remained. Jason's expectation (and the rest of the team's hope) was that the incoming *Purplecoat rookies* would cover all of the remaining tasks, maybe after a little training or shadowing if necessary. Jason went through the personnel details that Biddy had sent him to see what the new employees had to offer and consider which of these activities could best suit each *rookie*.

The four new *Purplecoats* were Tricia, Jane, Lenny and Callum. Jason read aloud Biddy's candidate comments:
1. Tricia - 'Mature for her age Brummie who's boyfriend is a drummer in a band with a summer contract in Torquay so asked to be placed in any nearby holiday centre.'
2. Jane - 'Intelligent but shy girl so may need training to increase confidence and fulfil potential.'
3. Lenny - 'Mature for his age, entertainment hosting experience so should be good for family-oriented activities.'
4. Callum - 'Keen candidate and confident Sports Organiser but a bit of a cocky 'Jack the lad' that will need careful management.'

With Biddy's candidate comments in mind, the assembled group discussed the pros and cons of each *rookie*:
1. Tricia seemed ideal for working with the Kiddies but Jason would have to talk to her to see if she would be staying at the purple flat alone. If she wanted to stay elsewhere with her boyfriend, she would have to guarantee that she will be punctual each working day at the *Seaview* and cover all the tasks required of her.
2. For Jane - the team would need to see how much help she needed and review how she gets on with any roles given.

3. Lenny appeared to be ideal to host any family-oriented activities that needed to be covered.
4. Callum should be useful for sports activities but all present were concerned about Biddy's 'Jack the lad' comment. Dale, never backward in coming forward, vowed to put Callum in his place to test if he could be as professional as he needed to be.

Even though Jason was in charge of training all the team, the new *Purplecoats* would still need someone to confide in, especially if they were struggling to deliver the tasks given. Jason had considered asking Dale to mentor the new boys but, after his arrogant threat to put Callum in his place, Jason instead lined up the ever-reliable Mike. Jeannette agreed to mentor the new girls.

Having got as far as they could until the *rookies* arrive, Jason told his senior team they could have the rest of the day and following morning to themselves so long as they come back refreshed and ready to welcome the *rookies* the next afternoon. Dale sarcastically said 'I can't wait'.

CHAPTER 4 - Lenny and Callum's journeys (3rd May am)

[Playlist Track: "Light Flight" - Pentangle]

Early morning May 3rd 1972, Lenny Eglin was driven to his local railway station by his dad. As he looked at his reflection in the side mirror, he recalled Biddy's haircut ultimatum. Up until a few days ago, he was proud to let his 'freak flag fly' by letting his hair grow as long as it could. He had however promised Biddy that he would definitely get it cut if he was taken on so made a rare visit to the barbers and got it trimmed. When the barber raised a mirror and asked if it was short enough Lenny said it was fine even though it still touched his shoulders. He hoped his new employers would agree.

Lenny carried the battered suitcase his mum had given him into the station. With less protection around his neck, he felt the cold much more and, after climbing the stairs to reach the platform, a blast of cold wind whipped through. He shivered and dropped his suitcase down so that he could warm his hands in his pockets. He was relieved to have narrowly avoided a sludge of chewing gum that was stuck on the platform.

The first train going to London was late arriving and made slow progress along the route, stopping for what seemed like an age at every station. Nearly an hour passed before it screeched to a halt at Seven Sisters station. Lenny hurried down the staircases to the London Underground, took two connecting tube trains then hopped up the escalator to the main railway terminus of Paddington Station. It immediately brought back memories of his misspent youth more than a decade earlier when he used to sprint up these stairs in excitement and anticipation.

As a wayward child growing up in a rough area of North London, Lenny soon became a foolhardy adventurer. From a very young age, he pretended to carry out secret missions to private and forbidden places and play cheeky tricks. Red Routemaster buses passed by the end of his road and he would enjoy jumping on the open platform of the bus as it briefly slowed around the corner. He couldn't afford to pay a fare so hid from the conductor by crouching down under the Used Tickets bin and hanging on to the handrail. He'd then jump off when it reached his intended destination or earlier if he'd been seen. Buses were fun but trains were his favourite form of transport. He remembered the excitement he felt climbing over fences and bridges to walk along railway lines. There was a seemingly impenetrable brick wall near his school that was alongside a railway bridge. He used to jump up it until his small fingers just managed to grip the shelf firmly enough to enable him to swing his slight body up to perch on top of the wall. The first time he jumped down onto the private land on the other side, his momentum caused him to slide along the damp ground and down the railway embankment. His heart was jumping in this forbidden world, much like the hundreds of grasshoppers that fluttered around him. He trotted along the railway lines, pretending to be a train while looking to avoid railwaymen and signal boxes. As soon as he heard trains approaching, he would jump commando style into the embankment. Hidden in the undergrowth, he kept absolutely motionless as trains thundered by so that the drivers or guards wouldn't see him, even if he was being scratched by the thorny bushes or attacked by insects – that was all part of his secret mission. Even as young as eight years old, Lenny thought nothing of travelling around the capital and beyond on all forms of transport to see new sights and sounds.

Lenny loved jumping on empty trains while they were parked up at the capital's mainline terminal stations, walking through carriages and asking steam train drivers if he could climb aboard the engine. They always obliged and even let him throw some coal on the fire or toot the whistle. Perhaps the most famous steam engine he boarded was the Flying Scotsman, but his favourite was Mallard due to its glamorous and aerodynamic curved nose.

Lenny mostly visited Kings Cross station as it was the main terminus for his local line. St. Pancras station was handily located right next door and Euston station just down the road so he popped in to all three to see different types of trains arriving and departing. All three were workaday, business-like stations supporting industry and commerce but, when Lenny visited Paddington station, he felt an extra frisson of excitement. It seemed to be the starting point for fun-filled holidays to glamorous destinations aboard brighter carriages pulled by smaller, shinier and cuter steam engines.

Lenny always dreamed of travelling from Paddington station to a renowned holiday resort on the west coast and now that dream was coming true. He purchased his ticket at the office then stood in front of the large Departures Board. Eventually, the dials clickety-clickety-clicked to display the platform number and the few stopping points for the English Riviera express train: Reading, Exeter Saint David's, Newton Abbot and Paignton. Just seeing the names of places he'd never visited added a level of excitement. Lenny got his ticket punched at the gate then proceeded all of the way down the platform to look at the engine at the front of the train. He was disappointed to see his train would be pulled by a bland but powerful diesel engine rather than one of the brightly polished steam locomotives he used to admire.

Walking back down the platform at Paddington station Lenny at least appreciated finding and stepping into an authentic classic carriage for his journey to the English Riviera. Although a little faded and worn, the carriage still retained some of the old-fashioned glamour of the golden age of the railways. Lenny was the first passenger in the carriage so; after carefully placing his similarly worn suitcase onto the overhead rack, he sat by the window looking frontwards to get the best view. A few passengers joined him in his carriage then the express train drew away from Paddington station at the start of its long journey, jerking from side to side as it clattered over many points like dozens of metal drums banging out ka-ching ka-ching ka-ching sounds to different rhythms.

The train built up speed through the London suburbs and the pull-down window catches of the carriage creaked from the wear and tear of thousands of trips over many decades. The swaying, banging and creaking eventually merged into one rhythm that curiously helped Lenny relax and think about the near fatal accident that ultimately led to him taking this journey ….

Lenny was nearing the end of an engineering apprenticeship which, although comprehensive, was unexciting and the wages were low. His dad had recommended he take this option when he left school saying 'Get a trade - you can always fall back on it even if you choose something else years later'. It was a five-year apprenticeship and he was longing for his final year to pass by quickly. Unfortunately, Lenny hated everything about it - the cold touch of steel, the swarf digging into his skin, the strain of standing up all day and the smell of the oil that permeated his clothes. He preferred the relative excitement of the evening job he took on to supplement his meagre pay -

working for the London Evening Standard. Speed was of the essence and Lenny became proficient at counting newspapers into reams while being jostled around in the back of a minivan, then, as his vehicle screeched to a halt outside high street shops, he would jump out of the sliding passenger door and deliver their orders. He was a fast runner but many times he only just avoided getting hit by a vehicle, cyclist or pedestrian as he sprinted in front of and around them. After one particular shift mid-winter, Lenny was cycling home in the snow when a car forced him off the road as it brushed past him on the entrance to a narrow flyover. He crashed his bike into a cement post, but despite somersaulting over the handlebars, he somehow survived with bruises rather than broken bones or a broken neck. The bike, though scratched badly, was still rideable. He happened to have placed a spare copy of that evening's newspaper in the basket to read later but it had fallen out in the crash. The pages scattered along the road so he quickly gathered them up before they could blow away. As he flicked the grit-stained slush off the pages, he noticed a slightly smudged advert announcing job vacancies that immediately got his attention:

WANTED -   ENTERTAINERS AND SPORTS ORGANISERS
**For summer season work at the famous *Funtime holiday centres*
located around the UK
* Perform with some of the UK's Top Personalities
* Accommodation and meals provided
* Great Career Opportunities**

Lenny believed the sequence of events that led to him reading this advert was some form of destiny and resolved to apply for an interview for whatever role was available. He imagined himself living life to the full, while working at a holiday resort. There was no doubt that he enjoyed all types of sport and hoped that, with appropriate training, he would be able to do a bit of entertaining, whatever that included!

The next morning, Lenny sneaked into an empty office at the engineering company. He crouched under the desk in reach of the phone then pulled from his pocket the crumpled advert he had torn from the newspaper. He needed to ensure he couldn't be seen making an unauthorised call on the works telephone so kept his eyes and ears alert while calling the number shown. His heart skipped a beat when a posh sounding lady answered and immediately thanked him for his call. Lenny put his best voice on to explain that he was interested in the vacancy published in the newspaper. The posh lady put him through to an even posher sounding lady who again thanked him for his call. She explained that she would be asking a number of questions to see if he would be suitable for attending an audition in London. Despite the distractions from hiding in an out of bounds office, Lenny answered all of the questions positively but as quickly as he could manage without sounding too keen just in case someone saw him on the phone. An interview was booked for the following week at the *Funtime* head office near London's Oxford Street.

At the interview, the Group Entertainment Director - Biddy Rand - interrogated Lenny on his suitability for the role of Sports Organiser. He put on a confident swagger and was ultra positive in claiming he could do whatever she asked of him. It must have done the trick as he was offered the job. It was tough leaving his friends and colleagues behind, but they shared his excitement at the career change he was about to commence.

While Lenny's train was just starting its journey from London to Paignton, fellow *rookie* Callum was already more than a hundred miles ahead along the same line and almost half way to the same destination. Callum's family home was near to Paddington station so he had been able to take the first express train of the day.

Since leaving school, Callum had been steadily working 9 to 5 Monday to Friday in the dark room of a photographic printing company but, for the last two years, he earned extra money a few evenings a week entertaining party people at a number of pubs and clubs in central and south west London. He soon built up a solid reputation as a popular DJ and event host, supporting the new trend of dance and dine evenings. One night an old schoolfriend came up to have a chat that would start a chain of events that would change his life. Callum always selected the latest popular songs that would be good to dance to for his set. He also played songs requested by his audience if he had them with him. Unfortunately, he was often asked to play songs he didn't really like. On Valentines Night 1971 he had been constantly bombarded with requests for one particular hit song that he hated more than any other - "Bridge over Troubled Water" by the American folk duo Simon and Garfunkel. As always, he relented to the clamour and eventually spun it on the deck. As soon as the audience heard the first few bars, there would be a rush to grab a partner to make the most of the slow and epic song. Callum yawned and cursed under his breath as he watched the dancers cuddling up close as they glided romantically around the dancefloor. Suddenly, he heard someone shout 'Hey Callum!' He peered down from the stage and recognised Vince - an old schoolfriend – standing there with by far the prettiest girl on the dancefloor. Callum raised his thumbs and eyebrows as if to say 'How are you?' Vince returned with the same and shouted 'I'll pop back later' as he spun away to once again concentrate on his beau.

At the end of his set, Callum was packing away his records when Vince returned saying 'Hi Callum, how's things with you?' As they shook hands Callum said 'I'm doing okay thank you. Haven't seen you since before Christmas – what have you been up to?' Vince explained that he'd had a fantastic time as a support chef at a *Funtime* Holiday centre over the festive period. The work was hectic but, in his spare time, he'd had loads of fun with loads of girls, including the one he was with now. After going through more graphic detail than Callum would have liked, Vince said 'I must tell you, the DJ there was nowhere near as good as you are. Maybe you should get a job at a *Funtime* Holiday centre as a DJ or better still, a *Purplecoat*. 'What does a *Purplecoat* do?' 'A *Purplecoat* hosts fun activities, sports and competitions, basically doing whatever the customers want in order for them to have a great time!' This turned on a light bulb in Callum's brain and a new life beckoned. Callum reflected on his own love life or lack of it. He'd had some fun with girls he met at the gigs he worked at but they just turned out to be girl-friends - girls who became friends - rather than girlfriends in a romantic way. He longed for something more and life at a holiday centre seemed to guarantee plenty of opportunities.

The very next day, Callum popped into the nearest travel agent shop and picked up a *Funtime* Holiday brochure to see the type of activities that *Purplecoats* were involved in. He was excited by and confident of carrying out the entertainment events mentioned so long as he didn't have to do the sports-related ones. He assumed they'd allocate tasks to *Purplecoats* based on their background and interests and Biddy had confirmed this at the interview.

After his successful interview, Callum had been delighted and excited to show to his family Biddy's letter offering him work as a *Funtime Purplecoat*. Better still, the *Funtime* brochure he'd picked up suggested that the most picturesque option was the very resort he'd been assigned to - The *Seaview* Holiday centre in Brixham on the South Devon coast.

Callum had earned a decent living from his day and night jobs but it had taken up all of his time and energy. Worst of all, he had got bored with the repetition of working in the dark. Callum felt guilty when handing in his notice but was now looking forward to working more in the daylight and hosting more varied activities. He didn't realise the work would be much more varied than he could ever had expected…

The English Riviera express train made its first stop at Reading station, then it built up speed as it progressed into the countryside. Lenny looked out at the views then dozed off dreaming of being surrounded by lots of excited and scantily clad teenage girls. Suddenly, he was rudely awoken by a sudden 'Shopa' sound. He guessed it was from the vibration of the shaking carriage window as the train shot into a tunnel at full speed. This was followed by a whooshing 'Showa' sound as the train swept out of the tunnel into bright daylight once again.

More stations, bridges, farms, fields, cattle and hours flew by until the train slowed down to make its next stop at Exeter St Davids station. All of the other passengers in Lenny's compartment disembarked without a word, leaving him on his own for the remainder of the journey. He took the opportunity to unlace and slip off his brown shoes then stretch his socked feet on the bench seat opposite.

Minutes after leaving the suburbs of Exeter, the view from the carriage opened up to a glorious sunlit vista, the like of which Lenny had never seen before. The train appeared to be surfing on top of shimmering waves above azure blue water. Lenny jumped up from his prone position and pressed his face to the window to fully take in what he was seeing. He realised that the train was hurtling alongside a sandy beach overlooking a beautiful section of the English Channel. It was nothing like the muddy brown waters he'd been persuaded to splash around in on family holidays around the Thames Estuary. Here on the South Devon coast, the multi-coloured boats bobbed up and down on sparkling bright water which perfectly complemented and completed the riviera look. This was pure seaside bliss and Lenny couldn't wait to immerse himself into this glorious environment.

The train left the seashore too soon for Lenny's liking and continued alongside a river before a brief stop at Newton Abbot. It slowed to a crawl as it passed through the next station enabling Lenny to glimpse one of the signs bearing the name *Torquay*. Just before the Devon seaside came back into view Lenny was amazed to spot something he had only seen on his one foreign holiday - palm trees! In England! No wonder this area is called the English Riviera, he thought.

Lenny put his shoes back on and pulled his case down from the carriage rack ready to disembark at Paignton station. Lenny's journey was not yet complete, however. He had one more train journey to take but it would not be leaving for half an hour so he walked along Paignton's high street to see what was there, even though his case was starting to feel heavy. Summer was many weeks away but the town was already festooned with colourful banners. Even with this adornment, the streets were not as stylish as Lenny had expected for an English Riviera town and the amusement arcades were no better than those he'd played in as a kid visiting Southend.

Lenny recalled one particularly eventful day trip to Southend when he was just ten years old. He'd saved the pocket money his mum had given him by not paying for a train ticket, avoided detection by hiding in the toilet when a ticket inspector walked through the carriages then sneaked around a crowd of passengers disembarking at Southend station while the ticket collector was busy taking their tickets. Once on the promenade, he took a ride on the dodgems, treated himself to a small plate of cockles then made the mistake of playing the slot machines. He kept losing but was confident his luck would change. It didn't and when he concluded that he was wasting his money he checked what cash he had left in his pocket. He realised he might have gone too far and wondered if what he had left would get him home if he needed to pay the return fare. It was still too early to make his way home so he took his mind of his predicament by amusing himself reading the saucy postcards displayed on racks outside gift shops. He also pretended to play in the bingo halls by sliding the covers over the numbers on the machines without putting any money in the slot. It didn't take long for the owners to realise what he was up to and tell him to buzz off (or worse). When he finally ventured back to the railway station, he could see he wouldn't get past the ticket checker and he didn't have enough money for the return journey. His solution was to walk into Southend police station with a made-up sob story saying that he'd somehow lost his tickets. He expected the police to take pity on him and drive him all the way home in one of the flashy Jaguars he'd seen on television. Instead, they made a phone call to the nearest police station to his home and got a bobby to go round and ask his parents for the money needed. Hours later, they handed the same amount to him to get public transport home. When Lenny finally got back home his parents had believed the sob story he'd spun and praised him for doing the right thing. He felt a little guilty but the quote 'Don't let the truth get in the way of a good story' came to mind and if it was good enough for Mark Twain it was good enough for him.

CHAPTER 5 - *Rookie*s in Devon (3rd May midday)

[Playlist Track: *"We've Only Just Begun"* - The Carpenters]

While the experienced *Purplecoat*s were relaxing before their afternoon meeting, each of the *rookies* were at different points in their journey to the centre.

Tricia brushed her hair in front of the dressing table in the plush suite of a Torquay hotel. Her boyfriend, Geoff was the drummer in a pop covers band that had been signed up to perform most nights at the hotel for the duration of the summer season. He was talking to one of his band members from the bedside phone and laughing along to something said. The rest of the band were just about to leave Birmingham to arrive mid-afternoon and start rehearsals by the evening. Geoff had arranged to stay the previous night at the hotel with Tricia before she would be moving on to start her own summer season at the *Funtime* resort in Brixham. When they'd checked in, the hotel had kindly given them their bridal suite for the night. He would then switch to a standard twin room to share with another band member when the rest of the group arrived. Geoff had organised the sleeping arrangements for the season to suit himself – he'd checked the allocated twin rooms and chose the best room to share with the cleanest band member.

As Tricia packed her clothes into her case, she looked at the champagne bucket and vases placed around their suite. They had remained empty for all of the short time they had stayed there. Maybe Geoff would bring her back to this otherwise luxurious room under different circumstances one day. She imagined him tenderly carrying her over the threshold as a just married couple, their delight at seeing the vases beautifully resplendent and bursting with fragrant flowers and the bucket containing a bottle of the best champagne chilled on ice ready for them to toast each other. She sighed before being shocked back to reality as Geoff put the phone down and started talking about his band members teasing him about their 'night of passion.' Geoff had no idea Tricia had been in dreamland as he helped lock her case. They reluctantly said goodbye to the room and it hit home that they were just about to start new adventures working and sleeping on their own for the whole of the summer season. They had vowed to get together whenever they could but were secretly concerned that their relationship might suffer from being apart – Geoff based here in Torquay and Tricia around the bay in Brixham.

Geoff dropped his case alongside the drum kit that he'd stored behind the hotel's stage then carried Tricia's bags to his Bedford van – its bright yellow colour divided opinions but it certainly stood out amongst the more mundane colours in the car park. He opened his RAC map on the bonnet and tried to work out the route for the journey to Tricia's new job. The map was old and didn't show the *Funtime Seaview* holiday centre but Brixham was only 10 miles along the coastal road so he planned to get to the harbour then ask the way. He could then return to the hotel to meet up with his bandmates and start rehearsals for their season.

Callum's train arrived at Paignton on time at 11:55. He then had to change platform to catch the connecting train to Churston but that did not depart until 12:35 so, by the time Callum disembarked at Churston station, it was almost 1pm. He politely asked the station manager how he could get to the *Seaview* Holiday centre in Brixham and was directed to walk over the bridge above the station and continue back along the main road to the entrance of

Churston golf course. Here he'd see a bus stop for a number 12 bus to Brixham. From Brixham town centre he could walk or get a taxi up to the centre.

Whilst driving along the A379 out of Paignton, Geoff couldn't help admitting to Tricia that he was really looking forward to the band playing its first summer season residency. He went through the songs they would be playing but stopped short when he realised Tricia had dozed off. As the car passed Churston golf course she snored loudly and woke herself up. Geoff was so distracted that he almost hit a young man crossing the road carrying a suitcase.

Callum glared at the bright yellow Bedford van speeding away then sighed with relief that he had made it to the bus stop in one piece. He plonked his suitcase down on the pavement and leaned on a wall waiting for the number 12 bus. It was that period in Spring when the weather can change quickly and a sudden cold breeze from Torbay's waters blew in over the golf course and chilled Callum to the core. In any case, his ears would surely have been burning had he known what had been unfairly said about him by the *Purplecoat*s he would meet later that afternoon.

Geoff and Tricia couldn't see any road signs to the *Seaview* holiday centre when they reached Brixham Town Centre so they asked a pedestrian for directions. Many hills later, Geoff drove through the entrance to the *Seaview* and up the steepest hill leading up to the reception building. He parked outside the entrance and jumped out of the car to take Tricia's bag out of the boot. Tricia surveyed her new working environment and, although it seemed tidy and quaint, she felt the first pangs of nerves. She wasn't sure what type of tasks she would be given and wondered when she would be able to see Geoff once the summer season kicked in and how it would affect their relationship.

Geoff was thankful to have found the right place without too much difficulty and placed Tricia's bag against the reception counter. There didn't seem to be anybody around as the season was yet to begin so they took the opportunity to embrace and kiss each other until noticing a lanky blonde-haired youth looking at them. They unconsciously let go of each other and the youth came up and said in a strong west country accent 'Oim Alan, Be you nu *Purplecoat*s?' Tricia introduced herself and her boyfriend then gathered that Alan said he was the son of the *Seaview*'s Head Groundsman but helped out where he could. Tricia saw Alan as a jolly but slightly soppy teenager as he went on to say 'The *Purplecoat*s be avin a meet'n in thikky TV room so I'll taake 'ee 'n join 'em now'.

Geoff and Tricia exchanged reception phone numbers and promised to call or leave a message for each other whenever they could. To avoid further embarrassment with Alan close by, they briefly embraced and kissed each other politely rather than passionately as they said goodbye for who knew how long.

Tricia waved to Geoff as he drove off for the journey back up the coast to Torquay while Alan was placing her suitcase behind the counter. He then led her out and around the side of the ballroom to reach a long wooden shed that had a sign out front saying 'TV Room.' Before Alan could open the door, Jason came out to meet them having heard them approaching. Alan introduced Tricia and Jason briefly welcomed her then asked Alan to go back to reception to bring the remaining *Purplecoat*s in as soon as they arrive.

After ensuring they were out of earshot of Alan and the *Purplecoat*s inside the TV room, Jason told Tricia he wanted a quick but private chat with her. He explained that he had lined up accommodation for her at the flat that all the *Seaview Purplecoats* lived in throughout the season but he understood if she planned to stay with her boyfriend instead. His main concern was that, if she decided to arrange accommodation elsewhere, she ran the risk of not being able to be punctual and cover all the tasks required at the *Seaview* centre. Tricia put his mind at rest by confirming that she was happy to stay with the rest of the *Purplecoat* team at their shared accommodation. Her boyfriend would be sharing a twin room with another band member at the hotel his band were working at for the summer, so they would only see each other when they had some time off. This was a relief for Jason as he wanted all the team to bond together under the same roof and had allocated the only triple room at the purple flat to the three females in his team: Tricia, Jane and Jeannette.

Jason introduced Tricia to his assembled team - Mike, Dale, Bill and Jeannette - then explained to her that they had agreed what tasks they would be covering and were now going through the tasks that would have to be covered by the *rookies* as they were called by the experienced *Purplecoat*s. As she was the first of the *rookies* to arrive, she had the benefit of being able to have a say in the tasks she preferred or was most comfortable with.

Outside the entrance to Churston golf course, Callum almost had hypothermia by the time a number 12 bus stopped. The bus took a slow and bumpy journey to Brixham town centre, then jumped into the only vehicle waiting in the taxi rank and was driven up the steep hills to the *Seaview* holiday centre.

Callum carried his suitcase into the reception area and placed it down by the counter. There was nobody to greet him on the other side of the counter but, in the adjoining lounge, a lanky blonde-haired youth put his cup and saucer down, walked through and said "Or'rite maakeral? Be you anova one 'o the thikky *Purrplecoat*s?' Undaunted by what sounded like a foreign language, Callum got the gist of the question and nodded. Despite the language barrier, they introduced themselves then Alan said The *Purplecoat*s be avin a meet'n in thikky TV room so I'll taake 'ee 'n join 'em now'.

Alan placed Callum's suitcase next to Tricia's on the other side of the counter then led him back out and around the corner to the TV room. Jason opened the door and Alan started to introduce Callum but, before he could finish, Jason cut him short and told him he'd best get back to reception to wait for the final two *rookies*. As Alan walked away, Jason shouted 'Be sure to bring them over as soon as they arrive because we've got a lot to get through.' Alan mumbled an obscenity which Jason didn't hear as he was already pushing Callum into the TV room to introduce him to his assembled *Purplecoat* team: Mike, Dale, Bill and Jeannette, plus Tricia who had joined the meeting only 30 minutes earlier.

Callum had expected a friendly showbiz-type welcome like when royalty meets the stars lined up after a Royal Variety Performance. Instead, there were no pleasantries beyond a friendly smile from Tricia. Worse still, he sensed a slight hostility from the experienced *Purplecoat*s. He listened attentively while they all discussed and reviewed the activities schedule and progress so far on allocation of tasks. Tricia had just been assigned to carry out roles in the Junior programme and help on other child-oriented tasks. Otherwise, there appeared to be a ton of slots to be filled by the remaining *rookies*.

Jason, Mike and Dale all agreed that Callum could take on all the sports-related activities that remained. Callum was surprised at this suggestion as he had hoped to be given hosting or family-oriented tasks. He liked football and was willing to take guests on rambles, but was no athlete and had no experience or desire to manage the sports activities they mentioned such as refereeing football matches, umpiring tennis tournaments, organising rounders or taking fitness classes. Callum realised he was bound to be thrown in at the deep end as one of the *rookies*, so thought it best to just go with the flow and not question any decisions, at least not until he'd at least settled in with his new colleagues.

Lenny soon got bored shuffling up and down the streets of what he thought was a surprisingly scruffy Paignton while waiting for his connecting train to Churston. He was happy to return to the station early to take his final rail journey of the day, especially as he got to see the steam engine being coupled up to the carriages. The engine, named *Braveheart*, was gleaming green in the livery of the Great Western Railway. He stood for a while admiring it before boarding the train for the twenty-minute trip around the bay. It featured even more spectacular seaside views than Lenny had seen earlier that day, but, when he finally jumped off the train at Churston station he was once again disappointed. The location was as dull as the cloudy cold weather.

Only a handful of passengers disembarked from the train and Lenny noticed that only one other passenger was carrying a suitcase. She was a rather plump and dishevelled teenager with short black hair. Lenny thought she might at least know the area so went up to her and politely asked if she could help him. He explained that he was trying to get to the *Funtime Seaview* holiday centre in Brixham and his ego forced him to state that he was due to start work there as a *Purplecoat*. He expected her to be impressed at meeting a potential star of the future but, to his surprise, she said she was also going to the *Seaview* to also start work as a *Purplecoat*! Her name was Jane Perfect, which was quite ironic as she would have been better described as Jane Plain! Without any obvious redeeming features, she nonetheless had the intelligence and forethought to have found out the telephone number of the *Seaview* which she fished out from her handbag. She suggested they find a phone box so that she could call the *Seaview* to get directions or, better still, get a lift.

The building next to Churston station may once have been a thriving hotel and pub but it was now boarded up so Lenny and Jane looked elsewhere for a phone box. They walked along the main road toward Brixham until they reached a petrol station. Jane persuaded the owner to kindly allow her to use his office telephone. She dialled the *Seaview*'s number and, after a long wait, got an answer from a breathless man with a strong west country accent. Fortunately, Jane had learned a lot about the Devon dialect from a schoolfriend who had once lived in Plymouth. She was able to establish that the man at the other end of the line was called Alan and he would drive down and pick them both up to bring them in to the *Seaview* holiday centre.

After less than 10 minutes, a minibus screeched onto the petrol station forecourt. It had horizontal purple and white stripes along both sides of the bodywork and every other space was filled with adverts for *Funtime* and the *Seaview* holiday centre. It was clearly the right vehicle for them! Larger than life, a lanky blonde-haired youth jumped out and cheekily said to Jane and Lenny 'Oi grockel *Purplecoat*s, or'rite?.' Lenny didn't understand what he'd said but they all introduced themselves. Lenny shivered and Alan immediately said "Eesfay! Tiz propper bliddy naish cos of the ooley thikky blaw'n. There tiz, can't do nort about it. Don weery, Seaview's only over the way and oil draish up there n this yer vecall t' join t'others up yonder 'es zoon 'es uz kin'!

Lenny jumped onto the first bench seat in the minibus followed by Jane. Alan rev'd up the engine and jerked the "vecall" out of the forecourt toward their destination.

As Alan sped the minibus back through Brixham, Jane explained what Alan had said. It was something like "He's right! It's proper chilly because of the cold wind blowing. There it is, can't do anything about it. Don't worry, Seaview's only over the hill and I'll get you there quickly in this vehicle to join the others as soon as possible'! Lenny said to Jane 'Us two must be the only remaining Purplecoats still to arrive to complete the team. They must think we're important if Alan has gone to the trouble of picking us up so that we can "join t'others up yonder 'es zoon 'es uz kin'!"' He chuckled as he repeated the way Alan said the phrase, trying not to sound like a pirate in case it upset their driver. Alan overheard him but didn't take offence, saying 'Dawnt 'ee worry, Uz talk praaper Deb'm yer 'n grockles dawnt knaw wat us be yappin' bout.' Jane started to translate but Lenny said 'no need – I've guessed that one!'

After proceeding through the town centre, the "vecall" picked up speed despite climbing up and up and up the steepest of hills. Jane and Lenny held on as best they could while sliding around on the bench seats then suddenly flew up in the air like synchronised divers as the minibus bounced over speed bumps.   They passed through the entrance gates and up one more hill to reach a building with a sign saying '*Welcome to the Funtime Seaview holiday centre*'. Before Jane and Lenny could check out their new surroundings, Alan jumped out and told them he would drop their bags off in reception while they're in their 'mee-ing'. He hurriedly led them down the side of the reception building into the TV room to join up with the rest of the *Purplecoats*.

CHAPTER 6 - Allocation of duties (Wednesday 3rd May pm)

[Playlist Track: "Turn, turn, turn" - The Byrds]

Jason was grateful to have finally got all of his team together so that he could complete the task allocations and instil the standards he wanted them all to adhere to. He reinforced Sir Albert's decree that on no account should holidaymakers coming to *Funtime* holiday centres ever be called "campers" - this was a term used by their main rivals. To reflect the higher standards expected, staff must instead call visitors to *Funtime* centres as *guests* and treat them as such. Jason emphasised that the key aim for every *Purplecoat* is to do their best to ensure every visitor has a fabulous time while at the *Seaview* holiday centre so that they will remember their experiences for the rest of their lives and look forward to returning again and again.

Tricia's involvement in the Junior programme and other child-oriented tasks meant that she would be working alongside Bill under Dale's instruction. The other *rookie Purplecoats* would work under instruction from Jason and his second-in-command Mike.

After all the tasks had been allocated, Jason recommended that the *rookie Purplecoats* learn from and make the most of the tremendous skills and experience that his senior *Purplecoat* team have to help them settle in and develop their skills. He also suggested they regularly talk to their mentor to review how they were getting along, especially if they have any work or personal issues. Jeannette was assigned to mentor the new girls whilst Mike would mentor the new boys.

Regarding Health, Jason explained '*Funtime* Holiday Centres employ a full-time Senior Nurse and Nursing Assistant to provide confidential advice and support to holidaymakers and staff for health-related matters. The Senior Nurse at the *Seaview* is Beryl and her Nursing Assistant Hazel. One or both of them would be available or on call for First Aid and First Response to any accidents and emergencies.

The *rookies* were split into male and female groups. Jeannette took the *rookie* girls to the dressing room and Mike took the boys to one of the offices behind reception. Each group were shown a rack of *Purplecoat* uniforms. They tried on a number of sizes before picking two sets that fitted them best. The daywear was purple sports coats, to be worn over white sports tops, socks and plimsolls with beige slacks or white skirts/shorts, dependent on the weather. In the evening the purple coats would be worn with white shirts/blouses, purple or black ties or bow ties, purple or black skirts/trousers and black shoes. When Lenny heard this, he pointed out that he didn't have any black shoes, only brown shoes. Mike mumbled something derogatory under his breath while pulling out a £20 note from his wallet. He handed it to Lenny and ordered him to go into Brixham town centre after breakfast the next morning to purchase a pair of smart black shoes. He made it clear that this was just a short-term loan and Lenny would have to pay it back within a few months or whenever his contract ended, whichever came sooner. That last comment was intended to frighten Lenny into submission but it was water off a duck's back as far as Lenny was concerned, such was his blind confidence.

The *rookie* boys picked up their chosen uniforms and hung them over the reception counter just as Jeannette led the *rookie* girls in, carrying their own freshly selected uniforms.

Mike asked Jeannette to take all the uniforms down to the purple flat so that he could give the *rookies* a tour of the *Seaview* to help them find their bearings.

The *Seaview* was built in a unique position at the top of a hill with picturesque views down each of its four slopes which matched the four cardinal divisions of a compass: north, south, east, and west.

Mike's tour started from the buffet lounge which featured a wall-to-wall picture window that made the most of the wonderful vista. From the comfort of soft chairs and sofas, the holidaymakers could sip tea or coffee whilst looking out over the roofs of brightly coloured chalets to a huge green expanse that gently sloped down to a cliff top with azure blue sea beyond. Mike then took the *rookies* into the dining room and pointed to the tables where they would eat with the holidaymakers and hear announcements and reminders of activities available for the day.

The tour continued through the ballroom, disco room, then a few steps down to the lower level of the main building to see the snooker, table tennis and other indoor sports and play rooms. Outdoors there were plenty of benches to relax in the sun while overlooking trampoline, bowls and tennis courts. The path led up to a large open air swimming pool set on a plateau that again made the most of beautiful sea views. Mike swung the group round to the north field past the kid's playground and rounders court then finished the tour on the west field, where football matches and the donkey derby would take place in season. The donkeys grazed beneath this field, between the entrance road and a scruffy Victorian building. Mike pointed at the dilapidated building and advised all the *rookies* to keep well away from it as the kitchen staff were housed there and they could behave like wild animals even before they'd had a drink or three.

Jeannette had already reached the purple flat and placed the *rookie*'s chosen uniforms into their appropriate bedroom - a twin room for the *Purplecoat* boys and the triple room that she would share with the *Purplecoat* girls. She had already selected the largest single bed with the most comfortable mattress as her own. It also happened to be nearest the window so she could open it to cool herself on hot summer nights. She tidied up her corner while waiting for her room-mates to arrive.

After Mike's tour of the site, the *rookie Purplecoat*s picked up their bags from behind the reception counter and followed him down the hill to the purple flat. Mike opened the front door and, as each *rookie* entered the building, he gave them their own keys, warning them to keep them safe as it would be an expensive mistake if they were to lose them.

It didn't take long for Mike to show the *rookies* the kitchen and bathroom that they would all be sharing - both were small and basic but clean. Mike then opened the door of the bedroom next to the bathroom and told Callum and Lenny that they would be sleeping there.

Callum and Lenny walked into the twin room that was intended to be their private sanctuary for 20 odd weeks. The room was tiny with single beds that were pushed right up against each side wall so tightly that they would have to be pulled back out in order to lift or change the sheets and blankets. This action would be further hampered by the proximity of a large chest of drawers squeezed up against the bedheads at the back of the room. Above it, a curtainless window looked out on to a small unkempt garden and a metal staircase, presumably leading up to an entrance at the back of the flat. Callum and Lenny looked at each other with a sense of dread. They had only just met and privately thought that this room wouldn't be at all suitable for very different reasons: Callum was concerned he'd be sharing a bedroom with some sort of hippie freak. Lenny was wondering how he could begin, let alone achieve, his intention to persuade girls to join him in this single bed whilst an old-fashioned 'straight' like Callum was sleeping just a few feet away.

Mike directed the *rookie* girls to the bedroom opposite the bathroom. Tricia was the first to enter and was pleased to see it was spacious with three single beds and a large window looking out onto a side street. Jeannette was already there, laying on the bed under the window reading a book. She was clearly well settled in and delayed putting the book down and getting up as if to emphasise 'this bed is mine – keep off.' Tricia read the signals and placed her suitcase on the bed on the opposite side of the room nearest the door. This left Jane with the middle bed between the other girls. In Jane's mind, this was a familiar pattern since she'd arrived at the *Seaview*: being the last one to everything and having to make do with whatever was left. She was already getting fed up with it.

Later that evening, the *rookies* got together in the kitchen to privately discuss how they felt about their first day, starting with their first impressions of their senior colleagues. The *rookie* girls believed Jeannette would be a good mentor and guide as she seemed like a genuine and friendly person. The boys thought Mike would be more like a stern parent – serious and somewhat cold. Jason seemed very professional, Bill a harmless old eccentric and Dale a showman or show-off.

They checked that none of the seniors could her them by whispering more private matters. Mike had warned the boys to watch out for the practical jokes that Dale enjoyed playing. Jeannette had told the girls that, in addition to tending to ailments and injuries, the Senior Nurse also provided a sexual health service to guests and staff that included contraceptive advice and on-site pregnancy testing. Apparently, the environment at any holiday centre - of teenagers living away from home for the first time while working and playing in close proximity to colleagues and holidaymakers - raised the risk of uninhibited activities to its highest level.

The girls avoided further embarrassment by steering the conversation away from sex. They admitted they were excited but daunted by the comprehensive schedule of entertainment and sports activities listed in the programme that they would need to help deliver.

Tricia said she was delighted to be allocated child-minding tasks at the *Seaview*. She didn't explain that the main reason for her delight was that the role would provide a good foundation for her plan to start a family with Geoff within a few years. She longed to tell someone of her plan but had only just met her colleagues and didn't want anything to distract from her working relationships at the *Funtime* resort or her private relationship with Geoff, especially while he was fully occupied with his band in Torquay. She therefore decided to keep her plan to herself.

Callum and Lenny were also keeping their true feelings a secret. They were really unsure that the tasks they had been given would suit them. Callum seemed to have been given lots of sports roles that Lenny expected to get and Lenny was given lots of family-oriented hosting roles that Callum expected to get.

Jane believed that all of her rookie colleagues were being remarkably positive so she kept her own negative feelings to herself and joked that she was just there to fill any gaps.

The moon shone through the curtainless window into the bedroom where the rookie boys lay just a few feet from each other. Callum asked 'Are you still awake, Lenny?' 'Yeah, I can't sleep, I'm thinking about all these tasks we've got to master. It's like going back to school.' 'Did you enjoy school?' 'Not really.' 'Did you stay on at school?' 'No, my dad persuaded me to leave school at 15 to start an engineering apprenticeship. He said I could do whatever I wanted once I'd got a trade behind me, so, as soon as I completed my apprenticeship, I applied for this job and thankfully got it. How did you get on at school?' I started primary school on my fifth birthday. My mum took me to a building I had never been to before, handed me over to a woman I had never seen before, waved goodbye and left. I think I cried most of that day, then, on my second day I did something wrong and was put under the teacher's desk as punishment. I remember thinking, I don't like this very much. Things eventually got better and in later years I was given the star role in the school play. I was Prince Brian. I have no idea who he was but sang "Brian is a happy boy; his eyes are always filled with joy". I am still waiting for my Oscar! Secondary school was rough. I'm not really a fighter so spent my entire time talking my way out of trouble.' Lenny was starting to feel drowsy but kept the conversation going by asking 'How did you get on with sports lessons?' 'I remember doing cross country running and, at various points you were handed special tickets to prove you did them then had to hand them in at the end. The resident school bullies leapt on runners and took the tickets from them but I somehow managed to avoid them. In 1963, I went on a tv show called Junior Criss Cross Quiz. On the day it was going to be recorded a driver from the tv studio came to my class and said he had come to take me to be a contestant on the program. The teacher just let me go, with this man, no questions asked. That would never happen now! I left school when I was sixteen, and spent most of my working life in Photography. London in the swinging sixties was the best place and time to join the photographic world'. Callum heard Lenny snoring lightly so didn't know how much of his story he'd missed but felt more comfortable about him being there and was sure there would be plenty of other opportunities to get to know each other better.

[Playlist Track: *"I Wanna Say Hello"* - Sir Hubert Pimm & Ellen Sutton]

Around 5 am, Callum and Lenny were woken up by sounds that were unfamiliar to them: a colony of seagulls screeching outside the window of their bedroom. The gulls were so loud that they drowned out the sound of a larger number of cooing pigeons. It was Callum and Lenny's first morning in single beds alongside each other and it took them a while to realise where they were and take on board that this was the new norm. When it was time to rise, they took it in turn to use the bathroom. Undressing and dressing in front of each other felt awkward, even though they would have to do something similar every week in front of all the *Purplecoats*, male and female, for shows they would be performing together.

As Callum put on his daytime uniform, he noticed Lenny was putting on casual clothes. He broke the ice by reminding his room-mate that he needed to go into Brixham after breakfast to get black shoes. Lenny said 'Thanks for the reminder, Callum, but it's too bloody cold to walk around in shorts so I've decided to wear casual clothes while I go into town to get my shoes. I can put my uniform on when I come back here on the way back up the hill'.

The two room-mates set off for their walk up to the *Seaview* for breakfast. One dressed smartly in uniform, one looking out of place in relatively scruffy civvies as if he was a rebel refusing to conform. They got to their table before the other *Purplecoat*s had arrived and got started on their breakfast rather than wait.

One by one, the other *Purplecoat*s joined them and ordered their breakfast. Lenny didn't notice their dirty looks at the state of his clothes. He was too busy dragging the edge of a piece of toast along his plate to wipe up the remains of his egg, bacon and beans.

Just as Lenny popped the soggy bread into his mouth, Jason came over to the table and announced that he wanted all his team to assemble in the TV room immediately after breakfast to go through the song and dance routines he'd put together for an old-time music hall show. They would be performing this show in the ballroom every Monday night, starting the very next week so time was of the essence.

Suddenly, Jason noticed Lenny's clothes and pointedly asked him 'Why on earth are you not dressed in your uniform?' Lenny nearly choked as he tried to reply while still chewing his last mouthful of breakfast. Callum saw his plight and bailed him out by interjecting 'Lenny's got to go into town to buy black shoes'. Jason looked at Mike, who nodded that this was true before adding 'Yes, I've loaned Lenny £20 to purchase something suitable'. Jason grunted and said 'Fair enough but, once you've got your shoes, drop them off at the flat, change into your day uniform and get back up to the TV room to join up with the rest of us as soon as possible.' Lenny nodded submissively as he finally gulped down his half-chewed mouthful of dredges. Jason briefly closed his eyes and shook his head in a disapproving way as if to say 'god help us, we've got a rough batch of *rookies* to train this season'.

After breakfast, Lenny took the long walk down the hills into Brixham town centre armed with the £20 note that Mike had loaned him. When Lenny reached the main shopping street, he sought the help of a local who directed him to the only establishment that could be described as a shoe shop. Looking in the window he could see just two types of black shoes on display so went in and asked the assistant what ranges they had. Without any embarrassment or apology, the shop assistant confirmed 'The two styles shown in the window are the only ones we have available at present. The brogue style shoes are what I call *bank manager* shoes and the smooth leather shoes are *young executive* shoes. Each model sells for just £10 a pair – would you like to try them on?'. Lenny could never imagine himself as a bank manager so tried on the *young executive* shoes. They seemed comfortable enough so he declined the offer to try on the *bank manager* shoes and simply said 'I'll take these *young executive* shoes please'. The shop assistant said 'Oh, Goodo!' as he put the *young executive* shoes back in their box, put the box in a plain paper bag, snatched the £20 note from Lenny's hand and stuffed it into his clunking till, lifted out a crumpled £10 note and handed it to Lenny in change. Lenny was astute enough to realise he would need to give Mike proof of his purchase so asked for a receipt. The shop assistant seemed a little put out but quickly wrote one out and popped it in the bag before handing it to what was probably his only customer of the day.

Lenny carried his box of apparently fashionable shoes back up the hills to the purple flat. Now that he was walking uphill, rather than downhill, he realised these roads were the steepest he had ever walked along - you almost needed ropes to climb them.   Lenny got his breath back as he changed into his uniform, then took the final climb to the summit.

When Lenny walked into the *Seaview*'s TV room, his colleagues were busy learning their moves in different groups. Dale was helping Tricia finesse her tap-dancing number to the tune of *Anything Goes*, Jeannette was leading Jane through her dance moves while Jason was showing Callum the boy's moves. Callum was frantically trying but failing to learn the correct steps for the Al Jolson classic cake walk song 'Waiting for the Robert E. Lee.' Jason had gone through the routine many times but Callum was still struggling to copy the moves. Jason asked Lenny to have a go and he quickly matched the routine. Lenny didn't have any professional dance training but had a big advantage in learning these moves - from a very young age he had been taken to family parties around North London that could best be described as 'cockney knees ups.' At these events, Lenny's aunts and cousins would show him how to dance to plenty of old-time songs as well as the basic steps for classic ballroom dances like waltz, foxtrot and quickstep. He'd therefore got used to learning dance moves quickly.

Lenny's ease at picking up the moves for the old-time music hall made Callum feel even more inadequate but a breakthrough came when Jason came up with a new approach. He stood to one side of Callum and told Lenny to stand the other side. The three of them then went through the dance routines one step at a time like robots. To an onlooker it would have looked more like a yoga exercise than a dance class but this approach worked and they used it to train Callum to dance along to all the songs in the show: 'I Wanna Say Hello', 'On Mother Kelly's Doorstep', 'My Old Man said Follow the Van', 'Daisy, Daisy, Give Me Your Answer Do', 'The Old Bull and Bush' ending with 'Waiting for the Robert E. Lee.' The vocal part of the act was easier to learn and perform because Jason and Dale led the singing and the other *Purplecoat*s simply had to harmonize alongside them as backing singers.

In addition to the song and dance routines, Mike went through a 'comedy' sketch called 'Mother, I Die!' that they would be performing in the weekly *Purplecoat* show. The sketch attempted to depict an acting rehearsal for a murder scene in a film. Mike played the part of a serious director, Lenny a wayward dishevelled boy, Jane was his deadpan mother, Callum a doctor and Bill an undertaker. The scene started with the mother sitting down knitting. When the director shouts 'Action', the boy walks on to and around the stage carrying a stick of rock then his face contorts as if he's been poisoned. He dramatically throws his arms wide and screams out 'Mother, I die!' After staggering around the stage so all the audience can see him dying, he collapses onto the stage, still holding the rock horizontally alongside him. The doctor strides onto the stage looking grim. He places his stethoscope over the boy's heart and gravely nods his head from side to side to pronounce him dead. The undertaker then walks on and stretches a measuring tape horizontally across the prone boy in order to get the right size coffin. The audience applaud, thinking that's the end of the performance, but the director stops the applause to say that he didn't like the way it was performed. He asks the actors to play it again with more emotion. They go through the same routine, slowly overemphasising each action until the director loses patience and suggests they do the whole scene faster. This time, the mother knits frantically, the boy runs around the stage, screams 'Mother, I die!' then drops to the floor like a sack of potatoes. The doctor runs on to the stage and nods his head quickly over the prone boy who now has the stick of rock in a vertical position. The undertaker trots up, scratches his head when seeing the erect stick of rock then stretches his measuring tape vertically up it. The *rookies* didn't think the sketch was that amusing but Mike assured them that this sketch would go down well with the audience - at least that's what he thought!

Having tired out his team with all the rehearsals, Jason gave them the afternoon off. Callum and Lenny still felt embarrassed walking around in their uniform so changed back into casual clothes. Not knowing where else to go, they went back up to the *Seaview*'s buffet lounge. Callum went up to the counter and bought a pot of tea and biscuits for the two of them to share. Lenny wished he had gone up instead because he was fascinated by the girl filling the pots. Her long flowing auburn hair surrounded a beautiful cherubic face and her dazzling smile greeted every customer.

As Callum picked up his cup from the saucer, he started humming a classical tune while crooking a finger. Lenny laughed at him and said the tune sounded vaguely familiar but he couldn't remember where he'd heard it. Callum said 'I think it's called "Minuet"'. Lenny said 'Are you into classical music?' Callum didn't want to seem any less cool than he already felt so replied 'No. It's just that the tune was featured in a film I liked, called *The Ladykillers*'. Lenny hadn't heard of that either, let alone seen it so Callum gave a brief synopsis. 'It's a comedy crime film. Alec Guinness plays the leader of a gang who stay in a guest house while they plan a robbery nearby at Kings Cross station. The gang carry musical instruments and pretend to play them to fool the little old lady who owns the guest house. She eventually realises what they've been up to which leads to a surprise ending'. Lenny said 'It sounds like fun, especially as it's set at a station that I spent a lot of my childhood in'. Callum recalled seeing a cine film projector and screen in the TV room along with lots of 16 mm films. He vowed to check if *The Ladykillers* was in the collection so that they could watch it together.

Lenny was still ogling the cherubic girl when Callum noticed a tanned but thin young man with curly hair walking in with a ton of photographic equipment. The stranger carefully placed his camera on the table alongside them, giving Callum the opportunity to ask 'Excuse me, is that an Olympus M-1?' The man looked Callum squarely in the eye and half-jokingly bragged in a cockney accent 'No way pal – you're talking out your arse, ain' cha? Olympus cameras are for bleedin' amateurs - this is a top of the range Nikon, used by professionals like yours truly.' He wafted the camera teasingly in front of Callum's face as if it was a rare and precious jewel then placed it back on the table before introducing himself with a handshake: 'I'm Kenny Tucker - *Seaview*'s exclusive photographer. My assignment includes taking photos of holidaymakers and selling memories on a variety of merchandise'.

In an attempt at one-upmanship Lenny told Kenny that he and Callum were new *Purplecoats*. Kenny's eyes lit up when heard this and he assured them that they would be seeing a lot of each other throughout the season. This was because he would be snapping holidaymakers participating in events and activities hosted by the *Purplecoats* around the *Seaview* most days and some evenings. He described how he would be sending his used film to a local processing company to be developed overnight and returned the next morning to Gillian Evans - his shop assistant in their photographic shop. She would go through each batch and select the best ones to display on the wall for would be purchasers. Kenny said 'I'll sell anything to the campers … sorry, guests' - he intentionally emphasised the words and paused to mock the unwritten rule of *Funtime* holiday centres.

Now it was Callum's turn to show-off and he surprised both of his new colleagues when he went through his extensive knowledge of photographic techniques. He'd gained plenty of experience of Kenny's world as a film developer at a photographic printing company. Alone in a dark room, he'd processed films from many famous advertising campaigns. He confessed that he felt that he didn't get the money or credit that the quality of his work deserved and eventually got fed up of being left to look after the studio while all his colleagues went out on exciting assignments or jollies around the world. That was one of the main reasons he'd applied to be a *Purplecoat*.

Kenny warmed to his new colleagues and said 'You two fancy a drink tonight?' Lenny said 'I remember seeing a bar alongside the entrance to the ballroom but we were told it won't open until the bar staff have been fully trained'.   Kenny said 'You're right. The only bar licenced to sell alcoholic drink on-site is *Inn Paradise* but it's not due to open until next week. I'll take you to the nearest pub called *The Three Elms Inn*. It's the favourite watering hole for *Seaview* workers who want a drink and chat away from the resort. They can make the most of the pub's cheap booze and behave or misbehave exactly as they want without the prying eyes of their managers'. They agreed to give it a try.

As they left the buffet lounge, Lenny looked out for the cherubic girl but sighed as another girl had taken her place behind the counter – this one thin and relatively nondescript despite her frizzy hair and orange tinted Lennon-style round framed glasses. He said to the others 'I'll just ask the buffet girl about her colleague' but they continued walking and Callum said 'It's probably the end of her shift but you're bound to see her another day'. Kenny added 'You've got twenty weeks to find out about her.'

CHAPTER 8 - Three Elms Initiation (Thursday night 4th May)

[Playlist Track: *"Black Magic Woman" - Santana*]

Kenny met Callum and Lenny outside their flat and led them down many hills to what looked like a grubby locals pub. When the three of them walked in, it was devoid of customers apart from a tiny old lady perched on a high stool alongside the bar. Kenny said 'Hi Lucy' to her, which seemed to surprise and annoy her. She mumbled something incoherent into her tankard then cackled a crazy laugh before taking another swig of scrumpy.

Lenny dared to sneak a look at Lucy. Her unkempt grey hair, leathery skin, pained expression and deep wrinkles made her look like an ancient witch from an Arthurian legend. Lenny imagined that her swarthy facial features had been caused by squinting against the sun and being windswept by surf spray from countless trips and wild adventures with fishermen out on the water around the bay. Lucy delicately dropped a paper skin onto a bar mat, spread a thin line of tobacco leaves onto it then rolled and licked it tight before lighting up the cigarette. Lenny noticed that her lighter was etched with a skull and crossbones logo so, with a sense of unease, returned to the conversation of his new pals.

Kenny insisted that Callum and Lenny go through the initiation ceremony of anyone visiting the pub for the first time. This was to drink 'Lemon Top followed by Neat.' Seeing their puzzled faces, Kenny added: 'Lemon Top is local scrumpy topped with a dash of lemonade to reduce the harshness of the flavour. New visitors have to down a pint of this as quickly as possible, then drink the next pint neat. Scrumpy is available in three flavours - Sweet, Medium and Rough – so which flavour do you wanna go for?' Callum and Lenny guessed that the medium option would be the safest choice so Kenny ordered pints of Medium Lemon Top for all three of them. The barman suddenly ducked down behind the bar and reappeared with full glasses. Callum asked Kenny why the scrumpy barrels were hidden from view. Kenny explained that the *Three Elms* would only serve scrumpy to locals and *Funtime* staff. Holidaymakers - called Grockles hereabouts - would instead only be offered the more expensive but weaker brand name cider. They swiftly downed their Lemon Tops and Lenny got the next round of neat scrumpy using some of the money that Mike had loaned him to purchase his black shoes. Each pint only cost 4p so it was by far the cheapest way to get merry.

The pub started to fill and 'Lucy' certainly seemed to be part of the furniture. Everyone who walked in said a polite hello to her, at least until a half dozen noisy teenage lads bundled in. The shaggiest member of the gang strode up to the bar and brusquely ordered six pints of rough scrumpy. While the barman was carefully filling their glasses, another lad in the group shouted out to Tommy 'What's the delay Tommy, tell the barman to get a bloody move on as we're gasping here.' Tommy simply returned a sinister stare as if to assert that he was the leader of the gang and took no orders from anyone else. Another member of the gang quickly defused the situation by involving the complainer in a rowdy conversation regarding a waitress at the *Seaview*.

Kenny recognised the lads as *Seaview* kitchen porters that were likely to cause trouble wherever they went. He led Callum and Lenny to a table well away from the bar with the excuse that the three of them could hear themselves talk. Swiftly glugging their scrumpy drinks down helped loosen their tongues and they spoke freely about themselves and their new life at the *Seaview*. Kenny laughed as he pointed out that the initials of all their first names and surnames sounded like girl's names when spoken: The initials of Lenny Eglin - LE - sounded like Ellie, Callum Carmichael - CC - sounded like Sissy and his own name Kenny Tucker - KT - sounded like Katy. They decided to use their initials as nicknames when they spoke to each other.

The conversation moved on to the financial packages they were on. All three of them received the usual *Funtime* benefits including free accommodation and food but Kenny could only get his food in the self-service staff canteen. The *Purplecoat*s were waited on along with the guests in the dining room, so the choice and quality of their food was much better. Lenny and Callum's wage was just £10 per week whereas Kenny's agency paid him commission on merchandise sales. He therefore had a keen interest in selling as many items as he could.

Kenny explained that, in addition to date-stamped photos of various sizes, a variety of supplementary mementoes could be made up by cutting out and inserting photographic prints inside small gifts like keyrings or placing transparencies inside viewers that looked like mini-telescopes. All merchandise was branded with the *Funtime* logo to ensure the company was promoted when guests returned home and showed off their mementoes to friends and family.

Callum and Lenny admitted that they were still trying to get used to sleeping alongside each other in a twin room at the purple flat. They'd got over the initial embarrassment of dressing and undressing in front of each other and other personal matters but it still felt weird. Kenny said his experience of sharing was not only more embarrassing than he could have imagined but also led to a mystery that hadn't been resolved.

Callum and Lenny leaned forward so that they wouldn't miss any part of Kenny's story:
'The *Seaview* management had placed me in a chalet with one of the security guards called Roy. My first night in that chalet was a shock, even for someone as broad minded as me. I was fast asleep late into the night when the key turning in the lock awoke me. I heard a male and female voice so it was obvious that Roy had brought a girl back to the room with him. Her voice sounded familiar but in the dark, all I could see was the silhouette of a tall amazon-like woman. I couldn't make out who she was but making out would be an understatement for what Roy and his mystery girl did next. It became clear that she was as horny as he was and the two of them went at it for ages, changing position with hardly a rest. Despite the gasps and moans, I eventually managed to drift off to sleep. When I woke up the next morning, the other bed was empty and I wondered if I'd dreamt the whole thing. A few days passed by and I was getting more and more concerned that I hadn't seen Roy since that noisy night. I eventually decided to try and have a conversation with Baz'.

Callum and Lenny looked blank so Kenny laughed and said 'You've not met Baz yet? He's Roy's part-time security guard colleague and quite a character - his long black hair and drooping horseshoe moustache make him look like a mad eccentric Hells Angel. When Baz tries to act like a professional security guard it comes out like a comedy act, especially when he introduces himself, saying "Hey man, I'm the camp fuzz!" He's a laid-back dude despite doing two jobs at the *Seaview*. He plays the trumpet in *Seaview*'s resident dance band led by Tony Garner but also works the odd shift on security. The extra money he gets is probably paltry but I guess it makes him feel more important. Anyway, after Baz listened to my toned-down description of the events surrounding Roy, he casually placed his hand on my shoulder and said "Don't worry man. Roy probably moved in with this bird or found another pad to take his bird to." Despite being a bit of a joke, Baz was probably right about Roy finding "another pad to take his bird to"!'

The scrumpy drinks made the three new friends drowsy but Callum was especially tired from going through all the dance lessons that day. He was anxious to get back to his room and recharge his batteries for more rehearsals the following day. Meanwhile, Kenny could see Tommy was getting more aggressive up at the bar and was concerned that he might start a fight. As if to prove the point, one of Tommy's drinking partners laughed sarcastically when Tommy mentioned the names Nick and Judy. This seemed to hit a raw nerve with Tommy as he instantly reacted by lurching towards the perpetrator, roughly wrapping his arms around his neck then pulling him down to his knees and tightly gripping him in a headlock until he forced out an apology.

With Tommy fully occupied, Kenny thought it was an opportune moment to get up and leave the pub so said 'Come on CC, LE - let's leg it before it really kicks off.' Callum and Lenny dutifully followed Kenny out the door, making sure they didn't make eye contact with the unruly kitchen lads. They made it safely outside, just as a group of girls were arriving. Lenny courteously stepped back and held the door open for them. He immediately recognised the girls as the cherubic girl he'd seen serving in the buffet lounge and her colleague with frizzy hair and orange tinted Lennon-style round framed glasses.

The cherubic girl and Lenny looked each other up and down as they passed each other. Lenny continued to gawp as the girls went up to the bar and he was having second thoughts about leaving until he saw they were clearly friends with the unruly kitchen lads.

Lenny caught up with Callum and Kenny as they chatted on the way back up the hill toward the purple flat. Callum was questioning Kenny. 'Hey KT. I saw from the expression on your face that you sensed trouble back there even before it started.' His brief reply was 'Let's just say I've experienced more than my fair share of danger and try to keep away from it wherever I can.' Kenny dared not elaborate further as he was sworn to secrecy about his Security Service missions. Luckily, CC and LE were too tipsy to question him further and they eventually reached the purple flat. They thanked KT for introducing them to the pub and tried to reassure him that his room-mate would soon turn up. They said their goodnights then walked up the path to their flat.

Kenny carried on up the hill through the resort gates alone and in the dark. As he approached the security hut, he wondered if his missing roommate would jump out and say hello or maybe his colleague - Baz - would be there to give him an update. No chance of either as the hut was empty and unlit.

Walking past the hut made Kenny shiver as it reminded him of the work he had undertaken for the Foreign Office. He definitely couldn't tell his new friends that he'd carried out an intelligence mission taking photos and reporting on military movements during a major conflict in a far-flung place. He had been full of excitement when being sent on his first mission but didn't anticipate being an on-the-ground witness to a major power struggle where thousands of people had to choose which side they were on, collect their weapons then fight to kill opposition soldiers and their supporters, even those who had previously been their neighbours and friends. Kenny's initial feelings of bravado soon subsided when he found himself in the midst of the action, dodging bullets and stepping over dead bodies, some of whom were women and children who happened to be caught in the crossfire. He even had to break into an abandoned border security hut to forge his visa papers in order to get past the soldiers on the other side of the barriers and reach a safe haven. Miraculously, Kenny completed his mission without a scratch but returned a wiser man. The Foreign Office tried to persuade him to take on another mission but he simply picked up his pay and ended his contract. He was determined to look for a safer way to make a living and signed up to an agency that assigned photographers to *Funtime* holiday centres. With no preference for any particular *holiday centre*, they'd placed him here at the *Seaview* holiday centre.

The moon peeked through the clouds to just about illuminate the way for Kenny as he continued up the resort's entrance hill but it was eclipsed by trees in the densest section so as dark as a Ghost Train ride. He was still deep in thought reliving the horrors he'd seen when a sudden gust of wind blew through the trees and the branches were thrown together violently. The crackling sounds instantly gave Kenny flashbacks of the gunfire he'd encountered but he held his nerve to reach the top of the hill. He still hadn't seen another person, let alone security staff, as he walked past the reception block and down the other side of the hill along rows of chalets to reach the twin chalet that he'd been allocated. Once inside, he saw that Roy's bed was once again empty. Flopping into his own single bed, Kenny thought that he might struggle to drop off while wondering what could have happened to his room-mate but the scrumpy and assurances from Baz, CC and LE soon induced a good night's sleep.

CHAPTER 9 - Practice makes good enough (5th to 12th May)

[Playlist Track: *"Let's Dance"* – Chris Montez]

Jason gathered all of the *Purplecoat*s together every morning after breakfast for the rest of that week and most of the following week. He insisted they practice all the dances and routines until they could deliver them as sharply as possible in time the first live performances when the season started the following Saturday. Lenny secretly gave Callum extra dance tuition in the empty disco room next to the ballroom so that he would be more confident at rehearsals and actual performances.

Despite or perhaps because of their different personalities and attitudes, Lenny and Callum confided in each other and started bonding as friends, rather than colleagues who happened to be sharing a bedroom. Their friendship included calling each other by the initials that Kenny had joked about that first night in The Three Elms pub. At the end of each day, they lay in their beds side-by-side and reviewed how their day had gone or discussed how they were feeling about the tasks allocated to them. Callum said 'Thanks LE for your patience in giving me extra dance tuition'. Lenny replied 'You're welcome CC. Fanks for coming to my aid when Jason had a go at me about not wearing my uniform on the morning I bought my shoes'. Lenny went on to describe his experience at the shop with the only choice being bank manager or young executive shoes. They had to stop themselves laughing too loud in case they disturbed any of the other residents at the purple flat.

The next night, Lenny admitted being disappointed that he hadn't been lined up to do the sports-related activities. Callum was equally surprised as he had hoped to be given the hosting and family-oriented tasks that Lenny had been allocated. They assumed that it was some sort of test to see how they got on when being thrown in the deep end with an unfamiliar task. They agreed to simply accept what they were asked to do without question but help each other as best they could.

Callum whispered so as not to be heard 'LE, how are getting along with our senior *Purplecoats*?' Lenny quietly replied 'I think I'm getting along okay CC, my only issue is with Bill. He keeps telling me to get my hair cut and calls me "poodle" in front of people'. Callum said 'You're lucky LE. That's nothing compared to what Dale said to me on the day I arrived at the *Seaview*.' 'What happened?' 'Well, he pulled me to one side and snarled in my ear "Watch out pal, you might be a Jack the Lad where you come from but I'm the stud around here and I don't think you've got the looks or intelligence to topple my crown!" I wasn't sure if he was joking but I was shocked - I didn't think I was a Jack the Lad and certainly wasn't planning to tread on anyone's toes or other body parts, especially Dale's!' Callum and Lenny agreed to try to keep a safe distance from Dale to avoid the risk of any more abuse or upset.

A few days before the season was about to start, Jason handed out copies of the *Funtime Seaview Weekly Program and Activities Schedule* to his team. Callum and Lenny sat down at a quiet table in the ballroom to read through it. Callum was the first to see both their names listed in the section titled: *Your Purplecoat Team* and smiled as he exclaimed 'LE, we're famous!'

Callum and Lenny visited *Inn Paradise* on the first evening it opened, just a few nights before the first wave of holidaymakers were due to arrive. The walls surrounding its long counter were daubed with colourful murals of palm trees and coconuts in an attempt to emphasise the intent when it was so named. It could hardly be described as paradise but it was handily located alongside the ballroom. Once the season started, the only non-holidaymakers officially allowed to frequent this bar were visiting entertainers, *Purplecoats*, *Funtime* managers and their guests. Prior to this, the bar was unrestricted so *Funtime* employees could spend time in it to relax and get to know each other.

Dale was drinking and holding court at the front end of the bar, surrounded by a bevy of girls and hangers on. He didn't notice Callum and Lenny sneak by him and walk up to the far end of the bar. Callum scraped together enough change for two pints of bitter which they sipped slowly to make the drinks last longer.

As Callum and Lenny surveyed the scene, two teenage girls smiled and walked up to them holding full champagne classes. Lenny smiled and said aloud 'Looks like we have a couple of royal princesses here!' One of them replied in a cute Scottish accent 'Thank you knaves but you don't have to bow - it's only Babycham'.

Ruby and Mary introduced themselves and seemed keen on telling their stories and sharing the gossip. They explained that the *Funtime* organisation used recruitment agencies to acquire the 100's of catering and kitchen staff needed across their holiday centres. In their case, an agency in Edinburgh assigned them to the *Seaview* holiday centre as dining room waitresses, even though it was located more than 500 miles from their family homes in Fife. They'd spent the whole of the previous day travelling down from the North East of Scotland to the South West of England on various trains and buses. Along the way, they had to ensure they got receipts for every stage of their journey so that they could get reimbursed by Jill Tully - the holiday centre's receptionist. Their trip down from the Firth of Forth to the English Riviera was the first time they had ever been south of the border but they seemed worldly in other ways.

Ruby said she'd heard that the *Seaview*'s Senior Nurse put any waitress asking about sexual matters straight on the pill 'just in case.' This included 17-year-old twins from Ireland that had already earned a reputation for making the most of their new found freedom.

Callum felt a little embarrassed at the way the conversation was going so tried to steer away from it by mentioning their night at the *Three Elms Inn*. He described their scrumpy drinking initiation and the gang of kitchen lads getting aggressive at the bar. Mary warned him, and Lenny, to avoid all of the kitchen lads and don't get into any arguments with them as they generally hate *Purplecoats*. Callum was amazed and curious so asked why this was the case. Mary reeled off many reasons: *Purplecoats* were served the best quality food in the main dining room with the holidaymakers while kitchen lads were squashed together in a cramped staff canteen fighting over junk food or leftovers from the main dining room. *Purplecoats* gadded about in smart uniforms with smug smiles. Kitchen lads could not get the smell of food and cleaning fluids off their clothes. *Purplecoats* seemed to have the pick of the staff as well as holidaymakers for any relationships. Kitchen lads were left with their rejects. Ruby's grin broadened as she added that being able to say you've 'Pulled a *Purplecoat*' was a big thing for holidaymakers and waitresses to brag about with their friends. Mary added 'Prepare to be very busy boys - hope you've got the stamina to keep it up for the whole season'. While Callum and Lenny were taking this news in, both girls giggled, clinked their glasses against the boy's glasses and said with a wink 'Cheers!'

The girls swiftly emptied their glasses and waved them in front of Lenny. He accepted them and said 'Same again?' While Lenny stood at the bar waiting to be served, he totted up the change left over from Mike's shoe loan. When the barman arrived, he asked him how much the round would be before confirming his order. He was relieved the girls were only drinking Babycham rather than real champagne as he only just had enough to pay for the round. He recalled Mike's insistence that it was a short-term loan that had to be paid back 'within a few months or whenever his contract ends, whichever comes sooner'. He hoped he would stay around long enough to test the girl's exciting claims and his own stamina.

Callum helped Lenny carry the drinks back from the bar and handed the Babychams to Ruby and Mary. Soon enough, two more waitresses joined them, introducing themselves as Jackie and Pauline. Callum was immediately attracted to the new girls, but in different ways. Jackie was a sweet 'girl next door' beauty with long wavy blond hair whereas Pauline had straight auburn hair, a dazzling smile and the figure of a catwalk model. While Callum was engaged in conversation with the other girls, Ruby turned to Lenny and asked where his digs were. Lenny said he and Callum shared a room at the purple flat right down the hill and just outside the *Seaview*'s entrance gates. Ruby whispered something in Mary's ear then turned back to Lenny and said 'Would you like me to show you around the chalet I share with Mary?' As soon as Lenny replied with 'Sounds interesting' she grabbed his hand and pulled him away from Callum and the other girls without another word. Ruby led Lenny through the *Inn Paradise* crowd, out past reception, and along a few paths to reach a long terrace of chalets.

Ruby opened her door and flicked a bedside light on while Lenny looked around the chalet. A tour wouldn't be necessary because the chalet was the size of a small studio flat: a bare rectangular room with just enough space for a single bed along and against the back wall and a single bed along and against the front window. Beside the head of each bed was a small table and at the opposite end of the room was a chest of drawers alongside an arched opening leading to a sink unit with a separate toilet cubicle. Ruby picked up a cylindrical tool off the bed and placed it on the sideboard. Lenny half-jokingly asked if it was some sort of sex toy. She giggled and said 'Don't be silly - they're curling tongs for my hair!' Just the way Ruby had said 'curling tongs' with her cute Scottish accent was enough to turn Lenny on but she then said 'Help me pull the curtains together so that we can be a bit more private.' Lenny was full of anticipation as he did as he was told. Ruby slid the curtains along from one end of the window while Lenny followed suit from the other end. As they, and the curtains, met at the centre of the window they looked in each other's eyes, kissed and embraced before flopping onto the bed. She started unbuttoning his shirt and could see he was ready for action as they finished undressing each other. They rolled under the sheets and his hard body thrust against her soft body. 'Damn, I haven't got a Johnny on me' he whispered ruefully. Ruby knew 'Johnny' was slang for a condom but assured him they would be fine so long as he promised to be careful and let her know when he was 'about to.' While Lenny was taking in this *laissez-faire* approach, she grabbed, pointed and poked his manhood into the right places to satisfy her lust. He had now become her sex toy and he felt like the whole of his body was dissolving into hers. They bounced against each other more and more urgently. Lenny's mind was racing. This was the real deal and nothing like the clumsy fumbling of his drunken bedding of a girl the previous year. Ruby was clearly an expert in this area as a sudden movement of her thighs ejected him from their union at just the right time before even he knew he was 'about to.'

Lenny and Ruby lay beside each other for a while slowly getting their breath back. Lenny noticed the time on the clock above the chest of drawers showed that ten minutes had passed since they'd left their friends at the bar. In a panic he said to Ruby 'I'd better get dressed and leave before your room-mate gets back'. Ruby giggled naughtily and admitted 'Don't worry. Just before we left the bar, I asked Mary to give us half an hour - there should be time to go again if you are up for it?' After more kissing and caressing they certainly did 'go again.'

By the time Mary was thoughtfully tapping on the chalet door, Lenny was just about dressed and ready to leave. Ruby had pulled on enough clothes to appear decent but Mary smiled knowingly at Ruby's knickers on the floor by her dishevelled bed and the flushed faces of the two of them as they kissed and said goodnight.

Lenny jogged back down the hill toward the purple flat clicking his heels while jumping in the air. He was full of macho self-satisfaction and hoped Callum had managed to have a similarly enjoyable evening with one of the girls he had been talking to. He then wondered if his roommate was with someone right now. When Lenny reached the purple flat, he thought it best to copy Mary's idea, lightly tapping on the bedroom door, just in case he was interrupting something. No such luck for Callum - he opened the door to let Lenny in and had clearly not been entertaining anyone.

Callum couldn't help noticing that Lenny was very flushed and grinning like the cat that got the cream so dared to ask him how he'd got on after Ruby dragged him away from the bar. Lenny tried to be tight-lipped but Callum was his new friend and he couldn't help but brag about his first conquest at the *Seaview*, and maybe his first ever conquest. Lenny added 'I was expecting to see you in bed with one of the waitresses you were talking to at the bar'. Callum held up his palms as he explained 'Mary introduced me to some lovely girls and we all had a good chat together but I think they were only looking for friendship rather than anything else'.

The next night, Callum said to Lenny 'LE, what do you want to get out of the season?' 'What do you mean?' 'Well, I want to get plenty of stage experience to work professionally and build up a reputation in the entertainment business, eventually becoming a TV or radio show host, interviewing celebrities. You know, someone like Simon Dee but better. How about you?' Lenny said 'I don't look to the future CC. I live for today not tomorrow so don't have any career ambitions. I just want to grasp every opportunity that comes my way and have as good a time as I can get away with. My golden rule is to live life to the full but don't get hooked on anything – drugs, money or love'. 'I thought hippies believe "all you need is love"'? 'That's what the Beatles sang but most hippies take it further and believe in free love that has no boundaries or restrictions and living each day as if it was your last. If that means bedding lots of girls with no strings attached then that's ideal as far as I'm concerned'. 'I don't feel the same LE. It may sound soppy but I really hope I'll find true love soon and there should be plenty of opportunities to meet my ideal partner at the *Seaview* whether it be a holidaymaker or a colleague … like Pauline' he sighed.

Lenny thought Callum was an old fashioned over sentimental gentleman who would always seek permission or approval before doing or going after something he wanted. Callum, on the other hand, thought Lenny was shallow, wild and impulsive - someone who would just throw himself into something without any thought for the consequences then maybe seek forgiveness after the event if he felt it warranted it. They didn't voice their initial assessments of the other's personality in case it hurt their feelings. If Lenny had opened up and confessed the reason why he wasn't seeking love, Callum would have better understood his new friend's negative attitude to it.

CHAPTER 10 - First day of the season (Saturday 13th May)

[Playlist Track: *"Mary Skeffington"* – Gerry Rafferty]

The first and last two weeks of the *Funtime* summer season were secretly named 'wrinkly weeks' by all holiday centre workers, especially the *Purplecoats*. This was because these weeks were marketed almost exclusively to old age pensioners wanting to take advantage of the off-peak cut price deals being promoted. The assumption, of the *rookie Purplecoats* at least, was that these weeks would be easier because the expectations and requirements of visiting pensioners would not be as lively, fussy and demanding as younger peak-time holidaymakers.

The activities schedule during 'wrinkly weeks' was necessarily reduced and many of the remaining activities would be cancelled, sometimes at the last minute, due to lack of participants as much as bad weather. The entire Junior Club programme was not needed, nor other family-oriented activities like Mini Circus. The swimming pool was outdoors and unheated so remained out of bounds during these weeks. The donkey derby did not take place, nor did more energetic sports activities like football, tennis, netball and rounders.

The first fortnight therefore served as a gentle introduction to the season with spare time and plenty of opportunities for experienced *Purplecoats* to show or share hosting duties with *rookie Purplecoats*. It also gave *rookies* their first chance at having a go at taking the lead themselves. Tasks were shared or handed over in front of a small elderly audience without the same level of pressure *rookie Purplecoats* might feel when entertaining supposedly more attentive and critical peak-time holidaymakers. Nonetheless, the pensioners were far from docile and not always easy to deal with.

On the first day of the season, the *rookie Purplecoats* were given the apparently simple task of welcoming holidaymakers at the start of their holiday at the *Seaview*.

Visitors came in on different forms of transport and Jane once again felt she had the short end of the straw, shivering and isolated on her own at Churston railway station from 10am to 2pm waiting to meet and greet holidaymakers who travelled in by train. As each train arrived, she stood on the platform alongside the exit gate and raised a board. It was painted in the purple and white livery of the *Funtime* organisation and said 'Welcome to *Funtime Seaview* Guests.' When the *guests* approached her, she pointed them to the *Seaview*'s mini-bus in the car park or asked them to wait in the car park where the mini-bus would shortly be arriving. Alan was driving the mini-bus to pick up and drop off the 'grockles' but sometimes it took longer than anticipated to deliver a trainload to the *Seaview* then get back in time for the next train. Jane had to placate guests complaining about being left out in the cold during these delays.

Back at the *Funtime Seaview* holiday centre, holidaymakers arrived using different modes of transport. Coaches brought in organised groups, the posh ones came in by taxi but most turned up in their own cars, vans or motorbikes with sidecars. All of these arrivals put a great strain on the entrance to the reception area. To avoid unnecessary holdups and delays, the remaining *rookies* were each given a particular bottleneck area to manage:

- Callum was given the duty of directing all arriving vehicles to the nearby car park as soon as the drivers had dropped off their passengers and baggage outside the reception entrance
- Lenny would carry bags inside and place them in front of the reception counter while the owners of the bags checked in
- Tricia would welcome newcomers after they'd picked up their keys, locate their chalets on the large map mounted on the wall outside reception and help direct them along the best route to get to them.

Things got chaotic on the first afternoon, especially when rain pelted down. The reception manager, Jill Tully, loaned Tricia a *Funtime* umbrella to shelter under while shouting directions to new arrivals desperate to venture out in the weather to get to their chalet. Unfortunately, the umbrella blew inside out every time the wind picked up. Bags were piling up outside and inside the reception area alongside increasingly lengthy queues of newcomers as counter staff struggled with the volumes. Callum helped Lenny get more than twenty bags off a coach then he jumped on board to avoid the rain and direct the coach driver up the hill to the car park. Lenny, meanwhile, guided the new arrivals to the check in queue as he carried their soggy bags right through the crowded reception area to place them down in the buffet lounge as it was the only remaining indoor space nearby.

When Callum ran back from the coach to the reception area, he saw an empty car parked right in front of the entrance door. It was blocking the entry road and causing a long queue of traffic up the hill behind it. He also noticed that the *Seaview*'s own mini-bus packed with new holidaymakers was in the queue. Alan was frantically waving from the driver's window to suggest he was desperate to drop his passengers and their bags off and get back to Churston station in time to pick up the next trainload of holidaymakers.

The owner of the dumped car did not appear to be in the vicinity, so Callum had to think fast. He noted that the car was unlocked so opened the driver's door, carefully put the gears into neutral, took the hand brake off and gently pushed the car forward a few car lengths. This allowed the traffic queue to move forward into the reception space. Just as Callum was putting the brake back on the vehicle, the owner ran up to him and screamed expletives saying he had no right to move his car.

Luckily, the *Seaview*'s Business Manager - Eric Arden - happened to have also been stuck in the traffic queue and saw everything unfold. He jumped out of his car and gave the car owner a stern talking-to. He pointed to the No Parking signs outside the reception building and said his actions had caused an unnecessary hold up. Eric went on to say that, if he persisted in swearing at staff trying to carry out their job, he would have to insist the man, and whoever he's brought with him, leaves the *Seaview* holiday centre immediately. This threat seemed to do the trick as the car owner got in his car and drove off to the official car park without saying another word, be it swearing or any apology. Eric Arden turned to Callum and commended him for using his initiative. Callum recalled Dale's verbal attack on his first night, so was relieved that he now had some sort of recognition, appreciation and respect from the top man at the *Seaview*.

Jane didn't have an umbrella for the duration of her shift at Churston railway station so was soaking wet, cold and exhausted when Alan drove her back to the purple flat. She longed for a hot shower and a lengthy siesta in a warm bed but she only had a short time in the bathroom before someone was banging on the door to say they were desperate. After covering her modesty with an already used towel, she hung her clothes up to dry overnight in the kitchen and returned to her bedroom for a rest. She cursed her luck when she saw Tricia and Jeannette already there, chatting noisily as they got changed and ready for the evening shift. Jane had already been struggling to be as positive as her colleagues. Now, she felt like she was running frantically on a treadmill against her will.

Jason had warned his *rookies* what to expect before dinner on the first evening of a holiday week. New holidaymakers were usually desperate to be first into the dining room in order to claim the best seats on the tables they'd been allocated for the duration of their holiday. This often led to a long queue early on at the entrance to the dining room. Family and friends of the early birds would invariably push in at the last minute if they could get away with it and this sometimes caused the odd altercation when someone objected. The doors to the dining room could not be opened until all the kitchen staff were ready and waitresses poised at their stations.

Callum and Lenny were given the task of opening the dining room doors and welcoming the diners in once given the all clear by Jason or Mike. Tricia and Jane would then help the diners find their allocated tables just like ushers at a cinema.

Thankfully, there had been no incidents by the time Jason gave the all clear to Callum and Lenny. They immediately opened the doors, then, as the throng of eager diners lumbered slowly into the dining room, they smiled to each other and hummed the refrain 'See them shuffling along' from the song 'Waiting for the Robert E. Lee.' Callum's smile turned to a nervous frown when he realised that he would be singing and dancing to this song in front of these people a few nights later.

Diners paused as they approached their allocated table to decide who they wanted to talk to and eat next to. They hardly noticed the waitress standing there until she introduced herself with a welcome. Each waitress had to look after thirty-two diners per sitting: eight diners at each of four tables. This was hard work, especially for the younger, leaner, girls where this was their first job and they were yet to develop any great muscle strength.

Once all the holidaymakers had made their way into the dining room, Kenny quickly followed behind, carrying his camera in one hand and flash unit in the other. As the *Seaview*'s exclusive photographer, Kenny's mission was to encourage holidaymakers to pose for photos to sell to them as mementoes on a range of merchandise. He'd happily snap holidaymakers around the holiday centre most days and some evenings but hated taking photos in the dining room because the holidaymakers generally didn't want to be disturbed while they were busy chomping away or talking. He invariably wasted a lot of film on distorted faces when his targets moved as the shutter closed on his camera.

The *Purplecoat*s ate all their meals alongside the *guests* in the dining room. They sat at two designated tables that butted against the back wall. This meant that they were in prime position to just about hear, from the other side of the wall, the muffled sounds of kitchen staff shouting to each other and clattering crockery as they prepared and plated dishes that the waitresses would soon rush in to pick up.

Jason waited until all the diners had settled at their tables before standing up with the microphone and officially welcoming them to the *Seaview* holiday centre. Ignoring the increasing noises coming through the wall behind him, he explained that he would run through the evening's entertainment schedule later on but for now 'please be nice to your waitress and enjoy your dinner.'

As soon as Jason flicked off the microphone, all the waitresses sprung from their sections like racing drivers at the start of a Le Mans race. They were not allowed to run but walked as fast as they could toward and through the swinging 'in' doors to the kitchen. Once inside, they picked up empty trays from the stack awaiting them then queued up at the serving stations to load plated food on the trays.

The sound of activity in the kitchen got more frenetic and louder as the production line and serving stations reached full speed. Waitresses soon kicked or pushed through the swinging 'out' doors from the kitchen into the dining room, carrying a full tray of starters to the first of the four tables allocated for them to serve.

The waitresses had to push their newly learned skills and newly found strength to the limit to ensure they didn't bump into each other, topple their trays or spill food in their efforts to serve up each course to their diners as fresh or hot as it could be. Invariably, plates or trays would crash to the ground, quickly followed by a loud cheer from the unforgiving diners to further embarrass the unfortunate waitresses.

Pretty soon, the decibel level reached a peak as the clatter of metal utensils hit crockery with great gusto and hundreds of pairs of teeth and dentures clicked to different beats as they were given an extreme workout.

The waitresses at least appreciated one positive of wrinkly weeks - there were no children running around that could get in their way, trip them up or spill anything. On the other hand, old age pensioners could be especially grumpy and complain about the slightest thing, such as waiting too long for their food to arrive or not having enough gravy. Guests had to be placated by the serving waitress, or her supervisor, even if the problems related to issues in the kitchen or something else that was outside of their control. *Funtime* waitresses were trained to provide the best service possible but they also realised that keeping their diners happy would generally increase the value of any tips they got.

As Callum started tucking into his dinner alongside Lenny, he noticed a holidaymaker get up and furtively approach the next table where Jason sat. The visitor whispered something in Jason's ear and handed him a slip of paper. Jason read and acknowledged the content of the note and the holidaymaker smiled and returned to his table. Almost a dozen more holidaymakers rolled up one by one and went through the same procedure.

The first evening meal of any week was Kenny's first chance to make an impression on his target audience. It was also the quickest way to snap a new batch of photographs for display the following afternoon around the walls and windows of his shop. He methodically approached each and every table with camera and flash unit at the ready, offering to take photos of the diners enjoying themselves. Maximum time was spent on the tables that were celebrating as they would offer the best chance of multiple sales and increased profit.

The waitresses had placed a serving basket full of bread rolls on each table to accompany the soup first course. As Kenny approached a particularly rowdy table, he noticed a red-faced man picking up a full basket from the table and looking menacingly at him. Suddenly, the man started throwing the rolls at Kenny one by one. As Kenny tried to protect himself and his camera equipment, a few rolls bounced off him onto nearby tables: one roll nearly caused an old lady to have a heart attack when it splashed into her bowl of soup, another knocked a glass off a table but it was miraculously caught by a quick-witted gentleman.

Kenny beat a hasty retreat out of the dining room and into the buffet lounge where the *Seaview's* Business Manager - Eric Arden – happened to be sitting. He breathlessly explained what had happened. Eric immediately got up and said 'Take me to the troublemaker and let's nip this in the bud before he causes any more problems.'

Kenny led Eric to the table where the rolls had been thrown from and Eric immediately recognised the culprit as the same holidaymaker that he'd spoken to earlier that day. The idiot that had caused a traffic jam outside the reception then swore at a *Purplecoat* who'd moved his car to resolve the problem. The other diners on his table were clearly in shock at his actions, especially as they were looking forward to eating the rolls with their soup before he'd thrown them at Kenny.

Eric concluded that this holidaymaker was going to continue to cause trouble so gently but firmly ordered him and his wife to leave the dining room immediately and follow him to his office. With the troublemaker and his wife out of the dining room, normal service resumed. The waitress serving the table where the rumpus had taken place nipped back into the kitchen and refilled her basket with rolls from a spare batch that the porters had put aside to munch on. Kenny mindfully took photos at other tables until returning when he could see that the disrupted diners had recovered from their shock and enjoying themselves again.

The waitresses had been trained to be attentive to the progress of their diners as they munched their way through each course. As soon as all the diners on a table finished what they could eat, the waitress serving them could move in to pick up their dirty plates and used cutlery, stack them up on her serving tray, transport them through the swinging doors then slide them onto the metal table where the kitchen porters would load them into the industrial washing up machines before drying and stacking them on shelves. The best waitresses strived to be the first in the queue for each course and the fastest to serve it to their diners as this would most likely lead to getting the best tips.

Once all the holidaymakers had finished their main course and chosen their desserts, Jason stood up with the microphone and asked his audience if they had enjoyed their dinner. Without waiting for a reply, he picked up the notes given to him earlier and said: 'Before going through the schedule for this evening's entertainment in the ballroom I have a few announcements to make.' Callum now realised that each visitor to Jason's table had asked him to read out the details on their notes to announce a birthday or anniversary of someone in their group.

'First of all, we have three couples celebrating their wedding anniversary here today ....' Jason read out the names of all of the anniversary couples from the notes he'd been given and encouraged everyone to clap along with the embarrassed couples, friends and family. Soon after the applause died down, Jason moved on to birthdays and got everyone to join in to sing 'Happy Birthday' to Iris, Ernie and Violet. Much to the relief of the rest of his audience, Jason returned to the evening's entertainment schedule: '*Funtime* fun starts in the ballroom at 7:30 sharp with cash bingo. From 8:15, you can dance to live music from Tony Garner's big band. I will introduce our wonderful *Purplecoat* team to you all at 8:45 then the special cabaret show will start around 9 o'clock. The star of tonight's cabaret act is Rodger Bodger. He's a tremendous one-man band and comedy entertainer. As if that wasn't enough *Funtime* fun for your first night, we'll finish off this evening's entertainment with a Singalong until 10:30. Will you all stay up for a Singalong with us?' Jason raised his arms to encourage a response from his audience but it was a little muted so he repeated loudly: 'Will you all stay up for a Singalong tonight?' This time, he got a resounding 'Yes' from the holidaymakers even though most of them were unsure if they would have the stamina to last that long.

As it was the first night of the season, Jason told his *Purplecoat* team that he would call out the bingo numbers, but asked Mike to show Lenny and Callum how to get everything in place. This would enable the rookies to take over bingo sessions as and when required during the season.

In the privacy of the *Purplecoat*/artistes dressing room, Mike showed Lenny and Callum where the bingo items were kept, got them to move two tables and three chairs to the middle of the ballroom, place the bingo rack and bag of balls on one table for Jason then place the tickets, cash box and float bag on the other table. Callum sat on one side of the table with the cash box and float bag ready to take the money while Lenny sat on the other side to hand over the appropriate number of tickets purchased. A queue of eager players built up in front of them while they were trying to get up to speed. They would soon get fed up of the banter and ubiquitous wisecracks especially 'are these the winning tickets?'

When the queue for tickets died down, Jason flicked his microphone on and started building rapport with his audience – he was a consummate professional who had learned how best to warm up an audience, get their attention and engage with them. Bingo, however, was a tough one to get *guests* on side but he did his best. He opened with 'Hello everybody' to which he received a muted response. Never one to give up, Jason increased the volume and repeated 'Hello everybody!' It had the desired effect and a hearty 'Hello' came back from most of the audience. Now he'd got their attention Jason continued without waiting for any response: 'Are you all excited to play our first game of bingo? I'll be starting to call out the numbers in a moment once we've finished selling the tickets. Have you all come up to buy tickets from our handsome young *Purplecoat*s, Lenny and Callum? If you miss this opportunity, it might be a bit frustrating watching everyone else having a great time playing and winning cash from their lucky tickets.' That persuaded a few more holidaymakers to rush up to the table and empty their pockets of change for their own 'lucky tickets.'

As soon as the queue had emptied, Lenny and Callum carried the cash box and tickets back to the dressing room so that Mike could show them how to tot up the cash receipts and determine the amount of winnings to be offered. Mike ensured they swore themselves to secrecy before explaining the difference between the official procedures and the actual procedures. Bingo cash prize values were calculated from the number of tickets sold, however, there was often some odd cash left over after the values had been rounded down. The leftover money should have been added to the cash float for inclusion in a subsequent game. Instead, it was snaffled away into a 'slush fund' bag that would be used for a *Purplecoat* team night out at the end of the season.

Jason had just finished explaining the rules to his audience when Mike gave him a piece of paper with the prize money amounts set out. Jason announced how much cash would be paid out for each round and, at every opportunity, managed to get every last ounce of excitement and humour out of the simplest things and make most of the audience titter in response. Jason shook his bag of numbered balls close to the microphone and said 'Look, I'm giving my ball bag a really good shuffle' … 'OK, turn your hearing aids up' … 'Here we go, your first number is (pause) 9, 0, top of the shop, blind 90' … '2 and 8, what a state, 28' … 'Ooh, what colour is this game's bingo tickets? Dark Red, Purple Brown, Brownish Purple?' … What's that you said? Puce? Is Puce a real colour or have you just made it up?

... 'Anyone getting close to it yet? I haven't been *close to it* for ages!' ... 'if your numbers aren't coming up feel free to shout out *Shake your balls again!*'

After the bingo session, *Inn Paradise* was at its busiest and the volume of the audience increased as the winners bragged about their good luck and losers cursed their bad luck.

Before the cabaret was due to start, Jason lined up his *Purplecoat* team on the stage in order of seniority. Looking out to the audience, he waited for the right moment - he didn't want to shock someone carrying a full tray of drinks – before speaking into the microphone 'Hello There!' It got the same muted response as earlier in the evening so he used the same strategy, shouting out 'Bloody hell, let's try that again - Hello There!' This stimulated laughter and elicited an enthusiastic 'Hello There!' reply from the audience.

Jason continued "OK, OK. It's now time to meet our wonderful team of *Purplecoat*s who will host your entertainment and sporting activities while you're here at the *Funtime Seaview* holiday resort". Jason walked down the line of his team and pointed toward each *Purplecoat* in turn while introducing them to the audience. Lenny was a little confused when Jason introduced him as a Competition Host and Callum felt the same when he was introduced as a Sports Organiser - this was the opposite way around to the roles they had signed up for! They obviously couldn't embarrass their boss by correcting him in front of the audience so smiled and believed that it was a simple error that would be corrected next time. There were very few sports activities planned that week so they didn't expect it to be a major problem. In any case, they had no time to discuss it with Jason because they had to quickly go to the dressing room and help the cabaret star get ready for his act.

Jason passed the time talking to the audience about activities due to take place the next few days and the weather forecast, interspersed with a joke or two. After more minutes than he would have liked, he was relieved to see Callum open the dressing room door wide and put his thumbs up to signify that the cabaret act was ready. Jason stopped waffling and started his introduction: 'And now ladies and gentlemen ... the moment you've all been waiting for ... The star of tonight's cabaret ... An amazing one-man band and comedy entertainer ... Let's hear a big *Seaview* applause for Misterrr ... Rodgerrrr ... Bodgerrrrr!'

The audience gave Misterrr ... Rodgerrrr ... Bodgerrrrr ... an enthusiastic reception as he clambered onto the stage carrying what looked like a ton of musical instruments, in weight as well as quantity. The instruments were clamped or strapped onto every possible part of his body: his banjo strapped over one shoulder, bass drum on his back operated by his feet, cymbals under his arms and elbows, harmonica, squeeze box, horns, pan pipes, whistles, tin cans and other paraphernalia clamped onto a metal frame straddling his body and strategically placed for use. Callum and Lenny crossed their fingers in the hope that they had helped attach all the pieces correctly.

After the applause died down, Rodger Bodger warmed up the crowd with a few funny quips. Soon he was launching into the first of a dozen classic ditties. While singing enthusiastically, he cleverly and energetically accompanied himself by strumming, thumping, tapping and blowing any instrument he could reach with his hands, feet, elbows or mouth. The ditties included 1950's classics like 'Freight Train' and 'Peggy Sue' as well as 1960's hits 'Rosie' and 'Blue Eyes' made famous by Don Partridge - the most successful one-man act to feature in the UK pop charts.

As Rodger Bodger was nearing the end of his eighth song, the *Purplecoat*s spread out around the perimeter of the ballroom floor to help the audience clap and cheer Rodger Bodger's performance and sing along to his encore: 'Let the Good Times Roll' where his cymbals were put to good effect. After a final crash bang wallop, Rodger bowed and waved to the audience as he clambered off the stage and back to the dressing room. Callum and Lenny followed him in and carefully helped him detach his instruments one by one. A barman came in and placed a pint of beer on a ledge at the back of the dressing room for him. Once he'd been fully 'disarmed' he picked up the pint wearily and took a few big gulps, burped loudly and remarked 'God, I bloody needed that!' Without another word or thank you to Callum and Lenny he sneaked out the back door for a smoke.

Jason had by now started his singalong session with the other *Purplecoat*s spread out around the dancefloor, encouraging the audience to clap and join in with the singing. Callum and Lenny quickly joined them in their pre-defined positions just as Jason started to sing Hava Nagila - the popular Jewish folk song. All of the *Purplecoat*s were meant to synchronise the same arm movements in time with singing the beat of the song then raising both arms in the air, then waving hands above their head while singing 'Hava neranena', etc. If any of the *Purplecoat*s sang the wrong words or missed an arm movement through not concentrating it was rarely noticed as most of the audience were by now inebriated, competing against each other or simply enjoying themselves too much to care. Callum was secretly relieved that Jane was even clumsier than he was at following the right words and arm movements.

Once Hava Nagila finished, the *rookies* anticipated a rest with a drink at bar but the *Senior Purplecoats* knew what was coming next. Jason squashed together all of his team in the dressing room but purposefully looked at the *rookies* as he said 'For the rest of the evening, and every night you're on duty in the ballroom, I want you to walk around and mingle. You should be *socialising with the guests at all times* or *socialising and dancing with the guests whenever and whatever music is playing*'. Jane had already made it pretty obvious that she was reluctant to do any *dancing* so the thought of encouraging strangers to get up and dance with her was daunting, in her mind at least. Thinking that it would be best to show her preference for the only remaining option she naively asked Jason what he meant by the term *socialising*. Before Jason had chance to respond, Dale jumped in and exclaimed 'Crikey Jane. Use your imagination. Ask *guests* how far they travelled to get here, how they got here, if they are on their own or with family or friends, if they are happy with the chalet they've been allocated, did they enjoy their dinner, will they be entering any competitions … do you need any other suggestions?' Jane was too embarrassed to respond beyond a meek 'No' but felt like bursting into tears until she felt Jeanette's hand touch her shoulder tenderly in sympathy and say 'Don't worry, you'll soon get used to it'. Jane assumed Jeanette was talking about the *socialising* but later wondered if she was sneakily referring to Dale's heavy handedness. The other rookies just made a mental note of Dale's suggestions until they got into the swing of this *Socialising* concept.

At the end of the first evening's entertainment, Jason got back on the microphone and asked the audience if they'd had a good time. Everyone clapped and cheered. He thanked them for their kind applause but, before closing proceedings with a *Goodnight*, he asked them to please return to their chalets quietly in due consideration for their fellow guests. The ballroom gradually cleared as the remaining holidaymakers emptied their glasses and tried to remember the best route back to their chalets while chatting and laughing along with old and newly found friends and neighbours.

Jason gathered his *Purplecoat* team together at one end of the bar for a final recap of the night. First of all, he advised them that the troublesome holidaymaker – the one who had shouted and swore at Callum when he arrived then threw bread rolls at Kenny during dinner - had already left the *Seaview*. Eric Arden had reluctantly reimbursed the troublemaker's holiday money, minus his deposit, then got one of the security guards to escort him and his wife to their chalet to ensure they packed their bags and left the holiday centre in their car – the same vehicle that Callum had pushed away from the reception area to clear it from blocking new arrivals.

Jason acknowledged that, despite the troublemaker's disruption, his team had handled the first day of the new season very well and it was really encouraging to hear the applause from the holidaymakers in appreciation of their efforts as much as the evening's entertainment. Dale sarcastically added that a bonus was that none of the old folks had died from the excitement. This shocked the *rookies* and they would recall his throwaway comment over the next few weeks.

While the *Purplecoat* team were at one end of the bar, Rodger Bodger was at the other end, talking to a couple of teenage girls - one tubby and jolly, one thin and shy. The jolly girl pushed herself toward Rodger and breathlessly told him that she and her friend had really enjoyed his show. In fake modesty he avoided staring at the breasts thrusting toward him and replied 'You're too kind. Thank you and please call me 'Bodge' - it's a nickname my closest friends use. What are your names?' He was now looking at the shy girl but her jolly mate got in first with 'my name is Brenda but my friends call me 'Big Bren' for some reason!' She opened her arms as if to emphasise the joke while belting out a loud and embarrassing shriek of laughter.

Bodge ignored Big Bren and went back to her friend 'What's your name and nickname then?' She smiled but before she could reply, Brenda butted in with 'her name is Polly but her nickname is Kettle 'cos she can get a bit steamy, especially when she's had a few too many drinks!' Brenda let out another shriek of laughter before continuing 'We've been the best of friends since we met at the same school in East London.' As Brenda took a breath, Polly took the rare opportunity to speak for herself and explain 'Brenda more or less rescued me when I was being bullied by a gang of older girls in the playground. We managed to keep away from the bullies for the rest of our time at school but kept bumping into them wherever we went around our neighbourhood. In the end, we decided to get away from East London and work as *Funtime* waitresses to avoid further trouble as much as have a good time.'

Rodger gently placed a hand on Polly's shoulder and put his most considerate face on while emphasising 'Don't worry Polly. You are entirely safe here. *Funtime holiday centres* are well protected by security staff and the *Seaview* holiday centre is in the most secluded position of them all.' Believing he'd pacified the girls; to further impress them he beckoned the bar waitress over and asked her to serve them drinks from his tab. As they sipped their vodka and lime drinks, Brenda started worrying that she wouldn't be able to afford to get her round in if she hung around. She could see that 'Bodge' wasn't interested in her in any case - he was having a deep and meaningful conversation with Polly. Swiftly finishing her drink, Brenda put her hand to her mouth and faked a yawn then made the excuse that she was tired before saying goodnight and walking back to the chalet she shared with Polly, or at least had done prior to that night.

As soon as Brenda had left *Inn Paradise*, Bodge asked Polly if she would be so kind as to help him carry his musical equipment back to his chalet. Polly was too naïve to smell a rat or too tipsy to care if Bodge had used this routine before. From the moment they, and his musical equipment, were safely back in his chalet they embraced passionately and, for the rest of that night, he delivered a very different kind of one-man performance. Polly had no complaints as she lived up to her *Kettle* nickname.

[Playlist Track: *"Blue Eyes"* - Don Partridge]

All Funtime staff had regular scheduled time off within their working week and the Purplecoats had one full day plus a half day off each week but they had to be flexible to cover for their colleagues as necessary. Generally, Lenny had all day Sunday and Monday morning off whereas Callum had all day Wednesday and Thursday morning off.

Facilities were very limited in the kitchen at the purple flat - there was no toaster so the only way Lenny and Callum could work out how to make toast was to utilise the top of a metal biscuit box lid that had been left there. By placing it astride two flaming hobs then carefully dropping a slice of bread down flat on top of the heated lid the bread would eventually turn brown. Unfortunately, the painted pictures stamped on the lid gave off industrial fumes when hot so, even though the resulting toast looked good, it had a metallic taste and the smell of burning paint permeated the flat. Still, it was marginally preferable to having to walk up the hill for food as they would be required to wear their uniform in case guests recognised them. They also ran the risk of getting extra work just by being there.

Each morning in the dining room, the scheduled activities of the day ahead were announced to the holidaymakers while they were having their breakfast. Requests from holidaymakers to acknowledge an anniversary or birthday continued to occur at every meal. Jason rarely handed over announcing duties to Mike or Dale so most often carried out this chore which interrupted his eating and ruined his appetite. No wonder he always looked thin!

Rain pelted down relentlessly and the weather forecast suggested it would remain that way for the rest of the week so all the outside activities were cancelled. Mike and Dale tended to run the Bingo sessions as they were well attended in bad weather. Lenny and Callum were on the other hand assigned the responsibility of setting up a cine film projector and screen in the TV room and show films from the limited pack of 16 mm film stocked there.

Callum was delighted to unearth *The Ladykillers* film. He'd mentioned it to Lenny when they had their first cup of tea in the buffet lounge. Now they got to enjoy it with the *guests* whenever it rained. It became a firm favourite of theirs and they always had a laugh humming the tune and crooking a finger in a posh way every time they had a cup of tea for a joke that only they shared.

Popular favourites with the *guests* were 'Doctor at Sea' and 'Doctor in Trouble' but 'Carry on Up the Jungle' was the most requested movie.

Lenny and Callum laughed along with the holidaymakers at the comedy sketches and jokes featured in these films but, after lots of repeated showings, they started to get fed up of the repetition. Hearing the same jokes over and over again eventually became tedious for them and the saying 'familiarity breeds contempt' came to mind. They did however adopt for their own use one of the catchiest words from the 'Carry on Up the Jungle' film: As Bernard Bresslaw leads a trekking group through the jungle, he suddenly stops, points to animal poo on the trail and shouts 'Oomballah!' to warn the trekkers to step around it. Holidaymakers and colleagues would be none the wiser when Lenny and Callum repeated this word to secretly communicate between themselves anything or anyone they didn't like.

Kenny was sitting alone in the staff canteen on Monday lunchtime. He watched the rain slapping against the windows. It was less depressing than looking at his plate of burnt burgers and reheated chips. Suddenly, he heard someone say 'Hi Kenny – can I sit here?' It was his missing room-mate Roy. Without waiting for a reply, Roy plonked down opposite Kenny looking like a long-lost ghost. The security guard had filled his plate with similarly disgusting food but Kenny thought Roy looked even worse than the mess he was preparing to eat. Roy had lost a lot of weight and his face was pale and drawn with dark circles under his eyes.

Kenny addressed the elephant in the room and said 'I haven't seen or heard from you for ages and you look knackered. Have you been ill?' Roy replied 'I haven't been ill in the normal sense but deprived of sleep since we last saw each other – I'm literally shagged out!' Roy explained 'I've lost count of the days and nights but a while back I got into a long conversation with Jeannette.' 'The tall senior *Purplecoat*?' 'Yes'. 'Go on'. 'Well, we teased each other and I thought she was just having a laugh but she seemed very keen to take it further so I took her back to our chalet. You were already in your bed asleep so I tried to keep it quiet but Jeannette didn't seem to care that she might wake you. She turned out to be a right nymphomaniac, demanding sex all through the night.' Kenny didn't let on that he'd heard most of the action so moved the story along by asking where Roy had disappeared to after that night. Roy was happy to go into detail about what happened next. 'Jeannette wasn't content with us banging away in the chalet. She wanted sex in flagrante.' Kenny said 'What the hell does that mean?' Roy explained 'It's intentionally seeking to perform sexual activities where there's a strong possibility of being seen. She persuaded me to do it on the playing fields while we could hear people walking along on the other side of the trees. She followed me on my late-night security walk around the holiday centre once she'd finished working in the ballroom. I've got a master key to all the chalets and most were empty this early in the season so we had plenty of opportunities for privacy but this wasn't daring enough for her. She preferred to do it up against occupied chalets where all was quiet apart from the sound of snoring from within. Jeannette really got a kick out of doing the business where there was a high risk of disturbing someone and getting caught!' Kenny laughed and said 'I look forward to hearing more about your frolics but I've got to shoot off to cover this afternoon's Granny contest'.

Mike was preparing to host the Elegant Grandmother competition and Dale was on to a promise so they told Lenny and Callum to take over that afternoon's Bingo session on their own. Dale said "Don't forget, when you're calling out the numbers; Wrinklies love to hear traditional bingo sayings and phrases being used such as Kelly's Eye - number 1; One little duck - number 2; etcetera etcetera ... You should know them all by now." Mike always put a serious spin on every briefing and said "Don't make any comments personal to anyone in the audience or offend anyone. For instance:

- When shouting out Legs Eleven - number 11 you can add the usual wolf whistle but don't direct it toward the girl you fancy or the one with the shortest skirt.
- If there are plump ladies in the audience, look elsewhere when you shout out Two Fat Ladies - 88!

Lenny called out the numbers and Callum checked the numbers of the guests' tickets and handed over the prize money. Even with the restrictions he'd been given, Lenny still dared to add risqué nicknames for certain numbers including 6 and 9 - Any Way Up – number 69, and their favourite: 1 and 2 - One Doz, if one gets the chance - number 12. They managed to get through the session without incident but Lenny's urban cockney accent came back to bite him when a gang of cheeky holidaymakers came up to him afterwards and mocked him by saying 'Fank you all the frees firty free!' They laughed as they walked away, leaving Lenny annoyed at being the subject of ridicule. Callum saw his mate was upset and said 'Forget your embarrassment LE. *Purplecoats* are here to entertain the guests, so that's exactly what you just did' With these wise words, Lenny learned to embrace the humour and even emphasise it for the extra laughs.

Monday night was Callum's turn to be embarrassed. During the Old-Time Music Hall show he completely lost track of the dance routine while singing along to Jason and Dale's lead on 'The Old Bull and Bush' number. Luckily, Lenny was close enough to put his arm around Callum's waist knees-up style and guide him back on track without anyone noticing. Callum's confidence was restored by the time they ended the show with 'Waiting for the Robert E. Lee.'

Most of the elderly couples got into the romantic atmosphere of the evening, dancing or reminiscing about their courtship a half-century ago or more. Others sat quietly alongside each other with arms folded having forgotten or missed out on these feelings - their only pleasure coming from another drink. For the rest of the evening, the *Purplecoats* chatted to as many guests as they could at all points across this spectrum.

Callum and Lenny had very little money, so soon worked out a crafty ruse to get drinks and cigarettes without paying for them. Most evenings, they would seek out guests to socialise with. The guests they targeted were based on how empty their glasses were rather than how much fun they were having although a tick in both categories would be ideal. The idea was to start a conversation with them when you don't have a drink in your hand and the glasses of the holidaymakers are almost empty. If you've endeared yourself to them, they would invariably ask if you'd like a cigarette when they light up or drink when they go up for their next round of drinks. After pretending to be surprised, you would simply offer to help them carry the drinks from the bar to their table but take up their offer of a drink while at the bar. Once sat back down with them you could usually escape after a carefully timed but not too obvious couple of gulps. The almost full glass could then be stashed away on a ledge in the dressing room so that you could get back out there to target the next table. After a half dozen or more table drop-ins you should have enough drink for your evening's pleasure.

Tuesday was big band dance and cabaret night and most of the senior *Purplecoats* took the evening off. Dale introduced the cabaret act and encouraged an encore at the end of his show. Late into the evening, he told Callum and Lenny that he was going off for a break, leaving them to look after things on their own. They were quite relaxed about being left in charge because there wasn't too much work for them to worry about beyond a watching brief and of course *socialising and dancing with the guests*. Lenny was chatting and cadging drinks off guests at the back of the ballroom and the dancefloor was packed with holidaymakers enjoying themselves. Callum smiled when he noticed a particularly dapper gentleman who clearly loved to dance. The gent must have been over 80 years old but was inviting and persuading different women to join him up on the dancefloor for every type of dance tune that the band played - ballroom dances, ceilidh dances and line dances.

The band leader - Tony Garner - enthusiastically asked his audience to get up on the dancefloor for the last dance of the night – the Gay Gordons. Callum knew that it was a Scottish ceilidh dance where couples follow the movements of the leading couple while marching around the dancefloor with their partner. Callum thought the Gay Gordons was quite an energetic dance for wrinklies but the dapper gentleman was clearly up for it. He'd almost worn himself out dancing with plenty of girls throughout the evening but this time his wife insisted he whisk her around. The Gay Gordons was her favourite dance, especially as Gordon was the married surname they shared.

The music started and Mr and Mrs Gordon closely followed the moves of a younger couple leading the dancers, spinning and turning with great gusto along to the music. Mr G tried to keep up with them while pulling Mrs G around but, just as the dance reached a crescendo, he clutched at his heart and fell to the floor, half pulling down his shocked wife. The nearest holidaymakers ran up to Mr G, who was now lying prostrate on the floor, and they waved to Callum for help. After a few seconds of panic, Callum had the foresight to shout out to Lenny to run and get the nurse while he answered the call.

As Callum rushed onto the dancefloor, he briefly believed he was a real doctor like the one he acted in the 'Mother, I Die' sketch. Unfortunately, when he stood over the poor man, he had no idea what he could do to help - this was one task none of the *rookie Purplecoats* had been warned about, let alone had any training for.

Callum stupidly asked the man if he was okay and what his name was. The man was limp and unresponsive but his wife, who was still holding his hand, said his name was Garry Gordon. Callum managed to avoid reacting to the irony of him having a similar name to the dance he'd just collapsed to but was mightily relieved when nurse Hazel arrived with Lenny. Hazel announced that an ambulance was on its way as she kneeled alongside the man. On feeling his pulse, she asked Callum and Lenny to carry him to the manager's office where he and his wife could wait in privacy for the ambulance to arrive. They sat the man up then Lenny held his ankles still while Callum put his arms under the man's armpits to help lift him up. Even though the old man looked relatively light, the sweat from so many dances made it difficult for Callum to keep a grip. Callum tried not to react to the pungent smell as he and Lenny carried the man out of the ballroom, followed closely by his distraught wife and Hazel. When they all reached Eric Arden's office, Callum and Lenny carefully flopped the man down onto the sofa. Mrs Gordon sat down alongside her husband to prop him up and Hazel told the *Purplecoats* that they'd better return to the ballroom.

As Lenny and Callum left the office, Hazel followed them down the corridor and tapped Callum lightly on the shoulder. He turned around and she said 'thank you for your help'. Callum was going to say 'You're welcome' but when he looked at her face, she was shaking her head from side to side to silently inform him that Mr Gordon had already passed away.

When Lenny and Callum got back into the ballroom, they were faced with concerned or just nosy holidaymakers asking how the old man was. They managed to hide their personal feelings and kept the tragic news private, simply stating that the ambulance was taking Mr Gordon to hospital.

The next morning, Jason gathered all of his team together in the TV room – even Callum despite it being his usual day off. He wanted to hear Hazel's update on the previous night's tragic incident.

> She started by thanking Callum and Lenny for helping carry Mr Gordon to Eric Arden's office. Minutes after they'd returned to the ballroom the ambulancemen arrived and confirmed Mr Gordon had died, most probably of a heart attack. They laid him out on a stretcher and covered him in a blanket for his final journey to the local mortuary. Hazel comforted his distraught wife and helped her contact family and friends with the sad news before helping her back to her empty chalet. Mrs Gordon's daughter was due to

arrive later this morning to help her mum set up the funeral arrangements. Eric Arden had thoughtfully offered another chalet to the daughter and her mum for as long as they needed. Hazel concluded by saying that the wife had told her that they'd booked a two-week holiday to celebrate their diamond wedding anniversary and he'd actually died on their anniversary night to a dance that was practically his name. Tricia said 'Oh, how awful' and she started sobbing with Jane. Lenny put his arms around the rookie Purplecoats to comfort them. Callum felt immensely sad for the family and was relieved that he had held back from reacting to the matching name when he'd first heard it. Dale tried to inject a positive note with misplaced humour by saying 'Wow, it's certainly a shock. A married couple for 60 years that were still enjoying being together!'

Jason always instilled into his Purplecoats the motto 'the show must go on.' The senior team understood and accepted this motto but this was a new concept for the rookies. Lenny spoke to Alan and Baz about the shock he felt over Mr Gordon's death. Alan simply but philosophically said 'There tiz, can't do nort about it. Us Devonians call 'eez weeks wakes weeks 'cos we expect some o the old uns to peg it while they be 'avin fun. Tiz better un pegging out 'avin no fun, dawnt 'ee knaw?' Baz added 'You just have to accept it's gonna happen, man. I've had to deal with plenty of peg its, picking them up from their chalets, the beach, on the beach steps and in the toilets – I've encountered sights and smells I wouldn't want repeated'.

Jackie saw Callum looking a little forlorn sat alone in the ballroom and said 'Hi, sweetie' as she delicately sat down next to him. All she got back was a murmur but undeterred, continued with: 'Look, you can tell me it's none of my business but I just wondered how you're coping after Mr Gordon's death'. Callum in surprise said 'Oh, I thought it was being kept a secret'. Jackie explained 'Well, I just told Hazel I was concerned at how sad you looked. I pretty much forced her to tell me about the death of the old man and your help in carrying his body out of the ballroom'. Callum finally opened up and confessed 'It was horrible. I took this job because I wanted to make people happy. I didn't realize I would have to deal with sad incidents as well'. Jackie could see the emotion in his eyes and went to clasp his hands and comfort him but Callum noticed Pauline walking up and jumped out of his chair to attend to her. Jackie knew it would be the latest episode of Pauline's long running saga about being upset about her boyfriend and Callum comforting her. She slipped away and left them to it.

No matter how melancholy the Purplecoats might have been feeling, they had to carry on with a smile for the sake of their guests. Jason snapped them out of any negative thoughts by pushing on with a final rehearsal for the surprise show they would be performing on Thursday night.

Lenny and Callum spent most of Thursday afternoon in the ballroom, setting alight long taper candles and melting them onto the necks of empty wine bottles before going back to their room to change into evening wear. Thursday night was Continental night and the Purplecoats were instructed to wear smart casual clothes instead of their usual evening uniform in order to emphasise the international theme. Lenny was glad to be able to at last wear his comfy brown shoes and matching trousers to go with a modern brown round collar shirt with white dots. Callum was preparing to wear an old-fashioned white shirt until Lenny playfully criticised his lack of fashion sense. Callum responded with his favourite catchphrase, 'I'm just an ordinary guy in the street, steamrolling along from day to day.' Lenny insisted that he shouldn't be so negative. He picked up one of his favourite shirts - purple with round collars - and held it up in front of Callum then handed it to him with the words 'Here you go CC, try this and, if it fits, you won't be an ordinary guy in the street anymore.' Callum put the shirt on and said 'Thanks LE, it fits perfectly and looks good'.

The dinner menu choices tried to reflect the evening's cosmopolitan theme but many holidaymakers struggled to understand one exotic option. The waitresses tried not to laugh when diners asked whether something called Paella was some sort of pie! When they found out it was sea food and chicken cooked with rice, they rejected it out of hand in favour of the more familiar stew and dumplings. A few asked their waitress if the rice could instead be cooked with milk or cream for the sweet course! The waitresses were thankful that their diners were happier with the actual dessert served to them – chocolate and vanilla ice cream with wafers. Lenny and Callum enjoyed their paella but had to scoff it quickly as they had to leave the dining room before the guests ate their desserts in order to carry out last-minute preparations in the ballroom.

Lenny said 'CC, shall we have a sneaky drink while we're doing this?' Callum replied 'No way, LE. There's no time. We've got to place *Continental Funtime* brochures on each table along with these empty wine bottles then set the candles alight before the guests roll up.' The brochures pointed to the reason for the Continental theme - the night was designed to promote *Funtime holiday centres* that were soon to be opened along the Spanish mainland and Mediterranean islands.

Lenny and Callum were still setting up in the ballroom when a few early birds turned up to claim their preferred tables. One even shouted across the ballroom 'What you up to Firty Free?!' Lenny politely forced a laugh to show he hadn't taken offence and shouted back 'I fink the magic will be revealed very soon.' Callum whispered 'LE - I told you there wouldn't be time for a sneaky drink.' As soon as they'd finished preparing all the tables, they shouted out to the early birds they were about to turn off the main lights. As they flicked the switches, the audience went 'ooh' then clapped or cheered as the ballroom was immediately transformed. The harsh bright fluorescent lights were replaced by the softer light of the burning candles and the flickering effect of the flames on the wicks gave the ballroom a sparkling romantic feel. Callum turned to Lenny and said 'Wow, the ballroom looks great LE. It's just a shame we missed out on that ice cream dessert.' Lenny laughed and told Callum to look out for his signal later on and be ready to follow right behind him – he had a surprise set up for him.

The rest of the holidaymakers streamed in to the ballroom and jumped on available seats like a game of musical chairs. Once they had settled in, Jason told his team to mingle with them to see how much they were enjoying their holiday at the *Seaview* and find out if there was anything they needed that hadn't been offered. He also told his team to ensure they recommend that the holidaymakers look through the Continental *Funtime* brochures and take advantage of the special code *Seaview5* to snap up a 5% discount if they decided to follow through with a booking. Callum was pretty sure that the Senior *Purplecoats* or management at the *Seaview* would get a bonus for any holidays booked this way, even though the *rookies* had put most of the effort in to make it a success.

While the other *Purplecoats* were busy chatting with their guests, Lenny saw the opportunity to carry out his plan. He waved to Callum and put his thumb up then pointed it toward the exit before striding purposefully out of the ballroom. Callum caught up with him just as he'd reached Ruby in the dining room. She said 'About bloody time' then, without another word, she skipped through the kitchen doors and brought back two platefuls of ice cream that she'd placed in the fridge especially for them. Callum's eyes lit up and he said 'Thanks Ruby, nice one, LE!' They did indeed woof the dessert down, even though it was so cold that it gave them a sudden brain freeze.

Lenny and Callum handed the empty plates to Ruby to wash up then made sure there were no ice cream stains around their mouths or on their clothes. Mike had just started looking for them but, luckily for them, he didn't see them sneak back into the ballroom. By the time he spotted them, they had already sat with the nearest approachable holidaymakers and were laughing along with their *guests* while pushing the brochures as commanded.

Just before 8pm, the holidaymakers were dancing and singing along to the big band's rendition of *Itsy Bitsy Teenie Weenie Yellow Polkadot Bikini*, unaware that all the *Purplecoats* were busy getting ready for a surprise performance. Squashed together in the dressing room, they changed into different fancy dress costumes. In such a confined space it was inevitable that they couldn't avoid elbowing or bumping into each other. This was ironical as they would be mimicking something similar in the sketch for comedic effect. In time with the music, they each took their turn to emerge from behind the stage curtains and sing the chorus then a rhyme about the job they would rather have if they were not upon the stage. As they sang their piece, they actively mimicked the actions from their imaginary job. The next actor would join the line, sing their piece and mimic different actions from their imaginary job. As the line got bigger, their movements would almost interfere with the alternative movements of the actors alongside them.

Lenny was first up, dressed as a chimney sweep with soot on his face and a long-handled brush. He sang: 'If I were not upon the stage, something else I'd rather be. If I were not upon the stage, a chimneysweep I'd be. You'd hear me all day long, and this would be my song …' then he thrust his brush forwards and upwards to emphasise the words he sang 'Up yer flue ma, up yer flue ma, 50 times a day.' Next was Dale in tennis gear singing 'balls to you sir, balls to you sir, service down the line' while swinging his racquet sideways and forwards narrowly missing the movements of the chimneysweep's brush. The rest of the *Purplecoats* joined the line one by one and did their piece. Jason was the last to join the fun and of course he was a ballerina. Dressed in a tight white tutu he pranced and pirouetted around the stage singing 'a jete here, a chasse there' then lifted his skirt can-can style to flash his frilly underwear as he sang 'Show my arabesque - ooh!'

After the show, the *Purplecoats* took it in turns to have a break, but Callum and Lenny managed a quick chat as they switched places. Callum reflected on his own love-life, or rather the lack of one. Lenny had a different mindset - he felt frustrated at spending so much of his time with all these old codgers while Ruby was probably ready and waiting for him in her bed, perhaps with yet more ice cream!

On Friday morning, Polly had just finished serving breakfasts in the dining room. She dropped off the last of her dirty plates at the washing up area and was looking forward to a rest before the lunch service. As she returned to her base in the dining room, she slipped on a greasy patch left by another waitress. Callum saw her fall to the floor and jumped up to help her. As he tried to lift her back on her feet, she screamed in pain. Polly's right wrist had already started swelling so Callum helped walk her over to the first aid room, just opposite the reception entrance.

The Senior Nurse at the *Funtime Seaview* Holiday centre - Beryl - was on her day off but Callum and Polly were relieved that Beryl's Nursing Assistant - Hazel - responded when they knocked on the door. Hazel looked at Polly's wrist and was quite sure she had sprained it.

Hazel put Polly's arm in a temporary sling and kindly offered to drive her to Brixham hospital to get an X-Ray and a more permanent solution. As the three of them came out of the nurse's surgery, Callum saw that Lenny and Kenny were gathering together that morning's rambling party for the walk to Berry Head. Callum had been scheduled to cover the stragglers while Lenny led the ramble and Kenny took photos. When Callum explained what had happened, Kenny said he and Lenny could cover the ramble while he helped Polly get herself sorted. So it was that Callum tagged along as Hazel drove Polly to Brixham hospital, thankfully only a mile or so away.

While Polly was having her X-Ray done, Hazel asked Callum if he was Polly's boyfriend. She seemed pleasantly surprised when Callum confirmed Polly was just a friend. Callum added that, as far as he knew, Polly's boyfriend was a one-man band and comedy entertainer. As soon as he mentioned the name 'Rodger Bodger' he was sure Hazel's face changed as if she was thinking 'Oh dear.' She quickly changed the subject and the two of them got onto more enjoyable topics before Callum got the nerve to ask her why she had looked that way at the mention of his name. Before she could utter another word, Polly returned from her X-Ray. They tried not to look guilty and pretended they were talking about Lenny. The doctor walked up to them, holding Polly's X-Rays, and confirmed that she had indeed sprained her wrist. Luckily, she hadn't torn any ligaments so surgery was not necessary but his nurse would put a more permanent sling on her wrist and she would need to rest her arm for at least three weeks.

When they all returned to the *Seaview*, Polly sought out Margot Medway - the catering manager - and updated her on the doctor's diagnosis. They both agreed that there was no way Polly could continue carrying heavy trays full with plates of food as a waitress in the dining room. Polly didn't want to leave the *Seaview* and return home so pleaded with Margot to find her some other work she could do, even if on a temporary basis. Margot had an idea and assured Polly that she would get back to her once she'd checked it out.

Margot was already planning for the season to get busier from the following week onwards. A new intake of waitresses would be arriving in a few days to help prepare for the increasing number of bookings but two girls from Ivybridge were already onsite, working in *Seaview*'s buffet lounge. Margot approached them to see if they would prefer to work in the dining room. She emphasised the benefits of the move, including a better chance of decent tips to supplement their meagre income. They agreed and, by the next shift, Connie and Judy had switched places with Polly and Brenda. To protect her wrist, Polly carried out the more genteel tasks of serving beverages and cakes to one or two guests at a time while Brenda did the more energetic tasks like carrying bulk supplies and clearing up tables.

That evening, Lenny was sat with Callum in the dining room. Ruby had the night off but he was surprised and delighted to see a new waitress working near to their table. She was the cherubic girl he'd first seen in the buffet lounge then practically bumped into her on his first visit to *The Three Elms Inn*. They hadn't spoken on either occasion but when their eyes briefly met a spark ignited. He hadn't realised how petite she was but now he couldn't take his eyes off her as she glided around the dining room with that dazzling smile. He then watched her lips move as she told her diners what choices they have for each course. He wondered what it would be like to kiss those lips. The saying *the best presents come in small packages* immediately came to mind. He asked Callum 'CC – Isn't that the waitress from the buffet lounge? Callum said 'Yes LE, she and her colleague switched jobs with Polly and Brenda after Polly sprained her wrist'. 'Oh wow - do you know her name?' 'I think her name is either Connie or Judy'.

As she walked by his table with a tray piled high with dinner plates, Lenny tried to break the ice, shouting out something relating to her stint in the buffet lounge: 'I'll have a cuppa tea an' a bun please!' She looked confused by the joke, his accent, or both. At the end of the dinner service, he walked up to her station as she was clearing up and tried to make up for the bad start. He already knew the answer but asked her 'How come you're not in the buffet lounge anymore?' She now realised she'd made an impression on him the first time he'd seen her but politely replied 'My friend and I were offered the switch for more money and a promise of better tips'. 'Is that what you got?' 'Well, I've only just switched so it's too soon to say but the hours are an elluva lot longer and the work is an elluva lot harder, that's for sure.' Lenny noted her use of the word *elluva* and couldn't think of anything else to say so put his hand out to shake her hand formally: 'My name's Lenny but my best friends call me LE - what's yours?' 'I'm Connie but my best friends call me Connie!' They both laughed together for the first time and when they shook hands it felt warm and cosy and neither wanted to let go. Callum hurried up to them and, after catching his breath for a quick introduction, stressed that he and Lenny should get into the ballroom straight away as Jason was waiting for him. Lenny let go of Connie's hand and said 'Sorry, Connie, gotta go but it was nice chatting to you.' It was hardly a chat but she politely replied 'Likewise.' He instinctively touched her arm briefly but tenderly and they shared another tinge of excitement from the contact before he followed Callum away. Their first *chat* had ended much sooner than they both would have liked.

Friday night was the last night of the holiday week so the evening ended with a *Purplecoat* singalong to thank the *guests* for holidaying at the *Seaview* holiday centre and see them off in style. Jason led the singing, accompanied by all of his team. They encouraged the audience to clap and sing along with them to familiar classics, like 'I do like to be beside the seaside', 'She'll be coming round the mountain' and 'I've got a lovely bunch of coconuts.'

As the evening neared the end, the *Purplecoat*s did their best to get as many *guests* as they could up onto the dancefloor for the last few tunes. They persuaded the participants to do all the arm movements to 'My Bonnie Lies Over the Ocean' then put their arms around the person on either side of them while singing along to Vera Lynn's wartime classic 'We'll Meet Again', swinging one leg out beyond the front of the other leg then swapping to the other leg in rhythm to the beat. When the final verse started with a "2, 3 4", they followed the *Purplecoat*s lead by kicking their legs up as high as they could in the good old tradition of the Tiller Girls.

While everyone was up on the dancefloor, the band played Auld Lang Syne. All the *guests* interlinked arms and swung them up and down while singing the lyrics. They stayed up standing to sing the final song of the week – 'God Save The Queen' - before returning to their chalets to start packing or wait until the next morning after they'd sobered up.

Once Friday evening's entertainment was completed, Jason always felt like he needed something else to celebrate completing another successful week of the season. His veins were still coursing with adrenalin and excitement but the holiday centre was generally closing up for the night. His number two Mike had a similar feeling even though their sexual preferences were in totally opposite directions. So it was that Mike would drive them both into Paignton to an infamous after-hours night club.

The Blue Bay nightclub was the infamous key hot spot for local showbusiness professionals to meet and be entertained by other professional entertainers. Mike and Jason would try and get to a front row table before the midnight show started - it was usually a drag act followed by dancers wearing progressively skimpier clothes until they required a fan or feather to hide their nether regions. Mike would eat a huge steak that didn't do his developing paunch any favours. When the cabaret finished, the bar was the place to be. Mike would generally hook up with older ladies that were well past their prime but could still remember how to have a good time. Jason, meanwhile, would mix with the latest batch of young men looking for male affection or money.

This particular night, Jason struck up a deep conversation with a blonde-haired androgynous teenager called Daniel. Jason found out that Daniel performed a skeleton dancing act at the Festival Theatre - the seafront entertainment venue located just down the road on Paignton's Esplanade. For his act, Daniel wore a black costume with fluorescent white bones on the front and back that matched a human skeleton. When he danced spookily around a dimly lit stage, the bones illuminated in the dark and looked like one of the skeletons that battled with the hero in the film 'Jason and the Argonauts.' Mike, meanwhile, struck up a deep conversation with a forty-something chorus girl called Dolores that smoked like a chimney. Mike and Jason succeeded in getting their new partners back to their bedrooms that night to consummate their relationships. Mike found out that Dolores hid her grey locks under a blonde wig and Jason found out that Daniel was super fit and a demanding lover.

CHAPTER 12 - Fashion, Scrumpy and Salvation (w/c 20th May)

[Playlist Track: "Dedicated Follower of Fashion" – The Kinks]

Jason washed and dressed early on Saturday morning, ready for the start of the second week of the season. As he came out of his suite, Dale happened to be walking up the corridor from his less salubrious bedroom. Jason quickly shut the door behind him - he didn't want Dale to see that someone was in his bed, especially a blonde naked teenage man.

They said their usual brief 'morning' to each other, but this time Dale grabbed Jason's arm and said 'Have you seen your neck?' Jason instinctively felt his neck but was none the wiser. Dale suggested he go back into his room and have a good look. Jason pretended to fumble for his room key until Dale was out of sight then re-opened his door.

Daniel was just rousing after the few hours of sleep they had managed to fit in overnight. Jason looked in the bathroom mirror and said 'Bloody, bloody hell!' Daniel, now wide awake, said 'What's the matter, sweetie?' Jason pulled the collar of his sports shirt down and said 'Daniel, I know things got passionate last night but you've covered my neck in love bites.' The teenager said 'I don't understand darling - what's the problem?' Jason replied 'What's the problem? What's the bloody problem? For starters, I'm the Entertainments Manager at the holiday centre up the hill and I've got a meeting with my boss in half an hour. I've then got to ensure hundreds of paying guests are entertained by my team while I've got sodding love bites all around my neck. That's the bloody problem!' The teenager said 'Sorry darling, I must have got carried away - you should take it as a compliment.' Jason didn't respond to Daniel's juvenile remarks but thought to himself 'Why do I go for these naïve young men?' He answered his own question as he stared at Daniel's bare muscular body and recalled what they'd got up to throughout their wild night together. Jason didn't want to miss out on another night like that so calmed down and said 'Never mind darling, what's done is done - I've just got to work out what I can do to hide these hickeys.' He searched through his wardrobe and stumbled upon something that might do the trick. After all, he'd used it to disguise himself while participating in marches with the Gay Liberation Front.

Jason walked up to the other *Purplecoat*s while they were having breakfast in the dining room. He tried not to look embarrassed by the long purple scarf wrapped tightly around his neck. Dale had secretly told Mike what he'd seen in the corridor but Mike decided to tease Jason, pointedly asking why he was wearing the scarf. Jason had prepared himself for just such a question, making up the story that Biddy Rand - the *Funtime* Group Entertainment Director - had asked him to try wearing it as a potential new uniform accessory. Mike and Dale stifled their sniggers until Jason had left for his meeting with the head of the holiday centre.

Jill Tully was leaning over the reception counter talking guardedly to Kenny. She warned him to tread carefully around Gillian Evans - his shop assistant in their photographic shop. He pushed her for a reason and Jill couldn't help but spill the beans. She had noticed that Gillian looked very upset when she came in for work that morning so asked her if she was okay, despite sensing that she wasn't. Gillian had previously confessed to Jill that she had been having arguments with her husband over his late nights coming home drunk. This morning, while she was getting dressed in the bedroom, he had woken up. Between groans from his latest hangover, he mumbled that he'd had a terrible nightmare about her bending all of his golf clubs. She left for work without responding but by now he will have found out that what he thought was a nightmare actually happened!

Jill and Kenny were still laughing about the golf clubs when Jason turned up. Unsure if they were laughing at his love bites, he quickly yanked his scarf up to his earlobes to ensure it was still covering them. Jill ushered Jason in to Eric Arden's office for their meeting. Inevitably, Eric couldn't help but ask why Jason was wearing the purple scarf. Jason spouted the same story that he had told his team earlier. Eric hid his disbelief in order to progress the subject of their meeting - bringing in some new entertainment to cheer everyone up while the weather was so bad. Jason had prepared a list of acts that might be suitable and started to go through them before Eric stopped him.

The entertainment budget had mostly been used up but Eric had an idea that wouldn't cost a penny. He handed Jason a letter, but without waiting for it to be read, summarised the content: 'I received this from Brixham Salvation Army just last week. As you can see, they've asked if their brass band can come up to the *Seaview* to play. No payment will be needed so long as their helpers can go around with donation tins that the *campers* can put their change into.' Jason squirmed when Eric said the word "campers" – a banned word in *Funtime holiday centres* because it's what the opposition calls their holidaymakers – then he realised his manager was just quoting from the letter. Eric continued 'If we arrange for the band to play in the ballroom after lunch, the *guests* ...' he emphasised the word for Jason's benefit'... will be encouraged to imbibe at *Inn Paradise* so we'll actually make money rather than spend it!'

Eric patted himself on the back for coming up with what he thought was a brilliant plan. Jason went along with it just to please his boss, but was concerned that neither of them knew how good or bad the Salvationist players were. Jason also recalled rumours from his Gay Liberation Front buddies that the Salvation Army hierarchy supported legislation against same-sex orientations. He couldn't voice any displeasure to his boss but was privately determined not to personally meet or support them.

The *rookie Purplecoat*s worked a daily rota to clear up and clean up the dressing room alongside the stage in the ballroom. Jason went up to one of them and said: 'Ahh, Callum. I've got a very worthwhile task for you to carry out'. Callum said: 'Sound's good, what do you want me to do?' 'Well, I've just arranged for the Brixham Salvation Army band to visit and perform in the ballroom on Tuesday afternoon, straight after the bingo session. I want you to help them set up and supervise the event.' Callum initially said 'I'm sorry Jason but I won't be able to do it.' 'Why not?' 'Because I'm already tasked with cleaning the dressing room at that time'. Jason had already thought this through and said 'The two of us are the only *Purplecoat*s on duty then and I'll be busy showing a VIP round'. While Callum was taking this in, Jason added 'This is a good chance for you to step up and I'm confident that you can fit in both tasks.' Before Callum could say another word, Jason explained: 'They are in the same location - and you'd have had to wait in the dressing room in any case while the band plays. All you have to do is introduce the band to the audience, go into the dressing room to do your chores and listen out for the bandleader to announce "This will be our final number." You can then emerge out of the dressing room as the music ends to do a big thank you, leaving everyone happy'. It all sounded plausible and Jason was adamant that Callum could do this without any problems so he walked away before Callum could come up with any counter argument if he dared.

Callum and Lenny enjoyed the company of Alan - the son of the *Seaview*'s Head Groundsman. Despite not being able to understand everything he said, he was a proper Brixham boy so could talk about local customs or places to get things. One day, the three of them were talking about the cost of booze when Alan said "I be gwain to my fay'vrit scrumpy farm soon – wanner tag along to try the best grog ooo can get?" He added 'Don't dare buy scrumpy anywhere else - It's a rantacket of a catchpenny!" He slowly explained that he knew the owners of a farm with an apple orchard that produced the best but cheapest scrumpy in the world, or at least in Devon, and buying scrumpy from anywhere else would be a waste of money.

The were all free on Sunday afternoon, so Alan borrowed the *Seaview*'s minibus and took Lenny and Callum on a white-knuckle ride down miles of windy single-track roads in the general direction of Totnes. Lenny and Callum closed their eyes in fear while Al told them he believed scrumpy was first made by pixies so he called it Pixie Juice. 'If someone drinks too much, we call it gettin shamfered up then, if their feet go backwards when they want to go forwards, they are accused of being 'Pixie Led'.

Alan said 'Yer Tiz' as the minibus screeched to a halt at the entrance to what looked like a ramshackle farm fronted by a charming thatched and beamed cottage bedecked with a half dozen hanging baskets already in full bloom.

As the three of them got out of the minibus, an organic smell hit their senses. The powerful pong of rural detritus was stronger than a sewerage farm. Callum wondered if the drink they'd come for would smell or even taste as bad.

Alan was a regular visitor to the farm so opened a wooden latch to one side of the shed and said "We'll go thru hikkety rather than ring bell". Alan shouted out 'Lo?' as they entered the shed but there was no answer. He walked them past the large sweet-smelling wooden vats and massive cider press through the back door that led out to the fields beyond. They could see the farmer on a tractor mowing the grass around what must have been a hundred or more apple trees.

Alan pointed to the orchard and said "Caw kin' 'ee zee 'th blooth on sum o them 'ole trees?" Lenny and Callum nodded in agreement, assuming he was referring to the late blossom. Callum didn't understand the life cycle of apple trees so said 'How can we get scrumpy if the apples haven't grown yet?' Alan laughed and said 'Don be silly – this year's scrumpy was pressed from last year's apples so its ad plenny of toime t ferment. Also, the alcol genrated firm the fermentation process kills off potentially armful germs from damaged apples riddled with maggots, wasps and even rats!' Lenny and Callum squirmed at the thought and Alan teased them further by adding 'all these pests just add me'eness to the flavour!'.
When the farmer saw Alan, he turned off his tractor, stepped down and walked up to him. They shook hands and Alan said "Ow be Nackin' Vore?" The farmer replied with 'Oi be gurt fine - 'ow be ee then?' Alan said 'purty vitty thank ee'. They mumbled something else in private before chuckling as they looked toward Callum and Lenny standing there. The farmer smiled toward the latest visiting 'grockles' and said 'Orr roit?' He was close enough for them to see that most of his teeth were missing and those that were left were stained yellow, presumably from drinking his own brew - not a great advert for scrumpy sales.

The farmer said 'Come on me boody - 'tiz time 't nip in ter shed t'wet yer oozle' which to the Londoner's ears sounded like 'wet your whistle' so they all followed the farmer back into the big shed. He picked up a well-worn and grimy plastic tumbler from a cracked wooden table, placed it under the tap of the biggest vat and poured a small amount of the amber liquid into the tumbler. He then swung the tumbler away from his visitors to eject its contents on the ground - in his own mind this sufficiently cleaned the tumbler ready for tasting. Looking at Lenny first, he said 'Wood yew loik to troy a drap?' Lenny just about worked out what he was saying and replied 'Oh Yea fanks, cheers ta.' The farmer looked astonished and said to Alan 'Ark at 'Ee - that's a funny acsunt" and they all laughed at the ironic amusement of trying to communicate with each other in their different regional dialects.

Alan asked Lenny if he wanted to try the sweet, medium or rough scrumpy. Lenny recalled when Kenny took him and Callum to *The Three Elms Inn* before the season started and insisted that they have their first taste of Devon scrumpy as part of an initiation ceremony. At the time, they went for the medium option as it seemed to be the safest bet. This time, Lenny didn't want to be thought of as a wimp grockle so boldly went for the rough scrumpy this time.

The farmer smiled knowingly and placed the tumbler under the tap of the vat containing the rough scrumpy and filled it to the rim. Al was first to drink the scrumpy and after gulping half the cupful in one go, said 'Zamzoi' which apparently meant 'Very Good'. The next to try the brew was Lenny. He briefly glanced at the contents, presumably to make sure there were no floating lumps or body remains in it, then bravely took a swig of the liquid. He smiled at the sweet and sharp flavour of his first authentic rough scrumpy taken straight from the vat. The farmer said 'Gurt lush, proper job, innit'. Lenny assumed he was asking if he liked it and suggesting that 'it's good isn't it.' After having the leg pulled on his accent last time, Lenny simply said 'Mmmm' and nodded in approval. Callum followed suit, although he had to stop himself from spitting it out from the initial shock of its powerful taste. The farmer elbowed him playfully and said 'More parrr to thee elbo, boi!' The alcohol hit their senses and encouraged them to try out all three flavours before agreeing that the medium was the best option after all.

The effect of the liquid was probably better than the flavour but they all reckoned this would be the cheapest way to get drunk locally even though they would have to pay the same amount for the reusable container as they did for the scrumpy. Lenny and Callum agreed to share an investment in a 5-gallon polycask container full of the medium flavour scrumpy. Callum handed the farmer a crisp five-pound note and cringed as the old man dug deep into his overall pockets and fished out two crumpled and filthy one-pound notes. The farmer said 'Thankin' 'ee kindly' as he handed the change to Callum. Alan handed all his change to the farmer and raised four fingers to which the farmer said 'Zactly roit'.

Lenny and Callum struggled to carry their single container to the minibus then waited for Alan to make four trips to bring four containers. Lenny said 'Blimey, Alan – you must like your scrumpy!' Alan said 'these 'tainers of rough r for t' kitchen lads'.

The journey back was very hazy after the scrumpy tasting but Callum and Lenny vaguely remembered having a good laugh with their driver who they renamed 'Big Al.' They even managed to understand some of the things he said! All three of them were aware that alcohol, especially the infamous scrumpy, was banned from all staff accommodation. Big Al's dad was the *Seaview*'s Head Groundsman, so he was taking more of a risk than Callum and Lenny by smuggling it in. He told his passengers that he didn't mind them telling anyone he took them to a scrumpy farm for a tasting but asked them to stay 'mumchance' about him bringing containers back 'speshly for them kitchen sprats'. Callum asked Big Al why he called the kitchen lads 'sprats.' He said 'well, they be oily, smelly and go round in gangs like shoals o' veesh!' No matter what the risks were and what he thought of the sprats, he was happy to make a bit of profit from selling them a few containers. Big Al explained the guards regularly raided the infamous big house where most of the kitchen lads were billeted. If they found any scrumpy, they would confiscate it but, instead of reporting it, they'd consume it themselves as a secret perk. This only made the kitchen lads buy more to quench their thirst for the stuff. Big Al confessed that 'them kitchen sprats' planned to hide today's batch of containers in the woods at the back of their house and top up their bottles as needed. He jokingly added 'I do 'ope thikky security men don't find the stash too quick, else I'll just 'ave to go and get some more for 'em and make a bit more profit!'

As they passed Churston station, Big Al told them about the dual use of the brightly coloured Wendy house opposite the *Seaview*'s reception entrance. It was of course put there for children to play in during the day, however, late at night it was a target for adults wanting claustrophobic sex. He'd often seen security guards shooing kinky lovers out and them running away clutching their clothes.

Despite the alcohol and laughter, Big Al managed to keep the minibus on the road and get them back safely, stopping right outside the purple flat. He helped Callum and Lenny lift their container of scrumpy out of the minibus and plonk it down on the pavement then drove off to deliver the containers to 'them kitchen sprats'.

Lenny grabbed one handle of their scrumpy container and Callum held on to the base to share the weight as they heaved it off the ground. It seemed heavier than when they'd first picked it up and they struggled to shuffle the booze along the entrance path to the front door of the purple flat. The after effects of the tasting session had hit them so they were mighty relieved that nobody saw them stagger in carrying 5-gallons of booze. They didn't dare store the scrumpy in the kitchen or anywhere else where the other *Purplecoat*s might see it so hid it at the bottom of the wardrobe in their bedroom. That evening, they managed to steal a couple of stacks of plastic glasses from the *Seaview* stores cupboard and bring them back to their room. They could then help themselves to their scrumpy hoard whenever they or their visitors wanted a drink.

Jason was sharing the bathroom mirror with his young beau early Tuesday morning. He had forgiven Daniel for the love bite debacle earlier in the week, especially now that some carefully applied makeup meant he didn't have to cover his neck with that purple scarf and continue the ridiculous charade that he was wearing it as a potential new uniform accessory. As he put on his uniform for his Tuesday morning stint, he thought it would be nice to give Daniel a glimpse of the environment he worked in so asked if he'd like to join him up the hill for breakfast and a tour of the holiday centre. Daniel was delighted with the offer but concerned that it would be risky for Jason to flaunt a boyfriend in front of his colleagues and holidaymakers. Jason assured him that it would be fine so long as he went along with whatever he said.

In the dining room, Jason formally introduced Daniel to his team, stating 'Daniel is an up-and-coming cabaret star who is visiting the *Seaview* to consider performing here at a later date'. Daniel nodded in agreement and Jason had put the story across so well that he almost believed it was true. There were a couple of spare seats on Jason's table, held in reserve for visiting acts so it seemed entirely appropriate for Jason to sit Daniel alongside himself for breakfast. Mike remembered driving the two of them back from the Blue Bay nightclub when he had his one-night stand with Dolores but went along with Jason's story. The other *Purplecoat*s took Jason's explanation with a pinch of salt but at least engaged in polite conversation with Daniel for the sake of keeping the peace with their boss. When Daniel mentioned that he was performing a skeleton dancing act at the Festival Theatre it certainly seemed believable that Jason would consider bringing his act to the *Seaview*.

Jason stood up and flicked on the microphone to give the morning's announcements to the holidaymakers. It included the latest weather report, warning that it will continue to rain for the rest of the day. After light-hearted boos died down from some of the diners, he continued 'Okay, okay. We can't change this typically wet English weather but I'm delighted to announce that we've arranged for special visitors that I'm sure will lift everyone's spirits.' Jason was relieved to hear the boos turning to excited Oo's so continued. 'Immediately after this afternoon's bingo session in the ballroom, the Brixham Salvation Army brass band will be playing all your favourite tunes'. The Oo's now turned to less enthusiastic Oh's.

Callum helped Lenny set up for that afternoon's bingo session then waited in reception until the minibus carrying the Salvation Army band arrived. A dozen players clambered out carrying brass and percussion instruments of various sizes. Then came a flag bearer and a half dozen Salvationist helpers carrying donation tins and cardboard boxes full of copies of the latest edition of The War Cry publication. The band leader went up to Callum and shook his hand saying 'Thank you for allowing us this opportunity to play for your holidaymakers. I'm afraid a few of our best players have had to cry off with bad colds but the show must go on as they say in your line of business.' Callum politely acknowledged the band leader's gratitude but chuckled to himself at his presumption that he was talking to a seasoned professional.

Lenny was in the midst of calling the bingo numbers as Callum led the band into the ballroom. They walked around Lenny's table and started setting up in front of the stage. Whilst the remaining bingo games were being played, brass instruments were sliding out of their bags onto the stage and percussion instruments were clonking and crashing on the ballroom floor. The noise not only put the bingo players off their game but Lenny was so distracted that he made an elementary mistake when calling out a number: 'two little ducks, twenty-eight!' Luckily, 22 had already been crossed off so Lenny corrected himself by saying 'Sorry, bingo players - I made a mistake there. Ironically that should be two and eight, what a state, twenty-eight!'

More holidaymakers arrived in the ballroom, shaking the rain off their clothes but anticipating that the brass band would *lift everyone's spirits* as promised by Jason. Lenny had to shout out the last few bingo numbers just to be heard above the noise of the band and the new arrivals settling down. He was relieved when a lady finally screamed out 'Bingo.' Callum helped out by going over to her table and reading out the numbers on her card so that Lenny could confirm they matched those on his board. Callum picked up her winnings from Lenny and gave it to the winner.

As the two of them moved the bingo equipment and tables off the ballroom floor, Lenny said to Callum 'Good luck, CC. I'd stay to help you but I told Ruby I'd spend the afternoon with her.' Callum watched Lenny walking briskly out of the ballroom and had a good idea what he would be up to for the rest of the afternoon. He started thinking it was about time he got his own sex life sorted out ...

The band leader had seen Callum deep in thought and whispered in his ear 'Please introduce the band quickly as we're all desperate to start, especially our bugle player as he has a particularly acute bladder problem. We don't want an accident to occur, do we!' Callum snapped out of his fantasy world. There was a job to do here and now - actually two jobs to do at the same time so let's get the first job started. As he flicked on the microphone, he looked around the ballroom and was overwhelmed by the size of the audience that had turned up. He reckoned there must be at least 200 *guests* packed into all the seats and standing areas.

Callum was determined to be as professional as the band leader thought he was when he first met him. Trying to be as witty as Jason would have been, he announced as bold and clear as possible 'Good afternoon, ladies and gentlemen. After that exciting game of bingo …' he paused for laughs but none were forthcoming. Undaunted, he continued '... we have come to the moment you've all been waiting for. Please put your hands together and give a big *Seaview* welcome to the award winning Brixham Salvation Army brass band!'

Callum sneaked into the dressing room to start his cleaning chore. He had got a bit carried away in his introduction making up the bit about the band being 'award winning.' He soon regretted that little white lie as he could hear the band's percussion instruments playing different beats and more than a few notes coming out of the brass instruments were off key. It reminded Callum of that classic sketch from the previous year's Morecambe and Wise Christmas special. The one where Eric tells Andre Previn - the great pianist, composer, arranger, and conductor - 'I'm playing all the right notes, but not necessarily in the right order.'

Callum was half way through cleaning and clearing up the dressing room when he found a pint glass that had been left on a shelf. It was full of yellow liquid that he was pretty sure was not beer, unless you include beer that's already been through someone's internal organs. In the middle of the day, *guests* could drink as much alcohol as they wanted but Jason frowned upon any of his *Purplecoats* being seen with an alcoholic drink, or anything that looked like an alcoholic drink before 8pm. Callum had no option but to climb up and open the small window in the dressing room then toss the contents of the glass out. Thankfully, no one was walking by outside the dressing room or they would have been drenched in cold urine.

The Brixham Salvation Army brass band were still in full flow so he couldn't take the empty glass to the bar as *guests* would see him and think he'd just drunk whatever was in it. Talking of *guests*, he wondered how many were still enjoying the cacophony. He peered through the gap in the dressing room door to check the audience. From his position he could only see one side of the seating area around the ballroom but noticed a lot of seats that *had* been occupied when the band started were now empty. He also noticed that the bugle player was shuffling around in an agitated way, presumably in an attempt to take his mind off his bladder problem. The audience probably thought it was the bugler's way of keeping a rhythm going but he would probably have appreciated Callum's empty pint glass at this moment!

The band leader realised it was a lost cause so announced that the next tune would be their final number. The bugler looked thankful that he would soon relieve the pressure on his bladder but Callum was caught off guard. He had to quickly take his rubber gloves off, put the cleaning products away and place the safe key in its usual hiding place, ready to emerge from the dressing room for the final thank you.

By the time Callum got back to the microphone, only 20 or so brave holidaymakers remained, nonetheless, he managed to get some sort of an appreciative applause from them. They must have been tone deaf, extremely generous, stupid or all of the above. They obviously hadn't seen the Salvationist helpers taking merchandise out of their cardboard boxes and hadn't foreseen what would happen next. As soon as the applause died down, the helpers pounced upon their audience, desperately trying to hand out copies of The War Cry publication and extract money by shaking their donation tins.

It took an age for the Salvationists to use the toilet facilities and pack up their instruments and merchandise. They couldn't have raised much money but the band leader appeared to be used to this, politely thanking Callum as they piled back into their minibus. Callum gave a sigh of relief as the vehicle disappeared over the hill and out of the holiday centre. He could now take that "used" beer glass to the bar so that it could be thoroughly washed. It was a wonder there were no outbreaks of salmonella or typhoid poisoning!

One show that the holidaymakers could always rely on for entertainment was the weekly *Purplecoat* show. Jason and Dale were fantastic comedians as well as being excellent and confident singers but their versatility and skills in both categories came to the fore in this show.

Jason started off with his song and dance act based on the swing era then Dale followed up with a couple of more contemporary songs including a rendition of Don McLean's 1971 hit 'American Pie.' Dale accompanied himself on acoustic guitar as he sang this classic folk/rock song about the loss of innocence of the early rock and roll generation. Most of the audience loved it but it got a bit repetitive for the other *Purplecoats*, especially when Dale milked the opportunity and went on past his 10-minute slot. When he finally came back to the dressing room, he pointed his guitar toward the stage and said to Tricia 'Okay, Tania Twinkletoes, over to you!'

The band started playing the intro and Tricia, AKA Tania Twinkletoes, bravely clattered onto the stage and went through her tap-dancing number to the tune of *Anything Goes*. As Lenny and Callum watched her, they were getting more and more nervous because their 'Mother, I Die' sketch was next up and it seemed to be the weakest part of the show. When Mike had gone through the sketch with them, he'd assured them that it would go down well. Despite their misgivings, they acted their parts as ordered by Mike in his role as film director. Unfortunately, the less than enthusiastic response from the audience confirmed they didn't think the sketch was that amusing either. They agreed to find a way to improve it but only after they'd settled into their jobs and were confident that they wouldn't be sacked for daring to change it.

The next act always went well. It was a quick-fire comedy duel between Jason and Dale. With the band providing a high-tempo musical beat, Jason would tell a short bawdy joke or ditty in time with the music then Dale would immediately respond and try to outdo him with an even more risqué pun. 'The Grand Old Duke of York, he had ten thousand men - Oooh!' could be followed by 'Mary had a little lamb - the doctor had a fit!' 'Georgie, Porgie, puddin and pie, kissed the girls and made them cry. When the boys came out to play, he kissed them too he's funny that way!' 'She offered her honour; he honoured her offer and all night long he was on er and off er!' 'Puff the magic dragon, lived upon the shelf, he couldn't play with little boys so Puff played with himself!' Dale's favourite was 'When I die, bury me deep, make it humble, make it cheap, upon my tombstone I want this wrote, a million drinks have gone down my throat, if you pass by where I lie, piddle on me, I'm always dry!' The music got faster and faster until one of them failed to come up with a new pun in time to the beat. At that moment, Mike ran on to raise the arm of the winner like a boxing champion and encouraged the audience to applaud them off the stage.

The pace increased further with the final act and highlight of the show. The band played Offenbach's Galop Infernal and the *Purplecoat* girls - Jeannette, Jane and Tricia - ran up onto the stage whooping in their can-can costumes. Jeannette looked the part as she was the only one with a tall slim body that might have got through a real audition at the Moulin Rouge. Tricia got into the fun of the show but Jane felt extremely uncomfortable - she hated flaunting herself in this way. The audience were oblivious to Jane's embarrassment and simply enjoyed the routine of high kicks, half splits, and cartwheels. They clapped along to the rhythm of the song and cheered whenever skirts and petticoats were raised and white flesh shown. The cheers turned to raucous laughter when Jason, Dale, Callum and Lenny ran on whooping in can-can costumes to join in the dancing. Callum and Lenny followed the movements of the girls as far as they could but Jason and Dale must have had ballet training as they could do expert cartwheels from one end of the chorus line to the other ending with full splits.

After wild and sustained applause, the *Purplecoat*s came back out for a brief encore. They waved to the audience in gratitude before turning round and simultaneously bending over while lifting their skirts and petticoats for a final glimpse of their rear covered by the frilliest of knickers.

Jason's young beau, Daniel, had watched the whole show and patiently waited while the *Purplecoat*s changed out of their can-can gear. As soon as Jason emerged from the dressing room, he minced up to him and patted him on the back, rather than where he wanted to pat him. Daniel excitedly told everyone how much he enjoyed the show. A pretty blonde girl went up to Dale and congratulated him with a kiss and a cuddle. He loved the attention but introduced his girlfriend to everyone present with the minimum of fuss, simply announcing 'This is Sue'. The four of them said their goodnights as they walked off to go back to the purple flat and celebrate in their own way. Bill said 'I'm knackered and off to my bed too' before trudging off in the same direction without any pleasantries.

With Mike's usual accomplices for his end of the week fix otherwise engaged, he had to look elsewhere so turned to Callum and Lenny. He offered to take them to the Blue Bay nightclub to watch a cabaret and have a slap-up meal with him – his treat. The rookies were tired but couldn't turn down such a generous offer so changed out of their uniform at the flat then Mike drove them at breakneck speed to the nightclub. Despite the rush, it was past midnight by the time they were tucking in to huge steak suppers. Lenny wasn't homophobic but didn't enjoy the drag act and was glad when they took a bow. As the applause rang out, he glanced at the excited faces around the room and couldn't imagine having anything in common with them. Next to take the stage were two unattractive middle-aged ladies. They gyrated to the tempo of the sleazy music and gradually discarded their clothes. Eventually, the only items remaining on their bodies were tassels hanging off their nipples. The audience went wild as the strippers closed the show by spinning the tassels faster and faster and in different directions. Lenny found this part of the show more interesting than the drag act but still didn't like the overt voyeurism or the seedy side of life that this place epitomised. The steaks were tasty but much too filling for an after-midnight supper. Lenny found the whole scene desperately sad and decided never to return. He was surprised that Callum seemed to be more tolerant of the people that frequented the place or perhaps he simply enjoyed midnight feasts.

CHAPTER 13 - Here Come the Families (w/c Saturday 27th May)

[Playlist Track: "Schools out" – Alice Cooper]

At the start of the third week of the season, the number of visitors arriving at the *Seaview* holiday centre increased by many hundreds, the majority of which were families with children of all ages. New employees also arrived to share the increased workload and provide additional services to a wider range of *guests*.

Midway through their first dinner sitting, Jason took to the microphone and formally welcomed the new batch of holidaymakers. He recommended they read through the programme they'd been given to see the host of games and competitions on offer throughout the week at the *Seaview*. Participating in these events would not only offer the possibility of a personal reward but also earn points for the *planet* they had been assigned to when they checked in. Jason added 'Even if you're not participating, please support those that do, especially if they're assigned to your *planet*!

When Jason finished going through the agenda for that evening, he noticed a few *guests* only just walking in to the dining room. Regular *Funtime guests* knew what they had to do to late-comers and they slow hand clapped them as they made their way to their table. When the clapping ended, Jason took the opportunity to mention that any *guests* arriving late for meals made it unnecessarily difficult for the waitress and kitchen to accommodate and disrupted the service to other diners. He then announced a rule that would be enforced from the next meal sitting through to the end of the week: In addition to the slow hand clapping, any holidaymakers arriving in the dining room after service had started would have to turn up at their next meal dressed only in their bed clothes. The thought of eating in a packed dining room wearing only pyjamas or a nightie was enough to make most people ensure they weren't late but Jason added that anyone failing to comply with the punishment would lose 10 points for the planet they'd been assigned to. Luckily, most *guests* supported the rule and even took the punishment in good spirit.

After dinner, all the holidaymakers moved into the bar and ballroom for drinks while they played bingo, then danced to Tony Garner's big band. To avoid having lots of kids causing havoc after their usual bedtime, Dale ran a *Goodnight Kids* send off. At 8:30pm, he stood in front of the stage and asked all the children to come up and join him - Uncle Dale – with Auntie Tricia and Uncle Bill - on the ballroom floor for the *official Junior Club Bedtime Song*. This song was used at all *Funtime* holiday centres to ensure the younger children of the holidaymakers were tucked up in bed by 9pm every night. While Tricia and Bill organised the kids to sit down in a semicircle around Dale, he told Mums and Dads to check the Junior Club schedule in the programme they'd been given for events taking place each day. Now all the kids were sat in front of him, Uncle Dale asked those who knew the song to sing along with them while the rest could hum along until they'd learnt the song in the Kids Club events. Dale strummed his guitar as they all sang or hummed along to the *official Junior Club Bedtime Song* which used the melody of *Pop Goes the Weasel*:

> Mary had some marmalade and Mary had some jam
> Mary had some Worcester Sauce and Mary had some Spam
> Mary had some lemonade and then some Ginger Beer
> And Mary wondered why it was that she was feeling queer

Whoops went the marmalade and whoops went the jam
Whoops went the Worcester Sauce and whoops went the Spam
Whoops went the lemonade and then the Ginger Beer
And Mary wondered why it was that she was feeling queer!

As they reached the end of the song, Uncle Dale, Auntie Tricia and Uncle Bill got all the kids to raise their arms and shout a final 'Triffic!' The audience gave the children a hearty round of applause to make them proud to have been well behaved. It would also hopefully encourage the kids to go to bed and let their parents enjoy the rest of the night.

Jason gave all the parents enough time to put their kids to bed, top up with drinks and settle in their seats before he led all his *Purplecoat* team on to the stage. He introduced them to the *guests* as he had done in the wrinkly weeks, but, now that parents were in the audience, he also spent time talking about the Junior Club. He kept looking around the ballroom until he sighted a little old lady who was familiar to him. Even though she was small in height, Nanny Muriel stood out from the crowd in the formal white overall that she always wore, even though it was hardly ever needed. The uniform gave her the appearance of a professional carer but those that knew her better were well aware that age was catching up with her, physically and mentally. Jason called for Nanny Muriel to join them on the stage and introduced her as '… a key member of the Junior Club team. In addition to providing valuable assistance to Dale's team during the day, Nanny Muriel will be on call every evening for *kids checks* … '

While the entertainment was in full swing each evening, the holiday centre's security guards patrolled the grounds, particularly checking chalet numbers that had been registered at reception for *kids checks*. If they heard a child crying inside the chalet or there was a problem, they would use their walkie talkies to contact reception. Whoever was on duty would respond to each call by chalking the chalet number on a black board at the side of the stage then flick the switch to a flashing amber light with the message *Baby Crying*. The parents that had registered that chalet number could then go up and switch the light off to confirm they were going back to their chalet straight away to deal with their child. Nanny Muriel would be on standby if any parent needed paediatric help or if the flashing light wasn't turned off within 5 minutes. Lots of parents made sure their chalet was included in the *kids checks* scheme so that they could relax every evening while their children were tucked up in bed at their chalet.

After the introductions had finished, Jason told his team 'Don't forget to walk around and mingle with the *guests*. Remember, it's all about *socialising and dancing with the guests whenever and whatever music is playing'*. Jane thought she'd got into the swing of this *Socialising* concept until she asked a couple 'Did you have a long and difficult journey to get here today?' She was taken aback when they said 'Not really, we only had to walk up the path from our chalet because we arrived a week ago!' Lenny was having a completely different experience. Guests asked him to pose for a photo with them so that they could show friends and family back home what a good time they had with a Purplecoat on their Funtime holiday. Later on in the evening, driven on by alcohol, some guests would take things further and Lenny would often end up with someone's girlfriend or wife being intentionally plonked on his lap for photos, a dare, quality time or risqué contact.

Kenny had developed a relationship with Jill Tully. As reception manager, she kept her ear to everything that was going on at the *Seaview* from the top management to the kitchen lads. The previous week, she had handed Kenny a letter that was addressed to a Mr K Tucker. It was marked Urgent so he didn't hesitate in tearing open the envelope and decided to read out the key points to Jill. The letter was from his photographic services agency. They were sending two bunny girls to the *Seaview* to help boost photo sales. The girls, called Diana and Violet, were due to arrive that Monday afternoon so accommodation needed to be arranged for them within just two days. Jill checked the Reservations folder and confirmed that holiday bookings were at an all-time high at the *Seaview* and all available twin chalets not already used by staff had been reserved for holidaymakers.

Kenny said he didn't think it would be a good idea for the girls to squeeze in with him and Roy in the chalet they shared. Jill didn't laugh at his attempt at humour and came up with a solution. The maintenance team had spare beds in stock so she would get them to squeeze another single bed into a single chalet that the girls could share when they arrive.

Two days later, Jill handed Kenny the keys to a single chalet at the far end of the holiday centre to be used by the two bunny girls. He checked it out and, as Jill had promised, the maintenance team had somehow managed to squeeze another single bed into this tiny chalet - he hoped the bunny girls were on the small side and would get on well enough to accept living together in such a tight space.

He couldn't dwell on his thoughts as he had to get back up to reception to welcome the girls' arrival. It was quite a long walk from the chalet they would be sharing but his mind was put at rest when he saw what the agency had sent him. Jill stayed behind the counter as she introduced the girls to Kenny. He tried to be professional in welcoming them but was distracted - they were petite but buxom and put their arms around one another as they spoke. Kenny thought they were attractive enough in normal clothes but he couldn't wait to see how they looked in bunny girl uniforms and he fantasised about how they would look squashed together in their single beds… Jill's glare snapped him out of his thoughts and he emphasised to the bunny girls that they should turn to *Jill* for anything to do with the holiday centre. Jill now raised her eyebrows expectantly at Kenny and, after a long pause, he remembered to mention that she was his girlfriend! If he thought that would stop her from being jealous it was already too late, especially after the bunny girls giggled childishly and said they liked to be called Di and Vi.

Kenny helped Di and Vi carry their luggage down to their single chalet. They didn't seem concerned that their accommodation was so small and admitted that they'd stayed in worse places. A few hours later, he returned to take them back up the hill for dinner in the staff canteen before their first evening of working together. They carried plastic shopping bags containing the uniforms they would change into after dinner, talking of which, they followed Kenny's lead in loading their plates with a salad and snack from the meagre buffet. The waitresses stared jealously and the tongues of the kitchen lads were hanging out when they saw these new pretty girls dressed in the latest summer fashions. Kenny saw the impact the girls had on his colleagues and wondered how much more excited they would be when they saw them in their uniforms. As it happens, a few kitchen lads had already spotted bunny girl uniforms peeking out of their bags and were salaciously imagining the girls wearing them.

After their meal, Kenny walked Di and Vi down to the shop where his photos and other merchandise were on display. There was no dressing room so Kenny stood guard at the door while the girls changed into their bunny girl costumes behind a counter. When Kenny saw them come out all dressed, or should that be undressed, in their outfits it was his turn to get turned on. The uniform consisted of a skin tight black strapless corset with white silk collar and cuffs, a black bow tie, bunny ears and tights, and a white fluffy tail.

Armed with his camera and flash unit at the ready, Kenny escorted the girls to the noisy dining room. Prior to the arrival of his new assistants, taking photos of the guests while they were eating was the least enjoyable task of his working week but a necessary evil to get early snaps. The reason why he hadn't enjoyed it was because he would waste a lot of film on photos that couldn't be sold. The faces of his targets were often contorted while they were eating and talking or they would intentionally mess about or make it difficult to get a good picture, sticking out their tongue or grimacing as if they were in a gurning contest.

This time, Kenny felt like Hugh Hefner parading his girls at the Playboy mansion as they sauntered into the noisy dining room. Immediately, the noise died down as the diners saw the girls, nudged their neighbours and pointed to the new arrivals. Kenny soon got his bunny girls to pose alongside groups of holidaymakers at one table after another. The repetitive flashing of his camera lit up the room like an electric storm and the level of excitement and noise increased again as more and more holidaymakers got a good look at the scantily clad girls. The waitresses could do without this distraction as they were trying to avoid unruly kids that were running around after refusing to eat the sickeningly lumpy dessert options of Strawberry Blancmange or Jam Roly-Poly and Custard.

Kenny was on his third roll of photo film and the mass photo shoot had gone extremely well by the time they reached the last table to be visited. The guests pointed to the oldest member of their party and said grandad was celebrating his 80th birthday. Kenny got the bunny girls to make a big fuss of him and lean in close either side of him while they posed for an amusing if provocative photo. The old man sneakily ran his gnarly hands down their backs and cheekily fondled their bottoms. Di and Vi were fun-loving girls who had been around the block a few times but were still dismayed when holidaymakers tried to take advantage of their close proximity when they posed with them. These men obviously assumed that, because the girls were dressed in sexy clothes, they were easy pickings so thought they could get away with a touch here or a grope there, even an octogenarian sat at a table with his family all around him.

Just as Kenny's camera shutter clicked, grandad's smirk changed to a grimace as he slumped forward and his face slammed into his Jam Roly-Poly dessert. His grandson was sat next to him and, like an automatic reflex, instantly reached across and yanked grandad's head out of the mush. The old man's face was smattered with jammy custard and his gaping mouth suggested the worst. Kenny ran to get the nurse and they soon returned with blankets ready to cover and carry grandad out of the dining room.

They were amazed to see that the old man had made a miraculous recovery. His face was all cleaned up and he was busy chomping away with what was left of his pudding as if nothing untoward had happened. He even made Hazel wait until he'd finished his pudding to check his pulse. She couldn't find any problem with his heart so suggested he book a thorough examination from his doctor when he gets home after the holiday. The family asked what might have caused his sudden collapse. Hazel suggested that he probably had an episode of vasovagal syncope. His family were frightened of these long unfamiliar words so asked "what is vasie veggie syncopation?" Hazel put their minds at rest by explaining that vasovagal syncope is simply fainting from getting over excited. His family were relieved and promised to make sure he calmed down and behaved himself for the rest of their holiday. That included keeping well away from those bunny girls!

Kenny saw that Di and Vi were still shaking so led them into *Inn Paradise* for a stiff drink to help them get over their shock. Such was their professionalism that, as soon as they'd knocked back large brandies, they were willing to pose for more snaps in the ballroom.

When the evening's entertainment finished, Kenny and the bunny girls had a few more drinks in the bar then he helped guide them back to their chalet. The three of them giggled as they staggered and swayed along the pathways. Their bonhomie, stoked by alcohol, encouraged Kenny to kiss both of them on their cheeks as he said goodnight at the chalet door. They didn't protest and he had an inkling that they wanted to take things further – maybe a threesome? He thought better of it and turned to take the long walk back to his own chalet as Di turned the key to open the chalet door. Suddenly, the three of them heard loud and rhythmic groaning inside - it was obvious what was taking place. Kenny, panicking, turned back, thinking that the alcohol had led them to the wrong door. He shouted 'Oops, sorry, we must have got the wrong chalet' but before he could recover his thoughts, a breathless voice he recognised called out from within: 'Is that you, Kenny? It's ok, It's Roy - we didn't realise this chalet was occupied.' The groaning stopped, replaced by muffled murmurs over the sound of clothes being put back on and zips closing up. Roy emerged from the chalet, closely followed by Jeannette. She looked dishevelled and very sheepish. Her cheeks could be seen blazing under the moonlight, rosy from aroused flushing as much as embarrassed blushing. Roy knew that Kenny was fully aware of what had just occurred but, to avoid further awkwardness for Jeannette - especially in front of two girls in bunny uniform … two girls in bunny uniform? Wow! His mind was racing but he managed to concoct a story that Jeannette was accompanying him on the security round when she suddenly needed to go to the loo and they thought that this chalet was unoccupied - sorry.

Tuesday morning was a special day for *Seaview*'s kids. They could choose to see a magic show in the ballroom or go on a coach excursion to Paignton Zoo. Uncle Bill and the children's Nanny, Muriel, looked after the kids in the ballroom while Uncle Dale and Auntie Tricia supervised the trip to the zoo. Although Tricia was a rookie, her responsibilities appeared to be pretty straightforward: Help gather together about thirty kids, get them onto a coach to take them to Paignton Zoo, help Dale supervise them for just a few hours as they look at the animals then get them safely back onto the coach back to the *Seaview* where their parents will collect them outside reception in plenty of time before the lunch sitting.

Tricia greeted parents and their children at the front of the coach for the trip to Paignton Zoo. Most parents told their children to behave as they handed them over. The kids were already too excited to listen and bounded up the coach steps to grab the seats with the best view or sit with their friends. Parents breathed a visible sigh of relief as they waved their kids off and the vehicle drove away. They had offloaded their charges to the *Purplecoats* and could now enjoy the rest of the morning as if they were on a second honeymoon.

Tricia walked up and down the aisle counting the kids and making a note of the total in her diary. The kids were very noisy on the half-hour coach journey to the zoo, but she was relieved that there were no major squabbles. When the coach reached the zoo's car park, Dale headed the group through the turnstiles and Tricia scooped up the straddlers at the rear. Kenny tagged along and took photos of the kids in front of lots of different animals.

The kids did as their parents asked them and behaved quite well. This was especially necessary when approaching monkey cages. The Monkey House building was long and narrow with only one entrance to an internal corridor flanked by rows of cages all the way to the exit door. The cages housed a variety of monkeys from around the world and Tricia did her best to shield the children's eyes from the ones that seemed to be engaged in some sort of sexual activity. A woolly monkey called Willow and a full-grown chimpanzee called Chumley were kept behind bars in the last two cages. Dale warned the kids in his group to stay silent or the beasts would get angry. When they reached the woolly monkey cage, a few kids made grunting noises which frightened Willow and he ran up to the bars screaming at them. Undaunted, they repeated their grunting at the full-grown chimpanzee. Human's closest living relative also didn't like the noisy kids so grabbed and threw at them whatever came to hand, luckily only banana skins and apple cores at this time. The kids, and their adult supervisors, just about escaped without getting covered in already chewed fruit.

The next stop was the Reptile House. Tricia was full of trepidation and dreaded seeing any of the inhabitants, especially the snakes. As soon as she saw one in a cage she had to escape immediately, shouting for Kenny to cover for her. He had no problem with this because reptiles were the least photogenic of all the animals at the zoo so he saved on wasted film. When Tricia rejoined the back of the group outside the Reptile House, Dale noticed and gave her a quizzical look. Tricia made the excuse that she suddenly had to go to the toilet. Dale assumed it was *women's problems* so didn't question her further.

As they all continued on the tour, Kenny sneaked up to Tricia and asked her if she was okay. She said 'I'm fine now Kenny and thank you for helping me back there. To be honest, I've been afraid of snakes or anything slivering since walking into a nest of adders while on a school trip. Please don't tell anyone, especially Dale, or I might lose my job'. Kenny agreed to keep her anxiety a secret and continue to cover for her whenever she came on this trip.

As they re-boarded the coach for the return journey, Dale asked Tricia to sit with a girl who was on her own and Kenny to sit with him. At first, Kenny thought he would get the third degree about Tricia going AWOL but eventually found out that Dale simply wanted his help that afternoon. Dale started with 'There's a *Hunt the Wicked Pirate* kiddies game starting at 3pm and I want you to be the leading man they'll be searching for'. Kenny said 'How come none of the other Purplecoats are taking the role?' Dale explained 'Bill is not fit enough to be chased and the others are playing in the *Guests versus Staff* football match. Look Kenny, you'll be *the star of the show* because I've got a brilliant pirate costume for you. I'll take it to the dressing room alongside the ballroom and explain everything if you meet me there at half past two'. Kenny said 'What's the catch?' Dale assured him 'No catch. Well, the only catch I suppose is when they catch you'. 'Yes?' 'Well, you have to allow them to push you into the swimming pool. The kids will be dressed up too and your costume is waterproof so you just need to wear underclothes that you don't mind getting wet. It'll be a lot of fun, especially in this hot weather.' Kenny didn't take much persuading to agree to be *the star of the show* because it did sound like it would be *a lot of fun*.

The coach was delayed by road works on the return journey from Paignton Zoo but arrived at the *Seaview* just in time for lunch. Dale and Tricia helped the kids disembark and made sure they were handed back to their appropriate guardians, no matter how begrudgingly for all concerned. They then followed them into the dining room for lunch.

Kenny went for lunch in the next building - the infamous staff canteen. As he scooped up a plateful of the second-class sustenance available, he saw Roy in the corner of the room and sat with him to eat it. Roy saw Kenny move two dirty plates and used cutlery to one side to make space for his own dish and said 'Ahh, Di and Vi have already had a snack and gone without clearing up their mess. You'll have to have a word with them, being as they work for you …'. Kenny noted that Roy had already found out their names even though he hadn't been properly introduced the previous night. The moment wasn't conducive to normal pleasantries because he and Jeanette had been too busy getting their clothes back on and making an excuse for their dishevelment. '… God, those girls are super sexy even when they're not in their bunny girl uniform …'. Roy was in full flow so Kenny didn't get the opportunity to admit that he agreed with Roy's assessment. '… They sat next to me to have their lunch and of course I apologised for 'using' their chalet the previous night. Apologies to you too, mate, if I gave you a shock.' Kenny, tried to use the term he'd learnt from a previous conversation with Roy: 'Would you say you were caught *in flagrante*?' Roy said 'I'm not sure about that but Jeannette was certainly gagging for *"it"* last night. Before you caught us in the bunny girls' chalet, we'd already been interrupted while trying to *do the business* in another chalet. Just as we started getting into it, bloody Baz suddenly came through on the walkie talkie shouting "Camp Fuzz here! Where are you, Roy?" then a frail female voice close by whispered "Hello? Is somebody there?" We'd woken up an old lady who happened to be in the next bed! In the moonlight, I could just about see that she was reaching out for her glasses on the bedside cabinet so, quick as a flash, I knocked them to the floor and we were out the door before she could find them and put them on. Hopefully, she'll have believed she knocked them over herself and was simply having a vivid dream!' Kenny said 'God, Roy. You take it beyond the limit don't you!' 'Don't blame me. I've never done anything like this before. It's Jeannette. She's a bad influence on me but I love it!'

As Kenny left the staff dining room to change for the Pirate game, he saw Baz and asked him about his part in the previous night's *walkie talkie incident*. Baz was only too eager to spill the beans. He and Roy were supposed to leave their walkie talkies on throughout their shifts in order to communicate with each other and respond to an emergency. The trouble with that arrangement was that he kept overhearing Roy getting up to all sorts. He got so fed up of hearing Roy gasping 'ooh, ooh Jeannette' and suchlike that he'd deliberately spoilt his fun to teach him to wait until he'd finished his shift and could officially turn his walkie talkie off. Baz promoted himself in every way when he summarised his stance on the matter: 'As Camp Fuzz Manager, I have to make sure everyone obeys the rules!'

Kenny continued through the ballroom to meet Dale in the dressing room. Dale picked up the pirate costume and propped it up in front of Kenny's chest. 'Put this on while I draw a map outside'. When Kenny came out of the dressing room Dale said 'That costume fits perfectly like it was made for you! Sit down while I go through the plan for *Hunt the Wicked Pirate*.' The costume was tighter than Kenny would like to admit but he managed to sit down without tearing the seams while Dale presented him with the map he'd drawn. It showed four locations around the holiday centre marked, not with an X, but numbered from 1 to 4, with the last one being intentionally near to the swimming pool. 'At the start of the game, you need to hide in location 1 while I deliberately lead the kids there. When you see or hear us, you've got to let the kids get a glimpse of you then, when they shout *"Pirate"*, you've got to run off to the next hiding place. At each location, let the kids get nearer to catching you until they finally *catch* you at location 4. When they all grab you, you've got to pretend to resist them before allowing them to pull you along and push you into the swimming pool.'

While hiding at location 1, Kenny was anticipating how excited the kids must be while searching for him as *the Pirate*. After what seemed like an age, he had a change of thought. Was Dale playing one of his tricks on him and nobody was looking for him at all. Just as he went to leave his hiding place and return to the dressing room, he heard the increasing sound of kids shouting rhythmically: *"Where is the Pirate. Where is the Pirate…"* When they got as near as Kenny dared, he let a few kids spot him. As soon as they screamed *"There is the Pirate…'* he made off to run to the next hiding place. As he looked back, he realised his chasers were all armed with pointed sticks. A few of them were quite speedy and Kenny only just managed to lose them by the time he got to location 4. As he awaited capture, he started to wonder what the kids planned to do with the pointed sticks. When he pretended to lose his balance and fell over on a grassy embankment he soon found out. They surrounded him and, cruelly urged on by Dale, prodded their pointed sticks mercilessly into him from every angle. Despite their young age and diminutive size this was quite painful. The scene reminded Kenny of the *Carry On Cleo* film often shown in the TV room were a group of senators stab Julius Caesar on the Ides of March. He went along with the similarity by quoting Kenneth Williams's line from it: "Infamy, infamy, they've all got it in for me" as the kids "forced" him toward and into the swimming pool with a big cheer of *Triffic!*'

The weather improved midweek so Mike and Dale started hosting a few outdoor activities. They handed over nearly all of the Bingo sessions to Lenny and Callum who saw this as a poisoned chalice when the weather was good for many reasons:

- Only the boring few would want to stay inside to play bingo when the sun was shining.
- The minimum number of players officially prescribed to run a bingo session was forty but, even when only twenty or so players turned up, there would always be a few bingo addicts who would desperately insist that the *Purplecoat*s go outside the ballroom and drag in more players so that the session could go ahead for their own amusement.

As more activities and events had to be hosted, *rookie Purplecoat*s had to quickly share or take over the load from experienced *Purplecoat*s. They usually learned how to host activities and events by watching an experienced *Purplecoat* do it for one or two sessions. The experienced *Purplecoat* would then watch while the *rookie Purplecoat* had a go, stepping in if and when necessary.

Based on the suitability profile provided by Biddy, Mike asked Callum to referee a football match with Dale's help while he would help Lenny compere the Most Elegant Grandmother contest. In reality, Callum could hardly kick a ball, let alone understand the rules and Lenny had never hosted any type of "beauty" contest.

Callum followed Dale to the football pitch, carrying eleven green and eleven blue coloured tabards. He didn't expect to need them all so was surprised that 18 holidaymakers had turned up to play. They all looked like they were in a contest for the biggest beer belly. Nonetheless, they were fully prepared for a football match in sports tops and shorts or track suits - some even wore football boots. Callum didn't own a pair of football boots, let along bring any to the *Seaview* so would have to make do with his white plimsolls. Dale split the teams corresponding to the 'planets' they had been assigned to when they checked in at the start of their holiday. After a terse reminder from Dale, Callum handed green tabards to the Saturn team and blue tabards to the Neptune team. As would so often be the case, the numbers didn't match up. There were 10 players in the Saturn team but only 8 in the Neptune team. The Saturn team refused to allow any of their players to switch to the opposition as they wanted to go all out for the 15 points on offer for the winning team's planet. To help even up the contest, Dale said to Callum 'Do you want to play for the Neptune team or would you prefer that I help them out?' Callum didn't fancy running around on a muddy pitch getting kicked so said 'I'd rather you help them out.' 'Alright Callum, I'll play while you referee!' Dale smiled sarcastically as he handed him a whistle and stopwatch and said 'Give the teams 20 minutes each half and a couple of minutes for the half-time break so they don't get cold'. Callum may have avoided getting kicked but was now kicking himself for not thinking through his options. In a panic, he practiced setting the stopwatch and blowing the whistle. The Saturn team took the sound of the whistle as the start of the game and kicked off before Dale had chance to take his place in the Neptune team. He had to run on the pitch and put on his blue tabard while he was running around.

The football pitch hadn't had a proper match played on it since the previous September so it was more like a paddy field than the hallowed grass of Wembley. Callum seemed to splash into the muddiest puddles as he tried to keep up with play, slipping and sliding in plimsolls that were getting wetter and heavier by the second. Dale was dismayed as he saw Callum stumble through the game, physically and from a refereeing perspective. Fouls and offside infringements were completely missed and Callum was clearly out of his depth. It all came to a head after just 12 minutes. Callum got too close to the action and collided with one of the players making a sliding tackle, losing his watch and whistle as he fell to the ground with the tackler. Of course, the tackler had to be Dale. The two of them struggled to get to their feet and recover the watch and whistle. Meanwhile, the Saturn team took full advantage and walked the ball into the net, unopposed. All hell broke loose as the teams argued with each other. Callum blew his whistle to try to stop the melee but it had too much mud in it to make a sound. Dale had to take charge to avoid a mass punch up. He snatched the whistle off Callum, shook the mud out and blew it long and loud over the main protagonists then shouted 'The game is over – it's being abandoned!' When the Saturn players protested, Dale blamed the state of the pitch rather than allude to Callum's mis-handling of the game. He quietly promised to award them 12 points for their planet – a point per minute - which they grudgingly accepted.

Dale was seething as he trudged back to the flat with Callum, both of them covered head to toe in soggy, cold mud. To make matters worse, Callum hadn't recovered all the tabards and failed to lighten the mood by saying 'It's amazing what people will pinch as mementoes!'

While Callum had been struggling on the football pitch, Mike was trying to help Lenny host the Most Elegant Grandmother competition. Only seven ladies entered the competition - they were all dressed in their best attire with lots of makeup slapped all over their faces to try to hide their wrinkles but this just made them look like pantomime dames. Mike lined the ladies up across the stage and gave Lenny the microphone in order to introduce each one to the audience. Lenny was not confident from the start. He did not feel suited for hosting family shows like an elegant granny competition. It crossed his mind that the only reason he would want to have a conversation with a granny would be to use her to get an introduction to her daughter or even her grand-daughter! He tried to banish these thoughts from his head while going through the motions of interviewing each contestant. 'Let's introduce our first contestant - what's your name?' 'Ethel Lane' 'Where are you from Ethel?' 'Pratts Bottom!' Lenny thought this was a wind-up and saw the audience sniggering but carried on just in case. 'Oh really?! Whereabouts is Pratts Bottom, Ethel?' 'It's in the London Borough of Bromley' 'Ahh, anyone out there from Bromley?' Muted cheers from a few people. 'Who are you here with Ethel?' 'My husband, Arnold, and my youngest daughter, Millicent' 'Ahh, she's lovely, I mean that's lovely …' Lenny tried not to focus on sweet Millicent too long and returned to the task at hand. 'Let's have a round of applause for Ethel, everyone' Polite clapping. As sweet as each old lady was, Lenny just couldn't add the excitement and personal quips that a professional like Jason, or even Mike, would have done. Mike took the microphone back from Lenny sooner than he'd anticipated, just to raise the tempo through the judging section. Without further delay, Mike announced that Ethel was the winner of the Most Elegant Grandmother competition and thrust the plastic crown into Lenny's hand. Luckily, the microphone was off when Lenny plonked it on her head more vigorously than she would have been expecting otherwise the whole audience would have heard dear old Ethel swear!'

Later that day, Mike and Dale met up with Jason to review how the *rookies* had got on in the tasks given to them. Jason was dismayed to hear that Mike was less than impressed with Lenny's performance then Dale said Callum had the distinction of being the first *Purplecoat* to cause a football match to be abandoned. They were puzzled as to the reasons why Biddy had recommended Callum for sports events and Lenny for hosting family events. If the two of them couldn't improve quickly, Jason would have to call Biddy to arrange for urgent replacements.

The *Purplecoat*s got their bedding washed by the *Seaview*'s laundry team but had to wash their clothes themselves, including their uniform. When Callum got back to the *Purplecoat* flat, he lathered and rinsed his muddy clothes in the kitchen sink then pegged them out on the washing line in the back garden, praying that it wouldn't rain before they dried. Lenny was relaxing on his bed when Callum returned to their room. At exactly the same time, they said to each other 'How did your day go?' They laughed momentarily before reviewing the horrific day they'd had. They still had no idea that their seniors had given them unsuitable tasks only because they'd been misled by Biddy's profile mix-up. Worse still, they were unaware that their performances were being discussed and they were in danger of losing their jobs.

Off their own backs, Lenny and Callum agreed that the best course of action to solve the problem was to switch roles. They anticipated that their senior colleagues would initially be annoyed that they took it upon themselves to do this but hopefully, they'd soon realise that Callum was much better suited for hosting family shows and Lenny much better for sporting activities.

One activity that Lenny and Callum enjoyed doing together was taking holidaymakers on rambles. During one ramble through the neighbouring *Funtime* resort, they noticed what looked like a charming little pub at the end of the site called the Barnacle Bar. They vowed to visit it at the first opportunity.

The star of Tuesday evening's cabaret night was a comedian, called Charlie Farley. The *Purplecoats* were not allowed to mingle with guests while any cabaret show took place, just in case they put the act off. Instead, they generally sat quietly and patiently in the buffet lounge. As Jason went up on the stage ready to introduce Charlie, an idea popped into Lenny's head. He said to Callum 'Hey, CC. This is the opportunity we've been waiting for. Rather than sit listening to the same jokes for an hour and a half we could sneak away and check out the Barnacle Bar. It's only a 10-minute walk each way. That gives us at least an hour to have a crafty pint and still make it back before Charlie's act finishes. What do you say?' As soon as the comedian stepped up to the microphone, Lenny and Callum were ready for the off. They left the buffet lounge as Charlie shouted out his opening pun 'Is somebody smoking turf?' They'd already passed the reception counter by the time Charlie followed up with 'I haven't always been a comedian. I used to be a traveling salesman, going door to door selling my goods. One evening, a housewife opened the door in her nightdress. I thought to myself "That's a funny place for a door"!' Lenny and Callum were over the first stile as they heard the audience getting the joke then the laughter faded as they continued over the grass to the neighbouring *Funtime* resort.

When Lenny and Callum walked in to the Barnacle Bar for the first time, they were delighted to find that it had a laid-back relaxing feel. An organist they recognised was playing soft music. It was Ian from the trio that regularly worked at the *Seaview*. They gave Ian a friendly wave and he nodded his head in acknowledgement while his hands were busy on the keyboard. Callum was just about to order two halves of bitter when Lenny tapped his arm and pointed at a wooden board hanging above the bar. On it were carved a lengthy list of local fruit wines on special offer. There must have been more than a dozen flavours listed, including blackberry, cherry, apple, damson, elderberry and strawberry. Lenny persuaded Callum to take advantage of the "special offer" and he ordered a glass of blackberry wine and a glass of cherry wine so that they could do a taste comparison.

As Lenny and Callum took it in turns to sip and compare the two drinks, they agreed that both flavours tasted refreshing and sweet as they went down but an alcohol kick came through soon after. They soon emptied both glasses and couldn't resist the temptation to try two more flavours. They revisited the list on the board, seeking inspiration. Neither of them had any idea what damson or elderberry fruit tasted like, let alone a wine made from it, so decided to save those flavours for another visit. Lenny instead ordered a glass of apple wine and a glass of strawberry wine for their second taste comparison exercise. These drinks seemed to be even stronger but sipping the third and fourth glasses gave them the Dutch Courage they needed to plot how to spice up the 'Mother, I Die' sketch. They came up with a change that they could put into their next performance in the *Purplecoat* show the following night. They also agreed to keep it secret in case they chickened out at the last minute. They'd got so engrossed in their discussions that they forgot about the time passing until Callum saw someone else look at their watch and followed suit. 'Bloody hell, LE – we're supposed to be back on duty when the comedian finishes his act and I reckon that will be in about 7 minutes time. It's a 10-minute walk back so we'll have to get our skates on or we'll be in big trouble!'

The journey back wasn't as simple as they expected because they hadn't allowed for the daylight to have gone but, despite the darkness, Lenny sprinted across the clifftop fields and vaulted the stiles while Callum did his best to keep up. When Lenny ran into the *Seaview* buffet lounge, he breathed a sigh of relief to have got back just as Charlie Farley was finishing his encore. Jason led the applause as the star left the stage for the sanctuary of the dressing room. Dale walked up to Lenny to ask where he and his rookie mate had disappeared to just as Callum arrived. He couldn't breathe a sigh of relief because he was so far out of breath that he couldn't speak. His head was thumping and the tastes of all the drinks were lingering in his mouth so badly that he had to stop himself from being sick. Lenny helped him out by doing all the talking and coming up with an excuse 'We nipped back to the flat because we'd left our money there. On our way back, we got chatting to some guests smoking outside reception. We came in when we heard the cabaret finishing'. Callum stifled a hiccup with his hand as Dale said 'Go mingle with guests in the ballroom where I can keep an eye on you two'.

At the end of their shift, Callum suggested that the next time they visit the Barnacle Bar, they keep away from the fruit wines or any other alcohol. Lenny said 'If you insist CC, but aren't you curious to find out what damson and elderberry wines taste like'? Callum smiled and shook his still throbbing head from side to side in acknowledgement of his mischievous roommate.

The *Purplecoat* show was in full swing on Friday night. The audience had already shown their appreciation of Jason's song and dance act and were singing along to Dale's rendition of 'American Pie' as Lenny and Callum were getting ready to perform the 'Mother, I Die' sketch with their fellow actors. The previous night, too many fruit wines in the Barnacle Bar had encouraged them to spice up the sketch. Now, Callum was having second thoughts about carrying out their idea without giving any warning to their fellow actors, especially Mike, who was playing the part of the film director. Lenny said 'What the hell, CC. If we don't try out *your* idea tonight, we'll never know if it would have made the sketch better or not'. Callum noted that Lenny didn't want to take any credit for helping come up with the idea of the change. Was this a crafty way of ensuring he would be blameless if it bombed? He'd just have to make sure it was successful.

So it was that the actors went through the same routine as taught by Mike, up until the section where, as the film director, he ordered them to do the final scene faster. Callum – as the doctor - ran up to the stage much faster than he'd previously played the scene, tripped over the kerb, slid up to the prone boy – played by Lenny - and karate chopped in half the stick of rock that Lenny was tightly holding in a vertical position. Unfortunately, as this was the first time Callum had attempted this manoeuvre at such a speed, he hadn't realised how far he would slide. Time stood still as his momentum forced his body to continue sliding past Lenny, all the way across the stage and off the other side straight into the director's chair, knocking Mike flying. As Callum helped Mike get back to his feet, Bill - as the undertaker - trotted up to the prone boy, scratched his head more vigorously than usual then stretched his measuring tape vertically up what was left of the stick of rock. The audience were in an uproar, thinking the collision and the broken stick of rock were all part of the act, but it was a shock, not just to the other actors, but also the watching *Purplecoats*. Dale said to Jason 'Callum seems to be making a habit of knocking over his seniors.' Jason replied 'True, but the extra drama at least made the sketch more enjoyable'!

The *Purplecoats* took a bow at the end of their show and the audience clapped and cheered. Jason stepped up to the microphone and thanked them for their appreciation. He then built up the tension for the "Battle of the Planets" by saying that the points tally between the supporters of the competing planets - Saturn and Neptune - was so close that they needed to play a final set of games on the dance floor to decide things. Unbeknownst to the audience, Jason made sure this was always going to be the outcome.

Jason promised there would be enough points from these final games to make the reward worth the challenge and whipped up the audience by raising his arms and shouting 'Which planet is going to win?' Cries of "Saturn!" and "Neptune!" drowned each other out and pennants in the planet's colour were waved frantically – green for Saturn and blue for Neptune. Some *guests* even dressed in these colours to show their support for their planet. Jason asked for volunteers from the Saturn planet to line up in front of Mike and Neptune volunteers in front of Dale. Spurred on by Jason's promise that the reward would be worth the challenge, many stepped forward, like gladiators entering the arena. Soon, there were two long lines of opposing players, willing to do all they could for their planet and mocking the opposing line of players in a firm but friendly way. Mike and Dale made sure the number of players in each team were the same then went to the front of their line and handed an orange to the first player. Jason explained that the first "Battle of the Planets" bonus game was a race to pass their orange down their line and the winners would be the team that gets their orange to the last player the quickest. The players immediately thought this would be easy until Jason said they could only pass it to the next player by trapping it under their chins without using their hands. Once Jason's whistle started the race, all hell broke loose as oranges slipped out of players grasp and bounced along the floor. If the wayward oranges got anywhere near the opposing team a sneaky kick would send them further away, thus eating up valuable time. Eventually, Jason blew the whistle when one team managed to transport their orange to the last player in their line, much to the annoyance of the losing team.

While the orange race was in full swing, Lenny blew up a green coloured balloon for the Saturn team and Callum blew up a blue coloured balloon for the Neptune team. After declaring Saturn as the winners of the orange race, Jason explained that the second "Battle of the Planets" bonus game was similar to the orange race because the winners would be the team that passes their balloon to the last player the quickest without using their hands. The difference is that they could only carry it and pass it to the next player by trapping it between their legs! On Jason's whistle, players waddled up to each other and coupled up like train carriages as knees hit knees. There was no time for embarrassment but the onlookers found it hilarious.

Neptune of course won the second game to bring the scores level again, thanks to a little bit of cheating from Dale. While walking up the line, he *accidentally* bumped into a player on the Saturn team just as they were passing their balloon, causing it to fall to the floor. By the time they'd retrieved it, Neptune's lead was unassailable.

Jason announced 'As each team has won a bonus game, the "Battle of the Planets" is still all square. The good news for the final game is that you can add players and finally use your hands. Don't forget, whichever team wins this game will win this week's "Battle of the Planets"'. Before he'd even started explaining the game, extra volunteers joined the queues to bolster their planet's chances of winning. The players looked confused as Lenny and Callum started handing them large cloth sacks. Were they prizes, was it a sack race or something else? The excitement reached fever pitch and Jason had to shout out the rules of the game to be heard over the noise: 'Listen up everybody. Can each player climb into the sack they've just been given?' This was given as a question but treated as an order so all the players complied. Now that they were psychologically trapped in their sacks, they were starting to wonder what they'd let themselves in for. Everyone gasped when Jason revealed the rules of the game. 'Each player has to discard as many items of clothing as they dare and place them top to toe along the ballroom floor starting from the front of the stage. The team with the longest line of clothes will win the bonus game and the "Battle of the Planets"'.

Jason blew his whistle and coats, jumpers, scarves, hats, ties, socks and shoes were the first items of clothing to be jettisoned. The strippers then had to hop up to their clothes and connect them end to end before the next stripper could line up their clothes in the same way. The more daring competitors added their shirts, blouses and stockings. Even though players were provided with a modesty sack to undress in, their grip often slipped as they threw off their most intimate items of clothing and laid them down, so a sight of bare flesh was guaranteed. It was hilarious for the audience, even when or especially when their friends or family members were stripping off their clothes. Both lines were so long that they started to snake back after reaching the perimeter of the ballroom. The drink helped break through inhibitions and persuade everyone to take desperate measures. A few bystanders bent the rules and threw whatever clothes they could spare onto the ballroom floor to extend the clothes line. It was hard to tell who had the longest line of clothes until a few competitors decided to go for broke and throw in their trousers, tops and the odd bra to help their team win the "Battle of the Planets".

[Playlist Track: "Goodbye T' Jane" - Slade]

Jane had finally had enough of feeling like she was the least respected member of the team and decided that the *Purplecoat* way of life was not for her. Before Saturday morning's breakfast, she handed a scribbled resignation notice to Jason. He wasn't at all surprised and accepted her decision without question. Jane hadn't taken over anything of note so Jason said she could leave immediately. She may have thought he was being unusually abrupt but he really wasn't in the mood to worry about her reasons on this day of all days. That morning when he woke up, he reached out for Daniel across the bed but his young beau was already up and dressed. Daniel looked upset as he confessed to Jason that he was leaving him. He had been offered a lucrative residency at a Blackpool theatre to perform his skeleton dancing act. He apologised for the short notice but had packed his bags while Jason was asleep and would be leaving right away to start the long journey north. They tearfully embraced and kissed before Daniel picked up his bags and left their brief but intense love nest. They waved to each other as Daniel reached the bottom of the metal stairs and once again when he got to the corner of the road. Jason sighed as Daniel disappeared from sight on his way towards the town centre. Daniel had promised to keep in touch but Jason was worldly enough to know that a pretty blonde boy like Daniel would soon find another lover *up north*.

As Jason made his way to the Business Manager's office, his professionalism kicked in. He told himself there was no time to lament Daniel's departure. He certainly didn't lament Jane's departure, especially after she'd got her rambling party lost while taking them around the harbour. The urgency was that the *Seaview* was about to be a whole lot busier and, even though a deadweight member of the *Purplecoat* team was off his hands, he urgently needed a replacement who could hit the ground running. Tricia could take over the harbour ramble and he would have to stick with Callum and Lenny for now and hope that they improve.

Jason updated Eric Arden on Jane's departure then they started phoning the other *Funtime* holiday centres in the Torbay area. After a few wasted calls, they struck lucky when they spoke to Joe Barlow - the Entertainments manager at the neighbouring *Warm Park* holiday centre.

Joe happened to be in a fortunate position: not only had all of his experienced *Purplecoat*s returned from the previous season but his team had been bolstered by the addition of a couple of excellent *rookies* who were settling in well. Joe admitted that rivalries and jealousy had built up in his team as relationships developed with other members of staff and artistes, including the resident band. To avoid or reduce the tension, he would be happy to transfer out one of his most experienced *Purplecoats* called Yvonne. Joe assured Jason and Eric that Yvonne was an excellent *Purplecoat* - she could sing, act and talk confidently to holidaymakers and artistes. They all agreed to the transfer and Yvonne would be told to report to Jason the very next day at the *Seaview* holiday centre.

Jason shuffled around his remaining rookies to cover for Jane's departure, beginning with the Saturday mid-day shift. He chose Callum to be the first *Purplecoat* to meet *Funtime* holidaymakers at Paignton station as they arrived on mainline trains from London, Bristol,

Birmingham and beyond. Standing behind the ticket collector at the platform exit, Callum raised a board saying 'Welcome to *Funtime Seaview* Guests.' Once tickets were checked, he guided *guests* to the separate platform for the connecting train to Churston. That's where Tricia would be waiting with her own 'Welcome' board. She in turn would direct *Seaview* guests to Big Al's minibus in the car park for the final leg of their journey to the holiday centre. Lenny was waiting outside the reception entrance to meet, greet and help *guests* bring their bags in for checking in.

Lenny and Callum were therefore the first male *Purplecoats* to see each week's new batch of girls starting their holiday at the *Seaview*. They tried to hide the thoughts in their head but couldn't help ranking each new girl they saw with marks out of ten for looks and sexual attraction. The behaviour of the girls was just as bad or even worse. They would stare and talk to their friends about each sighting of a *Purplecoat*, as if they were spotting celebrities for the first time. The summer day uniform for male *Purplecoats* was a purple blazer over a white tennis shirt, socks, plimsolls and tight white shorts which didn't leave an awful lot to the imagination. Bolder girls would be more than friendly by getting up close to a *Purplecoat* and asking silly questions then whispering to their friends the naughty things they'd like to do next. Cheekier girls would touch or pinch the leg or bottom of a *Purplecoat* before running off giggling.

During breakfast on Sunday morning, Yvonne arrived at the *Seaview* holiday centre following her transfer from *Warm Park*. She was formally welcomed by Jason and introduced to the *Purplecoat* team. In her late 30's with a long face under unfashionably short, mousy grey hair that made her look much older, she was lacking in beauty and star quality. Nonetheless, she had a very positive attitude that suggested she would soon deliver on all that her previous manager had promised and make life easier for Jason and the other *Purplecoats*.

Later that morning, after Dale had led the Keep Fit class, he picked up his guitar from the dressing room and placed a chair in the middle of the ballroom. He was still tuning his guitar when parents started bringing their children in for the Kids Club. Their smug faces betrayed the relief they felt in being able to ditch their babies with the *Purplecoats* for a few hours and get some peace and quality time together. Bill and Tricia greeted the parents then herded their children together to plonk down on the floor around Dale, so that the *Purplecoats* could teach them the *official Junior Club Bedtime Song* and other songs to sing.

Dale had learned that it was best to let his Junior Programme assistants do the initial rounding up of the children. In previous seasons, he had led from the front but too many incidents had discouraged him. He felt his nose as he recalled the day when a father brought his son to join the kids club and the boy was carrying a toy gun. The boy refused to let his daddy take the gun away so the then inexperienced Dale tried to act as peacemaker. He bent down to talk gently to the kid but, before he could say anything, the boy shot him on the side of his nose. The toy gun only fired suction darts but it was still quite painful. Dale appeared to remain composed, patting the boy on the head as he told the father that his child would be fine. Once dad had gone, however, he snatched the gun off the brat and, through gritted teeth, gave him what for in no uncertain terms. He told him if he ever did that again he would wring his neck and, if he blabbed to his daddy, he would make sure he didn't get any treats for the rest of his holiday.

Tricia and Bill helped Dale teach the children to sing along to a few songs, then kept a watching brief while the children were allowed some free time to play and talk with each other.

Dale yawned as he attempted to ignore the hubbub from the over excited kids shouting and screaming at one another. After a few minutes, Tricia went up to Dale to say that she'd noticed a boy, around nine years old, kicking one of the smaller girls. Dale sighed and said he'd deal with it. He went up to the boy and softly asked him what his name was. When the boy said 'Ivor Stump' Dale chuckled to himself and wondered if his parents had considered the connotation of the name and the likelihood of ridicule. It reminded him of another boy's name the previous season that contained five body parts when spoken – Tony Williams! 'Look ere, Stumpy. If you don't behave, you'll have to leave our Kids Club and go back to your family'. The boy responded by spitting in his face. Dale was shocked but, as he wiped his face, he asked him 'Why did you do that?' Stumpy simply said 'My daddy said I could do anything to the *Purple* people!' Dale realised that threats wouldn't work on this occasion but knew how he could get his revenge on Stumpy in a few days' time.

Dale got his own back on kids that misbehaved by bringing them into contact with one or two animals – a donkey and a monkey. Mishaps caused by animals would appear to show Dale completely innocent of any blame. He used a specific donkey for kids who were repeatedly naughty. Dale would ensure they were put on the back of the laziest and most unruly donkey in Thursday's donkey derby or Friday's donkey rides for the younger kids. In extreme cases of misbehaviour, the brat in question would get the monkey treatment …

On Tuesday morning, Dale switched his team around. He told Auntie Tricia and Nanny Muriel to look after the kids in the ballroom for the magic show while he took Uncle Bill with him on the coach excursion to Paignton Zoo. He then roped in Kenny to help him in his plan to get his own back on Stumpy. Without Auntie Tricia's calming influence, the kids were misbehaving on the journey and hyper-excited by the time they got to the zoo. As expected, Stumpy was leading the worst offenders. They followed him when he jumped over the turnstiles before Dale could sort out the tickets, then mimicked the noises that each type of animal made as they followed Dale and Kenny around the grounds. When they reached the Monkey House, Dale told Kenny to keep the entrance door shut while they waited for the rest of the group to catch up. Uncle Bill was way back and the stragglers were waiting for him rather than the other way. By the time he caught up with everyone he was gasping for breath. Dale had anticipated that this would happen in his cunning plan. He said 'You look knackered Bill. Sit down and have a rest for a minute. Kenny can lead the kids through the Monkey House and I'll look after the stragglers.' Uncle Bill was relieved to be able to sit on a bench and took the opportunity to light a cigarette. As Kenny led the kids along the corridor, the kids got rowdier and rowdier, especially Stumpy who delighted in pointing to the monkeys engaged in sexual activity and leading his gang in making loud grunting noises which frightened the animals as they passed them. Meanwhile, Willow and Chumley were getting ready to defend themselves in the last two cages. Kenny tiptoed past them and waited by the exit door at a safe distance from the front of their cages.

The kids were at their noisiest when they reached the cage housing Willow, the woolly monkey. Dale sneaked behind the kids and joined Kenny at the exit door while Stumpy stood at the front of the group nearest to the cage. He read the name Willow on the plaque and thought he would be clever by making grunting and screaming noises that sounded like "Ooohh, Ooohh, Ooohh, Willloooooww – I'm Willlly Arrrm, Arrrm, Arrrm,". The woolly monkey reacted by scampering menacingly to the front of his cage. That alone was shocking enough for Stumpy and his audience but then Willow started urinating through the bars. The ring leader couldn't escape a soaking, but he ran to the next cage where Chumley was also ready to attack. The chimpanzee grabbed something even more disgusting and threw it straight at Stumpy. Dale hide a smile as Stumpy ran up to him crying and covered in smelly monkey waste. His mates gave him a wide berth on the return journey and all the kids learned a lesson about misbehaving.

The kitchen at the purple flat could be used in place of a barometer. In dry weather, *Purplecoat*s would wash and rinse their clothes in the kitchen sink then hang them overnight on the line in the back yard. In wet weather, they would have to let their clothes dry in the kitchen. That's when male and female underclothes would be seen hanging alongside each other in any available space, over the back of a chair or on oven nobs, hooks or door handles.

Late one afternoon, after a particularly hot and sweaty day, Lenny decided his day clothes needed a thorough clean. He washed, rinsed and wrung out his day shirt, shorts and underpants then, as rain was expected overnight, hung them over the back of a kitchen chair to dry. The next morning, he jumped out of bed and went into the kitchen to recover his clothes for the day ahead. When he got there, he was dismayed to see that one of his female colleagues had left her soaking wet underclothes on top of his clothes. He carefully extracted his still damp day clothes from beneath lacy knickers and bras then carried them into his bedroom.

When Callum returned from shaving in the bathroom, he saw Lenny wafting a hairdryer over his clothes and said 'LE, what on earth are you doing?' Lenny grunted and explained what had happened. In unison, they chuckled 'Oomballah!' at the thoughtlessness of one of their colleagues.

The hairdryer had got Lenny's shirt reasonably dry but there was no time to dry his shorts or check who the culprit was because they had to get up the hill to have breakfast and start their work for the day. As they reached the halfway point Callum noticed something was wrong. He said 'LE, you put your shorts on inside out.' The nearest toilets were beyond the reception area alongside *Inn Paradise* so there was no way he could change there without being seen by colleagues or holidaymakers. He had to think fast.

Looking up and down the hill he couldn't hear any traffic or see anyone in either direction. Being sure that the coast was clear, he quickly pulled down his shorts and stepped out of them. Suddenly, a gust of wind blew them down the hill. He scampered back to collect them just as a minibus came around the corner past the entrance and proceeded up the hill toward them. About twenty pensioner ladies happened to be looking out of the windows as the minibus drove past the lads. They gasped as they saw Lenny on the verge scrambling for his shorts with only his tight underpants covering his modesty. By the time he'd got his shorts on the right way round, the minibus was up over the hill and out of sight.

When Callum and Lenny reached the *Seaview*'s reception building, they saw the minibus, now empty, parked outside. A sign was placed over the reception counter stating '*Funtime Seaview* Holiday Resort cordially welcomes the ladies of Paignton Women's Institute'. More embarrassment was yet to come for Lenny as he walked in to the buffet lounge area. All the old ladies had congregated there and, once he had been seen, they nudged elbows and pointed at him, giggling as they spread the word that this young man was the flasher on the entrance hill. Their tittering continued all through breakfast and Lenny assumed it was all to do with his unintentional impropriety.

If Callum or Lenny had a little spare money, they would treat themselves by buying and sharing a glass of brandy and a packet of ten cigarettes. They preferred Consulate menthol cigarettes as they tasted fresher and reduced the smell of tobacco when they were talking to guests. If they couldn't afford the menthol cigarettes, they would make do with ordinary cigarettes but suck a mint at the same time to aim for the same effect!

In addition to Callum and Lenny's crafty ruse to scrounge drinks and the odd cigarette off holidaymakers, whole packets of the Empire brand of cigarettes were given out during the Empire Olympics competition, held every Wednesday night in the ballroom. Empire Girls, dressed up in skin tight Superwoman-style costumes with the Empire logo on their chests, pushed their company's brand of nicotine to holidaymakers under the guise of a harmless competition. The Olympics consisted of a series of knock out games where contestants had to beat the clock. The Empire Girls carried wicker baskets full of packets of Empire cigarettes and handed out three packets as a prize to the winner of each game, two to the runner-up and single packets to losing participants. Once all the games had finished and prizes given, any packets remaining in their baskets, were sold at half price. Callum had all of that day off so Lenny tried to pinch a pack from the baskets while the Empire Cigarette Girls were distracted. They caught him trying but were friendly enough to let him off and hand him a pack each week.

Callum had become good friends with Pauline and Jackie. They were both pretty in their own way but Pauline could have been a model and was definitely his favourite. On the many occasions that Pauline was pestered by holidaymakers or kitchen lads she would pretend that Callum was her boyfriend and get him to escort her away from trouble. She appeared to covet his friendship, but every time he got her safely back to her chalet all he got was a quick peck on the cheek. She consistently told him she wasn't interested in any sort of sexual or romantic relationships with anyone at the *Seaview* because she wouldn't cheat on her boyfriend who was working at another holiday centre. It was frustrating for Callum as he really liked being with her and wondered if her boyfriend was being as faithful as she was.

One night, in their single beds alongside each other, Callum asked Lenny for his opinion on his pursuit of Pauline. Lenny agreed that she was very attractive but bluntly told him he was wasting his time trying to get off with a girl who's already told him he has no chance with. 'Look elsewhere and you never know, if Pauline sees you going with someone else, she might even get jealous enough to want you for herself'. Lenny drifted off to sleep, leaving Callum to imagine a scenario where she finally tells him she'll dump her faraway boyfriend just to be with him.

Ironically, Lenny had been wondering if he was also wasting his time with Ruby. Since that delightful double session on the first night they met, they had 'got together' plenty of times, mostly at her chalet but also in his room at the purple flat, whichever had the best chance of privacy. The sex was always great but after a week or so Lenny somehow felt that something was missing from their relationship and his thoughts kept returning to Connie.

Lenny tried to have more meaningful conversations with Connie but for some reason he felt nervous and wasn't very good at it: 'Are you a regular at *The Free Elms Inn*? I fink I saw you going in there the other night.' She smiled at his cockney accent while acknowledging his continued interest before confirming 'I go there an elluva lot after work'. Lenny continued 'I remember there were some rowdy kitchen lads at the bar on the night I saw you there. Hope they didn't give you any trouble.' Connie exaggerated her west country accent by replying 'Thank my boody zur for your conzern! That must have been Tommy's gang.   Tommy is the boyfriend of my roommate Judy.' As she said her roommate's name, she pointed across the dining room to a stick thin waitress with orange tinted Lennon-style round framed glasses. Lenny said 'I'm surprised she's allowed to wear sunglasses in the dining room'. Connie explained 'Judy's eyes are very light sensitive so they made an exception for her. Don't you think she looks cool?' Lenny blurted out 'Yes, but not as cool as you!' He pretended to be called by someone in the distance to hide his blushes but she noticed them as he swiftly departed. He didn't see her blush in response.

Over the next few days, Connie and Lenny couldn't resist smiling at each other and getting close together for a chat. Every time they did, their eyes lit up and hearts fluttered - this was especially awkward when Ruby was nearby.

Through lots of brief conversations, Lenny found out that Connie came from Ivybridge, that it's a small town at the southern area of Dartmoor National Park and that it's named after a hump-backed bridge covered in ivy. She was amused by his urban cockney twang and he found her mid-Devon accent to be charming – much softer than Ruby's *Skootish* accent. It reminded him of the difference between the cute steam engines traveling from Paddington to the west versus the bigger more industrial steam engines traveling from Kings Cross north. Whenever Connie saw Lenny, she called out to him 'orroit me luvver' and continued to say 'elluva' a hell of a lot - but no matter what their conversation was, they were happy just to be together. They seemed to have so much in common, including a love of rock music and sport.

One day, Connie introduced Lenny to her brother, Nick, and his girlfriend Anne. Nick had just started as a trainee chef and Anne had started as a dining room waitress. Anne sang the praises of Margot Medway. The *Seaview*'s catering manager had thoughtfully placed Anne's serving station between Connie and Judy's group of tables so that she could follow their lead to help her settle in.

Lenny was by now the main organiser of sports activities at the *Seaview* and a couple of star players from Torquay United - the nearest professional football team – had just helped Lenny run football training sessions with the holidaymakers.

Lenny assumed that Nick, Anne and Connie all supported Torquay United, so mentioned the names of the players as he thought they would be impressed. To his surprise, Nick frowned and started belting out (to the tune of H-A-P-P-Y):
'I'm Argyle till I die
I'm Argyle till I die
I know I am
I'm sure I am
I'm Argyle till I die!'

Then, Anne and Connie joined in with the anthem
'Arr-guy-all
Arr-guy-all'

As a finale, they sang in rhythmic echoes to each other:
Nick: Green army
Anne: Green army
Connie: Green army

Nick: Green army (clap clap)
Anne: Green army (clap clap)
Connie: Green army (clap clap)

Then a final drawn out 'Piiiiiilllllllllgrimmmmmms!'

They saw Lenny's confusion, so Nick explained that Plymouth Argyle was the nearest professional football club to their home town of Ivybridge and most of the inhabitants were loyal supporters of the team, known as the Pilgrims. Torquay United and Exeter City were bitter rivals of the Pilgrims so each set of supporters pretty much hated the other two teams and their supporters. Lenny told them that the rivalry sounded similar to supporters of his team - Spurs - versus their nearest top flight football rivals: Arsenal and Chelsea.

That evening in the dining room, Lenny and Connie chatted and laughed to such an extent that Callum whispered in his ear to warn him that Ruby had glared at the two of them. It was obvious that they were becoming more than friends – they got on so well and couldn't resist being with each other.

Ruby instinctively knew her relationship with Lenny was over and, when he came round to her chalet that evening, he confirmed it. She was very understanding about ending their trysts. He didn't divulge that it was because he wanted to be free to see Connie, but he had a feeling she realised this. Ruby agreed that they'd had a good time together but she'd harboured no expectation of it lasting and neither of them had made any false promises. They'd both enjoyed the ride, in fact, many rides, but now it was time for them both to move on.

Lenny went straight round to Connie's chalet to give her the news that he'd finished with Ruby so he could be with her. After checking that Ruby wasn't too upset, Connie wrapped her arms around him and they kissed tenderly before being interrupted by an excited shout: 'Hey – What be you two luvvers up to?' It was Connie's roommate, Judy. She lowered her orange tinted Lennon-style round framed glasses to look them up and down then said 'Don't worry, I'll leave you to carry on doing whatever you two be up to doing!'

Lenny cuddled and kissed Connie on her bed. He knew there was no chance that she would invite him to venture under the sheets with her in the way that Ruby had done. He realised that this would be no *wham bam thank you ma'am* but a gentle, slow courtship. He told himself that Connie was too precious a prize to rush things and she was worth the wait, nonetheless, he hoped it wouldn't take too long. Over the next few days, he got to learn more about her, her brother and her friends. Judy had attended the same school as Connie but was a year behind her so, although they were good friends they weren't best friends like Anne was to Connie. Connie's brother, Nick, was in the same class as Judy and always spoke well of her, even when Anne was present. Anne didn't mind her boyfriend speaking nicely about another girl because he always seemed to see the best in people and would help anyone out. After all, he'd helped her, Connie and Judy write their CVs to get their waitress jobs and even helped Judy's boyfriend Tommy, get a kitchen porter's job at the *Seaview*.

Tommy lodged with most of the *Seaview* kitchen porters in a big Victorian house, which they called *the Gaff*. It was situated at the end of a cul-de-sac downhill from the reception area, right alongside paddocks where the donkeys were kept. This rural setting made the building look like a normal farmhouse from the outside but it was a filthy tip inside. The kitchen lads were supposed to keep their shared bedrooms and communal areas of the house clean but they were a particularly rowdy bunch and had other priorities: These included getting booze and drugs into the house and sneaking in whichever waitress or holidaymaker they could persuade to venture there. The house had a mess of plates, glasses and cutlery in every sink, stains and dog ends on every carpet, fragments of unidentifiable rubbish everywhere and the unpleasant stench of a pub on the morning after a particularly messy party. There was no respite outside the house either due to the smell of donkey poo permeating the air. This was not an environment that any discerning female would want to stay in, even for one night. Even the donkeys would bray and say "Nay"!

Tommy took Judy to *the Gaff* when she first arrived to show her off to his housemates as if she was his trophy then expected her to share his bed. She didn't like the way his mates looked at her and squirmed when she saw the mess everywhere. She usually did whatever Tommy wanted but this time put her foot down and refused to stay at the house for another minute. She pleaded with Tommy 'Can't you wait until we have our own place?' She then took it too far when she added 'You know, Nick managed to get a chalet for himself and his girlfriend Anne.' Tommy reacted angrily, snarling: 'I've had enough of you banging on about bloody Nick. It's like he is held up as a vucking saint every time you're not happy with something I've done or said'. Judy pacified him by making excuses: 'I'm really sorry if you think I've let you down but my manager is expecting me to stay in Connie's chalet, at least for a while. Once I've settled in to the job, I'll push for a chalet that the two of us can share – OK?' Tommy calmed down and quietly mumbled 'Well you better make it up to me when we do get our own place.' It sounded sinister to Judy but at least he wasn't angry any more. Like most people that encountered Tommy, she didn't like him when he was angry. Perhaps even Tommy didn't like Tommy when he was angry.

At the end of the fourth week, Jason told Callum and Lenny that the disc jockey had arrived in reception and they were to help bring his record playing equipment in and set it up in the small room alongside the ballroom so that he could run discos for teenage *guests* that Saturday afternoon and evening. The room was a fraction of the size of the ballroom but just about the right size to give the younger holidaymakers enough space for dancing and fraternizing with others of their own age. It was also small enough to discourage parents from hanging around and stopping their kids from enjoying themselves.

Callum asked Jason what his name was and was told he answers to the name of DJ Sub. Callum and Lenny met the DJ in reception and introduced themselves. He confirmed his name was DJ Sub. He was small and slight so the moniker DJ Sub didn't seem to suit him but his light brown skin certainly suggested he was of Indian descent.

As the three of them carried the record playing equipment in to the disco room, Lenny couldn't hold back his curiosity and had to ask him 'Why do you call yourself DJ Sub?' He responded 'Well, you've heard of underground music?' 'Yes'. 'Well, I play underwater music!' They looked puzzled and the DJ couldn't continue the pretence. 'Ok, it's easier to spell than my real name'. 'What's that?' 'Nitin Subramanian'. He explained that he had used his stage name of DJ Sub wherever possible as he got fed up of missing out on bookings because the agents couldn't spell his real name.

When they'd finished bringing everything in, Lenny asked the inevitable 'Where are you from?' Callum and Lenny were surprised to find Nitin AKA DJ Sub was actually born and brought up alongside Battersea power station in South London. Nitin said 'How about that fairground accident. Wasn't it awful?' His helpers said they had no idea what he was talking about.

DJ Sub explained that the accident occurred 30th May on the Big Dipper roller coaster at his local funfair in Battersea Park. A train being hoisted up to the highest point of the ride broke loose and the brakeman couldn't stop it rolling backwards. Some of the carriages jumped the rails and crashed through a barrier. Five children were killed and a dozen or more others injured. The rumours are that the ride wasn't up to safety standards so the owners may be jailed.

Callum said 'Blimey, that sounds awful'. Lenny agreed, then added: 'We pretty much live in a cocoon here so don't hear about anything in the outside world unless somebody tells us. We can't afford newspapers and there's no TV or radio at our digs …' Callum finished the sentence '… and we're not really allowed to watch TV with the guests even if we could spare the time.'

Callum thought it best to change the subject so asked DJ Sub what experience he had and where he'd worked. The DJ gave a potted history of his brief career so far. As a teenager in Battersea, he'd gone to disco parties at the local pubs and hung around the side of the stage, watching the DJ working with the equipment and getting the crowd going. One DJ let him have a go on the decks and he soon got the hang of lining up music tracks, talking through an intro then flicking the volume up at just the right moment. That was just a year ago and he'd only played to a live audience a few times before getting this job at the *Seaview* holiday centre through a London agency, called *Deejays UK*. The agency supplied him with a new kit as part of their group contract with *Funtime* Holidays so DJ Sub only had 24 hours to get acquainted with it before his first *Funtime* disco was scheduled to start.

DJ Sub was amazed, and Lenny was impressed, when Callum casually said he had been working for *Deejays UK* for the last three years before coming to the *Seaview* to work as a *Purplecoat*. Better still, he knew the kit in front of them like the back of his hand so could easily show DJ Sub how to set it up and use it.

As Callum gave the *rookie* DJ tuition on everything he needed to know, he shared some of his experiences in the industry. Callum had been steadily working 9 to 5 Monday to Friday in the dark room of a photographic printing company but a few years ago, decided he wanted to earn some extra money while entertaining people. After a successful audition, *Deejays UK* sent him out to DJ at a number of well-known pubs and clubs in central and south west London. The most well-known venue was a Thames-side establishment called The Boat. In the swinging 60's, most of the up-and-coming bands had played there including Pink Floyd. Now it was Lenny's turn to be amazed as Pink Floyd was one of his favourite bands.

Having got the full attention of DJ Sub and Lenny, Callum continued to go through a potted history of The Boat. Gigs were well supported but drugs were rife and booze-fuelled fights took place there on a regular basis. The police warned the venue that they risked losing their licence if this continued. The management team of The Boat got together for a strategy meeting to review matters and plan what to do with the business going forward. They started by looking at the latest entertainment trends taking place across the country.

One trend was the increase in food offerings at pubs, in addition to dedicated family eating places, like steak houses.

Another new trend - Reggae music - was being heard more and more in the pop charts and increasingly popular with the UK's working-class youth and beyond.

The Boat had two floors to fill so the management decided to stop hosting live bands and have a different theme on each floor to take advantage of both of these trends. Soon after, they opened a late-night reggae music disco on the first floor and a dance & dine evening on the ground floor. The latter was advertised as 'Dance & Dine for 12 and 9' - a nod to the pre-decimal 12 shillings and 9 pennies, equivalent to 64 new decimal pence. This covered the entrance fee plus steak and chips or chicken and chips - drinks were extra. In addition to a choice of food, a DJ would play smooth romantic music so dance & dine evenings were ideal for courting couples and clandestine trysts.

Callum built up a reputation as the most popular DJ for these dance & dine evenings. He got a little bored with the repetition of being requested or playing the same songs, but the gig was much more civilised than what was going on upstairs.

On the odd occasion, Callum was asked to help out upstairs, especially if the DJ needed a break or simply didn't turn up. Callum wasn't really into reggae music and the crowd were generally out of their head. Despite the usually passive effect of marijuana, a punch up would invariably break out most evenings and Callum quickly had to learn how to avoid pint glasses being thrown as fights reached their peak.

Callum was relieved when *Deejays UK* got him new bookings at more salubrious establishments like plush hotels and private members-only night clubs. He especially enjoyed sharing the music bill with live bands in the hotels as it gave him a break where he could relax with a cigar and brandy given to him by the bar staff in return for him playing their favourite song later.

Callum earned a decent living from his day and night jobs but the time was right to give them all up to come to the *Seaview* as a *Purplecoat*. He didn't even mind that the *rookie* DJ he was helping was probably earning more money than him - the work of a *Purplecoat* was much more varied and fun. A certain *Senior Purplecoat* might not have been so positive at that moment…

The hot June sun shone down on the harbour area but there was an extra warmth in the air as local people and visitors alike were getting more and more excited leading up to the final preparations for the annual Brixham Trawler Race.

Tricia didn't just do child-minding tasks at the *Seaview*. She did tap dancing, can-can and sang in the Purplecoat Show, umpired the netball matches, called some bingo sessions and hosted many other adult activities, including taking over Jane's ramble into Brixham town. She stood on a bench overlooking Brixham harbour and told the guests all about William of Orange, the replica of the Golden Hind and the Trawler Race, but most of them weren't really listening to her history lesson. They sneaked away to escape to the nearest bar.

The Brixham Trawler Race wasn't due to take place until the following Saturday but dozens of boats were already decked out to celebrate the event with brightly coloured bunting and flags, especially the red, white and blue of the union jack and the white cross over a green background of the Devon flag. Bunting and flags were also being hung over all the approach roads and draped along the front of pubs, cafes, shops and other businesses. Participating boats would battle against each other for two laps around the Bay under a strict handicapping system. Additional fun and festivities would take place along the quayside, all raising hundreds or thousands of pounds for local charities. Such was the importance of the event that all the town pubs, cafes and restaurants were allowed to sell alcohol all day in return for donations to the pot. The carnival atmosphere on the quayside and around town guaranteed fun for all ages and the day was a great excuse for fishermen, friends and holidaymakers to have a catch-up and drink together.

Dale's fun-loving and pretty blonde girlfriend, Sue, had moved in with him upstairs at the purple flat. She was telling him how she would love to participate in the Brixham Trawler Race. All of the cleaning staff at the *Seaview* holiday centre lived in Brixham so Dale asked them if they knew how he could get seats on a competing boat for him and his girlfriend. As luck would have it, the son of one of the chalet maids would be skippering a boat in the race. She got back to Dale and tried to deliver a funny quip as she said 'I've pulled a few strings - or should that be netting ropes - to secure two passenger places on my son's boat for you.' Dale didn't think the quip was up to his standard as a professional comedian but muttered some sort of thank you as she explained the arrangements they needed to follow. Sue was delighted when Dale gave her the good news, but when he let his boss - Jason - know of his plans for that day, it didn't seem such a good idea. Jason warned him that a lot of booze is consumed at these events and the water around the bay gets very choppy. The combination of activities could lead to participants getting seasick, injured or falling overboard - he didn't want Dale to have an accident or be too ill to meet and entertain *Seaview*'s new guests later that day. Dale had initially liked the idea of taking Sue out on a boat race and certainly enjoyed booze but was now starting to worry about the risks involved. He didn't want to disappoint her or be seen to be chickening out of something she'd looked forward to. Maybe there was a way of getting himself out of the arrangement without losing face. He had the rest of the week to plan his escape.

Lenny and Callum had learned the routes of all the rambles and took over most of them from the senior *Purplecoats*. Kenny took photos of the holiday makers as they made their way along the route, with Lenny leading the group and Callum at the back looking after any stragglers.

The most popular ramble from the *Seaview* was the Friday morning walk to Berry Head. Kenny made sure he took along plenty of film on this particular walk because there were so many opportunities for holiday snaps. The route included country roads and clifftop paths with breathtaking views around the headland and across the bay. Once they reached their destination, the holidaymakers could wander freely among the Iron Age remains and Napoleonic fortifications that were strategically built between two bays:

- Tor Bay to the north, where trawlers come and go from Brixham harbour out into a sweep of bay that curves up the coast beyond Paignton to Torquay
- St Mary's Bay to the south, where porpoises and tall ships travel down to Sharkham Point on their way to Plymouth and the southern Cornish coast.

Lenny and Callum helped Kenny build up a stack of photographs to sell by suggesting each holidaymaker in their group pose in front of the stubby lighthouse - the smallest in the UK - or on the cannons pointing out through the turrets. They also got families, friends and the whole rambling party together for group photos overlooking the panoramic vistas from this vantage point.

While the holiday makers were free to walk around the site, Lenny and Callum took the opportunity to hide behind the ramparts for a brief escape and a chat. If their ramblers were especially difficult or miserable, they would stand over one of the cannons and pretend they were firing cannonballs at them. They would also smoke or share a cigarette from a pack of their favourite menthol brand or a cheaper ordinary cigarette while sucking a mint!

One day, as Callum lit Lenny's cigarette, he said 'LE, do you believe in fate?' 'Why do you ask, CC?' 'Well, something weird happened this morning. I came out of our flat and saw Tricia talking to a man in front of a bright yellow Bedford van that I instantly recognised. She introduced this man as her boyfriend, Geoff. He'd come round to see how she was getting on. He happened to be a really nice guy and gave me a lift up the hill in the back of his van with the two of them sat in the front. Along the way, he made a point of saying that he was pleased to hear Tricia was getting along so well with all her colleagues, especially me and you.' 'What's weird about that?' 'I'm getting to it, LE. Give me a chance. The reason why I recognised the van was because it nearly knocked me over. It happened when I was crossing the road at Churston station on my way to the Seaview for my first day as a Purplecoat. Geoff must have been driving Tricia for her first day as well. It got me thinking that I could have met them in very different circumstances, such as at a hospital or a mortuary!'

Lenny said 'That's quite a coincidence but I'm never surprised when I hear of these types of things because I totally believe in fate. In a split second, fate can make the difference between life and death. I've survived so many dangerous incidents that I definitely wouldn't be here now if it wasn't due to fate intervening'. Callum said 'What sort of incidents?' Lenny explained: 'Well, my earliest brush with death was when I was an unruly headstrong kid going to a primary school in a rough area of London. The school was a dump but there was a triffic sweet shop located just over the road from its gates. The shop was very popular at lunchtime and I got fed up of queueing for my favourite sweets then finding out they'd all been sold by the time I got to the counter. One day, I hatched a plan and was on my marks as the clock ticked toward the lunchtime break. As soon as the school bell rang, without waiting for the teacher to dismiss us, I sprung from my desk ahead of any other schoolchild and sprinted as fast as I could out of the classroom, down the steps and out through the school gates. Without breaking my stride or looking left or right I ran into the road toward the shop. Halfway across, I heard a loud continuous screech and turned to see a huge silver car skidding toward me as fast as an express train. There was no time to get out of its path, but, just as the front bumper was about to hit my knees, I instinctively thrust my hands forward onto the front of the bonnet above the grille. I must have been very supple because the action propelled my body up in the air, like a gymnast bouncing off a springboard in a vaulting competition. Luckily, the driver had been quick enough to bring his vehicle to a halt so I landed on the top of the bonnet like a cat jumping down from a fence. I would have been a goner if he'd have been a second slower to react. Anyway, I scrambled off the bonnet, spread my arms apologetically at the driver then ran into the sweetshop, relieved but only slightly shaken.

Just over a year later, on my way home from school, I was grabbed by a gang of bullies at a wooden bridge over a railway line. They apparently liked "Treasure Island" because their leader claimed his gang were pirates forcing captives to walk the plank. The gang roughly jostled me up onto the top cap of a fence that formed one side of the bridge. They then whipped my legs with plastic swords to try to force me along the bridge. Luckily, I knew the area well so, when I reached the point that was higher than they were I jumped down the other side of the fence and ran along the embankment to escape. A week later, I heard rumours that another kid from my school had been found dead on the tracks, apparently after jumping off the same bridge'. Callum asked Lenny 'Why on earth didn't you tell anyone what the bullies were doing?' Lenny admitted 'At the time I was being caned regularly and, with my reputation, thought I would be suspected, reprimanded or caned yet again'.

Callum said 'Wow, you definitely were lucky' but Lenny continued 'There's loads more incidents that I can recall. Even as young as 9 years old I used to love travelling around London by bus, train and the London Underground tube. One day, I was standing alone on the platform at Campden Town station when a man sidled up to me and said he'd give me a ten-bob note if I went down to the toilets with him and let him see my meat. I was totally confused as to what he meant because I hadn't been to the butchers and wasn't even carrying a shopping bag! He moved away quickly when a train came in and we were surrounded by passengers. I only found out what he was aiming to do when I got home and told my older brother about it. He reckoned I could have been murdered if I'd done what the paedophile asked. Later, that same year, a schoolfriend took me on my first visit to a lido. He could swim and showed off by diving straight into the deep end and swimming back to the edge, beckoning me to join him. I was yet to have a swimming lesson so declined the offer and made my way toward the shallow end, intent on keeping my feet firmly on the pool floor. I'd only walked a few feet when a rowdy group of teenage girls decided to push me in for a laugh. I splashed around frantically, trying to stay afloat and breathe air before sinking deep into the water. I remember looking up at the beautiful clear blue water and stretching my arms up toward the surface then blacking out. When I came to, a man in a tracksuit appeared to be French Kissing me while squeezing my nose. I pushed him off then realised I was surrounded by a crowd. My friend leaned over and told me I would have drowned had the lifeguard not seen what happened, grabbed my hands, hauled me out and gave me artificial respiration'.

Lenny continued 'I've had near misses with cars. I illegally drove my brother's car around London from the age of 14, then, within days of passing my driving test on my 17th birthday,

I wrote it off after another car hit it. When I tried to instal a radio in the first car I owned it caused a short circuit which set it alight. I managed to get out in time but the fire brigade arrived too late to prevent it being another write off. Then of course there was all the drugs. As a 19-year-old, I unwittingly sniffed heroin and cocaine at the same time'. Callum said 'Didn't you get hooked?' Lenny replied 'No, I was just violently sick and vowed never to get near the stuff again. Finally, to top up my meagre apprenticeship pay, I worked most evenings for the London Evening Standard. I used to jump out of the sliding doors on their minivans before they'd even stopped, sprint through traffic with reams of newspapers under my arms to deliver them to newsagents then get back to the van as fast as my legs would carry me. I cannot put a figure on how many times I just missed being hit by vehicles or motorbikes. To finally prove the power of fate, I only saw the advert for this job due to an accident while cycling home from my Evening Standard job earlier this year. I always put a spare copy of the latest edition in the basket of my bike for my parents to read. As I was riding home in the snow, a sports car forced me off the road as we both approached a flyover. My bike skidded into a cement post at the base of the flyover and I was catapulted over the handlebars. The snow must have cushioned my fall because I escaped with a few bruises rather than a broken neck.' Callum said 'Didn't the sports car driver stop to see how you were?' 'No, he just zoomed away, whether or not he realised what he'd done. Anyway, I picked myself up from the cold, wet road and just about avoided being hit by other vehicles as I gathered up the scattered pages of the newspaper. That was when I noticed the advert for summer season work at *Funtime holiday centres*. I applied next day and somehow got through the interview and ended up here with you!'

'Wow, LE. You're like a cat with nine lives all the near misses you've encountered!' Lenny replied 'I guess you're right, CC. I could have perished on each occasion but it obviously wasn't my time to leave this world'. He held up his arms in a muscleman pose like Superman and said 'Maybe fate has made me INVINCIBLE!'

Kenny shouted out 'Oi you two. The ramblers want you for a group photo'. Callum and Lenny ran down to join the group as Kenny was lining them all up. Once everyone was in place, he got them to raise their arms with thumbs up to make the photos look more theatrical. He smiled as he took the snaps, well aware that he would get a tidy commission when the printed photos were sold the next day or soon after. This didn't stop him looking for other ways to line his pocket.

As the group were taking the last few photos of each other or hanging around ready for their return journey, a stocky middle-aged man came up to Lenny, Callum and Kenny and introduced himself as Mister Bradshaw. He was the owner of a café on the site and had just finished renovating it. He'd seen their rambler group and forcefully insisted they all visit his café for cakes and drinks. Kenny didn't like the café owner's attitude and, never one to miss an opportunity, bluntly replied 'Okay *Mister Bradshaw*, what's in it for us?' The café owner was a little taken aback but offered to sneak them a free cup of tea or coffee each time they brought a party in. Kenny quickly estimated that they could bring in twenty to thirty holidaymakers each week, so suggested that a fiver for each visit would be more appropriate. Rather than be impressed by Kenny's business acumen, the café owner was shocked at his brazenness. He wouldn't let these whippersnappers get the better of him so said No to any deal. As they walked off and left him standing there, Kenny said 'That's his loss 'cos he's blown all that potential business for the rest of the season'.

On competition nights in the ballroom Kenny took all the usual photographs of the different entrants on the stage while the big band were getting prepared to play behind them. One night it was the Lovely Legs contest and Kenny was concentrating on showing just the right amount of flesh without it getting too explicit. The films were processed overnight, photographs printed and delivered to the shop the next morning.

Kenny's shop manager - Gillian Evans - helped him go through the photos to see which ones were best to display on the wall shelves to encourage customers to place their orders. Suddenly, she choked as she noticed something untoward on some of the photos. She told Kenny to take a good look at one particular band member behind the guests, pulling faces and making all sorts of animal gestures and sexual movements. It had to be Baz of course! Gillian had the bright idea of snipping off the offensive images so that the cut-down versions could be used for plastic mini viewfinders but this didn't work when Baz was right behind the subjects so most of the spoiled photos had to be destroyed. Kenny was livid and the next time he saw Baz he told him so. By way of apology, Baz took Kenny out on a fishing trip, after which, they visited his favourite quayside inn. Baz was known to have some disgusting habits, so he always had to be watched. One night in the ballroom, Kenny happened to be looking at Baz while he was playing trumpet in the big band. Suddenly, Baz paused, opened the valve on his trumpet and flicked out the residue of his spit towards guests as they danced alongside the stage. The guests were so engrossed in having a good time that they didn't notice the sticky dew on the backs of their clothes until they got back to their chalets so had no idea where it came from. Kenny kept a very close eye on Baz while he was up at the bar getting drinks for them both. He didn't want any additives from Baz in his pint!

Every evening that Lenny worked in the ballroom, Jason gave him a mission: to get as many people as he could up onto the dancefloor when the music was playing. Lenny was happy to teach a group how to follow the steps, kicks and turns of the Slosh or other line dance. He also looked out for women on their own but wives were also glad of the attention of a fit young *Purplecoat* who could give them a welcome break from their boring husbands and spin them around the ballroom like a princess to a traditional waltz, foxtrot or quickstep.

One evening, Lenny was teaching a middle-aged woman called Mabel how to dance the waltz. He went through the basic steps with her: 1:2:3, 1:2:3, turn:2:3, etc. No matter how slow and deliberate Lenny's tuition was, the woman was constantly stepping on his toes. The end of the song came as a relief for both of them and Lenny courteously walked Mabel back to her table. Her husband jumped up out of his seat and introduced himself as Eric. He insisted that Lenny sat with his wife while he went up to the bar to get drinks for the three of them – he said it was the least he could do after his wife had nearly crippled him. He returned with a tray of drinks and passed a whisky chaser to Lenny in addition to the pint of beer he'd asked for. As Lenny supped both drinks, Eric asked him if he would kindly teach them both how to dance basic steps together so that they could surprise their friends when they get home. Lenny didn't want to upset them, especially after they had been so generous with the drinks, so agreed to help. Eric told Lenny he and Mabel were too shy to practice in the ballroom in front of people, so wondered if he knew somewhere more private. Lenny suggested the TV room - it was generally unused when the weather was good. They arranged to meet there at midday the following day.

Eric and Mabel were already waiting for Lenny when he turned up at an otherwise empty TV room. Eric was eager to start while nobody else could disturb them so Lenny started going through the basic steps with Mabel then got Eric to take his place. Eric didn't seem to be following the moves at all and now it was his turn to tread on Mabel's toes. Eventually, Eric suggested Lenny go through the moves with Mabel while he followed the moves closely behind him. Lenny thought it was a little bit creepy but didn't like to say no to holidaymakers so went along with the request. As Lenny held Mabel and moved to the rhythm, she suddenly started pushing her crotch towards his and her husband seemed to be pushing his crotch into Lenny from behind. Lenny realised both their intentions were dishonourable and quickly detached himself from their clutches by pretending he had a coughing fit. He then made the excuse that he had to leave to get a drink of water for his throat.

That evening, Lenny was at the start of his shift in the ballroom. Eric came up to him and asked how his throat was. Lenny was confused for a second then remembered his earlier excuse and said, putting on a gruff voice, 'much better thanks.' Lenny pretended to recognise someone in the distance and started to walk away. Eric persisted by walking alongside him and saying how much he and Mabel appreciated the dance lessons and wondered if he'd like to visit their chalet for a drink when he finished his shift. Lenny made up another white lie by saying 'Sorry, can't stop to chat. I've got to catch up with that woman to give her a message' and he jogged off towards his imaginary target. Once he'd lost his prey, he made sure he avoided the kinky couple for the rest of their holiday.

One of the more unusual weekly evening entertainment shows was a table tennis display performed by two of the top British players at that time: Chesney Benn and Todd Fallon. They would play a demonstration game and Dale would do the commentary. Chesney would show his attacking skills by smashing the ball over the net using top spin. On the other side of the net, Todd would show his defending skills by running backwards up to twenty feet or more from the table to lunge for the speeding ball and slice a return using bottom spin. The game would usually end with Chesney jumping up on top of the table to smash a winner, illegal as far as table tennis rules were concerned but exciting as a spectacle. The crowd always showed their appreciation, especially when the encore was a game where Chesney and Todd replaced their bats with unusual objects such as plates and cups.

Lenny and Callum tried to be friendly with the table tennis stars but they seemed very stand-offish. It was no surprise to find out that they were very pally with Dale. Todd was quietly spoken and shy but Chesney was the opposite. He always drank a pint of beer before a show. One evening, Chesney had just downed his pint when Callum happened to go into the dressing room to pick up a microphone for Dale to do the commentary. Chesney brazenly relieved himself into the empty glass then tossed the contents out of the awning window. Callum recalled the dirty glass he'd found when the Salvation Army band visited and now knew who the culprit was.

One particularly wet day, the table tennis table in the sports room was unused so Lenny and Callum took the opportunity to play a few games. They started playing with the bats that were left there, then, for a laugh, emulated the encore that Chesney and Todd were to put on later that week. They switched their bats for plastic cups from the stack left for guests on the water tray. Lenny and Callum were surprised how quickly they got used to playing with the bases of the cups and they soon drew a small crowd who watched in amazement. Unfortunately, word got out that the two Purplecoats had copied the table tennis stars act. Dale took the side of his celebrity mates and protested to Jason, who couldn't disguise his amusement when he told Lenny and Callum that they had to stop their party piece or Chesney and Todd might register a formal complaint.

The dry weather had finally dried the grass on the playing field and Jason decided that the donkey derby should take place that Thursday morning. Dale continued to badger and bully Callum whenever he could. He told Callum to put reins on the tamest donkey in the paddock, lead it up the hill and bring it into the dining room during the lunch service. Dale explained that the sight of the animal would help promote the donkey derby and ensure the event was well attended. When Callum thought about it, he was worried the donkey might make a mess on the dining room floor so checked out Dale's suggestion with his boss. Jason laughed and told Callum that Dale was just having a little joke with him. Callum pretended to laugh it off but realised he alone would have suffered the embarrassment if he had fallen for the latest of *Dale's little jokes*.

Callum didn't escape another embarrassing situation on his next night off but for once it wasn't caused by Dale. Callum finally took on board Lenny's suggestion to stop chasing after Pauline and look elsewhere for love or something more physical. This led to him chatting earnestly to Hazel - the *Seaview's* Assistant Nurse. He started with 'Do you recall the time we shared together dealing with Polly's sprained wrist?' 'Of course.' 'Do you remember asking me if I was Polly's boyfriend?' 'Yes.' 'Well, you seemed pleasantly surprised when I confirmed she was just a friend'. 'I guess I was.' 'That made me wonder if you'd like to go out on a date with me'. 'Oh, okay, when?' 'Well, Wednesday is my day off so maybe that night, I mean that evening … if you're free?' 'Yes, I'm free that night.' Callum wasn't sure if she was intentionally suggesting the whole night but was chuffed that he'd got a positive response. The next obstacle to overcome was more delicate. He was desperate to avoid the chances of any mockery from his colleagues so suggested 'Why don't we spend our time away from the Seaview *for a change of environment*'. Hazel agreed and offered to drive the two of them to *Warm Park* - the nearby and largest *Funtime holiday centre* within the Torbay area.

That evening, Callum was in the kitchen at the purple flat ironing a brand-new white shirt that he'd bought earlier that day. He hoped it would impress Hazel on their first date. Just as he hung it up for a final inspection and turned the iron off, he heard a car arrive outside. Hazel had caught him by surprise by arriving early! He hurriedly took the shirt off the hanger, pulled it over his head and stuffed it into his trousers to greet her as she arrived at the front door. He looked a little flushed from the panic and the heat of the ironed shirt. She assumed his blushing was the excitement of their first date.

As Hazel drove the two of them to *Warm Park*, Callum cooled down and relaxed, safe in the knowledge that his colleagues were currently busy working back at the Seaview a mile or so away so couldn't play any tricks to embarrass him tonight. The two of them entered the large ballroom at *Warm Park* and stood under the very bright florescent lights, surveying the scene. Callum noticed Rodger Bodger beckoning to him while surrounded by a handful of girls at the bar. Callum confidently said to Hazel 'Oh look - *Bodge* is waving us over. He probably wants to buy us a drink for helping his girlfriend Polly when she sprained her wrist.' Unfortunately, once they got near enough, it became clear that *Bodge* wasn't looking to buy them a drink or even be at all friendly. He instead hissed at Callum 'Your flies are undone, man, and your white shirt is poking out of your trousers like a shiny white cock!'

Callum looked down to confirm *Bodge* was not joking. He fumbled to stuff the protruding bits of his shirt back in and do up his zip while bystanders looked askance. *Bodge* laughed at Callum unsympathetically and even Hazel couldn't hide her amusement. Sheepishly, Callum led her to the other end of the bar to avoid further embarrassment but their first night out together had already turned into a disaster. Hazel saw the disappointment on Callum's face and felt sorry for him. After an awkward drink or two, she knew how she could cheer him up and whispered in his ear 'Let's get out of here and go back to your place.'

Hazel was the first girl Callum had taken back to the purple flat. He nervously opened the front door and thanked god that all was quiet and they had the whole place to themselves.

Callum showed Hazel the kitchen and pointed to the bathroom before entering the inner sanctum of the bedroom he shared with Lenny. Even though Lenny wasn't there, he still managed to have some influence on proceedings as his single bed was unmade and his used underclothes thrown on top. Hazel had little choice but to sit next to Callum on his bed. She seemed happy to do so and they were soon kissing and fondling each other. Being a nurse, Hazel was well aware of the dangers of unprotected sex so asked Callum if he had a condom. Unfortunately for Callum he hadn't planned that far ahead but they managed to get as much enjoyment as they could while keeping their clothes on. It was such a shame that Callum was unaware Lenny's unopened box of condoms was just a few feet away from them in his section of the chest of drawers. Sometimes fate works against you.

When Lenny arrived back at the flat after his evening shift, he saw Callum asleep and alone in his bed. As he changed out of his uniform, he couldn't wait to find out how his mate had got on and excitedly shouted 'CC, you awake?' Callum was now very much awake so Lenny threw him a packet of cigarettes. 'I got you a packet of ciggies from the Empire Girls tonight. Now tell me, how did you get on with Hazel on your first date? I want to know everything and why she isn't in bed with you!' Callum was too much a gentleman to confess what they'd got up to before she left but just said she came back to their room and they had a nice cuddle. He had to tell Lenny about his dress malfunction. Hazel would probably keep the 'Warm Park incident' to herself out of respect for him, the Hippocratic Oath or whatever but Rodger Bodger would tell everyone he met just to get a laugh at Callum's expense.

Even Lenny couldn't help giggling as Callum explained how his evening unfolded, much like his shirt. Callum said 'You can laugh all you like but it wasn't funny for me. I bet you've never suffered embarrassment like that!' Lenny said 'Are you kidding? Don't forget, the ladies of the Paignton Women's Institute saw me chasing my shorts down the hill as their minibus drove past. I've also had an even more embarrassing evening during the first year of my apprenticeship'. Callum was intrigued and said 'Why? What happened?' 'Well, CC. One of my new workmates kindly invited me to the evening reception party for his forthcoming wedding, adding that I could bring a partner. I thought long and hard about who I could take then remembered a girl who used to be in my class at school the previous year called Lisa. I'd taken a shine to her so worked up the courage to drop by her house to ask her if she was free and would like to accompany me on the day. Lisa chuckled and thanked me for the invitation but couldn't accept my invitation as she herself was getting married that day ... and the groom happened to be the workmate who'd invited me! Word of my faux pas spread at the wedding reception and I stayed behind the bar all night washing glasses to hide from the embarrassment!'

Callum laughed at Lenny's story even though he thought it unlikely. Even if Lenny had made it up, Callum appreciated his attempts to make him feel less upset about the 'Warm Park incident' and of course the packet of cigarettes was a nice gesture.

Jason must have reprimanded Dale for trying to embarrass Callum when he asked him to lead a donkey into the dining room 'to promote the donkey derby'. Rather than learn the lesson, this just made Dale even more determined to *get* Callum for telling tales.

That evening's cabaret act was a comedienne who called herself Funny Fanny. Jason had a cold so asked Dale to get her set up and introduce her. Dale remembered that Callum had gone missing with Lenny the previous week and came back a little inebriated when Charlie Farley was performing. He would put a stop to that game by giving him a task where he had to stick around. Funny Fanny liked to work the audience by walking up to them and asking where they came from or how many kids they had. She would then respond with related anecdotes or jokes on the fly. Dale's twisted idea of a prank was to give Callum the shortest lead to attach to the microphone that Funny Fanny would use then see what happened. As Funny Fanny started to walk towards the audience, the lead jerked her back, mid-sentence. The audience laughed, assuming it was part of the act but Callum saw her concern and quickly reacted to the problem. When the comedienne saw him approach her with a bigger microphone on a much longer lead, she couldn't resist the opportunity to ad lib and said "Oo, can I have a lick of your lolly?" Callum uncharacteristically replied with his own ad lib "Is that a euphemism?" Those in the audience that knew what a euphemism was erupted, soon joined by everyone else. Once she took the bigger microphone and longer lead, she could continue her act. At the end of the show, she made a point of thanking Callum for coming to her rescue. Callum just wished she hadn't done so in front of Dale as he would just find another way to make him suffer at the next opportunity.

Early Friday evening, Biddy Rand - the *Funtime* Group Entertainment Director - paid a short visit to the *Seaview* as part of a tour checking out all the *Funtime holiday centres* in the Torbay area. She was staying at the nearby *Warm Park* resort as it was the largest holiday centre and central to all the others in Torbay. The management at Warm Park had pulled out all the stops to make her stay memorable, placing her in a luxury chalet and arranging for her to see Saturday's Brixham Trawler Race from a VIP lounge at the Harbour Masters office complete with an outside viewing platform.

Jason and Eric welcomed Biddy and her entourage at the reception then Jason took them into the *Inn Paradise* to introduce his senior team. Mike hadn't forgotten the story that Jason had made up about Biddy asking him to try out a purple scarf as a potential new *Funtime* uniform accessory. All the *Purplecoats* knew that Jason had lied to hide the love bites that a young beau had inflicted on him. Now that Biddy was in front of all of the senior *Purplecoat* team, Mike once again made Jason squirm by asking Biddy how the experiment of adding a purple scarf to the *Purplecoat* uniform had been received at the other resorts. Biddy looked mystified and said 'Sorry – I've got no idea what you are talking about.' Jason interjected 'Ok, take no notice Biddy. Mike must have misunderstood what I said at the time. It wasn't an official thing. I love fashion and just took it upon himself to try wearing a purple scarf to colour coordinate the regular *Purplecoat* uniform but the experiment hadn't gone down as well as I'd hoped so didn't bother suggesting it to you for the corporation'. Biddy nodded agreeably but her eyes suggested she didn't believe a word of Jason's excuse. Mike and Dale once again had to stifle a titter at Jason's expense.

Biddy looked out across the ballroom and saw a family laughing along to something Callum was saying and Lenny jiving with a woman on the dancefloor. She said 'I see that the *rookie* boys are getting along well with our guests'. Jason appreciated the opportunity to quickly move on from the purple scarf story by commenting 'Yes, they're both doing fine now that they've settled into the tasks that best suit them'. He deliberately omitted to mention that the boys had pretty much taken it upon themselves to swap the roles they'd originally been given because of the mix up with Biddy's suitability profile.

Biddy remembered Lenny's brashness at her interview and realised he hadn't got his hair cut as short as she would have hoped so asked 'Has the Jack the lad caused you any trouble?' Jason said 'No, he's been well-behaved since he's been here and...' pointing to Callum '... as you can see, he's keeping himself busy talking to a family over there.' Biddy was mystified for the second time in as many minutes. She said 'Callum wasn't the Jack the lad. It was Lenny - the boy spinning that woman around on the dancefloor!' Suddenly Jason,

Mike and Dale looked at each other as light bulbs lit up in their brains. They had been trying to teach the wrong *rookie* a lesson all this time and the real Jack the lad - Lenny - had got off scot-free. Dale felt particularly guilty as he had been bullying Callum incessantly and unfairly as it turned out. He knew exactly how he could repay him and get himself out of a personal commitment at the same time.

Jason gathered the rest of his *Purplecoat* team to say *Goodbye* to Biddy then walked her out through reception to her waiting limousine. Dale saw an opportunity to talk to Callum on his own so purposefully went up to him bragging that he had been given free places on a boat that was bound to win the following day's Brixham Trawler Race. Callum failed to smell a rat and politely but sarcastically said 'That sounds great … for you!' Dale added 'Yes, it is great but would you be interested in taking my place?' Callum: 'Yes, of course.' Dale: 'Okay, out of the goodness of my heart, I'll let you have my seat. You just need to keep my chick company and make sure she has a nice day. I was going to ask Mike or Jeannette to stand in for me but they're busy and I wouldn't trust Lenny to get anywhere near her whereas you're a safe alternative.' Callum wasn't sure if there was a backhanded compliment in there but he'd already been caught in Dale's trap. The overriding plus point was that the event would be a unique experience and great fun, especially with a girl as lovely as Sue. The down side was that it involved an early start and a tiring schedule - a long walk to get to the quayside around 8am before boarding the trawler at 8:30am, racing around the bay for around three hours then straight back to the *Seaview* so that he could start his stint on reception from 1pm. Callum had previously promised to spend that morning with Hazel so he went round to her chalet to let her know of the change of plan. He emphasised that Dale had ordered him to board a boat on the Brixham Trawler Race so he couldn't refuse. Hazel said 'Wow, that's great. Is anyone else going on the trawler with you?' Callum downplayed the part about keeping Sue company by telling a little white lie: 'I think Dale's girlfriend might be going – not sure, really'. Hazel seemed to take it very well, almost too well.

[Playlist Track: *"Into the Mystic"* – Van Morrison]

On Saturday morning, Callum's alarm rang out at 7am, waking both himself and Lenny in the opposite bed. A dazed Lenny asked 'What's happening CC?' Callum reminded him that he was going trawler racing with Sue that morning. Lenny murmured 'Oh yeah' and shivered at the thought of being bumped around the bay on a smelly boat rather than snuggling warm and cosy in bed.

Callum washed and changed in the bathroom next door then returned to the bedroom to peek through the curtains toward the staircase. A shaft of light shone in and woke Lenny up once again. He asked 'What's happening now?' Callum said 'Sorry LE - I'm just waiting for Sue to come down the stairs from Dale's room.' Lenny mumbled 'Okay - have a triffic day' before turning over and drifting back to sleep. When Callum saw Sue descending down the metal staircase, he lightly closed the curtains and bedroom door behind him, put his raincoat on and got outside the front door just as Sue came around the corner to the front path. Callum thought she looked damned good considering it was only 7:30 in the morning. Nonetheless, he knew he'd best keep any wayward thoughts to himself or it might spoil their day. Worse still, if Dale found out Callum fancied his girlfriend, he would kick him out of the *Seaview* quicker than he could say 'Oomballah!.'

It took a little over 20 minutes for the two of them to stride down the hills to reach the harbour. The trawler they were looking for apparently had the words *Oggy's Boat* painted on the hull. Of course, it was moored at the far end of the quay so they had to walk the entire length of the quayside past all of the pubs, cafes and restaurants. It wasn't yet 8am but all the eating establishments were already bursting at the seams and temporary tables lined up outside and along the quayside pavements were full of diners tucking into their English Breakfast, washed down with local beers, cider or a tot of something stronger. The air was thick with the smell of bacon, eggs, beans and booze on the dry side of the quay and the more usual stench of diesel and dirty saltwater on the wet side of the quay. Callum was already feeling nauseous and he hadn't even got on the boat yet!

When they reached the end of the quay, a burly fisherman was waiting for them. He had been told to look out for a pretty blonde called Sue with a man called Dale so he went up to the couple and asked 'Are you Sue and Dale?' Sue shook his gnarly hand as she confirmed she was Sue but, pointing to Callum, she cheekily added that Dale couldn't come so she brought her fancy man along instead. Callum laughed embarrassingly and shook the man's hand, trying not to blush or flinch at the roughness of the fisherman's hands and firmness of his grip. The fisherman introduced himself as Captain Hogg, but everyone called him 'Oggy' - the west country nickname for a pasty!

Captain Hogg helped Sue and Callum board the vessel and proudly explained that it was classed as a large beam trawler. He then gave a potted history of Brixham and its trawlers. This harbour was once home to one of the world's largest fleets of wooden sailing trawlers. More than 300 were built in the town's shipyards but only a few now remain seaworthy. Callum didn't pay full attention to Captain Hogg's talk because he was feeling more nauseous from seeing the oily water ricocheting off the jetty and slapping against the trawler's hull.

Captain Hogg continued with a tour of the trawler, named after his moniker, going through all the equipment and how it was used. Sue and Callum concentrated hard to avoid falling over as they clambered around and over the many obstacles on the deck, made more difficult by the rocking of the boat. Nonetheless, they still managed to say and get back a friendly 'Hello' from the crew busying themselves in preparation for the off. At the end of the tour, Captain Hogg sat his passengers down on a long wooden bench in the centre of the boat and handed them plastic cups, keeping one for himself. He then produced a bottle of rum and poured a good measure into everyone's cups as a welcome drink. The captain said *Cheers* while clinking their cups together and they responded. Without a second thought, Sue downed all of her cupful in one go. Callum was determined to stay as sober as he could because he had to look after Sue then work through the afternoon and evening shifts back at the *Seaview*. He thought he'd get away with a small swig, but Captain Hogg refilled their cups, insisting they both down another large tot for good luck. Callum was surprised to find that the rum dulled his feelings of nausea.

Captain Hogg explained that the Brixham Trawler Race began in 1963 and it's a massive time trial exercise based on the size and class of vessel and a handicap system that's too complicated to describe. The smallest boats set off in the first group so large beam trawlers like the one they're on are last to leave. The course is over two laps of a seven-mile course around Tor Bay from Berry Head to Hope's Nose so making a total of at least fourteen miles, depending how well you navigate around the other vessels. Each class has a first, second, and third prize and the best place that *Oggy's Boat* had managed so far is fourth place.

The crew of *Oggy's Boat* would be doing all the work so Callum and Sue simply had to keep out of their way, stay seated in the centre of the boat so as not to fall overboard and enjoy the race. A long bench facing the front offered the best view so they carefully timed the rise and fall movements of the boat to flop onto it. No sooner had they settled than the vessel was let off its moorings and started drifting away from the jetty as the engine burst into life - there was no turning back now!

The vessel joined dozens of other bedecked trawlers making their way to the starting point. As they were passing the Harbour Masters office, Sue elbowed Callum to point out the VIPs waving from an outside viewing platform. Callum followed Sue's lead in waving back – he thought he recognised a few celebrities then spotted none other than Biddy Rand - the *Funtime* Group Entertainment Director who had given him his *Purplecoat* job! He doubted that she would spot him amongst all the boats and crews but, if she did, he felt sure she wouldn't mind him enjoying the day as much as she was.

As *Oggy's Boat* to manoeuvre around but the views of Brixham all around them were incredible. Callum was surprised to spot big black seals flopped out lazily along the cement walls that protected the harbour from storms. As the boat chugged past, a few of them half opened one eye as if to say 'How dare you disturb my nap' before they snuggled back down to continue their slumber.

Oggy's Boat was directed to its starting point for the race. Soon after, a blast from some sort of gun was heard from a hill on the headland to signify the start of the race but *Oggy's Boat* remained afloat where it was. The race marshals sent out all of the smallest vessels in the first group, then the next size or class followed after them and so on. *Oggy's Boat* was in the largest size group, so by the time it was sent off there were many smaller vessels to manoeuvre around. All the engines on all the vessels strained to reach their top speed as quickly as their skippers dared to force them, crews battled against other crews to push their trawlers to the limit to do the two laps in the shortest time. Porpoises joined in like pacemakers leading the race boats around the bay. As the vessels splashed up and down through the surf, the jolts projected Callum and Sue up and down and along their bench. Callum hit the arm rest on the left of the bench, bounced back against Sue then she hit the arm rest on her right and bounced back into him. It was exhilarating and frightening at the same time. Sue, encouraged by the effects of the rum, grabbed Callum's arm as she slid into him and held on tightly. He couldn't decide if she was allaying her fears or teasing him again as her breasts briefly rubbed against his arm with the swaying of the boat.

Once the two laps had been completed, the trawler slowed to a gentle pace and headed back to the quay. Once safely moored up, Captain Hogg went below deck and came back with a fresh bottle of rum and clean cups, insisting that his passengers finish it off with the crew. Callum managed to get away with a few small sips but Sue knocked back three full cups in quick succession as they drank and chatted and drank some more. The race marshal turned up and confirmed Captain Hogg's boat had finished in second place. The Cap'n and crew were delighted as it was their best placing in many attempts. Another bottle of rum was fetched from below deck for everyone to continue celebrations, including rowdy shouting of the chant 'Oggy, Oggy, Oggy, Oy, Oy, Oy' while raising their cups to Captain Hogg.

The time had flown by and it was almost 12:30 when Callum finally managed to persuade Sue to say goodbye to the crew so that he could get back to the *Seaview* in time to start his afternoon shift. They thanked everyone for a wonderful time and the crew helped them clamber off *Oggy's Boat* to start their long walk back.

Callum and Sue made their way through the crowd of people celebrating the day and enjoying the shanty songs being sung at the many inns along the quay. It seemed like everyone was drunk, especially a gang of men that waylaid them outside the loudest pub. One of the men tried to grab hold of Sue and kiss her until Callum bravely pulled her away. The men were too intoxicated to respond as Callum and Sue got away from them to eventually reach quieter streets. Callum was well aware he would likely be late for his afternoon shift but his attempts to pick up the pace were thwarted by Sue. She couldn't stop giggling as she struggled to walk in a straight line, blurting out something about the voyage giving her sea legs and she hadn't got her land legs back yet or was it the other way around? They both knew it was the rum that was making her legless. Yet again, she decided to hold on tight to Callum's arm as they staggered up the steep hills towards the purple flat. Callum thought Dale would hit the roof if he saw them like this so he made sure she wasn't quite so close to him as they turned the final corner. That was a wise decision because Dale was stood outside the flat with his arms crossed, glaring at them.

Callum handed Sue over like a freed hostage at a checkpoint and she tittered as she slumped into Dale's arms. Callum explained that they had just fought their way through a frenzied crowd. He could see that Dale was really angry at how sozzled and dishevelled she was but left them to it by saying he had to rush off to his room to change and get up to the *Seaview* to start his shift.

As Callum switched out of his jeans and into his *Purplecoat* uniform, he heard loud clanging on the rear staircase. Peering out through his bedroom window, he could see Dale almost dragging Sue up the stairs to his room. Dale was sternly admonishing her but she just kept giggling and burping - she would be suffering later and not just from a rum hangover. Callum managed to find the energy to run up the hill to *Seaview*'s reception just in time to start his Saturday afternoon shift at 1pm. He still felt a little unsteady from the trawler trip and rum but at least the ground wasn't moving under his feet anymore!

It was the first week of the summer peak season and the *Seaview* was fully booked. Callum was struggling to cope with the pace after his exciting but tiring morning out trawler racing with Sue. He was relieved to see Lenny arrive early for his 2pm shift. Two coach loads of guests had arrived at the same time and the bags from one coach had been piled on top of the bags from another coach. Lenny immediately helped sort out the chaos by finding and handing out the correct bags while Callum dealt with other queries. Eventually, all the guests from the two coaches had scattered toward their allocated chalets and the reception was briefly empty. LE and CC took the opportunity to sit on the bench outside reception to have a breather and try to catch up with each other. Callum puffed as he slumped down and Lenny said 'CC - You look absolutely knackered! Did you overdo it with the lovely Sue at the Trawler Race?' Callum blushed at the comment then gave Lenny an account of his day so far. The chat was necessarily fragmented into brief slices due to frequent interruptions from yet more holidaymakers arriving. Callum eventually finished his review by saying how angry Dale was at the state Sue was in when he handed her over to him. Like synchronised swimmers, they both fell back on the bench and said 'Zezeze' simultaneously in a fit of laughter!

By 3pm, there were only a few guests yet to check-in but Lenny could see that Callum was really flagging so persuaded him to go back to the flat for a power nap while he managed reception duties on his own. Callum said 'Thanks LE. I *will* go back to the flat, after I've popped round to see Hazel and let her let know that I didn't drown in the bay'. Lenny quipped 'And you didn't run off with the lovely Sue!' Callum shook his head as he headed off to Hazel's chalet.

Lenny sat on the bench outside reception waiting for the last guest to arrive. It gave him time to think about his own emotional and physical situation. When Lenny was with Ruby, Callum probably thought he was shallow and cynical, without a romantic bone in his body. Being with Connie was totally different - exciting and frightening at the same time. The strong sentimental feelings he'd been desperate to avoid came flooding back into a heart that had got used to being numb. The fear - that his heart would be broken again resurfaced and reminded him of his time with *Lizzie* …

> Lenny first met Elizabeth in 1967 when they were both 15 years old. He was only a few days into his apprenticeship in an engineering tool room, but already hated everything about it. The noise of the machines, the smell of the oil, the coldness of the metal and pain from the swarf that kept cutting into his fingers. He'd just finished filing the sharp edges off a slab of cold steel when his manager told him to nip out to the nearest shop to get 'a packet of 20 Embassy'. The reward, once delivered, would probably only amount to one cigarette out of the pack or the odd small change. He didn't mind because it gave him a brief respite from this hell hole and released him out into the open air or what passed for it in the smoggy vicinity of the factory. As Lenny walked out through the security gates, he set eyes on Elizabeth for the first time. She was amongst a group of noisy girls, presumably on their way to a local grammar school, but she stood out from the rest in her smart school uniform. He was immediately captivated by her beauty like a love arrow striking his heart. For the rest of that week, he made sure he sneaked out at that same time every day, whether cigarettes were

needed or not, just to see her again and again. Eventually, he plucked up the courage to go up and talk to her. Lenny was surprised that she stopped to allow him to talk to her and delighted to find that she lived just a mile away from his home. He was immediately certain they were destined to be together, especially when she agreed to go out with him, despite her snooty friends cruelly giggling at the obvious mismatch in looks and class.

When Lenny first called round to Elizabeth's home, he was full of trepidation because he was clearly punching above his weight. As if to emphasise their cultural differences, her abode was a huge rural Regency mansion whereas he slept in the box room of a semi-detached council house on a notorious housing estate on the poor side of town.

Much like the steel he worked with, Lenny's cockney accent and manner were rough around the edges and the only jeans he owned showed oil stains from his work. Elizabeth's father took one look at Lenny and made it obvious that he didn't want his beautiful princess to end up with a good-for-nothing like him. It especially annoyed daddy that Lenny kept calling Elizabeth by the name of *Lizzie* as if she was the low-class market girl in *Pygmalion*. Despite daddy's annoyance, *Lizzie* continued to go out with Lenny. On the odd occasion that he would dare to visit the mansion, she would steer him away from her parents by taking his hand and leading him down the spiral staircase to their basement billiard room. Even with these precautions, daddy still found ways to interrupt the couple's attempts at kissing whenever he heard a pause in the sound of billiard balls being hit. To get away from prying eyes and disapproval, they made do with walking around the area or going to Lenny's humble home. Lenny's sister's bedroom was the only relatively private room in the house that allowed them to kiss and cuddle while listening to the latest music through an old Dansette vinyl record player.

A few years into their courtship, Lenny bought a sampler album called Bumpers - a showcase of artists signed up by the Island record label. When Lenny first listened to it, he was sure the softer tracks would finally create the right romantic atmosphere to help Lizzie want to move on beyond kissing and cuddling to something more passionate. When she next came round, he excitedly dropped the needle on the album then lay beside her on his sister's bed. When Bronco sang 'All the love I save' Lenny looked at Lizzie but sensed she wasn't getting into the romantic groove – maybe there were too many 'Ooh oohs' at the end of the song. He swapped the record and when John and Beverley Martin trilled 'It's yours - go out and get It' Lenny hoped tonight would be the night when he did get it!

With Lenny's mind working overtime as they lay close together, he failed to notice that Lizzie was unusually nervous. This wasn't due to Lenny's hardening body against her – she'd managed to fend off his more amorous advances all the time they'd been going out with each other. No, she was nervous because she had to tell Lenny something that may well break his heart. She looked for the right opportunity to tell him the news of her big adventure but he was too busy humming along to the music and trying to wrap his legs around her.

When Lenny got up to flip the record over, Lizzie saw her chance. He was busy taking care to place the needle down on the flip side of the record as she blurted out the words quickly in fear of failing to offload them. 'I passed all my exams … with the grades needed to go to university … daddy helped arrange for me … to get placed at

Southampton University ... set me up in digs ... overlooking the Dell football stadium ....' Lenny meanwhile had started jigging around the room to Fairport Convention's 'Walk Awhile'. He hadn't really listened to what Lizzie had said. She then struck the hammer blow 'Daddy persuaded me it would be best if we don't see each other so that can I concentrate on my degree'. Lenny couldn't think straight and his mind was oscillating between the music and the conversation. His subconscious mind kicked in and he heard himself say 'Maybe you're right.' Lizzie thought Lenny was being surprisingly mature until Cat Stevens sang exactly the same words from the record on the player. She thumped Lenny hard on the chest and said 'can't you take anything seriously?' then they tearfully hugged each other tightly. Lenny realised she was saying goodbye to him for the last time.

Lenny was distraught - he now understood what the blues singers were wailing about. He briefly contemplated suicide but, after hitting his head against his bedroom wall a few times, found it just added physical pain to his emotional pain.

Lenny finally came to his senses when he realised how lucky he was just to be alive. It didn't seem right to throw his life away but he vowed to live in the moment, never dwell on the past or wait for the future and never ever again allow anybody to break his heart in the way Lizzie had – this would be *Lenny's Golden Rule*.

Back on the bench at the Seaview, Lenny realised he was getting dangerously close to falling head over heels once again. His feelings for Connie thrilled but also frightened him as he was getting close to breaking the vow he'd called *Lenny's Golden Rule*. The other complication was that, since Ruby was no longer in the picture, the lack of activity in the physical department had pushed his libidinous appetite to an all-time high. It was definitely getting harder - harder to ignore the opportunities that were presenting themselves. He envisaged that the temptations would increase substantially during the peak period ahead.

Just as Lenny's shift was due to finish, a taxi turned up outside the *Seaview* office and an elegant thirty-something brunette stepped out. The taxi driver carried her bags in and gratefully accepted the tip she gave him before leaving her and her bags at the reception desk. After checking in and getting her chalet key, she saw that Lenny was the only *Purplecoat* still on duty so walked up to him. Peering at the name on his badge, she said in a posh husky voice 'Hello Lenny, I'm Samantha. Can you please help guide me to my chalet?' Lenny politely smiled and checked her key number. He said 'Of course Samantha, follow me and I'll show you the quickest way.' He picked up her luggage and led her out and around the back of the reception building.

Samantha toddled behind Lenny along the high path above the tennis courts, trampoline and bowling green. From here, the path overlooked the rooftops of the chalets cascading down the hill before grassy fields continued down to the clifftops, with sea and sky sharing the horizon. Samantha said 'Wow, what a fab vista - the photos in the brochure were impressive but this view looks even better in reality.' Lenny acknowledged that it was a fab vista but he was also thinking, what a fab voice! Samantha changed the subject and asked him what star sign he was. When Lenny said it was Aries, she immediately said she was Sagittarius. Samantha gazed into his eyes as she mischievously explained that their star signs were part of the Fire Trigon so extremely compatible. Perhaps they could have an astrological merger?! Lenny had no idea what she was talking about so moved the subject onto the weather forecast.

They reached a bench at a junction that led downhill to the superior chalets with sea views. Lenny placed the luggage down on the bench so that he could point out the remainder of the route to her chalet. It was relatively straightforward but she said 'I'm afraid I'm hopeless at directions. Would you be so kind as to take me all the way?' Lenny's work shift had now finished but he didn't want to disappoint a new guest, especially a very attractive one, so agreed to continue. He was slightly shocked but pleasantly surprised when she gave him a lingering peck on the cheek and said 'Oh, thank you, Lenny. You're a darling.' He tried to hide his blushes as he continued to carry Samantha's luggage down the hill.

As they criss-crossed the remaining set of paths to Samantha's chalet, she opened up about her life in the West End of London. Her mega rich daddy had acquired a posh apartment in Knightsbridge at the end of the swinging 60's and gave it to his beloved Sammie in 1970. It soon became clear that she preferred to live the life of a debutante rather than follow a career. She revelled in a hedonistic lifestyle amongst London's jet setters, going to parties and top-end night clubs. Her favourite haunt was Tramps, where she met stars of film and fashion including Michael Caine, Mary Quant, Sean Connery and Joan Collins. Joan's sister, Jackie was always there with her husband who was part owner. Lenny marvelled at her lifestyle but asked: 'With all the high life you enjoy in London, why on earth did you want to come to the *Seaview* holiday centre?' For the first time, she looked a little sad and came across as a little bitter when she confessed 'To be honest, I became disillusioned with my two-faced and shallow friends. I wanted to get away from a world where what you had in the bank was more important than love or kindness so decided to get away from it all for a week and get to know real, genuine people in this beautiful corner of the world'.

They reached Samantha's chalet and she opened the door so that Lenny could bring her bags in. The chalet must have been exclusive to VIP guests because it was the only one that Lenny had seen with a double bed rather than two singles. He placed the bags down and went to leave but Samantha stood in his way. Her sexy voice said 'Stay awhile, Lenny' and she cuddled up close and kissed his neck and lips. He was a little shocked but intoxicated by the aroma of exotic and no doubt expensive perfume merged with her own sweet sweat from the journey. She did not consider, let alone ask Lenny if he was in a relationship, but just treated him like a very personal member of staff there to serve her in any way she pleased. She continued with her seduction, cupping one hand around Lenny's buttocks to pull him toward her. Her other hand rubbed up and down the front of his shorts, like a Cuban factory woman might roll up tobacco leaves to make a cigar. Samantha was certainly turning a Cigarillo into a Corona Grande. What could Lenny do? His heart whispered to his conscience 'No, no, no, don't let Connie down' but his excited bulge shouted to his brain 'Yes, yes, for God's sake, yes!' They fell on the bed and went at each other voraciously like wild animals mating for the first time.

When Lenny made his way back to the purple flat, he felt supremely satisfied but very guilty. He didn't even say anything to Callum about his extreme meet and greet activity because he felt terrible at cheating on Connie. Callum didn't notice Lenny's demeanour but Lenny noticed Callum seemed very jolly and told him so. Callum couldn't hide anything from his roommate and soon admitted what had caused his jolly mood. 'Do you remember when you let me finish my shift early and I said I'd pop round to see Hazel and let her let know that I didn't drown in the bay?' Lenny immediately asked: 'Did you tell her you'd been on a trawler race getting drunk with the lovely Sue?' 'I didn't say Sue was lovely but I did confess the rest'. 'How did Hazel take it?' 'Well, LE. She must have felt a bit jealous because she responded as favourably as you could imagine!' 'Great, CC. You've finally broke your *Seaview* duck and proved your manhood!'

Lenny next saw Samantha at the bar of the *Inn Paradise* that evening. She looked even more elegant, dressed in what looked like the latest fashionable evening clothes. She was clearly engrossed in a conversation with a debonair 30-something gentleman. When she saw Lenny, she whispered something in the gentleman's ear while sneakily giving Lenny a cheeky smile and raising her eyebrows as if to say: 'thanks for the brief encounter but I've moved on now.' Lenny had to accept that wild animals often go back into the jungle after just one mating session but he would have loved to have found out more about Samantha's high life in London - had she met any Beatles or Stones at the swanky night clubs she frequented? If she had met Marsha Hunt, he could have told her she once chose him from the audience to dance with her during a performance of *Hair*. Unlike the rest of the cast, she didn't take her clothes off but she was so stunning that she didn't need to.

Biddy Rand's declaration - that she had recommended Callum for compering duties and Lenny for sports activities was a shock to all the senior *Purplecoats* and they realised her candidate comments had somehow been switched. They all thought Jason had mixed them up but he knew that wasn't the case. Nonetheless, he wanted to put things right straight away so he met up with Mike and they revised their plans. They could finally give the rookie boys the tasks that they were best suited to, at least as far as Biddy had envisaged.

That evening, Jason introduced his *Purplecoat* team at 9pm as usual, only this time he actually confirmed Lenny was a Sports Organiser and Callum was a Competition Host. They were happy that they had at last been officially given the roles that they had signed up for. They would soon find out that no time had been wasted in assigning suitable but extra tasks to them.

Once the evening cabaret show had begun, Jason and Mike took the rookie boys into the dressing room to give them an update on their workload. Callum would host the Miss *Funtime* beauty competition the following afternoon - Sunday - and the Man of the Week competition Monday evening. For Lenny, in addition to the sports tasks that he had already taken over from Callum, he would umpire tennis tournaments, organise rounders and take after breakfast keep fit sessions each morning apart from his day off on Sunday, however, Dale was taking an extra day off that Monday for an unexplained reason – rookies don't ask - so everyone had to cover his duties that day. This included Lenny taking the keep fit session on Monday morning – his usual half day off which he would be owed and could take at a future date - and Monday afternoon's coach excursion to Buckfast Abbey.
 The *Seaview* offered excursions to Paignton, Torquay, Dartmouth, Widdecombe-in-the-Moor and Buckfast Abbey. The senior purple coats always liked to take the *guests* on these trips as it got them out of the holiday centre and they often got tips that they kept to themselves. The rookies would usually be left behind to host the more mundane activities onsite like bingo, whist drive and trampolining, but none of the senior purple coats were available for that particular trip so this was a treat for Lenny.

That night, Callum and Lenny lay in their single beds alongside each other, thinking very different thoughts about their latest sexual encounters. Callum was still buzzing over moving to the next stage with Hazel and looking forward to developing the relationship further. Lenny was recalling the voracity of Samantha's seduction and realised that the yearning from his libido was so intense that it had ignored his deepest emotions and would probably gorge on sex 24 hours a day given the chance.

Overnight and by the following morning, Lenny had invented plenty of excuses to reduce his feelings of guilt: He and Connie had not yet started having sex, getting relief elsewhere would reduce the pressure on them both and he always said his job was to entertain the customers, whatever that entailed.

On Sunday afternoon, Callum was a little nervous. He had only seen Mike hosting the Miss *Funtime* beauty competition one week earlier so was relieved that he would be helping him get through his first event as the compere. Mike got all the girls to line up along the stage and pose in their swimsuits to let the judges and audience rank them on their looks to start with. The second official criteria to rank them was on their personality. Mike urged Callum to walk along the line of girls and ask each contestant their name, where they were from and throw in a trite question that they had to answer immediately, such as:

- How would you describe your personality?
- What philosophy or value do you hold dearest in life?
- How do you see yourself fifteen years from now?

Mike's tip to Callum was to cue up the applause from the audience after each answer and wait for the noise to die down before moving on.

The first contestant was a Susan Jackson from Manchester and Callum asked her 'Who is the most influential person in your life.' Susan said 'My mum!' It wasn't the most original answer but the audience loved it and applauded appreciatively, especially all the mothers.

Next up was Julie Harris from Bristol. Callum asked her 'If God should grant you one wish, what would it be?' Julie tried to sound sincere when she said 'I would ask god to maintain peace in the world and ensure that nobody was hungry.' The audience applauded respectfully. Callum was thinking that, if he had been a judge, he might have disqualified her for giving two answers instead of one.

Vicki Cuff from London was next and Callum immediately thought she was way prettier than all the other contestants put together. Struggling to avoid saying 'Wow', Callum pulled himself together and asked her 'If you won thousands of pounds on the football pools, what would you do with it?' She said that her parents had looked after her and her twin brother for all of their 17 years squashed together in a tiny council flat so she would love to buy them a nice house that they could all relax in. The audience applauded wildly and Callum felt sure that this must have clinched the win for her.

Callum went through the motions of introducing the remaining contestants to the audience then it was down to the judges to come to a decision.

Mike's next tip to Callum was to pause for effect when he receives the slip of paper from the judges and announces the results one by one in reverse order from 3rd, 2nd then first place.

After a longer deliberation than Callum expected, the judges finally wrote down their choice of winner and the two runner-up places then passed the list to Callum. When he sneaked a look at the slip of paper, he was surprised to see that his favourite was last on the list. He carried on regardless and hid his disappointment as he announced the result in reverse order 'In 3rd place is ... ' (pause for effect) '.. Vicki Cuff from London!' This was greeted with a mixture of cheers and murmurs of shock and disbelief from the more discerning viewers. 'In 2nd place is ..' (pause for effect) '.. Susan Jackson from Manchester!', Greeted with cheers from positively-minded family and friends, murmurs of 'she should have won' from negatively-minded family and friends plus polite applause from everyone else. 'In 1st place is ..' (longest pause for effect) .'.. Julie Harris from Bristol!' This was greeted with raucous cheers from her family and friends but silent shock followed by polite applause from everyone else.

As soon as the judges heard the announcement, they quickly waved Mike over and told him that Callum had got the 1st, 2nd and 3rd places in the opposite order. Mike realised the judges had written the places in 3rd, 2nd then 1st order whereas Callum had read the slip given to him believing that it was in 1st, 2nd then 3rd order. Officially, the decision had to stand as it had been announced publicly but Mike covered up for the mistake the best that he could. The girl who should have won was being comforted by her family, so Mike went over to them, explained and apologised for the error and promised that she as the rightful winner would be compensated. That very evening, he handed her an official invitation to compete in the Miss *Funtime* grand finals at the end of the season, adding 'You're bound to win the top prize, love.' Ever the charmer.

When Lenny had been tasked with looking after *guests* booked on the coach excursion to Buckfast Abbey he'd immediately thought of how he could make the most of the opportunity. He told Connie to book that Monday afternoon off and promised to sneak her along for free but she couldn't tell anyone or they would both be in trouble.

As Lenny was strolling up the hill with Callum for Monday morning breakfast, he mentioned his plan to take Connie on that afternoon's coach excursion to Buckfast Abbey, confident that Callum would keep it to himself. Callum said 'That's a nice thoughtful thing for you to do ... Have you checked if there are enough spare seats for the two of you?' Lenny said 'Damn!' and, in a panic, ran ahead, not stopping until he reached reception, red faced and puffing heavily. Jill Tully was behind the counter and said 'Morning Lenny, where's the fire? How come you're in such a rush?' He replied, breathlessly: 'Hi Jill. No rush. I was just warming up for my first keep fit class after breakfast then I'm escorting *guests* on this afternoon's coach excursion to Buckfast Abbey ... Just out of interest, how many *guests* have booked seats?' She looked at her register and came back with 'Twenty-eight.' 'And how many seats are there on the coach?' 'Thirty-four. Why do you ask?' 'Oh, I'm just making sure it's not too cramped for the *guests*, especially if they buy anything to bring back.' 'That's a nice thoughtful thing for you to do'. 'Yes, that's the second time someone's said that to me today!' At that moment, Callum walked in to reception and said 'Morning Jill.' Before he could say another word or spill the beans, Lenny grabbed his arm and led him into the dining room, whispering 'All sorted.' He said the same to Connie but reminded her to keep schtum about it – he could just imagine lots of waitresses gatecrashing his coach trip like a scene from a St Trinian's movie.

After breakfast, Lenny stretched and limbered up in the ballroom in readiness for his first keep-fit exercise class. He'd previously watched Mike and Dale run a couple of sessions in their own way, but no formal training in sports exercise was considered, let alone provided. The classes were supposed to offer light physical training for relatively fit pupils but participants often turned up with a wide variety of fitness levels and body sizes. It was therefore more by luck than judgement that there were no serious injuries. Nonetheless, Lenny was confident, having experienced many variations of training routines at school and with football teams he'd played for. This morning's *guests* covered the whole spectrum of fitness and body sizes but Lenny managed to cater for everyone. He finished the exercises with a 'Well done, enjoy the rest of the day and hope to see you back here same time tomorrow' and was heartened when they applauded him.

Callum had thoughtfully suggested to Jason and Mike that he helped Lenny load the *guests* on to the coach for Monday afternoon's excursion to Buckfast Abbey. They immediately agreed as it was one less job that they would have to do. Lenny was pleased as it would hopefully mean only the two of them would see that Connie was also coming along for a free ride. As the boys helped the last few *guests* to board the coach, Connie turned up looking sensational. The weather forecast more or less guaranteed a hot sunny day so in place of her waitress uniform, she wore a check blouse, yellow loons and pink sandals. She gave Lenny a sneaky kiss when nobody was looking and he directed her to the front seats that he'd saved so they could sit together. His duties were mainly to ensure everyone that had booked the excursion turned up, enjoyed the afternoon and got back safely. Lenny climbed up the stairs, armed with a register of the *guests* who had booked, ready to tick their names off and ensure all were aboard. Callum followed him with paper brochures that summarised the history of Buckfast Abbey and included a map. Connie said she'd be happy to hand them out to save him the trouble. Lenny thanked Callum who promised he would report back that all was well, but obviously not mentioning his unofficial helper. When all the holidaymakers had settled in their seats, Lenny walked up and down the aisle asking the incumbents either side for their names then ticking them off his list. Connie followed him and handed out the brochures with her beaming smile. A few passengers recognised her as their waitress but assumed she was employed to do this job as well or was taking part in cross-departmental training. All the names that the *guests* shouted out matched Lenny's register so he told the driver he could leave and the coach drove off exactly at the scheduled departure time.

As the coach bumped down the hill and out of the *Seaview* past the purple flat, Lenny was relieved that Callum's plan had worked. There had been no sign of any other *Purplecoats* checking on the departure so they would not have seen that Connie came along for a free ride. 'So far, so good' he thought. Now that he could relax, he thanked Connie for handing out the brochures. She cuddled up to him and lifted his arm to wrap it around her then whispered 'To be honest, I enjoyed helping and it made me want to help you more - I might even apply to become your full-time assistant!'

The coach made good progress and, as it passed Churston station, Lenny noticed Connie had already dropped off to sleep – the morning breakfast shift must have tired her out. She, and most of the other passengers, didn't wake up until an hour later when Lenny announced: 'Wakey, wakey, everyone! We're just arriving at the parking area for Buckfast Abbey. The path in front of you as you get off leads directly to the abbey and gardens. You'll see it on the map in the brochure that my beautiful assistant Connie gave to you'. Hearing her name mentioned thrilled Connie and made her even more sure that one day she'd escape the drudgery of being a waitress and become a *Purplecoat*. Lenny snapped her out of her daydream when he added 'Please remember or write down on your brochure that the number displayed on the windscreen of this coach is 7. This will help you return to the same vehicle before we leave for the return journey at 5pm prompt. In the meantime, you are free to enjoy the abbey and grounds. Please don't be late back to the coach as we want to get you all back to the *Seaview* in good time for dinner, unless of course you *want* to risk wearing your nightclothes as a forfeit!'

Lenny and Connie helped the passengers off the coach then followed them as they headed towards the abbey. When they all reached the entrance gate to the abbey there was a long queue waiting to go in. Neither Lenny or Connie were that bothered about seeing inside the abbey and decided to get away from the crowds. They wandered hand in hand through the pretty gardens, chatting about anything and everything – family, school, colleagues, likes, dislikes. They were happy to just enjoy the freedom of being alone together, like they were the only people on earth. They eventually came upon a large watermill and Lenny said it would make a great backdrop for a photo. He lined Connie up for various poses as he moved around trying different angles and distances while snapping away on his camera. He knew the results wouldn't be up to Kenny's standards because his Brownie 127 was the cheapest camera on the market. Nonetheless, the images of Connie that he saw through the camera's viewfinder appeared to be just perfect and he couldn't wait to see how the photos turned out. He would ask Kenny to put his film through the express processing agency he used but that would still mean waiting until the following late morning at best to see the results. He desperately hoped that at least one of the resulting photos would capture Connie's beauty and charm.

Mike gave Callum another chance to compere a competition without any incidents. This time it was the Man of the Week competition on Monday night. Callum was determined to get it right this time, even though he had only seen Mike hosting the show once, the previous week. He remembered Mike had lined up the contestants along the front of the stage and used the microphone to share with the audience a quick chat with each man before giving them an apparently random task to do. One was told he had to imagine he was a fireman and rescue a woman on the front row by throwing her over his shoulder in a fireman's lift and carrying her around the ballroom. The next contestant was told to pretend he was asking a woman he'd never met why she should let him date her daughter. Another was told to pretend he was asking a woman to marry him. It was a bit embarrassing for all concerned but a bit of a laugh for the audience.

Now it was Callum's turn to be the host and he started off brilliantly. He skilfully used the microphone to introduce the competition and invite volunteers onto the stage, lined them up and shared with the audience his conversations with each contestant. He established their name, found out where they were from and what job they did, then gave them a unique task, all the time encouraging the audience to respond and cheer. By the time Callum got to the last two contestants, he could only remember two tasks that he hadn't already used:
1. the one where the contestant had to imagine he was a fireman and rescue the woman on the front row by throwing her over his shoulder in a fireman's lift and carrying her around the ballroom
2. the one where the contestant had to pretend to ask a woman that he'd never met why she should let him date her daughter.

The next contestant was a creepy 80-year-old so the dating option was not ideal but he looked too frail to carry anyone around the ballroom. Luckily, the last contestant looked burly in comparison so Callum was sure he would be able to mimic the fireman task. Callum got the octogenarian to sit up close to a woman he'd never met and try to persuade her to let him date her daughter! The old man tried not to sound like a sex pervert when acting out his task, but the harder he tried, the worse it sounded and the audience squirmed in embarrassment. Callum looked at Mike and wasn't sure if he was laughing or grimacing. Never mind, Callum thought, the show must go on. Surely the last contestant would save the day and the competition would finish on a high note. Callum asked 'What is your name?' 'George Edwards.' 'Where are you from?' 'Waltham Cross'. 'And what is your job?' 'A Fireman'! Callum looked at Mike and said through the microphone 'I've got it wrong again, haven't I!' Mike nodded in mock agreement. Callum couldn't conjure up a different task, so got the fireman to show the audience how a professional would rescue a woman on the front row. The contestant went along with the humour of the moment and brought the house down by throwing the unfortunate woman over his shoulder in a fireman's lift, running her right around the ballroom then returning her back to her seat. He easily got the loudest applause in the audience vote to be crowned a worthy Man of the Week. The creepy old man never did get a date with the woman's daughter!

After Tuesday morning's football match, Lenny kept dropping in to the photographic shop until Gillian Evans confirmed the package he wanted had arrived. It contained the photos he'd taken when he and Connie went on the Buckfast Abbey excursion. Resisting the temptation to open the package himself, he went straight round to Connie's chalet and let her open it. She told him to sit next to her on the bed so that they could go through them together. As they looked at each photo, they laughed and recalled that moment. He could only afford the smallest size photos but Connie didn't mind. Thankfully, most of them came out as well as he'd hoped they would, especially those he was most looking forward to seeing – Connie in front of the mill. One in particular really did capture her beauty and charm, topped with that special smile. When he told her this, she got very emotional and got up from the bed with the photo in her hand. Lenny was concerned that something was amiss but realised the opposite was true when she picked up a pen, carefully wrote something on the back of the photo then handed it back to him. She'd written 'To my darling Lenny - All my Love, Connie'. He put the photo down on the bedside cabinet and they enjoyed a few minutes of passionate kissing until they heard tapping on the chalet door. Judy walked in and sat on her bed. She was so excited that she didn't notice Connie and Lenny were excited too, but in a different way.

Judy said 'I must tell you me news, me luvvers. I wuz walking dan the hill to see Tommy and bumped into 'iz mates walking up the hill carrying 'iz things. I asked them what they wuz doing and they said they wuz helping Tommy move in to 'iz new chalet. When I caught up with him at the Gaff, I asked 'what's this about you be gettin' a chalet and why did'n ee tell me. Well, ee was quite annoyed with me at fust n' said I'd spoilt 'iz surprise as ee was gonna take me to 'eez new chalet once ee'd moved in, bless 'n. Makes a change for 'ee to plan any surprise for me, let alone a nice one like thaat, but there tiz. I told 'n cuz I would move in with 'n tonight so Connie dear, could you please be a luvver n' help me pack?' Connie agreed to help so Lenny left them to it.

As Connie put Judy's bathroom items into a bag, she had a number of concerns that she kept to herself, for now at least: Judy had found out about the move almost by chance, not from Tommy but from his mates. Was Tommy really planning to surprise Judy or was it an excuse because he'd been caught out. Did Tommy really want Judy with him on the first night at his new chalet or did he want the place to himself, at least for a while, before committing to have her move in with him? Has Judy made herself look too desperate to be with him? Would Tommy take advantage of this and brag about it to his mates or the other waitresses he spent time with? While Connie was thinking about all these negatives, Lenny was simply thinking that this turn of events was one huge positive: It would enable him to enjoy total and unlimited privacy with Connie in her chalet.

Late that evening, after he'd finished his ballroom shift, Lenny went round to Connie's chalet. As they cuddled and kissed, he told her he was glad that she liked the photos as much as he did, cherished her gesture of writing words of love on the back of his favourite one and confessed that he felt the same way about her. He added that he was glad the photo was small enough to fit in his pocket because he would always keep it with him and kiss it whenever she wasn't right by his side. It reminded him of his favourite Elton John song that included the lyric: "Tiny dancer in my hand".

Connie let Lenny stay for their first night in bed together. When she undressed shyly in front of him, he couldn't help but marvel at how cute she was. Her skimpy pink panties were tightly wrapped around her ultra slim hips and when she unclipped her gossamer bra, her breasts popped out delightfully. He knew they were on the small side - she had recently allowed him to caress them over her clothes - but now he saw them in the flesh he could see that they, and her nipples, were perfectly shaped.

She lay on the bed waiting for him to join her. With her thick and curly auburn hair cascading down her shoulders, he thought she looked like Botticelli's painting of Venus but sexier with her geisha-like hips. He also sensed her shyness and anxiety but he couldn't wait to feel her naked body against his and was full of expectation as he undressed and climbed into bed alongside her.

They kissed and cuddled lovingly and he caressed those perfect breasts then his tongue tickled those perfect nipples. They both got more excited but when it was time to go on to the next stage of passion, Lenny was shocked to find that he literally hit a problem. Lenny was not particularly well endowed but, each time he tried to enter Connie, it was like hitting a firmly closed door. She sensed his concern and blurted out that she was still a virgin. Lenny had no experience of breaking a girl in and no idea how to get around the impasse. He tried to put Connie's mind at rest and stop her tears by telling her not to worry as there's no rush. They held on to each other in silence and contemplation before eventually falling asleep.

The next morning, they didn't say much as they got dressed. Lenny only had his evening uniform from the previous night to wear so needed to run down to the purple flat to change into his day clothes. It was Callum's day off and Lenny woke him when he barged in through the bedroom door. Lenny threw off his evening clothes and put on his day uniform as quickly as he could. A bleary-eyed Callum couldn't help but ask 'LE, how was your first night in Connie's chalet?' Lenny couldn't divulge the details so changed the subject 'Look at this fantastic photo I took of Connie at Buckfast Abbey'. Callum agreed that she looked beautiful then Lenny told him to turn the photo over to see where she'd written 'To my darling Lenny - All my Love, Connie'. 'LE, you're a lucky so and so.' 'I know that, CC. Best be off otherwise I'll miss breakfast. By the way, I'll be passing here with a rambling party later on. Do you want me to bring you a bacon sandwich or anything else?' 'No thanks, LE. To be honest, I stayed up at Hazel's last night and didn't get in this bed until a few minutes before you arrived so I'm having a lay in to get my strength back up!' Lenny laughed as he flew out the door, saying to his sporadic roommate: 'CC, you're a lucky so and so as well!'

Lenny reached the dining room just as service was ending but the waitress brought him a chunky egg and bacon sandwich. She leaned forward and whispered 'the extra bacon is from Connie for last night!' Lenny blushed but suspected she was joking and that maybe Judy had put her up to it by incorrectly assuming his relationship with Connie had been consummated.

When Lenny took rambling parties, he tried to add a trick, dare or game as the mood took him to make the trips more fun, at least he thought it was a bit of fun. He often pretended that he was lost, sending the ramblers the wrong way down a cul-de-sac then calling them back. Other times, he would get them to compete against each other or their opposing planets in silly games such as spinning around on a playground roundabout, climbing up a slide the wrong way or pushing someone the highest on the swings. When Kenny came along on these rambles, games like these gave him plenty of opportunities for amusing photographs that could be sold to the targets and beyond. Lenny also gave Kenny the nod by shouting 'Quick, KT!' to give him enough time to get in a prime position to snap a girl showing more leg than usual, especially when she was climbing over one of the many stiles along the route. Saucy photographs sold very well even when the purchasers had never met the girls starring in them!

One Wednesday morning, Lenny happened to be the only *Purplecoat* leading the rambling party on a visit to Warm Park. Visits to other *Funtime* holiday centres helped holidaymakers gauge how theirs compared. It was a 'win:win' as far as *Funtime* executives were concerned because, if any holidaymakers preferred the alternative holiday centre, they could simply choose to book it for their next *Funtime* holiday.

The ramble to Warm Park was a steady walk of a few miles each way along reasonably flat roads, apart from the descent down the hill out of the entrance gates. As the rambling party passed the *Seaview's* entrance gates, Baz flashed his security badge and pretended to scrutinise them while making imaginary notes on his pad.

Even though the ramblers were walking downhill, gravity forced them to go faster than they would have liked and some of them were puffing heavily. Lenny suggested they all sit on the wall outside the purple flat for a short rest. As they were getting their breath back, Lenny had an idea to play a trick on his room-mate. He asked the ramblers if any of them would like to see inside the flat where all the *Seaview Purplecoats* live. Around twenty of them said they would love to. Lenny took them through the front door, pointed out the kitchen and bathroom, which some of them were in need of, then he couldn't stop himself opening the door to the bedroom that he shared with Callum.

Callum was in a deep sleep getting over the previous night at Hazel's chalet when he was rudely awoken by Lenny opening their bedroom door while a multitude of voices were emanating from the hall. One by one, Lenny invited the visitors from the rambling party to walk in to say 'Good morning' to Callum as he lay in bed. They may also have been wondering why Lenny's evening clothes were strewn across his own bed. The more enlightened would have realised he'd had no time to hang them up when he'd changed uniforms earlier that morning. After the last holidaymaker had said 'Hello!' to Callum, Lenny poked his head back into the bedroom. His roommate now sat up in bed seething, said 'LE you bastard, they've all seen me in my pyjamas.' Lenny replied 'That's better than seeing you without pyjamas, CC!' After hearing Lenny laughing hysterically, Callum saw the funny side and told him his laugh sounded like he was saying 'Ze-ze-ze'. From that moment on, they always said 'Ze-ze-ze' to each other whenever anything hilarious occurred. After 'Oomballah!' and the nicknames 'LE', 'CC' and 'KT' they were developing their own secret language.

On Wednesday evening, Connie popped down to the Three Elms Inn with her brother, Nick and his girlfriend, Anne. Tommy and his gang of worshippers had commandeered the far end of the bar and Judy was standing alongside them looking a little bit out of place. Tommy was even more obnoxious than usual. He'd already upset pub regular Lucy by picking up her cigarette lighter from the bar in front of her to look at the skull and crossbones etched on it. With a growl, she snatched it out of his hands before he could read the inscription. Before he could retaliate, his mates distracted him by pointing out that his favourite song was playing on the juke box - Chubby Checker's hit: *Let's Twist Again*. Fully diverted, Tommy led his gang in singing along, only he'd changed the words *Let's Twist Again* to *Get Pissed Again* … He soon ran out of ideas for his own brand of crude humour and one by one his mates gave up on the song. Tommy's most loyal follower – Terry – was the last to realise this, or his mates mocking his crazy dancing and tone-deaf singing of *round and round and up and down we go* … all on his own.

Tommy leaned across to Judy as if to whisper in her ear but instead let out a deafening burp. His mates almost fell on the floor laughing. Judy was unimpressed and retreated to the other end of the bar to find solace with Connie's group. It was nice to share a normal conversation away from Tommy and his mates. They were busy having a burping contest when Anne and Connie went off to the toilet. Nick took the opportunity to have a quiet word with Judy. He asked her if she was happy being with Tommy … She secretly wanted to ask him the same question about Anne but, more importantly, confess that the man she was now sleeping with had been bullying her incessantly since she'd moved in with him, complaining about everything she did, punching her hard when he felt she wasn't paying him enough attention and even pushing her head under the covers when he'd farted. Instead, with a sense of loyalty or fear, she simply said "Some people think he's brash and vulgar but it's just his way that's all".

Nick wanted to talk further to Judy but one of his colleagues came up to him. Phil was a trainee chef, lucky enough to have been given a car by his dad. He wasn't too good at changing gear using the manual transmission so wanted to sell it so that his dad could get him an automatic instead. Judy got fed up of the two men going through the technical details and noticed Tommy was giving her a critical look so returned to him, trying to hide her disenchantment. Anne and Connie returned to the bar just as Nick said 'I'm not sure I want the responsibility of owning a car'. Phil in desperation said 'You can take it out for a trial drive on Sunday if it will help you decide'. Connie whispered in Nick's ear 'Let's make the most of the opportunity and nip home to see mum and dad'.

By the time Sunday came along, Nick had invited Anne at the same time as Connie had invited Lenny to join them. They really did plan to make the most of the opportunity by not only popping in to their homes in Ivybridge but then going to a gig in Plymouth. Nick knew the owners of the Van Dike club and they promised free entry for the four of them to see a German progressive rock band called Amon Duul.

Connie and Nick's mum and dad were delighted to see them and relieved to hear that they were enjoying life at the *Seaview*. A huge bonus for Lenny was that they seemed to like him, despite his cockney accent. Nick's dad checked over the old beat-up car and believed his son when he lied that the car was insured.

Nick managed to find a parking spot quite near to the Van Dike club and Lenny thought Amon Duul were brilliant. As he immersed himself in their unusual sounds, he realised how much he missed listening to progressive music like this. He'd got bored of having to listen to the schmaltz played in the ballroom and teenage pop in the disco.

After Lizzie had broken his heart, Lenny found solace in blues and progressive music. He spent the rest of his teenage free time going to folk clubs, rock clubs in and around London and the odd festival with mates or on his own. He still didn't have much money but managed to get into some venues by back doors or being let in for free just because his hair was the same length as the guy at the entrance. He also queued up for free entry to BBC radio shows hosted by John Peel. These sessions enabled him to get up close to see and hear the top acts of that time including his favourite rock band, Pink Floyd.

Alongside the London music scene was a burgeoning drug culture. Lenny smoked a lot of weed and took LSD at weekend acid tripping parties and excursions with his hippie friends. For the next few years, he tried everything that was offered - not to escape his world but to 'find his inner self', or at least that was what he believed at the time.

After inadvertently sniffing heroin and cocaine off of playing cards at a party, he coined *Lenny's Golden Rule Number Two* - he would steer clear of addictive drugs and never encourage anyone to get hooked on anything, not even alcohol.

The deafening sound of the frantic honking of a lorry and three people screaming 'Kinnell' woke Lenny from his semi-conscious state. He realised he was slumped alongside Connie in the back seat of a speeding car. She shouted to the driver and passenger in the front seats 'Nick, Anne. Are you okay? That was an elluva close shave. I thought that juggernaut was gonna hit us head on! Lenny – did you see it?' Lenny mumbled 'No, I must have rested my eyes for a minute'. Connie said: 'You *rested yer eyes* for an elluva lot longer than a minute - more like an hour. You've been asleep since we left Plymouth and I think my big brother just dropped off at the wheel!' Nick shook his head and rubbed his eyes as he responded 'If I did drop off for a second, then I bloody blame all of you'. They all said in unison 'Why?' 'Because you'd all promised you'd keep me alert.' The passengers felt guilty and made sure they all stayed awake by keeping the conversation going for the rest of the journey. Nick also felt guilty for not getting insured to drive the car so any type of incident would have been even more catastrophic than his passengers realised. They discussed the music they heard. Anne said 'Amon Duul were too weird for my liking'. Lenny countered 'They're supposed to be one of the top krautrock bands and I really like weird stuff like that.' 'Krautrock?' 'Yes, krautrock. It refers to progressive rock acts from Germany. If you want something softer than what you heard tonight, you should check out *Monster Movie*.' Anne said 'Which actors star in that film?' Lenny laughed and explained 'It's not an actual movie. It's a psychedelic album from Can - they're my favourite krautrock band. I'm going home in a few weekends so I'll bring back my record player with *Monster Movie* and some of my other favourite records to play to you all'. Connie looked concerned 'This is the first I've heard of you going home. What's happening?' 'Oh. Before I left home, I promised to return for my friend Bernie's 21st birthday.' 'Is that a male or female Bernie?' 'Male'. 'Has Jason allowed you the weekend off?' 'I haven't asked him yet but I'm owed time off because I worked extra shifts when Jane left and Dale asked me to cover him for the Buckfast Abbey excursion that I took you on.' She realised he was pointing out that he'd tried to include her even when he was supposed to be working, so changed the subject with 'How will you bring everything back?' 'Well, the record player has a carrying handle and instead of taking my suitcase, I'll just chuck a few clothes into a shopping bag then squeeze some records into it for the return journey'. Connie looked sad that Lenny was leaving her, even for a few days, so he put his arm around her like a warm blanket and whispered words of reassurance that their relationship would not be affected in any way. He wasn't to know that something would soon enough happen that *would* affect their relationship.

One morning, after his keep fit session, Lenny went round to Connie's chalet and noticed that the front door was ajar. He tapped on the window and walked in, only to find Judy sobbing on Connie's shoulder. Connie gave him a darting look to communicate that she needed some privacy to console her friend. Lenny got the message and quietly said to Connie that he would maybe see her in the buffet lounge. As he left, he failed to notice the bags on the floor and under Judy's eyes.

Ten minutes later, Connie met Lenny in the buffet lounge and led him by the hand into the empty dining room so that they could talk privately. She gripped both his hands and explained what had happened, or at least what Judy said had happened...
Apparently, Judy and Tommy had been arguing ever since she'd moved in with him. Tommy had insisted that the single beds be put together so that he could force himself on her whenever he pleased. That was bad enough but, after the beds kept sliding apart, Tommy used a rope he'd had found washed up on the beach to tie them together. Judy hated the smell of it but Tommy was insistent as it made it easier for him to roll away straight after he'd had his fun. Judy would have liked a cuddle after pleasing him but he seemed to want to be

as far away from her as he could as if the act was a necessary release for him without any emotions. The situation came to a head when he told her he wanted to go out with the other kitchen lads … without her. As he was leaving, she grabbed and hung on to his arm begging him to stay with her. He twisted around to push her away, but accidentally caught her with his elbow. Instead of seeing if she was okay and apologising, he ranted that she was suffocating him so much that he wanted her to move out. He even threatened to throw her out, along with all of her clothes, if she was still there when he returned. Judy took his threat seriously, packed her bags and left the *love nest*.

'Judy was sobbing as she asked me if she could move back into *our chalet* at least for the time being. Lenny, I couldn't turn my friend down but I did tell her I really wanted to continue to share my bed with you. She thought about it and agreed that the three of us could share the same chalet.   Would you be okay with this arrangement?' Lenny said 'I just want to be with you, Connie, so will go along with whatever that takes.' Connie put her arms around Lenny and said 'Tommy's been an elluva bastard to Judy and I'm not sure if her bruise was an accident. Why can't he be as caring as you are, me luvver?' Lenny knew this was a question he wasn't expected to answer so he didn't.

That afternoon, Lenny popped round to see that Connie had helped Judy move her things back in to the chalet that he would now be sharing with them. The sun came out and Connie tried to cheer up Judy, and Lenny, by spreading blankets on the grass outside the chalet. The three of them laid down alongside each other to enjoy the warmth from the sun rays. Within a few minutes, Judy's bruises started stinging from the heat and the sweat so she went inside to the shade. Moments later, she returned, carrying glasses of water for Connie and Lenny. As she handed the drinks to them, she smiled and told them they looked like a Sun King and Sun Queen with their long flowing sun-bleached hair and newly tanned faces. She was glad they got on so well but the smile she put on couldn't conceal the sadness she felt that her own relationship with Tommy was in a bad place. Despite his selfishness and cruelty, she really missed him and couldn't stop talking about him. Through misplaced love or blind faith, she was determined to win him back but hoped he would be begging for her to return after he had a few days and nights on his own.

Having Judy sleeping just a few feet away from their bed turned out to be a real passion killer for Lenny. Cuddling up to Connie every night was nice but Judy was regularly disturbing them, going over something Tommy had said or did and asking for their advice on how she should try to get back with him.   After a couple of nights like this, Lenny realised that, in this environment, there was zero chance that he would get a good night's sleep, let alone pop Connie's cherry. He even suggested to Connie that he move back into the purple flat to get some sleep and leave her to better comfort Judy, at least until her relationship issues had been resolved, one way or another. Connie was torn but said she'd talk to Judy.

At that evening's dinner service, Connie called Lenny over and told him the wonderful news that Judy had made up with Tommy and was moving back in with him that night.

While working his evening shift in the ballroom, Lenny was looking forward to returning to Connie's bed but concerned that they still hadn't consummated their relationship. He had swapped a sexual expert for a virgin and wondered if it was because he treated Connie like a delicate and precious flower that he was finding it impossible to deflower her. In a few minutes he would hear of a potential solution.

Lenny had for some time noticed the Irish twins laughing and chatting to men as they went up to the bar at *Inn Paradise*. He'd remembered Ruby telling him that the Senior Nurse had put them on the pill the first day they had arrived as waitresses and they had soon earned a reputation for making the most of their new found freedom. Both girls were plain-looking but had an indefinable magnetism and they certainly got the full attention of all the men they spoke to. They seemed to be competing with each other to get free drinks or more from their targets. Their techniques ranged from slight gestures using different parts of their body to just short of an assault. Subtle movements included a gentle bite of the lower lip, a slight raising of a shoulder or lifting a hand to their or their target's neck. More obvious ploys included holding a gaze or raising eyebrows to show interest. If they didn't gain attention, their more desperate actions included almost spilling a drink alongside their target, dropping a purse for the target to pick up or simply bumping into them *by mistake*. They could then engage in suggestive conversations and take it from there.

Lenny thought the girls were a bit too rough and ready for his liking so he hadn't spoken to them before but he was intrigued by them so finally went up to them when they were on their own. One of the girls said in an Irish accent but provocatively 'Hello Lenny! I'm Cara and this is my twin sister, Etain.' Lenny responded 'You know my name, then.' Cara said 'Oh, we've heard *all* about you from Ruby but Connie is more tight-lipped, if you know what I mean.' She elbowed Lenny playfully and both sisters giggled. Lenny was unsure if this was a crude barb about Connie still being a virgin. Cara said 'So, how are ye getting on with our girl Connie then?' Lenny meekly said 'She's great – lovely'. Etain brazenly chipped in 'When my sister said *how ye getting on*, she meant *are ye getting' plenty*!' He didn't respond, beyond blushing, so she probed further. 'Okay, spill the beans. Are ye getting *any*?' He fobbed them off with 'A gentleman never tells' then tried to switch the conversation away from this touchy subject but the twins were insistent 'Look, Lenny. We know some techniques that might help'.

In strong Irish accents that Lenny could barely understand, the Irish sirens took turns to go through their impromptu sex education class. 'Some girls get put off when the bed bangs against the wall when they're going at it. Before ye get started, jam a pair of soft shoes, socks or a blanket between the bed and the wall to stop it making a racket and disturbing her or the neighbours.' 'On the other hand, if she's into listening to someone else going at it, get her to put an ear up to an empty glass that's pushed against the wall'.

The twins also introduced Lenny to a subject he'd never heard of before. Etain said 'Ya really gotta find her erogenous zone'. Cara agreed 'Oooh Yeah.' Lenny said he thought that was a Dutch painter. The girls laughed and Etain said 'No silly, that's Hieronymus Bosch!' After they stopped laughing, they took it in turns to explain that erogenous zones are nerve endings located all over the male and female body. The most sensitive areas provide special titillation when stimulated through touching, kissing, licking, caressing or biting. The pleasure felt can lead to sexual arousal or even orgasm for the receiver. The girls said 'You've gotta tickle the tree to get the cherry' then warned Lenny he had to be careful when trying to find the most sensitive area as it can be tricky if handled badly. A rough touch or clumsy bite in the wrong area can put the recipient off, so it's best to go gently starting with the arms, hair, lips or neck then proceeding with the hands, forehead, shoulders, ears or belly to see what reaction you get. Lenny stopped himself from churlishly suggesting it was a 'suck it and see' approach. Instead, he thanked the girls for their intriguing advice before leaving them at the bar to continue to enjoy themselves with new targets. He couldn't wait to try out their teachings with Connie as soon as his shift finished.

CHAPTER 18 - Red cards and tragedies (w/c 23rd June)

[Playlist Track: *"Judy In Disguise - John Fred & His Playboy Band"*]

Friday was fish and chip day. Lenny and Callum were getting fed up of the longer than usual delay. They could hear noises coming from the kitchen so decided to go through to see what was going on and help themselves or at least help their waitress. When they pushed through the *In Doors,* they nearly bumped into the back of an already squashed up queue of waitresses. The scene was utter bedlam. Bodies were rushing around the steamy kitchen like a manic party in a Turkish Bath. Tureens of chips and piles of plates loaded with fish had fallen off the serving counter to the floor at the front of the queue. Judy was in tears and waitresses were helping clear up the mess she'd apparently caused due to her glasses fogging up. The kitchen lads on the other side of the counter were jeering and swearing at her so noisily it was a wonder that the guests didn't hear it. Callum pulled Lenny's arm and said 'LE, let's leg it out of here.' They retreated back through the *In Doors*, and sat back at their table to wait for their very flustered waitress to eventually serve them.

Connie wasn't responding to Lenny's latest jokes. He asked 'Are you okay? What's the matter?' She said 'I'm worried about Judy - she's having more always been thin but she's looking more and more unhealthy each day and she seems to have developed a slight nervous twitch after today's accident'. Lenny said 'Maybe you should get her to talk to the nurse. I'm sure Hazel could soon sort her out medically but having a boyfriend like Tommy probably doesn't help'.

Lenny refereed most of the football matches and Callum would help him go through a routine that added to everyone's enjoyment. In the match between *Seaview* staff and guests, Callum came on for the staff team and pretended to play really badly, which he found easy to do. After a few minutes, he gave Lenny a secret 'thumbs up' signal then deliberately handled the ball in the penalty area. Lenny blew his whistle loudly, walked up to him, raised a red card in his hand and dramatically sent Callum off. Callum pretended to be outraged, saying 'Oomballah!' but Lenny replied with 'Ze-ze-ze' then manhandled him off the pitch. The whole act was designed to bring back memories of the 1966 football World Cup when the Argentina team's captain was sent off in a crucial match against England. All the onlookers loved the histrionics and it was the first of many ways Lenny and Callum pretended to cause a scene for dramatic effect.

Talking of red cards, a philanderer was about to receive his red card too, but which one?

Brenda and Polly had been working together in the buffet lounge as usual. During a quiet moment, Brenda noticed her friend looked troubled so asked her how she was getting on recuperating from her sprained wrist at Rodger Bodger's chalet. Polly admitted that she had to stop sleeping in the same bed as *Bodge* because he kept bumping against her wrist and they were having more frequent arguments, especially when she complained of the pain. Brenda decided Polly needed a change of scenery to cheer herself up so took her off to the nearby *Funtime* holiday centre, called *Warm Park*. While at the bar there they got chatting to some girls who worked there as waitresses. Brenda made a point of asking them if they'd seen Rodger Bodger's one-man-show, only so that she could then brag that Polly was *Bodge*'s girlfriend. The waitresses looked disgusted to hear his name mentioned. They confirmed that they'd seen him perform on stage but added that he was just as famous for performing off stage as well. Polly asked them what they meant and was told that he was well known for bedding girls in every holiday centre he worked in. One of the waitresses pointed to a girl at the other end of the bar and whispered that the scoundrel had been with her the previous night. Polly recalled *Bodge* returning late from his gig that night and blaming the *Purplecoats* for delaying him. As soon as Brenda and Polly returned to the *Seaview*, they went down to Bodge's chalet. Luckily for him, he wasn't there but Polly left her key with a note calling him a philandering rat and confirming that she'd dumped him. Brenda then helped bring Polly's belongings back to the safe haven of their chalet.

Judy was deep in her own thoughts as she was walking from Tommy's chalet to the dining room to prepare to serve dinner to her tables. Since moving back in with him, instead of making up for their time apart, they'd continued to argue and seemed to be drifting further apart than ever. Judy couldn't help comparing her relationship with Tommy against the love lives of her closest school friends. Theirs all appeared to be going from strength to strength. Connie with Lenny and Anne with her dear friend Nick.

Judy recalled the moment when Nick asked her to go out with him. It was in their last year at school so Sod's law that he waited too long - Tommy had asked her out just minutes earlier and, urged on by her friends, she'd agreed to go out with him. She was torn at the time as she felt good in Nick's company and Connie had warned her that Tommy was a terrible flirt. Her other schoolfriends persuaded her that Tommy was a better catch - they liked his rough round the edges self-confidence and swagger whereas Nick had a soft personality that her friends thought was wimpish and less attractive. A year had passed since then but it seemed like a lifetime and Nick had moved on with Anne. When Judy saw how well Nick treated Anne, it confirmed that he was a much nicer human being than Tommy and this became more and more obvious the longer she got to know them both.

Nick's name kept coming up in the many arguments Tommy had with Judy. Tommy saw the way his so-called girlfriend and Nick looked at each other, even when he or Anne were present. Eventually, Tommy whined that she probably wished she hadn't turned Nick down only to be stuck in their crappy relationship - perhaps Tommy understood Judy better than she knew herself.

It was 6pm but the late afternoon sun was still blazing brightly and keeping the temperature hot and sticky. Judy definitely wasn't looking forward to working up a sweat under her uniform while serving hot food to her 4 tables. She felt that her waitress life wasn't all it was cut out to be and the tips she got were hardly worth the extra effort.

Three young boys suddenly ran up to Judy and pleaded for her to go with them straight away to the swimming pool as it was an emergency – Timmy had fallen in the pool. She could really do without this interruption to her hectic day and wasn't sure if the boys were playing a trick on her but they seemed desperate so she grudgingly went along with them.

The swimming instructor and attendant for the outdoor swimming pool at the *Seaview* had yet to start his season. In the meantime, signs around the pool warned visitors that using the pool was at their own risk and the whole area was out of bounds to unaccompanied children.

The boys practically dragged the reluctant Judy to the swimming pool area until she recoiled in horror as she noticed a small lifeless body floating on the surface. She ran up to the edge of the pool but couldn't proceed further as she couldn't swim. All she could do was scream for help in all directions. A middle-aged man came out of the nearest chalet to see what the noise was about. Judy waved frantically and cried out for him to help them as quickly as he could. The man ran over, saw the boy they were pointing to, jumped in fully dressed without hesitation and dragged Timmy to the side of the pool where Judy helped to haul him up onto the grass. The boy had stopped breathing and was unresponsive as the two of them desperately tried to revive Timmy by shaking him.

A few more holidaymakers came over but none of them knew how to carry out any form of resuscitation so they all felt totally helpless. Someone had run to reception to get the nurse or an ambulance as quickly as possible but, by the time help arrived, it was too late. The professionals confirmed Timmy's death, covered his body in a blanket and carried him away on a stretcher.

A policeman turned up and had to ask Timmy's sobbing friends what had happened. Stumbling to talk through their tears, they explained that they lived just outside the holiday centre but sneaked in through a hole in the hedge. The four of them had been playing by the pool and had an urge to cool off in the water. None of them could swim but, for a dare, they agreed to hold hands and jump in the shallow end of the pool together. When they lined up along the pool length, Timmy was nearest to the middle of the pool. They all jumped in together but the boy holding Timmy's hand lost his grasp with the pressure of hitting the surface. All of the boys tried to grab hold of Timmy and pull him back from the brink but he slid away from them down into the deep end. Once they realised that they couldn't help their friend, they ran for help.

The boys walked off with the policeman to take him to the home of the unfortunate lad's family so that he could convey the tragic news. Nobody thought to ask Judy how she felt. She was still shaking from the shock but had been left to get over the incident all on her own.

When Jason heard about the tragedy, he quickly gathered all the *Purplecoat*s together and passed on the terrible news. Before anyone could even think of getting upset, Jason insisted that tonight's show must go ahead with all of their support.

At an appropriate moment during that evening's dinner, Jason had the difficult task of making an announcement to the holidaymakers regarding little Timmy's death. He covered all the bases corporate-wise by confirming that a gang of local boys had trespassed into the *Seaview* holiday centre and ignored the warning signs around the pool, leading to one of the boys tragically drowning in the water. He allayed potential fears that this tragic accident might happen again by explaining that a swimming instructor would be arriving in a few days as scheduled. The instructor would guard the pool during most of the day but, when no guards are present, all parents needed to be vigilant regarding their children, as advised by the warning signs around the pool.   Jason confirmed that tonight's show would still go ahead and ended the announcement by saying that the thoughts of all the staff at the *Seaview* holiday centre go out to Timmy's family and friends.

Judy stood at her serving station listening to Jason's speech. She had managed to stop shaking but couldn't stop tears of sadness from dribbling down her face onto her waitress uniform. She kept telling herself that she had to hold herself together and maintain a stiff upper lip but helping guests stuff food into themselves had become a nightmare for her. She didn't just hate serving food, she now couldn't stand to look at it, smell it or even eat it.

Another complication was that it would be her birthday in a few days and, for the first time in her life, she was dreading it.

Waitresses wore a day uniform for breakfast and lunch and a darker set for the evening dinner. This was just as well because they always celebrated the birthdays of their colleagues with an amusing ritual. As soon as the birthday girl or girls had cleared up after the lunch service they would be carried to the pool and thrown in. When poolside, birthday girls could plead to take off as much of their uniform as their modesty would allow to stop it getting wet. If they declined this opportunity, they would be thrown in fully clothed. Their uniforms only had the rest of the afternoon to dry off so, if the sun wasn't shining, they would still be damp next morning.

Judy knew she couldn't refuse to go along with the birthday celebration ritual but was well aware that it would bring unwanted attention to her physical and mental state. Her colleagues would realise just how frail she had become when they picked her up and see the many bruises caused by Tommy that she had been concealing. Her orange tinted glasses, precious and necessary to avoid the glare she otherwise suffered from, might get damaged, stolen or lost. Most terrifyingly, no one in their right mind would ever want to go anywhere near a swimming pool ever again, let alone be thrown into the one where they'd witnessed a drowned child. Tommy had not been as supportive as she'd hoped and Connie was fully occupied with Lenny so she felt like she'd been left to suffer entirely on her own.

If Tommy had made any plans to treat or celebrate Judy's birthday with her, he hadn't said anything so far. She broached the subject while he was getting changed but he didn't respond favourably. It seemed like he'd either forgotten or simply didn't want to celebrate it with her. He gruffly said 'I'm not in the mood to talk about this now. I'm off to the pub with me mates. They don't nag at me like you do'.

In Tommy's mind, Judy's upcoming birthday was a huge irritant rather than an opportunity. She was a great lay and inviting her back into his bed satisfied his physical need briefly but he never really had any romantic feelings for her. He regretted his generosity because, outside of sex, he found her eagerness to please him really annoying. He fantasised over the Irish twins. They could snare any red-blooded man with their personality and cheek. Then again, they could fight their corner and would not be so easy to manipulate. He welcomed the challenge.

Tommy and his mates had visited quite a few pubs by the time they got to the Three Elms. It was packed and the barman had just rung the bell and shouted 'Last Orders' by the time they'd pushed their way to the bar. They ordered and downed a Lemon Top in one go as if it was medicine, then persuaded the barman to get them a Neat scrumpy as he rang the bell to say the bar was now closed. As the crowd dispersed, Tommy was excited to see the Irish twins enjoying the craic with some friends. He went up to them but couldn't remember which twin was which. It didn't really matter to him as either would be pleasurable as far as he was concerned. Fuelled by the alcohol that he had consumed, he put an arm around one of them and said 'You're looking sexier than ever tonight!' Cara squirmed then, as he tried to kiss her, he spilt a little scrumpy on her blouse. She jumped back and said 'Ehh – Watch Out, ya silly bastard!' Her twin sister, Etain, intervened and said to Tommy 'Is it a feck yer afta?' Tommy thought he'd struck gold and, drunkenly nodding like a dog waiting to be fed, said 'You Bet!' Having laid the trap, Etain followed up with the line 'Well feck off!

Tommy's mates burst into laughter at their leader being ridiculed until he launched himself at Terry - his most loyal follower of all people. The alcohol lessened the impact of his punch and, after a brief scuffle, the barman threw Tommy, Terry and the rest of his gang out.

When Tommy returned to *his* chalet, Judy was sat up in *his* bed with her glasses on and a face like thunder. Two empty bottles of *Babycham* were on the bedside unit beside her. He asked her what the celebration was but it came out like 'Washercelebrashun' from the alcohol he'd consumed. Judy said she had been looking forward to opening them with him on her birthday but he didn't seem interested and she had needed their comfort tonight. She asked him how he got the bruise on his face. Whether it was the drink loosening his tongue or another mark of his cruelty, but he confessed the whole incident with the Irish twins including them telling him to *feck off*. He finally laughed to himself at their trick on him, but Judy burst into tears at his candidness and lack of respect for her. While reaching for a handkerchief, she accidentally knocked over the bottles and fell out of bed while trying to recover them. Rather than help or comfort her, Tommy misread her demeanour and said 'Bloody hell, Judy. You're more 'pished' than I am. I'm going down to *the Gaff* for a game of cards with the rest of the lads … unless I get lucky elsewhere!'

As he put his coat back on, Judy crawled across the floor on her knees and wrapped her arms around his legs, pleading with him to stay. He dragged her along the floor with such force that he knocked her glasses off. In trying to avoid treading on them, he inadvertently propelled one of the bottles against the front door causing it to smash. Tommy shouted 'Bollocks to this - you can clear your own mess up and pack your bags for all I care.' He carefully kicked the largest fragments of the broken bottle out of the way of the door, only so that he could escape. He didn't even bother to close the door as he fled down the path.

Left alone again, Judy recovered her beloved glasses but they were bent out of shape. She didn't have the strength to bend them back so left them on the bedside unit and crawled back to pick up the broken fragments of the bottle and shut the door. She felt that her life was a pathetic mess and desperately wanted an escape from her misery as she sobbed uncontrollably. The tears blinded her and a shard of glass cut her thumb. The pain was no worse than the pain she felt about Tommy. He obviously didn't care if she lived or died so why should she? She visualised the boy who had drowned telling her that any life in heaven would be better than the hell she was suffering on earth. The bloody shard was in her hand and she started switching it from hand to hand and wafting it over her wrists. Swaying from side to side, she repeated the actions and couldn't resist moving the sharp edge closer and closer until she went for broke and dug the shard into one wrist then the other. The jets of warm blood awoke her from her discombobulation and panic took over her. What had she done? Did she really want to kill herself? Could she find a way to survive this? Where could she go for help?

Lenny was excited but exasperated in bed with Connie. It was past midnight and he had been trying to find the holy grail that the Irish twins had told him about called an erogenous zone. So far, all he'd managed to do was confuse Connie as he touched, tickled and licked different parts of her body in a more and more frantic search for her *special area*. It stubbornly remained a secret to them both and he could picture Cara and Etain laughing at him for believing the tale they must have made up. After half an hour of trying, his libido urged him to give up on foreplay and once again try the direct approach. Connie seemed to be ready for him and he thought he was just about to penetrate when they both heard weak but insistent tapping on the glass of the front door and a faint but haunting cry that sounded like 'Help'.

They both jumped up out of bed at the same time. Lenny started to open the front door but quickly hid behind it to avoid flashing his erection at the late-night caller. Connie screamed as she looked out of the door and saw Judy slumped on the doorstep with blood seeping from her wrists.

Lenny, now flaccid from the shock, knew from his experience with Mr Gordon that getting the nurse's help was the most urgent priority for a life-threatening incident like this so he swiftly put his shorts on and ran to Hazel's chalet. She reacted just as quickly by phoning the security number to report an emergency. While Roy was arranging an ambulance, Hazel grabbed some towels and ran after Lenny in a desperate sprint to Connie's chalet.

It must have felt like an age to Connie but it had only taken Lenny a few minutes to get the nurse and return. They saw a semi-conscious Judy half sat up on the doorstep, with Connie holding her and trying to keep her talking to stop her from drifting away completely and terminally. A pile of blood-soaked toilet paper was all around them. Connie had tried to stem the flow of blood with the paper but it hadn't worked. Hazel got Lenny to hold Judy's arms steady while she tied the towels in the tightest of knots around each of her wrists. As Judy grimaced with the pain, she kept saying 'I'm sorry, I'm sorry, please don't let me die.' It was as if, in taking herself to the brink of death, she realized her life was actually worth fighting for.

When the ambulance medics arrived, they confirmed the temporary tourniquet had stemmed the flow and briefly praised Hazel's actions while placing Judy on a stretcher. They couldn't judge if their patient would survive, especially in her frail condition.

Just then, Connie's brother - Nick - came out of the chalet he shared with Anne to see what the commotion was all about. He saw Judy being carried off to the ambulance for the dash to Brixham hospital, thankfully less than a mile away. Nick's mind was racing but he tried to keep a level head and insisted on driving Connie to the hospital there and then. She gratefully accepted and quickly explained to Lenny what she was doing while Nick did likewise to Anne.

Lenny washed the blood off the door, floor and sink the best he could while trying not to wake the neighbours. He had only just got back into bed when Nick and Connie returned. They confirmed Judy was stable, thankfully, but they would go back to the hospital after their breakfast shift to see her. It was around 3am by the time Lenny was comforting Connie in their bed. She was so exhausted that she immediately fell asleep in his arms. Less than four hours later, the alarm woke them. Connie forced herself to dress and get back to work to do the breakfast shift. Helped by the early morning light, Lenny finished cleaning the remaining flecks of blood that he'd missed in the dark.

Connie was putting on a brave face as she served breakfast in the dining room. Her diners were unaware of the trauma she'd been through but Lenny could see the pain and tiredness she was hiding. As she passed by his table carrying a fully laden tray, she smiled philosophically to let him know that she was just about managing to keep herself together.

In the kitchen, Nick noticed Tommy was looking even scruffier than usual and pointedly said 'What happened with you and Judy last night?' Tommy narrowed his eyes and said 'What's it to you and, by the way, where is she?' Nick ignored the question and said 'I thought you would've been up all night worrying about her'. Tommy gruffly replied 'Why should I? I played cards at *Vics Place* and fell asleep. When I woke up, it was too late to have a shave let alone return to my chalet. I haven't seen her this morning so assumed she was still in bed suffering from a self-inflicted hangover.' Nick explained that she had been rushed into hospital after cutting her wrists. In a matter-of-fact way Tommy said 'Whatever that silly cow got up to is nothing to do with me'. Nick was taken aback that even someone as cold-hearted as Tommy would have a total lack of concern for Judy. Nick dared to ask if they'd had an argument. 'Well, if you must know, Judy was drunk and being a right pain and I told her so. She's a bloody head case and I want nothing more to do with her. I tell you what, Nicky boy. I'll drop her belongings off at your chalet. I can just imagine the cosy set up with you, Anne and the nutter in the same bed!' Nick had never been violent in his whole life but he tore into Tommy with such ferocity that it took three kitchen lads to separate them.

On their way to the hospital, Nick told Connie about the fight. He was still seething about it but pleaded with her not to tell Judy as it would upset her. When they reached her ward, they were surprised but relieved to see that she was sitting up in bed. The only sign of anything untoward were the bandages around each of her wrists. Connie and Nick carefully put their arms around Judy as she said 'I'm really sorry for all the trouble I've caused everyone, especially you two'. Connie said 'Never mind, get yourself better.' Nick enquired 'What have the hospital said?' Judy replied 'The doctor told me I was very lucky that I hadn't cut deep enough to sever a radial artery I think he called it. Also, the tourniquet applied by Hazel had prevented me from losing too much blood so I hadn't required a transfusion.'

Her physical scars would heal in a few weeks but Nick asked about her mental state, bluntly asking 'Why the vuck did you do it?' Judy opened up to them both, confessing 'I'd felt depressed, upset and lethargic, probably because I hadn't eaten properly since finding that child dead in the swimming pool. I'd hoped Tommy would have been more understanding to my feelings but, instead of soothing me, he got even nastier. It all came to a head last night when he came back drunk and we had our worst argument. He told me to pack my bags and go to hell. He then bent my glasses and smashed a bottle – accidentally I think - before leaving me crying on the floor while he went down to *the Gaff* for a game of cards – at least that's what he said he was doing. My self-confidence was at rock bottom and I decided I had nothing to live for, hence the attempt at killing myself'. She laughed ironically as she added 'I couldn't even get that right!'

It was the first time Judy had opened up about her true feelings and Tommy's mistreatment. Connie and Nick put their arms around her again to comfort her. Connie assured her 'You've had an elluva bad time but you'll soon find a nice boy that treats you the way you should be treated.' Nick blurted out 'Tommy is a selfish pig and a vucking idiot if he doesn't appreciate what a wonderful human being you are'. Still in tears, Judy said that she realised how stupid she'd been to give up on herself but was thankful she'd managed to survive and lucky to have the two of them as loyal and supportive friends. Connie had never heard her brother say that swear word in front of her but now he'd used it twice. She wondered if Nick's feelings for Judy were stronger than he realised.

A doctor entered the room which snapped everyone out of their own thoughts. He asked Judy how she felt and she said 'I'm fine, thank you'. A nurse arrived to carefully take the bandages off each wrist then the doctor inspected each wound. He confirmed that they should fully heal in a week or two, so long as Judy kept them dry and didn't carry anything heavy. Better still, she should be okay to leave the hospital the following day. The doctor wrote and handed Nick a letter to pass on to the *Seaview*'s nurse to thank her for applying the tourniquet and asking her to look at Judy's wounds every few days to ensure they were healing okay. The nurse could then decide when Judy was fit enough to go back to work.

On the journey back to the *Seaview* Nick and Connie were talking about Judy. Connie left out the swear word when she said 'I agree with your comment that Tommy is a selfish pig and an idiot if he doesn't appreciate what a wonderful human being Judy is but I was surprised to hear you talk so emotionally. You're usually calm and polite, even with Anne. You've always spoken well of Judy and I'm wondering if your feelings for her are deeper than even you realise'. Nick changed the subject 'Thank god I got this car so we could quickly get to the hospital and back again'.

Once Nick had updated Anne on Judy's condition, she wanted to know why a rubbish bag containing what looked like Judy's belongings had been dumped outside their chalet door. Nick said he'd had an argument with Tommy and he'd threatened to do something like this. Anne mirrored Connie's comment: 'I know you feel sorry at how Tommy has treated Judy and you're being kind as usual by helping your sister look out for her friend but are you being totally honest with me about your own feelings for Judy?' Nick blushed and confessed that he wasn't sure himself how he felt but promised to sleep on it. That night, Nick couldn't sleep on it because he was too busy thinking about it. How could Judy return to the *Seaview* after what she'd been through? She was admittedly a little eccentric but a lovely, lovely, girl. He hadn't realised the depth of his feelings for her until he'd nearly lost her. His mind had been confused for so long but now it was crystal clear - his relationship with Anne was just a cover for his deep feelings for Judy. The next day was Nick's Day off so Anne left him in bed. As soon as she'd gone, he dressed and wrote a note for Anne to read, plus letters to be handed over. He then gathered everything he needed to take with him to the hospital.

Nick walked in to the private ward and said 'Happy Birthday Judy!' He couldn't help notice that her kiss of gratitude lingered on his lips longer than he'd previously experienced. As they embraced, he was reluctant to let her go. She said 'With everything that's happened, I completely forgot that it's my birthday. Thank you for remembering and thank you for bringing a bag with my belongings. Was there any trouble getting them back from Tommy?' Nick hid the fact that the bag had been dumped at his door and simply said 'I persuaded him in my own way'. He then presented her with her beloved orange tinted glasses. 'I gave these a good clean and bent them back into shape as best I could. Let's try them on to see how they fit.' He placed them over her ears then carefully made final adjustments until she confirmed they were just as they had been when the optician first gave them to her. She kissed Nick once again and said 'Thank you so much - you're an angel'.

The nurse came in and said 'Ahh, I see that your boyfriend has brought your clothes. You've got the all clear so are you okay for him to help get you changed so you can leave the hospital straight away?' Nick was about to tell the nurse that he wasn't actually Judy's boyfriend but Judy cut across him with 'Thank you nurse, we'll be fine, thank you'.

The nurse left the room, not noticing Judy sniggering at her mistaken assumption. Nick said 'Are you sure you're okay for me to help you dress?' She said 'I'm fine with it if you are!' 'Of course I'm fine with it. You know I'd do anything for you.' 'I probably didn't appreciate how good you've been to me until now.' 'Do you know, when you laughed just then it was the first time that I've seen you happy in quite a while. It takes me back to the girl I knew at school. You were zany but fun-loving and shone like the brightest star. I wanted to be with you forever' 'Why didn't you do something about it?' 'I was a bit shy and, by the time I plucked up the courage to ask you out, that thug had got there first.' 'If you felt that way, why did you help Tommy apply to come to the camp'? 'If you remember, I helped you apply to come to the camp first because I wanted you near me but you insisted on my helping Tommy apply as well. I reluctantly agreed as it was the only way I could at least see you in case you needed me. They say that you're never more than a few feet from a rat but I didn't anticipate that you would move in with one!'

Nick carefully helped her out of her hospital gown. He tried not to show his shock at her bruises but she saw through him and said 'Don't worry. Bruises will heal and I will too now that I've done with Tommy'. Nick draped the dress over Judy and said 'I'm glad to hear you've finally finished with him. You were always making excuses for him. He should have been worried sick about you, especially as his bullying pushed you to harm yourself. If we had lost you - If I had lost you - I don't know what I would have done, probably murdered him! Damn it Judy, don't you know I love you!' Judy flung her arms around him, ignoring the pain from her wrists, and confessed 'I love you too'. They kissed and held each other as if they had fallen into a deep but wonderful well of wanting and comfort. Nick whispered in her ear 'I finally decided that I had to tell you how I felt when I nearly had a head on crash with a juggernaut on the way back from the Van Dike club in Plymouth. I just wish I'd told you before you did what you did'. 'What stopped you?' 'I held back because you seemed to have forgiven Tommy and I didn't want to complicate things just before your birthday or spoil whatever he had planned to celebrate it'. 'He hadn't planned anything but you telling me that you love me is the nicest present I could ever have!' Now she was fully dressed, Judy said 'I don't think I can return to the *Seaview* so what do we do from here?'

[Playlist Track: *"Albatross" – Judy Collins*]

When Anne read the note that Nick had left for her, her fears were realised. He said he was eternally grateful for the good times they had spent together but he had to follow his heart and leave her and the *Seaview* to be with Judy. The note also asked her to please hand over the two letters he'd left underneath the note. She delivered one letter to Nick's boss. It was Nick's formal notice of his resignation with immediate effect. The letter went on to thank him and his colleagues for the great working relationship they'd built up and apologised for any disruption caused. The other letter was for Connie. It explained his feelings, his decision and ended with a promise to call her whenever he could.

That evening, just as Connie was clearing up after her dinner guests had gone, Lenny ran in to tell her that her brother was on the public phone wanting to speak to her. When she got to the phone, Nick said 'Hi, sis – did Anne hand you a letter from me?' 'Yes, you're an elluva dark horse, baint 'ee!' 'Maybe so, but I just couldn't bring Judy back to the *Seaview*. There were too many reminders of personal issues and tragedies for her. After my fight with Tommy, I also had good reason not to return so Judy and I agreed to go back to Ivybridge to start a new life together'. Connie said 'That's all very well bruv, but how will you two earn a living?' 'Well, that's where fate gave me a helping hand. Do you remember when we went to the Van Dike club for the Amon Duul gig?' 'Yes.' 'And do you remember I got chatting to our old schoolfriend Vernon at the bar?' 'Mmm.' 'Well, Vernon mentioned that he was opening a restaurant near Ivybridge in a couple of weeks and needed a chef. I told him what I was doing at the *Seaview* and he said he would offer me a great package if I would be his chef'. Judy jumped in on the conversation and said 'Hi, Connie, darling. Your wonderful brother has been a knight in shining armour. He called Vernon from the hospital before we left and told him he'd be his chef so long as Vernon also took me on as head waitress and I get a share of the profits. No more relying on the paltry wages and rare tips I got there.' Nick felt Judy was showing off a bit too much so said 'Sorry, sis. Got to go. We're racking up mum and dad's phone bill and they've been supportive enough as it is. They've even let Judy use your bedroom until her wrists heal so her parents don't find out. Speak soon. Love you.' Connie just about heard Judy also shout 'Love you' as the call ended. It gave Connie no time to comment about Judy's use of her private bedroom back home but she would in any case have allowed it if asked.

The Brixham Trawler Race event had been a tremendous success for the organisers, raising thousands of pounds for local charities. This increased the pressure on the organisers of the next big event in the area - the annual Cow Town Carnival and Fete, due to take place on Wednesday 12th July.

Brixham is made up of two distinct areas - Lower Brixham, known colloquially as 'Fish Town', and Higher Brixham, known as 'Cow Town'. Fish Town is the working fishing port generally referred to as 'the town of Brixham' whereas Cow Town was the original rural Saxon settlement which became an important farming area before a less rural community developed around its medieval parish church of St. Mary's.

The carnival organisers had got together many times over the last few weeks to review the arrangements and considerations, most of which were repeated from previous years. A procession, led by the mayor's float, would start from Higher Brixham and travel down to the harbour in Lower Brixham then back up to Higher Brixham ending in St Mary's Park. Volunteers would be recruited to walk alongside the floats, shake their tins and collect the all-important donations from onlookers. As well as advertising local businesses, the floats generally reflected popular films, TV programs and fashions. Local beauty queens, marching/brass/pipe bands and Police, Fire and Ambulance services would also be in the procession and Shetland ponies for the kids to enjoy. A variety of activities would take place in the park including a fete, traditional fairground attractions like coconut shy and dart throwing at playing cards, dog obedience competitions, tug-of-war and shows featuring folk, shanties and more contemporary music.

Most of the decorations that had adorned the boats for the Trawler Race had already been stored away but the colourful bunting and flags remained on dry land locations, still hung over all the main roads and draped along the front of pubs, cafes, shops and other businesses. Cow Town was a mile or so from the harbour area, so new decorations would go up all along the route and around the park.

The organisers were delighted to announce that:
- The actor/comedian Bernard Bresslaw - currently starring in a comedy play at Torquay's Pavilion Theatre - would open proceedings
- The all-round entertainer Ken Dodd and his Diddymen would be the star guests for the procession
- Regular supporter, *Funtime* Holidays, would once again donate a substantial amount towards the event and had decided to enter two floats this year: one from the Warm Park holiday centre - who were awarded best float last year - and one from the *Seaview* holiday centre.

By way of thanks, *Funtime* Holidays would be given guest of honour front row seats in a VIP stand to be erected at the end of the procession route in St Mary's Park.

That same day, Jason Peters represented *Seaview* at a monthly meeting of all the Entertainment managers of *Funtime* holiday centres within the Torbay area. After all the regular topics were covered, the next item on the agenda was a review of the recent executive management tour of *Funtime holiday centres* in the Torbay area. Joe Barlow - the Entertainments manager at Warm Park Holiday Centre - the largest *Funtime* resort in the area - said that he was honoured to read out a letter of thanks from Biddy Rand - *Funtime*'s Group Entertainment Director. In the letter, she praised the hospitality and professionalism of management and staff at all the holiday centres she visited. Joe beamed and tried not to boast, but failed, as he quite loudly announced that Mrs Rand gave special praise to Warm Park. He emphasised every word in the next sentence of her letter: '*Warm Park could not have done more to make my stay more memorable. This included accommodating me in a luxury chalet with a full-time valet and arranging for me to see the Brixham Trawler Race from a VIP lounge at the Harbour Masters office. My tour was so well organised that group management have decided they will send another executive to stay at Warm Park mid-July. This is in order to revisit the local holiday centres and represent the Funtime organisation at the upcoming Brixham Carnival and Fete'*. All the Entertainment managers were giving themselves a pat on the back until Joe revealed the last line of Mrs Rand's letter: '*The executive chosen for this tour is Mrs Burren and I trust you will extend the same level of professionalism to her as you all have shown during my visit to this area.*'

Mrs Burren was *Funtime*'s Group Business Director - Biddy's boss and the managing director's sister-in-law. She had a fearful reputation for finding fault and sacking people on the spot if they crossed her. Even if everyone kept their jobs, it would be a much tougher proposition to attend to her every need and get a positive report from her. Her intended presence added importance and pressure to everyone's preparation for the Brixham Carnival.

As soon as Jason got back to the *Seaview*, he gave his boss - Eric Arden - a *'warts and all'* update of his meeting with the other Entertainment Managers. He started with the very complimentary report from Biddy congratulating the management and staff at all the *Funtime holiday centres* within the Torbay area for their hospitality and professionalism. A wide grin appeared on Eric's face. Jason went on to say that Biddy picked out Warm Park - the *Seaview*'s neighbouring rival - for special praise and was so impressed with her stay there that she recommended that another executive stay there to witness the *Funtime* organisation's participation in the Cow Town Carnival. Eric's smile turned to an envious frown until Jason revealed that the visiting executive would be Mrs Burren. Much like those attendees who heard Joe Barlow read through Biddy's letter, Eric's frown turned into a look of fear and he was no longer jealous of Warm Park. Despite the kudos of having a *Funtime* executive staying at their holiday centre, Mrs Burren would be sure to find something she didn't like.

Jason got back to the subject of floats and confessed that all the other Entertainment managers looked at him disdainfully when the Warm Park manager bragged that they were going all out on their float to win the top award for a second successive year, especially now that the *Seaview* had decided to 'have a go' with their own float. Eric puffed in annoyance at Warm Park's arrogance and he was determined that they wouldn't just 'have a go.' Warm Park had laid down the gauntlet and everyone at the *Seaview* should go all out to create a float display that would not just give Warm Park some healthy competition but beat their float at the first attempt. There would never be a better chance as Warm Park would be distracted while looking after Mrs Burren. If the *Seaview* float could beat Warm Park's float, they would get further praise at the executive level without having the negative impact of Mrs Burren's presence.

The initial problem with designing, funding and producing a winning float was that Eric and Jason hadn't yet come up with a theme. Jason said he would get his *Purplecoat* team together to kick around some ideas and report back later that day with a winning theme and plan on how they could deliver it.

Jason's brainstorming session with his *Purplecoat* team wasn't yielding any decent ideas from his Seniors for a theme for the float. In desperation, he turned to the rookies. He asked Lenny and Callum which films had been the most popular when offered to guests during wet weather. Instantly and telepathically, they both thought of their secret word 'Oomballah!' but said, in unison: 'Carry On Up The Jungle.' Jason's face lit up for a number of reasons. Firstly, one of the stars of that film - Bernard Bresslaw - just happened to be the celebrity chosen to officially open the Cow Town Carnival. Secondly, he remembered there were lots of tins of non-permanent black dye left over from minstrel shows his team had presented in previous seasons. He'd often wondered whether to throw the whole lot away just to clear the space. Instead, he could make use of it to paint the skin of float volunteers and make them look like jungle tribespeople to match the theme. The only costumes they would need to get made were loin cloths plus modesty tops for the ladies.

Mike didn't want the rookies to steal the show and saw an opportunity to raise his profile by offering to be the float manager. He also suggested Jeannette help him throughout the day. Jason insisted that the two of them play active roles on the float as well as manage everyone else. He initially thought they could be the male and female leaders of the opposing cannibal tribes but glanced at Mike's protruding belly and had second thoughts. Jeannette would look the part dressed only in a loin cloth but Mike would be an embarrassment - he had enjoyed way too many late-night steak suppers at the Blue Bay club. Instead, Jason said Mike could play the part of one of the white trekkers glorified as a potential love god by the all-female *Lubby-Dubby* tribe and Jeannette could play the tribe's leader. Mike liked the sound of acting the part of a love god so fully agreed to the plan. Everyone else realised Jason had only suggested it so that Mike's paunch would be well hidden under a safari suit.

Jason went through the theme and plan with his boss - Eric Arden. He estimated that there was enough dye to paint more than one hundred volunteers. Eric wondered if the float would take that many and where on earth would they get that many volunteers from. Jason's imagination was firing on all cylinders. He pointed out that around six hundred guests were due to arrive at the *Seaview* on the week of the carnival so he would simply get his *Purplecoat* team to recruit up to one hundred of the fittest guests to dance on or alongside the float. It would reduce the load on the float and increase the number of participants to a level only seen in an epic film. It would surely beat whatever Warm Park could deliver. Eric realised that it would be quite a coup to beat their biggest rival and be a feather in his own cap business-wise so agreed to fund the venture. Eric ordered authentic fancy dress outfits and props from a local supplier and asked his site maintenance men to design and construct a professional looking decorated float.

Lenny was, temporarily at least, in Jason's good books for helping suggest the theme for the carnival float. He took advantage of this fortunate circumstance by asking for and getting permission to take the following Saturday as well as his usual Sunday off so that he could go to the 21st birthday of one of his friends back home. He had just about saved up enough money to be able to afford a cheap weekend return ticket on the train and maybe enough for a round of drinks and his share of a joint.

Lenny felt guilty leaving Connie so soon after Nick and Judy had departed but he said it was Bernie's 21st and emphasised that he was fortunate to be given the two days off. Connie was very good about it, saying she appreciated that a friend's 21st birthday is important and the date obviously couldn't be changed. Lenny had already softened her up by introducing her as his *bird* when he phoned his parents to let them know he was coming home for the party. He only needed his bedroom at home on Saturday night because he had to start the return journey to the *Seaview* on Sunday afternoon. Connie said that she'd miss him of course but knew he'd be pleased to see his friends for the first time since coming to Brixham. Lenny aimed to return on the last train from London to Paignton then hitchhike the rest of the way. It would be way too late to get a bus or beg a lift from Big Al so Connie agreed that it would be best for him to sleep in the purple flat that first night back. An unfortunate complication with this plan was that a new swimming instructor - Richard Head - was due to move into the purple flat while Lenny was away. When Jason negotiated for Yvonne to be transferred in to replace Jane, he promised her own chalet on the resort as a sweetener for helping him out at such short notice. That chalet had previously been earmarked for the swimming instructor so he would now have to move in to the purple flat after some shuffling around. The bed that Jane had used in the girls' triple room was now available, so Jason ordered Lenny and Callum to move out of their twin-bedded room and cross the corridor to share the triple-bedded room with the swimming instructor while

Jeannette and Tricia move in the opposite direction into the twin-bedded room. Lenny and Callum had got used to just the two of them sharing a room so it was a shame that they would have to get used to having a stranger sleeping alongside them. Their apprehension was made worse by rumours they'd heard from Kenny – via Jill presumably - that the new guy was a bit weird and eccentric.

On the morning that Lenny was due to catch the train home, Big Al kindly offered to give him a lift to Paignton station in the *Seaview*'s minibus. Before they left, they helped Callum secretly lift the half full container of scrumpy out of its hiding place in the wardrobe in the twin-bedded room and drag it into a previously empty kitchen cupboard. They covered the contraband with blankets, clothes and games as a camouflage until they could safely move it to their new bedroom, assuming the swimming instructor would be amenable. Callum looked at his watch and said 'LE, you'd better get off to catch your train. Don't worry about your belongings. I'll carry them into the triple room when the girls have vacated it'. Lenny thanked Callum adding 'I hope the switch goes smoothly and you get along okay with the swimming instructor while I'm away'.

The roads were busy on the journey to Paignton but Big Al managed to get Lenny to the station just in time to catch the express train to London. Lenny felt weird heading home for the first time but couldn't wait to catch up with his family and friends. He also looked forward to hearing heavy music again, especially after going to that Amon Duul concert in Plymouth with Connie. He remembered his promise to bring back his favourite albums from his collection to play to his new friends, especially Connie. He hoped he wouldn't regret saying he'd carry back *his record player*. For a start, it wasn't *his record player* – it was his sister's, so she might not allow him to borrow it for the summer. Another issue was that, even with a carrying handle, it would still be a weight for the long journey back, only balanced by carrying his clothes bag stuffed with records in his other hand. Nonetheless, apart from DJ Sub's decks in the disco, there was nowhere else to play records at the *Seaview*.

Bringing back a record player was the only way Lenny could play *his music* in *his room*. *His room*? Moving to the triple bedded room added an unwelcome complication but Lenny didn't foresee any problems. The swimming instructor was an unknown quantity but he was also in his 20's so Lenny anticipated that he would be of like mind and enjoy the heavy music he was going to bring back. Callum was a DJ so he should be delighted to have a record player in their room, especially if Lenny chose something lighter for him to listen to. He just needed to think of where the player could be placed in that room. He remembered seeing a large chest of drawers between two of the three beds when the girls left their door open and he glanced in. He reckoned it would surely have enough space on top for the record player to sit on.

Soon after Lenny got home, he barely had time to wash and change, let alone chat to his parents, before his best friend Derek knocked on the door. They embraced like brothers and set off to Keith's car which was waiting on the corner. Derek jumped in the front passenger seat and Lenny climbed in the back. Keith started the engine and took a big drag of the joint he'd just rolled. Keith adhered to the unwritten but totally reasonable rule shared by most joint smokers that the maker of the joint is allowed the first and second drag before passing it on for the rest of the group to have their own drag.

Derek said 'Welcome back, mate' to Lenny as he passed the joint to him. Lenny sucked through the already damp tip then settled back in his seat to feel the effects of the THC being absorbed into his bloodstream. He smiled as he looked at his two hippie friends in front of him. Derek was a true friend and Keith was a pal with a unique skill - he could roll and smoke a joint even while he was driving. They all smoked enough of Keith's latest creation to get seriously mellow. Derek said 'Hey man, we must come down and see you at the camp sometime'. Lenny was too stoned to bother explaining that it was called a *holiday centre* rather than a *camp* so simply said 'Yeah, that would be triffic, man!' When they arrived at Bernie's house, his 21st birthday party was already in full swing. The three of them said *Happy 21st Bernie* as he welcomed each of them with a slice of his "special" birthday cake. The "special" part of it was the high content of cannabis. They already had *the munchies* from the joint they'd smoked in the car so gobbled up their slice as if they'd just ended a hunger strike then washed it down with beer from a Watneys Party Seven tin barrel they found in the kitchen. After slugging a glassful down in one go, they topped up their glasses then rejoined Bernie in a corner of the lounge with their other hippie friends. They updated Lenny on who was going with you and the latest football news. Lenny took the opportunity to brag that he'd been running football training sessions and matches for holidaymakers helped by star players from Torquay United. The football experts were not impressed and one of them pointed out that Torquay had just been relegated to the Fourth Division. The Tottenham supporters then said Spurs had thrashed Torquay in the League Cup the previous October. The conversation moved on to drugs and they reminisced about the parties they'd been to and acid trip excursions they'd taken. Derek chuckled as he recalled Lenny's unlawful detour into the jungle at London Zoo:

> The gang had taken a trip to London Zoo, literally, and the acid effects took hold of them as they walked into the tropical bird aviary. With the drug cutting out any filter for normally acceptable behaviour, Lenny followed his deepest impulse and jumped off the official footpath to venture into the forbidden area of the realistic but man-made jungle backdrop to get up closer to the humming birds flying around there. They were his favourite birds for many reasons: their brilliant colours, faster than sound wing speed and their ability to fly backwards and upside down. He somehow managed to find his way through the jungle without being arrested and, while looking for his mates, came upon the cage that housed Guy the gorilla. Guy was rightly the top attraction at the zoo - a magnificent beast and highly intelligent. When Lenny came face to face with him, he was convinced that Guy spoke or telepathically communicated with him and vice versa as they stared into each other's eyes from the opposite sides of the reinforced glass. When his mates caught up with him, all communication ended, replaced by a few grunts and snorts.

Just as Lenny was enjoying that memory and feeling good about himself, his nemesis turned up. Damien was always direct and insulting to Lenny, especially as Lenny always seemed to have been the one who missed out on getting laid while his mates got lucky or at least said they did. 'Ho there, Lenny. You still a virgin?' Lenny tried to fob off the insult with 'What are you on about, Damien.' 'Well, Derek told me you went to the camp to lose your virginity. Did it work out or are you still pure?' Stung that his best mate would divulge such a secret, Lenny over egged the bravado in responding with 'Don't worry, I've been getting loads – sleeping with one waitress after another and getting plenty more from the guests!' 'The guests?' 'Yes, the holiday makers.' He hoped his exaggeration would stop any further insults but Damien then said 'Well, if you have been getting your end away, I bet they were all rough ole dogs'. 'Actually, they were all gorgeous, especially the waitress I'm currently bedding'. Damien was not convinced and said 'So you say, Lenny, so you say.' Lenny had had enough and couldn't resist putting his hand in his pocket and pulling out his beloved photo of Connie. He proudly showed it to his tormentor to shut him up. Lenny winced as Damien grabbed the photo from his hand and studied it intently under a lamplight. Briefly flummoxed on how to continue his verbal attack, Damien settled on 'Well, if you really are bedding her, she's way too good for you!' He slapped the photo back in Lenny's palm with 'If you're with her, why are you going off with the holidaymakers as well?' Lenny's bravado was in full flow 'Well, I'm contractually obliged to entertain the customers 24 hours a day!' Finally defeated, Damien walked away to annoy someone else. Lenny carefully wiped the photo with the cuff of his shirt - as if Damien handling it had defiled it in some way - then slipped it back into his pocket.

The music being played at the party was new and unfamiliar to Lenny and he thought the atmosphere could do with a lift. The chemical reaction from the cannabis in Keith's joint and Bernie's cake might have given him a false level of confidence when he reasoned that he'd raised spirits back at the *Seaview* so why not do the same here amongst his old friends? He attempted to get a singalong started but his plan backfired. All the party-goers looked at him askance as if he was playing the part of an entertainer from an older generation. He recalled the quote that Callum often said about himself: 'I'm just an ordinary guy in the street.' Lenny felt the same, as if any perceived super powers vanished upon leaving the holiday centre.

Later on, when Lenny went to the toilet, he noticed huddles of people in different bedrooms, some indulging in drug taking with needles. Lenny had only ever taken drugs to relax with like-minded people or discover things about himself and the world around him. It was all peace and love, listening to psychedelic music, joint passing and having philosophical group discussions about the world we live in. The only time he stepped over the mark was a holiday in Bournemouth where he stupidly followed his mates in picking up a straw and sniffing grains heaped on playing cards that turned out to be cocaine and heroin. Now, it seemed that his hippie friends were taking all sorts of drugs to lose themselves and escape from the world. Drug taking had 'progressed' from euphoric smoking of marijuana and cannabis joints or swallowing tablets of speed and LSD psychedelics to the more sinister injecting of hard drugs like cocaine and heroin. He saw his mates' drug scene in a new light and didn't like the way it was going. It was not a trend he personally wanted to follow and he certainly wouldn't want Connie to be anywhere near dangerous drugtaking like this.

Back in Brixham, Connie was thinking about Lenny back at his home having a good time with his mates. Would he be talking about her in a loving way or would he be telling them she hadn't been able to fulfil him sexually. She really needed to do something about it but what?

Callum welcomed the swimming instructor to the bedroom they would be sharing at the purple flat, or at least he was trying to welcome him. On the plus side, Richard Head was 6 feet tall with a trim figure, blonde hair and a drawl he perfected from the beach boy lifestyle in Australia. On the minus side, he wore really thick glasses and Callum couldn't imagine him being able to see someone struggling in the pool let alone rescuing them, especially if his glasses got knocked off.

Rather than engage in conversation and get to know his room-mate, Richard looked disapprovingly around the room. Callum continued to try to make social conversation, so asked what he thought of the room, taking the opportunity to remind him that another *Purplecoat* called Lenny was due to join them the following evening. Unsurprisingly, Richard admitted 'I'm definitely not impressed with this room, man.'

Richard held out his arms as he moved forward and Callum initially thought he wanted to embrace him in some sort of weird welcome ceremony. Instead, Richard brushed past him and paced around the room, mentally guessing its dimensions and the closeness of the beds. Finally, Richard concluded 'This is definitely not on man. There should be at least 20 cubic feet between each of us or we'll be starved of the oxygen levels we need to stay healthy.'

Callum couldn't comment beyond revealing that he and Lenny had been happy and settled in the twin-bedded room opposite this room but they had been ordered to move to this room by Jason. The saying 'put up or shut up' flashed though Callum's mind as he emphasised that Richard had also been ordered to move to this room by Jason.

Richard realised he wasn't going to get a satisfactory resolution from the conversation so ended it and headed for the bathroom while grumbling to himself, leaving Callum totally underwhelmed by his demeanour and lack of social skills. When Richard returned, he said he was going to have an early night to ensure he got his minimum 8 hours sleep – another stipulation of his rigid health regime. Callum was a little shocked as Richard took all his clothes off in front of him – pyjamas were clearly not fashionable or necessary in Richard's world. He jumped into his bed, instantly complaining that his mattress was lumpy and uncomfortable. Once under the sheets, Richard carefully placed his ridiculously expensive divers watch on the dressing table then took off his ridiculously expensive designer glasses and placed them alongside the watch as closely as he could tell in his blurred vision.

Callum lay on top of his new bed and started reading a book until Richard asked if he would mind turning the light off so that he could get his 8 hours of sleep. Callum adhered to his lordship's wishes and, after getting his pyjamas on in the dark, lay in bed quietly so that he didn't further disturb his fussy room-mate. Despite Richard whining about his bed, the room and cubic feet, Callum soon heard him snoring which was marginally preferable to hearing him complain.

The negative vibes from Richard were in stark contrast to the fun and banter Callum had experienced with Lenny. Callum only now realised what a good room-mate and friend Lenny was. He wondered how he was getting on with his hippy friends and what he would make of Richard when he returned.

The next morning, Lenny awoke with a hangover from the previous night's drinks and drugs so was glad he had kept away from the heavier stuff that was being taken. Lenny surveyed his bedroom and thought it was nothing more than a box room and a fraction of the size of the twin-bedded room he shared with Callum at the purple flat. He corrected himself as he realised that he and Callum were now in a triple-bedroom with a new swimming instructor he had yet to meet. Lenny enjoyed sharing a room with Callum so hoped the new dynamic of the three of them would be as good or better.

After Lenny had breakfast with his parents on Sunday morning, his mum presented him with a carrying case to carry some of his vinyl records back to the *Seaview*. His sister's bedroom was much bigger than his so, while she wasn't there, he laid out all his records on her bedroom floor then sat on her bed contemplating which ones to take. He reckoned he would be able to squeeze a dozen albums into the record carrier. After careful consideration, he gathered together his favourites before ranking them into the top dozen to take to the *Seaview*. He had to include Can's *Monster Movie* album as he'd promised this to Connie on the journey back from the Van Dike club. The other records that made it into the vinyl carrier were albums from Jimi Hendrix, Frank Zappa, Pink Floyd, the Rolling Stones, the Beatles, Led Zeppelin, Doctor John, Genesis, Yes and Terry Riley. To complete the selection, he unselfishly included a softer album from Simon and Garfunkel called 'Bridge Over Troubled Water' that he was sure Callum would like.

The sun was shining Sunday afternoon as Lenny stood on the platform of his hometown station. He recalled how he shivered in the cold weather the last time his dad had dropped him off here. It was two months earlier at the start of his journey toward a new adventure in the West Country. He'd seen and learned "an elluva" lot since then and somehow fallen in love despite trying his best not to. He'd carried a battered suitcase last time. This time, he was carrying a bag containing the minimum of essential clothes and toiletries along with carefully selected records in a new carrier box and his sister's record player. She wasn't too keen on him borrowing it for the rest of the summer until he promised to replace it if it wasn't returned, fully working, at the end of the season. The London-bound train had arrived late the previous time and this time it was even later. Whatever the reason for the delay, Lenny was getting more and more concerned that he might not make it to Paddington station in enough time to catch that last train back to Paignton.

Lenny wondered if the sun was shining over the *Seaview*. He yearned to get back there as soon as possible. He wanted to return to the life he had there and desperate to see and lay alongside Connie again. His unplanned and unexpected devotion to her led him to accept, even treasure, the fact that she remained as pure as a pearl in an oyster. Moreover, he cherished the idea that this was a charming secret the two of them shared.

An hour later, Lenny only just managed to squeeze himself and his belongings into the packed carriages of the London Underground tube trains enroute to Paddington Station. There seemed to be a hundred or more male protestors filling them up waving signs saying "Gay Liberation Front". He had no idea what the slogan meant or their aims and didn't dare to ask. To slow him down even more, the escalator from Paddington's underground station to the mainline station was out-of-operation. His record player nearly slipped from his grasp as he strode up the steps and quickly glanced at the departures board. He ran as fast as he could to get to the right platform but all his efforts to make up the time lost along the way were in vain as he saw the tail light of the Paignton train departing down the platform and out into the darkness beyond.

Puffing heavily, he thought 'If only I had a time machine to be able to warp back and get an earlier train into London - I would have been snug as a bug and settled on that Paignton train.' Instead, he was standing on a cold and draughty London terminus with no idea how to get to his destination. He went to the ticket office that looked like it was closed but he knocked on the window in the hope that someone would help him. The hatch slowly went up and a man in railway uniform reluctantly placed his mug of tea down on the counter. Lenny apologised for disturbing him but explained his situation and asked for advice. Luckily, the clerk was kind enough to suggest that he get the last train heading for Plymouth but disembark at Newton Abbot. Great Western Railway would accept his Paignton ticket for this train without further charge. The clerk added that the train was scheduled to arrive at Newton Abbot at 10:30pm and he could then get a taxi from there. Lenny didn't like to admit he couldn't afford a taxi but figured he'd just have to hitchhike from the station to get as near as he could to his destination.

The train arrived at Newton Abbot just a few minutes late. There was no-one to collect, let alone question, Lenny's ticket so he walked straight out of the station. Lenny had never been to this area before so looked around to try to find his bearings. Outside the station, a man was puffing away on a cigarette while leaning against his cab on an otherwise empty taxi rank. The taxi driver flicked the stub in the road and stood up straight when he saw a potential customer approach. Rather than waste time, Lenny deliberately ignored him and walked on past his taxi and the still smouldering stub. The taxi driver lit another cigarette as he watched Lenny trying to get his bearings. Luckily, a road sign opposite the station pointed left to Torquay so Lenny walked down the road in that direction until he was out of sight of the taxi rank and reached a well-lit spot to start hitchhiking towards Brixham.

Lenny plonked his luggage down on the pavement and stood alongside the road waiting for oncoming traffic before stretching his left arm out and pointing his thumb forward as they drove up. In the darkness around him, he could make out what appeared to be a park on the opposite side of the road. A cool wind blew through and Lenny shivered as he contemplated spending the night on a cold bench in that park if he failed to get a lift.

While waiting for vehicles to approach, Lenny began humming Simon and Garfunkel's song "Homeward Bound". It was a tune that had always helped him get through the boredom, survive the cold weather and somehow bring him good luck every time he'd hitchhiked on late night journeys home, especially when returning from a gig or a girlfriend in London. Lenny recalled the time when his hitchhiking luck peaked earlier that year. The background to the story started 10 years earlier:

Lenny's dad first took him to Tottenham Hotspur's White Hart Lane stadium on April 1st 1961, a day before his 9th birthday. Spurs, nicknamed the Lilywhites because of the clean white shirts they proudly wore, were the top football team in the country at the time and on their way to a league and cup double. Lenny's dad sat his boy on top of a 5-feet high wall overlooking the pitch so that he could see the match. It was April Fool's Day and Spurs made fools of their opposition.

Spurs had a flying Welsh winger called Cliff Jones and he bagged a hat-trick as they thrashed Preston North End 5-0. As soon as his third goal hit the net, a dozen or more young fans ran on to the pitch to congratulate him. Lenny, not knowing any better, got into the spirit of the occasion and sprung from the wall to join them in patting Cliff Jones on the back. Lenny had a huge smile on his face as a policeman escorted him back to his section, but his dad gave him a dirty look and a right rollicking as the policeman lifted Lenny back onto the wall. The policeman laughed and the surrounding supporters told Lenny's dad to leave the kid alone as they wished they could have done the same.

A decade later, Lenny was thrilled when a swanky Jaguar car stopped while he was hitchhiking home and a lift was offered from none other than his first football hero - Cliff Jones! Football players didn't make lots of money in the early 1970's and Cliff was now scraping a living by managing a school football team in North London and teaching Physical Education. As well as being a great player for his beloved Spurs football team, Lenny was amazed how sociable Cliff Jones was.

Lenny told Cliff that he was a devoted Tottenham Hotspur football team supporter and had patted him on his back when he scored that famous hat trick in 1961. Cliff was flattered and happy to talk about the heroes of his time - Dave Mackay, John White, Bobby Smith and captain Danny Blanchflower - and the heroes that came through in the years that followed - Martin Chivers, Pat Jennings, Steve Perryman, Alan Gilzean and of course Jimmy Greaves. Even though Cliff was undoubtedly one of the best players that Spurs had at that time, they both agreed that Jimmy Greaves was the most lethal finisher of all time. Lenny admitted that he'd also patted Jimmy on his back after scoring many of his goals at White Hart Lane stadium. Cliff continued chatting until dropping Lenny off within walking distance of his home. Lenny always treasured that chance meeting with a football legend and thoroughly nice gent.

Lenny must have looked weird singing 'Homeward Bound' to himself while standing on the kerb late at night in Newton Abbot with a record player box, a record carrier box and a makeshift luggage bag at his feet. He pondered where 'home' was as he went through the lyrics:
'Home, where my thought's escaping
Home, where my music's playing
Home, where my love lies waiting
Silently for me'

He was taking his music to play at the *Seaview* holiday centre so was Brixham his new home and was Connie the love who 'lies waiting silently' for him?

Lenny's lucky song did the trick and a big car stopped beside him. A smart looking man wound down the window and asked 'where do you want to get to?' Lenny said 'I'm trying to get to Brixham'. The driver said "I'm only going to Torquay but at least that will get you most of the way'. Lenny replied 'that would be fab, fanks very much.' The driver detected but wasn't put off by Lenny's cockney twang as he carefully placed his belongings in the boot. They had a good chat on the way to Torquay and the subject soon got on to football. The driver was a Torquay supporter and was so impressed that Lenny did football training with one of his star players that he decided to take him the extra 9 miles to the purple flat.

It was almost midnight and starting to rain as the big car pulled up outside the purple flat. The driver opened the boot to get Lenny's belongings out and Lenny said 'Fank you so much for your kindness, especially going out of your way for me - please accept this.' Lenny tried to hand over the few coins in change from his pocket but the Samaritan simply waved his arms to confirm no payment was necessary. Lenny didn't want to argue in the rain so shook his hand and promised him that he and his family would be most welcome to visit the *Seaview* holiday centre where he would personally show them around and buy them all a drink (even though he probably would have to borrow money to pay for it!).

As Lenny turned the key to the front door of the purple flat, he could hear the rumbling sounds of a developing storm threatening to sweep in from the bay. He had struggled to carry his record player carrier full of records and bag of essentials all the way from home so was glad to have finally got them inside the flat before they could get too wet. He almost opened the door on the left to the double-room he had shared with Callum before remembering just in time that it was now occupied by the girls. He instead had to turn right into the triple-room he and Callum were sharing with the swimming instructor - Richard Head.

This was the first time Lenny had entered the triple-room in the dark so was struggling to get his bearings. He could just about see Callum fast asleep in one bed and the new man snoring loudly in another bed. To avoid his room-mates bumping into or tripping over his record carrier, he carefully slid it along the floor under the only empty bed - Richard's snores turned into grunts. Lenny then tried to place the record player on top of the chest of drawers but the gap was tight for space. As Lenny tried to manoeuvre it into position, he slid in his wet shoes and stubbed his foot. The shock caused the record player to slip out of his grasp and crash down onto the chest of drawers. It only fell a short distance but, as Lenny lunged for it, his hand knocked Richard's fancy diving watch onto the floor. Both his roommates woke up with a start and Callum instinctively put his bedside lamp on to see what was going on.

Callum was groggy but happy to see his old room-mate but Richard stared madly in the direction of Lenny from huge bleary owl-like eyes. He reached for his glasses and, as soon as he'd put them on, saw what he thought was a long-haired stranger scrambling on the floor in the middle of the night with his precious watch in his hand, much like Gollum's Precious in the Lord of The Rings. Callum had already sussed out Richard's personality and could see he was about to explode so quickly said 'LE, welcome back - this is our new room-mate Richard Head!' Before Richard could calm down, Lenny clasped his hand and forced a handshake out of him. He soon let go when he realised Richard clearly slept with no clothes on at all.

Lenny regained his composure and apologised for the accidental noise. He explained that he was late back because he'd missed a connection but managed to hitchhike from Newton Abbot. He hadn't put the light on because he didn't want to disturb them while they were asleep but his plan backfired when he tripped up in the dark. Richard appeared to grudgingly accept Lenny's apology and, without another word, turned over to resume his rigid 8 hours sleep schedule, man. Callum looked at Lenny, pointed a hand out toward Richard and shook his head from side to side as if to secretly say 'LE - we're stuck with a right one here!'

Lenny changed into his pyjamas and carefully nudged the record player fully onto the chest of drawers so that it wouldn't fall off then slid into the only empty bed by the window. It was the first time he'd slept in this bed but, even with the curtains closed, he was surprised to hear the rain lashing down more loudly than he had ever heard it before from the other bedroom. He thought no more of it as he fell asleep, totally exhausted from his journey.

[Playlist Track: "Gimme Shelter" – The Rolling Stones]

Outside the purple flat, the storm continued through the night of Lenny's return. Callum and Richard were snoring alongside him in the single beds they'd claimed in his absence. After his lengthy journey from home then the mishap with the record player on arrival, Lenny was too exhausted to hear the noises emanating from them or the tempest outside, even though his bed was right under the only window in the room. Memories of seeing his friends back home taking heavy drugs invaded Lenny's subconscious mind and his dreams became increasingly troubling:

Lenny saw himself as a spaced-out drug addict slouching on a rough mattress on the floor of a dirty threadbare room. Connie is lying beside him half-sleeping. Suddenly, he springs forward and plunges a hypodermic needle into her arm, injecting something sinister into her bloodstream. They both shiver as dirty dark grey damp smears run down the walls around them. Their faces contort with demonic vibrating smiles as the drugs overpower them. Lenny somehow managed to escape that nightmare but moved on to a new danger: *Lenny lay on an inflatable li-lo floating out to sea. A storm developed and he was thrown off the li-lo. He sensed cold water permeating all over his body. To avoid freezing to death, he attempted to swim toward a light that he thought was a beacon for safe shore but his limbs felt paralysed and he didn't seem to be getting anywhere.* The scenario changed again: *Lenny was flat on his back, underneath a wild waterfall that was flicking drops of cold water on his head to the sound of: 'tup', 'tup', 'tup', 'tup' followed by the spray of a sudden gush. Lenny suddenly had the feeling that this was not a strange dream but some sort of cold wet reality. His shivers increased until his body shook so violently that it forced him to wake up.*

Now back in the real world, Lenny realised that his whole body, indeed the whole of one side of his bed, was soaked through with cold water. The curtains above the bed were drenched and flapping heavily in response to the gusty squalls outside. The sodden curtains acted like a sponge. Whenever the wind happened to blow them together, they dripped cold rain water over Lenny then, every time they swung open, a gush sprayed him and his bed. Lenny jumped up and pulled open the curtains to see what was going on. The dawn light flooded the bedroom much like the rainwater and the remaining puddles on the window sill flushed onto him and his bed like a waterfall.

Lenny shouted 'Ye Gods' in shocked surprise, immediately waking his room-mates for the second time in six hours. Richard glared at Lenny and complained that his sleep had been disturbed yet again. Lenny looked back at him even more angry and said 'Who the fuck opened the window over my bed last night?' Without any emotion or compassion, Richard brazenly admitted 'I opened the window, man, because we all need at least 20 cubic feet of our own space to breathe in enough oxygen, man. There's only 12 cubic feet in this bedroom for all three of us, man, so it has to be ventilated, man!' Lenny felt like wringing Richard's neck but, instead, looked at Callum and they said in unison 'Oombalah'! Richard didn't understand their secret swearword and he soon settled back in his bed, snoring once again. He obviously believed that his sleep was more important than the welfare of his wet and shivering room-mate. Luckily, his other room-mate was more thoughtful. While Lenny was towelling himself dry in the bathroom, Callum found some blankets in the kitchen and lay them on the floor so that Lenny could try to get an extra hour's sleep. It must have worked because Richard had sneaked out of the flat by the time Callum woke Lenny up. The sun was shining bright so Callum helped Lenny haul his wet mattress out into the garden and hang the sodden bedclothes on the washing line to dry.

Callum and Lenny walked up the hill for breakfast, both seething about Richard's behaviour. Lenny tried to lighten the mood by mentioning that he couldn't wait to see Connie again. Unusually, Callum didn't respond – he seemed deep in his own thoughts so Lenny said 'You're quiet, CC. It's no use staying angry over Mr Oombalah.' Callum shook his head and confessed 'It's not that, LE. Hazel left the *Seaview* yesterday'. 'Blimey. What happened? Did you two have an argument?' 'No, not at all. Apparently, news of her quick thinking in helping save Judy's life got back to management. They decided that she deserved a promotion to head nurse so, when a vacancy came up at another *Funtime* holiday centre, she was offered an opportunity she could not refuse'. 'Is it close enough for the two of you to continue seeing each other?' 'No. It's in Somerset but it's a great career move for her so I wished her well'. 'There's no way that I would have let Connie go that easily'. 'I just didn't feel that I could stand in her way or stop her. We promised to write to one another and hopefully we'll always be friends but maybe not lovers like you and Connie'. 'That's a shame, CC. So, you're back to square one then'. 'Yes, but I'm still hopeful I'll find that special one someday soon.' Lenny placed a hand gently on Callum's shoulder 'I hope so, mate, you deserve it.' Callum tapped Lenny's arm in gratitude 'Thanks, LE.'

As soon as they entered the dining room, Lenny went over to Connie's station and Callum continued toward the tables allocated for *Purplecoats*. Connie had just taken the breakfast orders from her diners and was about to collect them from the kitchen. When she saw Lenny approaching, her smile just got more dazzling. They both desperately wanted to embrace but this was not the time and place to do it. Instead, he went to whisper something in her ear but gave her a sneaky kiss before communicating that he had lots to tell her when she finishes serving. She squeezed his arm gently then hurried off to the kitchen to load her tray with the breakfast items that would keep her guests happy enough to tip her at the end of the week.

Lenny caught up with Callum while he was speaking to Jason and Mike. Callum had already explained how demanding Richard had been and complained that his weird and unacceptable behaviour had led to Lenny and his bed getting an overnight soaking. He'd then left the two of them to dry everything out without offering any help or apology. Amazingly, without further argument or discussion, Jason confirmed that Richard would no longer be staying with them at the purple flat. He then gave them permission to make appropriate arrangements with the girls to reverse the switch and get their twin room back that very day!

As soon as Connie's diners had left the dining room, Lenny was by her side. She smiled and said 'Did you miss me, luvver?' 'Of course! I missed you - all the time we were apart'. 'How did you feel going home and being with your mates again?' 'It felt different. I'm different. They've changed and so have I. So much has happened to me here, especially meeting you'. Now they *had* to embrace and they didn't care who was watching. Lenny carefully kept quiet about his dismay at the drug-taking with needles that he'd witnessed but told her that his mates were pleased to see him and they hoped to visit him at the *Seaview* sometime soon. He also told her about having to hitchhike from Newton Abbott, luckily getting a lift from a Torquay supporter, waking up Callum and the swimming instructor after dropping the record player in the big bedroom, then getting soaked in the early hours. On the last point, he bragged 'Jason must think a lot of me and Callum because, when we told him what happened, he kicked the swimming instructor out of the purple flat and gave us our old room back without any argument'.

As Lenny walked through reception, he spoke to Jill about the night he'd had and how Jason and Mike had apparently kicked Richard out of the purple flat so that he and CC could get their room back. Jill laughed and gave Lenny the lowdown on what had really happened.

'It's a complicated merry go round but I'll try to explain. Firstly, Jeannette and Tricia had complained to Jason that the double room they'd been forced to move to was way too small for them. Stunk of scrumpy and didn't even have a dressing table for them to apply make-up. Jason understood how important a dressing table was (!) so agreed that they could return to their triple-bedded room.

As for Richard, his girlfriend was due to arrive soon and he had already asked Jason to move him to a chalet they could share near to the *Seaview* pool. Jason and Mike were only too willing to oblige him because, after the sad death of little Timmy, they wanted to do all they could to ensure the pool had adequate monitoring. Keeping the swimming instructor happy and near to it made sense so Jason asked Yvonne if she'd mind moving down the hill to stay with the other female Purplecoats when they move back into the triple-bedded room. That would enable Richard and his girlfriend to move in to her now vacant chalet. You played right into their hands when you complained about Richard – they were going to ask you to move back in any case!'

Lenny somehow felt less important but the arrangements seemed to work out best for everyone involved. That afternoon, Connie kindly helped Lenny and Callum move their stuff back from the triple-bedded room into their old twin room while all the *Purplecoat* girls moved their belongings in to the triple-bedded room. There were lots of *excuse me's* and *after you's* as they tried to avoid bumping into one another while moving their belongings back to the rooms they came from. Eventually everything seemed to be where it should be, then Callum remembered the scrumpy! Connie kept watch of the corridor while Lenny and Callum threw off the blankets, clothes and games that were hiding the half full container of scrumpy in the kitchen cupboard. When Connie put her thumbs up to say the coast was clear, they dragged the container past her to *plonk* it back in the wardrobe of their twin-bedded room.

Lenny didn't tell Connie or Callum about his nightmare - but he could still visualise plunging a hypodermic needle into Connie's arm. To take his mind off those unsettling thoughts, he filled up some cups of scrumpy to say Cheers for a job well done then went through the albums he'd brought from home. As expected, Connie looked forward to listening to the heavier albums but Callum was less enthusiastic. Lenny thought Callum was still sad over Hazel leaving so expected to give him a nice boost when he presented to Callum his Simon and Garfunkel album called *Bridge Over Troubled Water*. It was a lot softer and more melodic than the other albums so Lenny was pretty sure it would at least cheer his roommate up. Instead, Callum shook his head and tutted as he looked at the album as if it was the worst thing he'd ever seen. Lenny said 'What's the matter CC?' Callum confessed 'Sorry, LE, but when I was a DJ, I was forced to play that title song so many times that I ended up loathing it'. Lenny said 'Oombalah' and they all laughed it off!

Midway through Tuesday morning, Jill left her reception desk on an urgent mission to find Jason. She soon found him, sat at a table in the buffet lounge. He'd grabbed a moment to relax and sip a cup of tea while looking out the picture window over the roofs of the brightly coloured chalets, the gently sloping green leading to the cliff top and the azure blue sea beyond. Jill's interruption was not welcome, especially when she told him that their boss wanted to speak to him immediately. Jason was full of trepidation as he walked back with Jill toward Eric Arden's office. He knew full well that, whenever the Seaview holiday centre's business manager summons you, it is generally bad news. Eric motioned for Jason to sit down but, before his bottom could hit the seat, explained 'I just had a call from the agent of the star cabaret singer Ray Starlight to advise that he has a throat infection. Jason said 'Who has a throat infection - Ray or his agent?' Eric wasn't sure if Jason was trying to make a joke but continued 'Ray Starlight of course! Anyway, his doctor has insisted that he cancels all his shows until he's fully recovered'. Jason said 'Ray Starlight was due to perform tonight as the star of our cabaret night'. Eric said 'Yes, that's why I called you in as soon as I heard the news to give you time to do whatever it takes to get someone else in to fill the gap on the bill'.

There was no time to spare so Jason left the office without any further conversation and went off to seek out his senior Purplecoats. If they couldn't offer any advice or inspiration, he'd have to phone round the other holiday centres to see who they'd put in his place. As he walked through the ballroom, he heard a magician called Uncle Frank just finishing a show for the kids. Uncle Bill and Auntie Tricia jumped up from the huddle of kids they had been sat with and Bill said 'Come on children let's all give Uncle Frank a triffic round of applause'. The kids, encouraged by both Purplecoats, duly obliged. Jason saw an opportunity for an easy solution - just get Uncle Frank to step in!

Jason went up to Uncle Frank, shook his hand and said 'Well-done Frank and thank you'. The magician was a little surprised that Jason was being so nice to him. He usually left the Well-dones and Thank you's to one of his team. It was only when Jason explained his predicament and asked him if he could help by performing in tonight's cabaret slot that the compliments made sense. Uncle Frank had to think carefully about the offer. He had been a magician for twenty odd years but his act had always been a gentle run through of simple old-fashioned tricks designed for a very young audience. It wasn't in any way sophisticated and he had never performed to adults, let alone as the star of an evening cabaret show. On the other hand, Jason seemed desperate and promised him double his day rate. Uncle Frank agreed to give it a go and even accepted the stage name Jason had made up for him.

That evening, Jason gave the magician a big build up and introduced him as 'Frank Lee Magic' at the start of his act. Uncle Frank's daytime act for the kids included find the ball in the cups plus sleight of hand tricks with string, playing cards and money with the audience at his feet. Unfortunately, these tricks were not very visual when considering the longer distance between the magician on the stage and the audience on the far side of the ballroom floor.

The night went from bad to worse when the embarrassed and increasingly desperate Frank Lee Magic dropped his playing cards midway through one trick then one of the hidden balls fell out of a cup and bounced off the stage. Callum was on hand to chase after the ball as it continued bouncing along the ballroom floor toward the table of a family in the front row until it came to a halt under the seat occupied by a very large woman. Callum crawled under the legs of said woman to recover the ball but she thought he was taking liberties and hit him with her handbag. The audience couldn't stop laughing as Callum returned the ball to the embarrassed and increasingly desperate magician. Unfortunately, that was the highlight of the show. The rest of the act was a bit like a Tommy Cooper show with unintentional mistakes that were cringing rather than amusing. Jason had named the stand-in magician

Frank Lee Magic but he was proving to be Frank Lee Awful. Everyone was relieved when Jason ended the show earlier than planned.

The storms of the weekend were a distant memory and the *Seaview* holiday centre was at its busiest with around 600 guests having fun under a baking hot sun belting down. Lenny was now the regular trainer for the after breakfast keep fit sessions with holidaymakers. After finishing his Wednesday morning session, he walked through reception and Jill called him over. She told him that someone called Derek had phoned in to speak with him but, when she explained that he was running a keep fit session, Derek said he would phone back at 11am.

Lenny had mixed thoughts about getting a call from his hometown hippie friend so soon after seeing them when he went home for Bernie's party. He was excited but also concerned that it might be bad news, especially after seeing the needles being used there for hard drugs. He waited by the public phone and 11am came and went, adding to his concern. At 11:05 the phone rang and he sprang up to receive the call. After the usual pleasantries, Derek said 'Do you remember at Bernie's party when we said we must come down to visit you there?' 'Yeah.' 'Well, a gang of us will be doing just that this coming weekend!' Lenny was a little shocked at the suddenness of the planned visit but robotically said 'Wow, That's great! When you say *a gang of us*, how many are you talking about? Derek said 'Oh, it's just me, Keith, Bernie and maybe Damien' Lenny's heart sank at hearing the last name but continued: 'Where will you all be staying?' 'Don't worry, we've booked a triple-bedded family room at a Brixham guest house for the Saturday night and will top and tail if we have to but you did say you might be able to get us a chalet. If not, we'll all have to pull a bird for the night and end up in their chalets!' Lenny now wished he hadn't bragged about the opportunities hereabouts but, with a sense of reality, said 'We're into the peak period of the season so I don't fink there will be any spare chalets available. I may be able to shuffle around and get one or two spare beds or a floor with blankets to crash on if you're all coming for one night only'. Derek said 'It'll be great to get together, especially as I'll be armed with the latest gear that I can't wait to try out with you on a day trip'. Lenny knew that Derek's use of the word 'gear' was code for drugs and 'trip' was another reference to hallucinogenic drugs like LSD. 'Keith's car is being fixed so Bernie will be driving us down in his dad's car. If you hang around your reception area to look out for us, we'll toot the horn when we get there.' Before Lenny could talk further, the phone line started bleeping then hung up, presumably because Derek had run out of change at whichever public phone box he'd rung from.

On the one hand, Lenny was looking forward to seeing his best mate Derek as well as Bernie and Keith but he was unhappy that Damien might be joining them. He was already making the plans more complicated by coming along uninvited. Lenny then remembered that he had stupidly bragged to Damien about his sexual encounters the last time he'd seen his nemesis and even showed him a photo of Connie. Another concern was regarding Derek saying *I'll be armed with the latest gear that I can't wait to try out with you on a day trip*. Drugs like cannabis were one thing but Lenny would have to be extremely careful if his mates planned on taking anything stronger. *Lenny's Golden Rule Number Two* meant that he himself would refuse to take and discourage anyone else in his presence to take heavier drugs like cocaine or heroin but he didn't want to risk his job by being around users of such drugs. Most importantly, he didn't want a heavy drug experience to be inflicted on Connie. Thoughts of his nightmare where he and Connie shared a needle came back to haunt him. He decided he *had* to do something that would possibly upset Callum but definitely hurt both Connie and himself.

The first part of Lenny's plan was to get Saturday afternoon and evening off. Jason must have been in a good mood when he asked as he agreed that Lenny could have the time off so long as he worked Saturday morning and, instead of taking Sunday as his usual day off, took the Sunday morning ramble and helped Callum run the afternoon bingo.

The second part of Lenny's plan was to get sole use of the bedroom he officially shared with Callum at the purple flat. That way, he and his hippie friends could spend an evening there in private while all the other *Purplecoat*s were working up the hill at the holiday centre. His gang could listen to Lenny's music, smoke a joint or two and drink whatever was left of the scrumpy - it was starting to taste a bit stale so needed finishing or flushing away in any case. At the end of the night, one or maybe two of his friends could sleep there if there wasn't enough room at their guest house, they didn't want to walk back there or physically couldn't walk back there!

When Lenny walked into the bedroom he shared with Callum at the purple flat, his roommate was holding some sort of a doll. 'What you got there, CC?' Callum handed the doll to Lenny as he said 'After I hosted the Most Elegant Grandmother competition, the family of the winner gave me this as a present. Wasn't that nice of them?' Lenny needed a favour from Callum so tried not to recoil as he briefly held the floppy rubber King Kong doll in his hand before handing it back with 'Oh yea CC. Nice.' Callum proudly stood the toy up on the chest of drawers alongside the head of his bed.

While Callum was in a good mood, Lenny tried his luck: 'CC, old pal ... Would you be able to help me out on Saturday when my hippie friends visit?' Callum naively said 'Of course, LE' despite having no idea what his roommate wanted help with. Lenny explained 'They've booked a B&B down the road for the three of them but then had a last-minute addition so one of them may need to sleep over in our bedroom on Saturday night. In case they do, could you find another room to sleep that night in?' Callum asked 'Why aren't you staying at Connie's chalet?' 'Because my mates will probably want to smoke a joint and listen to music on my record player here'. 'Will Connie be staying here as well as one of your mates?' 'No, I've decided I won't be seeing her over the weekend as my mates can get a bit wild and I don't want to risk her being persuaded to take a heavy drug'. Lenny didn't mention his chilling nightmare about injecting Connie with a drug but thought to himself 'It's the only way I can ensure no harm can come to her'. Callum seemed to read his mind: 'If your friends can't be trusted as far as drugs are concerned why not just tell them not to come?' Lenny shrugged: 'They're my best mates and I couldn't turn them down, especially as they'll be traveling hundreds of miles to see me.'

Callum had a good think about Lenny's request and how he should respond. He was a little annoyed that Lenny wanted to evict him at such short notice but understood the bond of friendship. So where could he spend the night? He knew whose bed he would love to be in for the night but Pauline was unlikely to accommodate his wish. He had an idea of a potential alternative but didn't want to blurt it out to Lenny until he'd checked if it was acceptable to the resident.

Callum reluctantly agreed that, *if* he could find another bed for himself *and* Lenny ensures his mates don't take heavy drugs or make a mess then he could have the room to share with his hippie friends for that one night. Lenny boldly said 'I guarantee they will only smoke a joint or two in the room and it will be left neat and tidy'. Callum knew Lenny couldn't guarantee anything despite his best intentions but didn't want to spoil the weekend for him.

The sun shone brightly into all the chalets on Connie's block mid-Friday morning so it wasn't unusual for her curtains to be pulled across at this time. Connie pulled off her knickers and lay on her bed. The rays of the sun pushed through the thin curtains to light the room and warm her half naked body. Her old roommate Judy had left the *Seaview* with her brother and she could just about hear Lenny organising a game of rounders with holidaymakers in the field on the other side of her chalet block. She was confident she would not be disturbed for an hour or more, nonetheless, she had carefully pulled the curtains tightly together to prevent any passers-by seeing what she was about to do.

Connie and Lenny had shared a bed since his return but they still hadn't been able to consummate their relationship. Every time they tried, they seemed to be reminded of Judy's tapping on the glass, her haunting cry of help and her bloody wrists. One morning, after waiting on her tables in the breakfast session, Connie decided to visit the *Seaview*'s Senior Nurse and ask for her advice. She didn't mention the flashbacks of Judy so the nurse just looked at the physical rather than psychological aspects. She gave Connie a tube of personal lubrication jelly and described an exercise that she could try on her own that should help make her supple enough to attempt intercourse without the pain she had encountered. Since her mid-teens, Connie had, on the odd occasion, pleasured herself but this exercise went further. Even with the lubrication jelly, she felt a little sore afterwards. She was nervous at the prospect of losing her virginity but sure that Lenny was *the one* to help her become a woman. She looked forward to surprising and delighting him that very night. Another benefit of consummating their relationship would be that it would prove that it was the 'real thing' and give her more confidence when being with Lenny's friends from his home that weekend. She was really looking forward to their visit and hearing more about Lenny's background and home life. When Lenny last spoke to his parents on the phone, he'd introduced Connie as his "bird" and insisted on her talking to them. They seemed really nice. Would Lenny continue to call her his "bird" in front of his mates or perhaps promote her to "luvver" or even "wife"?!

Callum had been a thoughtful colleague and reliable shoulder for Anne to cry on after Connie's brother left her and the *Seaview* to return to Ivybridge with Judy. Since then, Anne and Callum had built up a solid friendship, sharing similar interests and points of view. It seemed like the right time for them to move their relationship up to the next level. Even so, Callum felt a little nervous when he knocked on the window of Anne's chalet. When she opened the door, he meekly asked her how she was. She said she was fine and Callum just stood there not knowing how to make the next move. She sensed there was something else on his mind so invited him in. With only the single beds to sit on they each chose one and sat awkwardly facing each other. Callum took an age just skirting around the subject in idle chit-chat before finding what he thought was a suitable moment to pop the question: 'Anne, could I stay with you here this Saturday night?' It wasn't the most romantic approach and he made it worse by adding too soon '… The thing is, I'm being kicked out because Lenny needs our room at the purple flat that night.' 'Why are you being kicked out by Lenny?' 'So that one of his friends from home can stay there with him.' Callum tried to inject some misplaced humour by suggesting that he would probably have to sleep in the disco room if she couldn't help.

Anne was totally confused. Did Callum simply want to use the spare bed he was currently sitting on to kip in for the night or was he making up a story to sleep in her bed for a more romantic relationship and, God forbid, sex? Anne definitely liked Callum but wasn't sure if she was ready to go the whole way with him. Nonetheless, she thought to herself - what the hell - let's see how the mood takes us on the night. When she agreed that he could stay, they kissed and embraced but looked vacantly over each other's shoulders as neither of them had any idea what they were getting into.

Callum left Anne's chalet and found Lenny still umpiring a game of rounders in the field on the other side of the chalet block. The game was being played by holidaymakers from the two opposing planets and a few of the competitors were taking it way too seriously. Lenny had tried to persuade the main offenders to calm down and prevent a brawl from starting. He clearly had his hands full but Callum stepped in and helped keep the warring parties apart. The main offenders calmed down and even shook hands, allowing the match to continue without any further incidents or fisticuffs.

Anne went round to Connie's chalet to tell her about Callum's visit. The curtains were closed and it took a while for Connie to open them slightly and peer through. Anne assumed Connie had just woken up after a late morning nap. Connie looked a little flustered as she let her friend in. They sat opposite each other on the single beds while Anne went through her conversation with Callum in great detail, including the news that Lenny wanted the purple flat all to himself on Saturday night, apparently so that he could be alone there with one of his friends.

Connie didn't tell Anne that she had planned to lose her virginity to Lenny that very night but did say she was surprised he planned to stay overnight at the purple flat with one of his friends rather than be with her. She surely didn't expect him to stay there as well, did he? Over the last few weeks, the gossip coming out from kitchen lads and other waitresses was that Lenny had been seen walking holidaymakers down to their chalets and sneaking back late at night. She hadn't believed the rumours but wondered what Lenny was up to on Saturday night - was he planning to see another girl and take her back to the flat?

Once the rounders match finished, Callum told Lenny he'd managed to get a room for the night. Lenny was relieved but of course wanted to know who had helped them both out. When Callum confessed that it was Anne, Lenny called him a cunning fox and said he didn't realise they'd got a thing going. Callum admitted that he definitely liked Anne but they hadn't really *got a thing going* - not yet anyway. Callum went on to say that even though Anne had agreed that he could sleep at her place he had no idea if it was in the same bed. Lenny said 'What the hell - see how the mood takes you on the night!'

The first two parts of Lenny's plan had been achieved. He now had to deliver the third and most difficult part of the plan.

Lenny tapped on Connie's chalet window. She opened the door and they kissed in their usual way but both of them hid their anxiety as to what was to come on Saturday night. Connie was feeling a little sore after her exercise so delicately sat on her bed but Lenny remained standing. He was trying to concentrate on what he was going to say so didn't notice her discomfort. Trying to lighten the mood, he asked 'Have you spoken to your brother lately? How's he and Judy getting on since they left the *Seaview*?' 'They're getting on great – Tom is loving the chef job and creating new dishes at our schoolmate's restaurant while Judy has turned the corner and enjoying food again as the senior waitress there'.
Having broken the ice, he reached out and held her hands as he reminded her that his hippie friends were coming to stay this weekend. She said 'Of course I remember. I can't wait to meet them'. That comment made it harder for Lenny to continue in an organised way. Instead, he blurted out that his hippie friends were a wild bunch and he'd prefer that the two

of them didn't see each other while they're here. He wanted to explain that he didn't want her to get mixed up in heavy drugs or dangerous confrontations but the words just wouldn't come out.

Connie assumed Lenny didn't want his mates to meet her. Was he dumping her so that he could be with another girl? Maybe it wasn't a colleague or local girl. Maybe his friends were bringing a girl that Lenny wanted to be with. Maybe he had been with her when he went to the 21st birthday party. Had he been cheating on her back then?

Connie could not hide her emotions and burst into tears. When Lenny tried to put his arms around her and explain further, she elbowed him away and screamed 'Just vuck off, please.' Crestfallen, he gathered up the rest of his uniform and wash bag from her bathroom and left Connie's chalet with his tail between his legs. He knew that he hadn't explained himself very well to her but had at least kept her safe from harm. Carrying his uniform and wash bag away felt like it was a permanent break but the rift was practical and necessary.

When he got back to the purple flat, Lenny told Callum what happened and how upset Connie was. "I should have told her that I didn't want her to be exposed to the hard drugs my friends might be having" Callum said 'I'm not surprised she was upset. Why didn't you tell her that instead of letting her believe you'd rather get stoned with your mates than be with her?' Lenny explained 'I tried but messed it up. I just wanted to keep Connie safe, away from my friends. Once they've returned home, I'll make up with her, move back in and all will be forgiven and forgotten.' Callum said 'It might not be as easy as that, especially if your so-called mates cause trouble – why take the risk?' Lenny sighed 'It's too late to change anything now'. Callum continued 'Talking of risk, what happens if you get drawn into taking hard drugs?' Lenny countered with 'I'll never take anything that would risk me getting hooked and don't forget I'm invincible. You said yourself that I have had so many lucky escapes I'm like a cat with nine lives.' Callum said 'I did LE, but if you've used up your nine lives already you have none left to protect you!' Lenny didn't take Callum's warning seriously and stupidly said 'Celery' – it was his little joke at not quite saying *C'est La Vie*, French for 'That's Life!'

Connie eventually dried her tears and went round to Anne's chalet to tell her that Lenny had broken up with her. Anne was shocked and put her arms around Connie as she tearfully went through what was said. Anne spoke from the heart and with venom as she summarised 'Men can be right bastards and none of them can be trusted. Remember how badly Tommy had bullied Judy then your own saintly brother dumped me and took Judy back to Ivybridge with him. At least Lenny told you face-to-face rather than leaving a note like Nick did. I had to toughen up after that and told myself *Bollocks to love* - it's not worth the heartache.' Connie wasn't listening as she was still getting to grips with seeing Lenny in a new light. He'd thrown away something she thought was special between them. She remarked 'Tommy told Judy he didn't want to be with her the night she nearly took her own life. Maybe Lenny is no better than Tommy'. Anne said 'Crikey Connie! Lenny *is* a bastard but nowhere near as bad as Tommy'. Connie tearfully said 'Okay, Okay. I guess I'm so shocked and disappointed that he dumped me so easily'. Anne said 'Forget about him if he doesn't realise how special you are. Do you remember when your brother left me for Judy, you took me to Torquay to get some new clothes to cheer me up. Let me do the same for you'.

[Playlist Track: *"Purple Haze" – Jimi Hendrix*]

On Saturday morning, just four days before the Cow Town Carnival, Jason primed all his *Purplecoat* team to be on the lookout for guests who would be fun-loving enough to wear skimpy fancy dress costumes and fit enough to dance and wave on *Seaview*'s jungle-themed float for hours. Lenny was therefore juggling three priorities while working his shift on reception:
1. welcoming new holidaymakers in the usual way
2. trying to persuade the more youthful and high-spirited ones to star on *Seaview*'s float
3. looking out for his hippie friends.

He hovered outside the reception area to be in the best place to see his mates arrive, excited and nervous as to how the weekend would go. He still felt really guilty about making Connie cry but, once his mates had gone back home, he'd explain the reasons why he didn't want her around that weekend, they'd reunite and everything would go back to normal.

He was nearing the end of his shift, helping pensioners carry their bags in, when he heard a loud beep, beep, bee-eee-eep. He turned around and saw Derek and his other mates from home waving out of the windows of a big, old but shiny American-looking car. The pensioners had been troubled by the car noise but Lenny ignored their concerns, plonked their bags down by the reception counter and gave his mates a quick thumbs up as he ran out toward them. By the time he'd reached the car, his mates had all got out to stretch their legs. One by one, they hugged Lenny and looked each other up and down. Lenny had been fearful that they would turn up so scruffy and outlandish that camp security wouldn't let them onto the site or word would get back to management of a hippy invasion. He kept to himself how relieved he was that were dressed reasonably smart, by their standards. Damien wasn't so reticent. He looked disparagingly at Lenny's uniform and sneered 'Oooh, get you, carrying bags in for old people in your purple school blazer!' Lenny hit back with 'Good to know you're still an arsehole, Damien!' He said it half-jokingly but inwardly thinking it was true. Damien always seemed to have it in for him. Derek sensed the hostility between them so lightened the mood by pointing at the car they'd arrived in as if introducing a special guest to a royal party. He said to Lenny 'What do you think of the *spliffmobile*?' The '*spliffmobile*' happened to be a 1960 Ford Zephyr with a two-tone colour scheme - light blue/grey around the top half and bright cream around the bottom half. Lenny said 'It's a classic beauty, that's for sure.' Bernie stroked the bonnet lovingly and explained 'It's my dad's pride and joy but he was good enough ...' Damien jumped in to finish the sentence '...stupid enough to let his lucky bastard son drive it further than it has ever been before with his crazy mates!' Bernie ignored Damien's barb and calmly explained 'My dad said I could borrow it for the weekend as a treat for my birthday'.

Keith asked Lenny when he would be able to get away from work as they wanted to drop their bags off at the guest house then go to the seaside and get stoned. At that moment, Lenny saw Callum arrive at reception so called him over and introduced him to his mates - they were all polite as they shook his hand and even Damien decided against ridiculing the *Purplecoat* uniform a second time. Callum could see that Lenny was desperate to finish his shift and start his day and a half holiday. He thoughtfully said he'd be okay covering reception so that Lenny could get away with his mates.

They all jumped in the *spliffmobile* and Lenny was surprised how roomy the car was for the five of them. Bernie drove the car down the hill a little too fast for Lenny's liking, especially when they bounced over the speed bumps and out past the entrance gates. Luckily, Baz had fallen asleep in his sentry box otherwise he might have jumped out in front of them shouting 'Camp Fuzz!'. Lenny pointed out the purple flat for Bernie to stop outside while he nipped in to change into something more casual. While there, Lenny grabbed one of four large plastic bottles full of scrumpy lemon top that he had pre-mixed in his room in anticipation of the weekend. He'd got used to quick changes from the weekly *Purplecoat* shows so was back out in the time it had taken Bernie to read through the directions to the guest house. Minutes later, Bernie parked the *spliffmobile* as near as he could to it and Lenny's mates went in to drop their bags off and check in. Derek stayed in the car with Lenny as only three of them could check in for the triple-bedded family room they'd booked. When they moved on, Lenny pointed out *The Three Elms Inn* as they passed it, commenting that this pub was the favourite watering hole for all the staff who wanted a drink and chat away from the holiday centre.

Bernie drove them a few miles down the coast to Broadsands. On their journey in from home to the Torbay area, Derek had glimpsed a sign pointing to the small seaside resort. He suggested they all spend time there as it should be less crowded than the more well-known beaches in the area. The *spliffmobile* turned off at the same sign then descended down a winding hill above the resort. A vista opened up to an elegant railway bridge precariously perched on top of towering slim brick arches that loomed up from the ground like one of Dali's paintings. The gaps between the arches peeked through to the azure bay beyond. The timing could not have been better as a passenger steam train chugged along the top of the viaduct to complete the surreal picture. They already felt like they were tripping but they hadn't even taken an *acid tab* yet! Bernie managed to find a vacant spot in the car park and they got out and walked down and along the promenade overlooking the sandy beach. They needed a relatively private place to take their drugs so jumped down onto the beach in an area that was well shielded from the other holidaymakers. They sat up against the sea wall and Keith - who else - rolled a big fat joint for them all to smoke. Bernie and Damien didn't want to drop any acid, so Derek handed one piece to Keith, one to Lenny and kept one for himself. The three of them downed their tablets with a few swigs from the bottle of scrumpy lemon top that Lenny had picked up from his room.

The hallucinogenic effects of the drugs soon took hold and they were grinning and laughing mischievously. Lenny looked at the beach around him and saw hundreds of waves and millions of sand granules expanding and pulsating in a spectacular kaleidoscope of blue and gold sparks and dots, interspersed with pink and black blobs apparently sliding out from the bodies and clothes of other beachgoers. His fellow trippers must also have seen something similar as they pondered thoughts that may have been pointless but felt, to them, like philosophical concepts or metaphysical discoveries such as: Does water merge with sand or sand merge with water? As fascinating as the discussions appeared to be, Lenny's mind went elsewhere when his eyes refocused beyond the beach and out across the bay. A low-lying chunk of land jutted out to separate this bay from the next and it was packed with tall, lush trees. Their brown branches and green leaves constantly changed colour as the sun and clouds fought to dominate the light and shade. To Lenny, the forest was a separate world, a living entity, full of tints and tones. Even though it must have been a mile away, he believed he could hear the god of the forest, roaring like a loud rasping and vibrating snore as the wind blew through the branches and the leaves flapped back and forth. It was a beautiful wonderland and Lenny wanted to converse with the forest god but he couldn't understand its language, much like the meeting of minds he'd had with Guy the Gorilla at London Zoo when tripping a few years earlier.

All too soon, Bernie and Damien got fed up with watching their spaced-out friends marvel at the world around them. The joint had made them thirsty and Lenny's bottle of scrumpy lemon top was now empty. They wanted to leave the beach to go on a pub crawl so led their reluctant and still hallucinating friends back to the car park and bundled them into the back seats of the *spliffmobile* like hijackers might dump hostages they'd drugged.

Bernie decided to by-pass Paignton and head towards Torquay. The Zephyr hummed and throbbed as it sped along while Keith, Derek and Lenny shared their visions of the streets, buildings and sea-views. Bernie and Damien couldn't wait to get to a pub for a drink and diversion away from the delirious and increasingly tedious musings coming forth from the back seat. Bernie had the bright idea of stopping off at a pretty village called *Cockington*. Whether tripping or not, this village was like stepping back in time with its narrow lanes, forge, cricket pitch, water mill and thatched properties including the Drum Inn.

The gang piled in to the pub and immediately felt like everyone inside had turned around to look down their noses at them. They realised that they must have looked a dishevelled bunch, with sand still stuck on their clothes from sitting on the beach and eyes still bulging from the drugs. As the driver of the *spliffmobile*, Bernie was the soberest of the gang so was brave enough to go up to the bar and order 5 pints of their best bitter. Damien helped Bernie carry the drinks to Keith, Derek and Lenny who had slipped back outside to slouch on a bench in the beer garden to get away from the accusing glares. The gang didn't risk a second pint and returned to the car to continue their journey.

The view along Torbay Road into Torquay was epic, even for Bernie and Damien who weren't out of their heads like the back seat trippers. Luxury hotels on one side of the road looked out onto a huge sweep of the bay on the other side of the road. Bernie found a convenient place to park the car, opposite Torquay's Princess Theatre. They crossed the road and walked through Princess Gardens then followed The Strand to Elizabeth Parade. It was a buzzing destination with a marina full of pretty boats bobbing up and down on the sparkling water overlooked by plenty of bars. Derek led them into the first two pubs they came across. They had one drink in each but didn't tarry because neither establishment had the right atmosphere. The third pub was completely different. It was one huge room full of teenagers and twenty-somethings enjoying themselves and the music banging out loud and clear in stereo through massive speakers. Lenny was still tripping and a tune he'd never heard before began to play that absolutely blew his mind. The opening beats from the drums shook him and the ground where he stood like an earthquake. The twangy metal guitar hinted at the melody then the initially sparse vocals began with gruff voices shouting 'Hey' like a sacred chant. Damien said it was a huge Glam Rock hit from someone called Gary Glitter and it was called 'Rock and Roll.' Lenny had not been able to keep up with the latest pop trends while cocooned in the *Seaview* but this music didn't sound anything like rock and roll to him. It sluiced through his body like hot waves and he was amazed that nobody else seemed to notice the 'Hey-y-y-y' words stretching, floating and swirling around the room and bar area like rampant ghosts or devils, sweeping through the furniture and bodies of anyone that stood in their path.

Reluctantly, Lenny followed his mates as they made their way through the crowd in order to leave this pleasure palace, the last venue on their Torquay pub crawl. As they opened the front doors, they were instantly blinded by the afternoon sun. Once their eyes became accustomed to the brightness, they walked along the promenade heading back toward the car. On reaching Princess Gardens, they realised that the drink, drugs and walking had absolutely knackered them. The sun-dried grassy areas in the gardens were just too inviting to ignore so they all lay down alongside the perfectly manicured flower beds and felt a cool breeze from the fountain as they crashed out for a while. Lenny dozed off thinking of Connie and looking forward to getting back with her once his mates had gone home.

Lenny was woken by a prod followed by the sound of excited girls talking in a foreign accent. As he rubbed his eyes and opened them, he couldn't believe what he was seeing. A mass of bronzed legs above and around him. The legs eventually reached tight miniskirts, but some were hiked so high that from Lenny's prone position, he saw more than was intended. He sat up and blinked in case he was still dreaming then realised he was surrounded by a half dozen blonde and tanned teenagers. Their apparent leader was leaning over him with a pencil and piece of paper in her hands while talking gibberish. Derek explained 'These girls are English Language students from Norway. They were asking questions about the local area and its history for something called a Treasure Hunt. While you were asleep, we looked at the questions but couldn't answer any of them so I told the girls to wake you up because you should be able to help, seeing as you take holidaymakers on excursions in the area'.

Lenny went through the questions on their list. Like the rest of the gang, he knew nothing about a Saxon settlement called 'Torre' and couldn't guess the year when Torquay hosted the water sports events of the Olympic Games. He also didn't know the stories behind famous locals such as John Babbacombe Lee. He remembered an English folk rock group - Fairport Convention - had released an album about him but the album cover looked so old-fashioned that he took no interest in it.

Lenny was relieved to be able to at least answer a few of the questions on their list:
1. *Where is the nearest miniature village?* Babbacombe Model Village;
2. *What type of railway is Babbacombe Cliff Lift?* Funicular;
3. *What is the name of the nearest prehistoric cave used by ancient humans including Neanderthals?* Kents Cavern;
4. *What is the difference between stalagmites and stalactites?* Stalacmites point up and stalagtites point down.

Lenny cheekily suggested to the students 'The easiest way to remember which way stalagmites and stalactites point is to think about the spelling of the words. *Stalacmites* ends with "mites" so think of mighty mountains…' He raised his hands above his head and touched the points of his fingers together to indicate the pointing up, then continued. '… *Stalactites* ends with "tites" so think of "titties" drooping down! The girls didn't understand so Lenny cupped his hands in front of his chest and bounced them up and down as he repeated the word stalactites while emphasising the "titties".' The girls burst out into fits of giggles and wanted to chat a while longer but their group leader turned up to take them off to their next destination.

Anne and Connie were on a bus heading back to Brixham after a successful shopping spree in Torquay. Anne was pleased that her plan to cheer up Connie with retail therapy appeared to have worked. She'd also made sure they grabbed the front seats upstairs to take in the lovely views. Anne knew the answer but couldn't help giggling as she asked Connie 'Should I let Callum see the new underwear I've just bought when he stays with me tonight?' Connie replied 'Didn't you say that men can be right bastards and none of them can be trusted?' 'I'm not saying that I'll invite him into my bed but it would be nice to think he'd be desperate to join me while he spends the night in the other bed!' Connie had stopped listening. She was too busy looking out of the window as the bus made a stop alongside Princess Gardens. She saw Lenny surrounded by a dozen blonde girls making what looked like rude gestures and laughing with them. He obviously wasn't feeling heartbroken or even guilty. She wondered if he'd dumped her for one of the girls he was talking to or was just playing the field enjoying having no trappings. Until that very morning, she was sure that *she* was the trapping he wanted but she'd obviously been misled.

The sun had gone down by the time Bernie parked the spliffmobile outside the Guest House in Brixham. A couple of hours later, the gang were trying out the local brew in the third pub they'd fallen on. Lenny was struggling to keep up with the alcohol consumption of his friends - crikey, could they drink! It was well into the evening and Lenny was once again thinking of Connie. Would she be alone in her chalet missing him? Perhaps she's having a drink with her friends and being chatted up by kitchen lads? There was only one way to find out. When he could get a word in, Lenny suggested to his mates that they move on to *The Three Elms Inn*. To persuade them, Lenny reminded them that it was just around the corner from their guest house and the best place to chat up girls. The second point seemed to have the desired effect as they swiftly downed their pints and said 'OK, let's go!'

Lenny felt nauseous as the gang reached *The Three Elms Inn*. He'd forced down that third pint too quickly just to try and keep up with his mates. They seemed fine and went straight in through the front door of the pub but Lenny had to run down to the outside of the toilet block to be sick. Still groggy, he staggered in to the pub and saw his mates at the bar. Damien had already ordered five pints of Newcastle Brown Ale and asked the barman to flick open the caps on the bottles then place half, not full, pint glasses upside down on top of them. They each carried their own drinks over to the only empty table at the far end of the room. Once sat, they turned the whole assembly the other way up then carefully lifted the bottles slowly until the glass was full of the brown ale topped with a good head of foam. This routine ensured the same amount of ale and foam would be preserved in the bottle when ready for the second filling.

Lenny scanned the area in case he recognised anyone and was absolutely gobsmacked when he saw Connie - she looked like every inch a rock chick with her hair curled to the maximum so that it was cascading over a fluffy faux fox fur coat. He'd never before seen the black bell-bottom jeans she was wearing but couldn't help noticing that they were so tight at the waist that it accentuated her slim figure. She seemed to be having a great time in amongst a gang of kitchen lads and waitresses so Lenny was torn as to whether he should approach her. He didn't want to spoil her night, especially as he was still feeling sick from the effects of the drinks and drugs and his breath probably stunk like a camel's rectum.

Derek and Keith saw that Lenny was looking rough and admitted that they were also coming down hard from the day's drink and drugs and this noisy pub was doing their head in. Derek furtively pulled out of his pocket a small bag containing what looked like brown pepper and said 'This'll pick us back up.' Lenny said 'What on earth is that?' Derek explained that it was a new hallucinogenic drug called desert dust that he'd been holding back all day. He suggested they all take a little dust before going back to Lenny's flat to enjoy the effects in private. Bernie and Damien hadn't taken any acid all day and declined both the offer of the desert dust and excursion to Lenny's flat. They were happy to stay at the pub drinking for the rest of the evening. Derek wasn't put off by the lack of support as he was keen to try out the dust for himself. He dipped a finger into his beer to wet it then poked it into the desert dust before removing it from the bag and sucking the accumulated dust off his fingertip. Keith took the bag and sucked a half finger of dust using the same method as Derek. When Lenny plunged a whole finger of dust into his mouth, Derek said 'Watch out tiger, that's strong stuff.' Apparently, a few specks were all that was needed to get high. Bernie was the only one still responsible enough to think about arrangements the next day. He said to Derek and Keith 'If you don't make it back to the guest house tonight, I'll pick you up outside Lenny's flat at 11 in the morning.'

Anne whispered in Connie's ear 'I'm off after I've finished this drink. I need to get back to my chalet and change into my new underwear before Callum turns up to spend the night with me. Do you want to walk back with me?' Connie said 'I'll stay a while longer.' She was willing to give Lenny one last chance to come over to her to see how she was. Anne broke her thoughts with 'Will you be alright, here on your own?' Connie replied 'Of course!' Anne swigged down her drink and said 'I'll be off then. You sure you don't want to walk back now?' Connie held her emotions in check to joke with her friend 'No, you get off for your date with Callum. I'll be fine with these rogues' referring to the few remaining kitchen lads and waitresses. As Connie gave Anne a goodnight kiss on the cheek, she whispered 'Good luck with the new underwear!'

Soon after Anne left, Connie saw Lenny trudge off with two his friends without even bothering to speak to her. So much for giving Lenny one last chance to come over to her to see how she was. Connie thought that if their sexual impasse had caused him to dump her, then he wasn't worth worrying about and she should forget about him and move on. She was certainly getting plenty of drinks and attention from the kitchen lads but didn't fancy any of them. Then she noticed one of Lenny's mates staring at her. She ignored him at first but, when she looked back, he smiled and walked over to her. Now they were close up, Damien was sure that this was the girl in the photo that Lenny had shown him when they were at Bernie's 21st. Ignoring introductions, he said 'Ain't you Lenny's bird?' The alcohol Connie had been plied with made her as bold as brass and she spitefully replied that she *had* been Lenny's *bird* but he dumped her that very morning, apparently, just to be with them or maybe another girl. She sarcastically added that, whatever the reason was, she hoped it was worth it. Damien's tongue had also been loosened by the booze and he found himself confessing 'I can't believe Lenny would be playing the field instead of being with someone as gorgeous and sexy as you!' Connie took in the compliment but asked Damien what he meant by 'playing the field.' Damien treacherously blurted out 'Oh, Lenny bragged about shagging holidaymakers while he was with you because it was part of his contract as a *Purplecoat*, or something like that'.

Callum relaxed on a luxurious sofa, tapping a large cigar between his fingers. Pauline walked in carrying a newspaper and a lighter. She was wearing a black negligee and Callum delighted in what he saw through it. She bent forward in front of him, kissed him on the forehead and lit his cigar before passing him the newspaper. She remained standing in front of him, as if obediently awaiting her master's next instruction. He puffed away on the cigar and settled down to read the latest news. The headline was … *Funtime Purplecoat found dead after drug fuelled weekend on the English Riviera.* The story mentioned the *Seaview holiday resort* and Lenny's name was there in print… Callum felt another kiss on his forehead…

Suddenly, Anne's voice said 'Rise and shine, *Sleepy Head* … I had to kiss you twice on the forehead to wake you up'. While Callum was gathering his thoughts, Anne continued: 'I left you sleeping while I washed and put on my waitress uniform. Didn't realise I'd worn you out that much through the night but we eventually managed to get some sleep in separate beds!' Callum said to himself *Thank God it was a dream*. As he came to, he must have still looked confused. Anne guessed that Callum was still comprehending his new surroundings as much as their new relationship. She said 'I've got to get off to the dining room to set up for the breakfast sitting but don't worry, you don't have to rush to get up. Just slam the door shut when you leave.' Callum watched Anne do just that. Looking around the room, he saw that Anne must have placed his shorts and top hanging over the end of the bed. He was glad he had brought them up to the chalet the night before, along with the rest of his day uniform and electric shaver.

Callum obviously couldn't have told Anne about his dream, but it made him anxious to know how Lenny had got on with his hippie gang. If they stayed overnight in Lenny and Callum's room at the purple flat, how much of a mess would they have made? Callum recalled Lenny admitting that he and his hippie friends would probably get drunk and take some sort of drugs the night before but he vowed he would not personally over indulge. Callum trusted Lenny when he was sober but worried that he might do something stupid after a few too many drinks with persuasive friends. That must have been in his thoughts when he dreamed about the newspaper headline. To put his mind at rest, Callum got up earlier than he needed to, washed, shaved and put on his *Purplecoat* uniform. As he left the chalet, he slammed the front door shut as Anne had requested. Walking briskly toward the dining room, he convinced himself that the newspaper article was just his own silly thoughts and he'd laugh about it when he saw Lenny at their breakfast table.

Callum was the first to sit at the *Purplecoats* table in the dining room. He smiled at Anne as she glided past with plates of English breakfast for her diners. Callum still couldn't work out how he felt about their night together and she probably felt the same. Callum's breakfast arrived but he struggled to get through it. He kept looking at the empty seat opposite where Lenny should be sitting. Sunday was Lenny's usual day off, but he'd agreed to work this morning and afternoon in return for getting Saturday afternoon and evening off so he could be with his hippie friends. The one-off arrangement included Lenny taking that morning's ramble which was due to depart in an hour or so. LE would surely need to get some food down him if he'd had a skinful the night before.

The breakfast service ended and the waitresses took away all the dirty plates but Lenny still hadn't shown up. Callum went to reception to see if Lenny had left a message but Jill confirmed nothing had been left there. A dozen or so holidaymakers turned up early for the ramble but there was still no sign of Lenny. Callum was now hoping Lenny had simply overslept and was on his way up the hill to get some scraps from the kitchen before taking the ramble – he'd laugh at Callum's concern with a Zezeze.

By the time it got to the scheduled start time of the ramble, a large group of holidaymakers had gathered and were tapping and pointing at their watches, restless to be led off. Mike turned up to see why they hadn't left yet. Callum instinctively felt that something was seriously wrong so asked Mike if he would mind taking the ramble while he went down to the flat to wake Lenny up. Mike looked a little disgruntled but agreed to help, so, while he gathered the ramblers together, Callum set off down the hill.

Once out of sight, Callum picked up the pace. He was still hoping he'd see Lenny jogging up but there was nobody around. Callum ran as fast as he could down the hill all the way to the purple flat. When he opened the door to their bedroom, he couldn't believe his eyes. All of his monopoly game's fake money had been scattered around the room and the board had been ripped in two and dumped on the floor by the wardrobe. Derek was fast asleep and snoring in a blanket on his bed and Keith was making puffing noises as he slept in a blanket on the floor. Lenny was making no noises at all and looked deathly white in his bed. Callum carefully stepped over Keith and whispered 'LE, wake up' in his ear but LE was unresponsive. Callum put his hand on Lenny's shoulders and recoiled because his body felt icy cold. In that moment, Callum reimagined Lenny's story of his childhood in the back streets of London.

> A seven-year-old boy runs out through the school gates on to a road, straight into the path of a speeding car. The driver sees the boy and hits the brakes. The car screeches and skids closer and closer toward the boy. In the final scene, the boy is laid out on the pavement covered in a blanket. It looks like the car failed to stop in time and the boy has departed this world. Then an ordinary guy in the street steps up to shake the boy and become a hero by miraculously reviving him.

Callum will never know if he saved Lenny's life that morning but he was mightily relieved when his vigorous shaking helped bring LE out of the very deep place he'd sunk into. As soon as Callum was sure that Lenny was okay, or at least alive, he just wanted to get out of that room. It had been turned into a rubbish tip and the stench of the previous night's drugs, scrumpy and sweat of the three young men permeated the air. Callum also wasn't in the mood to hang around and have an argument with Lenny or his mates that were still asleep. He quietly told Lenny he was going back up the hill to cover for Mike and try to stop any of the other *Purplecoats* coming down to see the mess. Lenny mumbled some sort of thank you to Callum and said he was a true pal.

Lenny resisted the urge to drift back to sleep and forced himself out of bed. He stepped over Keith while he lay on a blanket spread along the floor and inadvertently disturbed him. Keith's murmuring then woke Derek in the other bed. After the minimum of pleasantries, Lenny reminded his temporary squatters that the bathroom was next door and they all needed to wash, shave and get dressed, ready for Bernie to pick them up at 11. His mates were hungover but understood the urgency so they took it in turns to wash while Lenny wearily put on his day uniform. They all stepped out of the purple flat and waited until Bernie arrived in the car. Derek was the first to notice that he was alone so asked why Damien was not with him. Bernie explained that Damien had got chatting with a girl who happened to work at the *Seaview* holiday centre. As Damien left the pub with her, he had told Bernie that if he didn't come back to the guest house that night then he would wait for him in *Seaview*'s car park this morning around 11:30am.

Bernie drove the gang up the hill to the car park and, sure enough, Damien was already there. He couldn't wait to tell them that he'd got lucky with an auburn-haired girl called Connie who happened to mention that she used to be Lenny's girlfriend. Lenny's heart sank - he couldn't believe that Damien was bragging about his pure and innocent Connie. Bernie asked Damien if he had gone all the way with her and he looked at Lenny as he replied 'Of course I did!' Lenny protested 'but she was my girlfriend, you bastard!' Damien came back with 'Yea, but you just admitted she *was* your girlfriend, past tense. She told me that you'd dumped her!' Lenny was too shocked to question Damien's story further but couldn't believe this cruel twist of fate - his clumsy attempt at protecting Connie from being corrupted by his hippie friends had led to the opposite result. He had practically thrown Connie into the arms of his nemesis.

Lenny tried to fight off his emotions and put on a phony smile as he said goodbye to the gang before they headed off in Bernie's car to pick up the remaining belongings from the guest house then take the long journey home.

Lenny shuffled sluggishly into the dining room. He immediately thanked Mike for covering for him on the ramble and apologised for oversleeping. At the lunch table, Lenny managed to fend off the inevitable questions about his time with his friends and pretended to take an interest in other discussions. He should have been starving but kept recalling Damien bragging of going *all the way* with his so called *luvver* and telling him their relationship was *past tense*. This put him off all the food that was placed in front of him.

The weather was baking hot after lunch and both Lenny and Callum were still feeling fragile from the night before for very different reasons. They carried two tables and the bingo equipment out to the centre of the ballroom ready for their afternoon session. While the two of them were on their own, Lenny took the opportunity to put his arm on Callum's shoulder and say 'CC. Thank you for getting Mike to cover the ramble I was supposed to have led then coming down to the flat to make sure I was okay'. 'To be honest, LE, when I touched your shoulder to wake you up, you were so cold that I thought you'd died!' 'I guess I must have got cold because I left the windows open all night to try to get rid of the stink of tobacco, dope, booze and three sweaty men'. Callum noted that Lenny didn't end his sentence with his now customary *Zezeze* suggesting he was sad about something. He had to bide his time before finding out what that something was because a handful of holidaymakers turned up to chat with them before the bingo was due to start.

The holidaymakers patiently waited to start playing the afternoon bingo session but the scheduled start time came and went without any more arrivals. Callum tactfully told them that there were not enough guests for the game to go ahead. They left feeling disgruntled. As Lenny helped put the equipment and tables back, he asked Callum how he'd got on staying overnight at Anne's place. 'I enjoyed myself but the whole evening was weird - we chatted, had a laugh and then they had what might be described as a night of passion – but I would still rather be with Pauline'. Lenny felt his mate was wasting time worshipping someone who was stringing him along but was in no position to give advice on relationships so kept quiet. Callum broke the silence by saying 'LE, will you be making up with Connie now that your friends have gone home?' Lenny snapped back 'Forget it CC - Connie and I are definitely *past tense* and never getting back together.' He didn't have the heart to tell Callum what had taken place between Damien and Connie, or at least what Damien said had taken place as he didn't really want to believe it himself. Lenny held back the tears by changing the subject 'I'm going to make the most of this extra time by clearing up our room as promised' Callum insisted on helping him so the rookie room-mates made their way down the hill to do it. When Lenny had dressed in the room that morning, he had been surrounded by and distracted by his hippy friends. Now, with relatively fresh eyes, he was mortified at the mess. The scrumpy container had been emptied dry. That was no surprise, but the board from Callum's monopoly game was ripped in two and debris from the game was scattered all around the room – the only items beyond furniture that were still intact appeared to be the records and the record player.

Callum couldn't help tutting as he gathered up the monopoly money but could only find two of the metal playing pieces – the racing car and top hat. This meant that quite a few were missing from the set. Before he could work out the missing items, Lenny diverted his attention by giving him a roll of Sellotape, holding the two halves of the monopoly game board together and asking him to tape over the join as a make do fix. They continued clearing up the mess and Callum saw his beloved King Kong rubber toy, or at least two bits of it. He picked up the bits and thrust them in Lenny's face, crying out 'LE, what kind of people are your so-called friends to do something as crazy as this?' Seeing King Kong's head separated from its body jogged Lenny into remembering some of the shenanigans that had occurred the previous night in the room. As memories came flooding back, he confessed all to Callum:

Lenny, Derek and Keith had left Bernie and Damien in the pub to go back to Lenny's flat. Keith started rolling yet another joint while Lenny opened the wardrobe to put his coat away. Lenny's guests saw the container of scrumpy so he was honour bound to fill a glassful for each of them. Keith took a few deep drags of the spliff and passed it to Derek for his turn. By the time it reached Lenny, Keith had downed the scrumpy in one go, opened the wardrobe and helped himself to a refill. The drink and drugs may have given Keith a sense of melancholy for his youth as he got excited when he saw Callum's monopoly game propped up alongside the scrumpy. He opened the box, laid the board out on the floor and demanded that they all play. Lenny didn't like to stop his friends from enjoying themselves and thought *what could possibly go wrong?*

The monopoly players started by each choosing their favourite playing piece for the game. Lenny picked up the small metal racing car for himself but when Keith picked up the iron Derek said he wanted it. As the two of them childishly wrestled with each other to get the metal iron, Keith had an irresistible urge to prevent Derek from getting it so gulped the iron down with a swig of scrumpy! As Keith laughed hysterically, Derek took the opportunity to grab the top hat piece to use. Lenny thought Keith was crazy enough to try to consume the rest of the monopoly pieces so hid them under his mattress. When Keith stopped laughing, he looked around for a replacement and let out an unconvincing roar as he picked up the rubber King Kong toy that Callum had proudly placed on the chest of drawers alongside the head of his bed.

The game commenced, and every time Keith threw the dice and moved his substitute piece, he let out the same silly roar. Eventually, King Kong landed on a property where he was supposed to pay a large fine. Dramatically, Keith said that King Kong was really, really, angry and, with a final roar, bit off his head! At this point, the psychedelic effects caused by the second acid hit reached their peak so the monopoly game was abandoned to allow each of them to marvel at their own drug-twisted hallucinations before they fell asleep. Keith should have had indigestion from the iron he'd consumed!

Lenny recovered the monopoly pieces from under his mattress and reunited them with the racing car and top hat before placing the box in the wardrobe. Callum had to get back up the hill to compere the Miss *Funtime* beauty competition with Mike. Lenny had the rest of the day off so completed the clean-up of the bedroom then lay on the bed thinking about the events that had unfolded over the weekend and what was left for him now. He'd lost Connie through his own stupidity; He'd played a part in pushing Callum into some sort of relationship with Anne that neither of them seemed ready for. Even Ruby had moved on and moved in with a fellow Scot from the kitchen staff. Lenny was now most definitely on his own.

When Lenny woke up, he couldn't face going up the hill for dinner so instead went into town for a bag of chips and managed to eat most of it. He then decided to drop in to *The Three Elms Inn*, reasoning that a drink, potentially in the company of colleagues from the *Seaview*, would cheer him up. He also wondered if Connie might turn up there. Even though the two of them could never again be *luvvers*, they could at least be civil with each other and maybe emerge with some sort of friendship.

Going back to the Three Elms was not the best idea for Lenny – it brought back too many memories. Their paths first crossed at the front door of the inn then, once they were seeing each other, they'd spent many happy evenings together in the bar when it was packed with people. This time it was empty apart from a creepy looking barman. Even the old lady everyone called Lucy was absent. It was too late to turn around so, without thinking, he ordered a Newcastle Brown Ale. As he sipped the froth, he regretted picking this particular drink. Its bitter taste reminded him of the previous night. It was the last drink Damien had ordered for him and his mates before his act of treachery. Once again, a girl had broken his heart. In the same way he had consoled himself after the split with Lizzie, he resolved to cheer himself up with music. Unfortunately, when he got to the juke box, he couldn't stop himself pressing buttons to songs that had more bittersweet memories for him. Eric Clapton's 'Bell Bottom Blues' reminded him of the tight flares Connie had worn the previous night, just before he lost her, and she lost herself, to his nemesis. "Ain't No Sunshine" followed. He couldn't stomach the rest of his ale so left the unfinished drink and walked out, just as Michael Jackson was singing '*Ain't no sunshine when she's gone. Only darkness every day…*'. Once back to his empty room at the flat, he immersed himself in his favourite tracks from the albums he'd brought from home. He just wished he'd brought back a Blues album.

In the days leading up to Wednesday's Cow Town Carnival, Lenny and Callum were in totally different moods. Lenny was still feeling downhearted after losing Connie and spending nights alone at the purple flat. Callum was upbeat after spending his nights in Anne's bed. All the *Purplecoats* had been tasked with recruiting teenage and twenty-something guests to participate on *Seaview*'s float for the procession through the town. With Callum's confidence soaring, he was the most successful at persuading targets to participate.

On Tuesday morning - the day before the carnival was due to take place – Kenny saw Callum hanging around in reception to talk to families who had just offloaded their offspring for either the excursion to the zoo or the magic show in the ballroom. He hoped that a mum, dad, uncle or auntie would love to take part in the carnival and wave to their kids or just be grateful to get away from them for a few hours. Kenny said 'Hey, CC – never mind all these families with kids - how you getting on recruiting volunteers for the float?' Kenny would be taking photos of *Seaview*'s participation over the whole day so had good reason to ensure it would be a success. Callum was delighted to confirm 'It's looking really good KT. I've already secured more than 50 willing volunteers …' he pointed to his brain as he continued '… through my powers of targeting and selling'. Kenny took this with a proverbial pinch of salt 'Okay CC. How have you used your powers?' 'I just tell them I'm only looking for *good looking party people* like them to *star* on *Seaview*'s float in a procession around the harbour, waving to the crowds at *Torbay's biggest carnival event of the year*. By boosting their egos, I got plenty of positive responses'. Kenny laughed and said 'Well done CC, I think you deserve some sort of sweet treat as a reward. Tell me what you fancy and I'll get it for you.' Callum salivated when confessing he had a sudden craving for a jam doughnut. Kenny wished he hadn't made the offer, as no pastry options were available in the *Seaview* shop and he hadn't seen them in any other *Funtime* holiday centre he'd visited. Like an addict trying to get a fix, Kenny was compelled to go into town straight away, just to find a shop selling jam doughnuts and bring back a few for them both to scoff.

Kenny ran down the hill to try to fulfil his mission as quickly as possible. As he reached the *Seaview*'s gates, Baz stepped out from the sentry box and raised his arms in front of Kenny. Baz of course knew Kenny as a friend as well as a colleague - he'd even taken him on a sub-aqua dive in the bay. Nonetheless, he shouted out his stock phrase 'Whoa, Man, Stop. I'm Camp Fuzz.' Kenny said 'Baz, I can't stop. I'm in a rush.' Baz ignored his urgency, continued his serious act and said 'Well man, I'll just have to issue a speeding ticket to you.' As Baz went back into his sentry box to fill in an imaginary ticket, Kenny ran off through the gates to catch up on the time he'd just wasted.

Kenny bought the last three doughnuts from a bakery in Brixham town. When he returned to the *Seaview*'s entrance gates, he saw Baz sitting in the sentry box sewing up one of his sub-aqua dive boots and cursing to himself. Out of curiosity, Kenny asked him 'What's up, Camp Fuzz?'. Baz mumbled 'That stupid bitch next door and her stupid bitch dog.' Baz was billeted in a chalet next door to Muriel - the *Seaview*'s long-standing but aging screwball nanny - and her equally mad dog. After a dive the previous day, Baz had hung his wet dive boots on the washing line between his and Muriel's chalet to get them dry. Minutes later, Muriel let her dog out to do its business on its own as she didn't want to venture out in the windy weather. The gusts blew the boots back and forth which must have fascinated the dog so much that it jumped up and sunk its teeth into one of them. It then wrenched it off the line and ran off with it still in its mouth. Baz was pretty sure that Muriel had watched the whole thing transpire and made no attempt to stop her stupid mutt. It took Baz an hour to find the dog and wrestle his boot out of its mouth, by which time its teeth had ripped the material so badly that he wasn't sure if sewing it up would work.

In sympathy, Kenny picked one of the doughnuts out of his bag and handed it to Baz to cheer him up. Baz grabbed it and stuffed it in his mouth like a chimpanzee, murmuring 'Mmm, Camp Fuzz likes doughnut!' Kenny left Baz chewing away as he continued up the hill to share the two remaining doughnuts with Callum and so complete his mission.

Baz was halfway through consuming his doughnut when a chauffeur driven Rolls Royce turned up at the gates. Despite having his mouth full and the remaining half doughnut in his right hand, Baz raised his arms in front of the car and shouted: 'Whoa, Man, Stop - I'm Camp Fuzz.' The driver pulled over and wound down his window to remonstrate with this weird looking apparition with long black hair and a drooping horseshoe moustache who dared to delay his journey. As Baz approached the car, the occupants could see that his moustache was splattered in sugar and jam. He nearly spilt what was left of the doughnut in his hand as he placed it on the car window, looked in and said to the driver 'Who's the old bird in the back?' The shocked driver took out a handkerchief and wiped off the splattered crumbs and sugar from the front of his uniform before assertively responding 'This lady is Mrs Burren' expecting a dutiful response. Baz was just about to say 'I don't care if she's the Queen of Bloody Sheba ...' but kept his thoughts to himself as he realised that a chauffeur in a flashy car suggested that the passenger might actually be someone important. The driver continued 'You had better let us through without further delay if you know what's good for you.' Rather than continue arguing with the driver, Baz stepped back and nonchalantly waved the car through, spraying sugar granules off the remains of the doughnut that was still in his hand. Mrs Burren was livid at the sheer impudence of this so-called security person and glared at him as the car sped away. She gritted her teeth while hanging on to the leather straps in the back seat of the car as it bumped up the hill toward the *Seaview*'s reception.

Callum was leaning on *Seaview*'s reception counter when Kenny walked in, handed him one of his doughnuts and said 'Here you are, CC – my mission was successful!' Callum said 'Wow, thanks, KT' and excitedly stuffed as much of the squidgy delight as he could get into his mouth. Kenny was going through his conversations with Baz when Callum happened to look outside. He noticed a man in a posh driving uniform opening the back door of a Rolls Royce to let an elegant old woman out. In a panic, Callum stuffed the rest of the doughnut in his mouth, wiped the sugar off his hands and tried to look professional as Mrs Burren walked in. Unfortunately, like Baz, remains of the doughnut could still be seen. His cheeks were bulging like a trumpeter's and his lips were covered in sugar streaked with jam. Mrs Burren stormed past Callum and went up to Jill behind the reception counter. She demanded to speak to the business manager immediately. Jill did as she was asked and Mrs Burren walked straight into his office as if it was her own. Eric Arden was initially caught by surprise as she ignored formalities and demanded that the *Purplecoat* on reception duty be reprimanded over his messy appearance and the idiot on gate security be sacked. She ended her tirade by snootily posing the question 'Does everyone eat doughnuts while on duty at this place?'

Somehow, Eric Arden calmed Mrs Burren down by persuading her to relax on his sofa while he arranged for a buffet waitress to bring in a fresh pot of tea and plate of biscuits. Mrs Burren reluctantly nibbled the end of one of the bland biscuits and said with the first glint of a smile 'Don't you have any doughnuts?' In case she wasn't joking, Eric explained that doughnuts were not in the list of items stocked for sale at *Funtime* snack bars. Mrs Burren suggested maybe they should if they were that popular. Ever the businesswoman, she'd disregarded her personal annoyance at being affronted and recognised a potential profit opportunity. Mrs Burren got Eric to immediately write an internal memo to the executives stating her idea of having a shop that just sold doughnuts in every *Funtime* holiday centre. They continued talking business for what seemed like an age until Jason arrived to give her a tour of the site. He also took the opportunity to show her *Seaview's* carnival float. It had been constructed on top of a low loader trailer to be pulled by a prime mover tractor unit. Eric Arden had negotiated a deal with a local haulage company to provide the vehicles and a driver for the day in return for *Funtime Holiday* vouchers. Mrs Burren seemed impressed but, as she would be one of the judges on the day, was unable to make a comment even if she wanted to. The centrepiece of the float was two thrones - for Mike and Jeannette – and stools for handmaidens, set underneath an arch of flowers and vines. The rest of the float was festooned with jungle-style garlands stretching all the way toward and along the edges of the float.

Eric and Jason smiled as they waved off the Rolls Royce driving Mrs Burren to continue her tour of *Funtime* holiday centres in the Torbay area. She would soon be raising hell at Warm Park in preparation for her VIP trip to the Cow Town carnival on Wednesday. As for the doughnut reprimands, Eric had words with Baz and Jason spoke to Callum but both kept their jobs and the executives had a potential gem of an idea if they had the foresight to support Mrs Burren.

To the relief of everyone involved, all the preparations for the *Seaview's* carnival float came together by Tuesday afternoon. The float looked better than anyone could have hoped for. The fancy dress boxes contained 100 male/female loin cloths plus plenty of plastic shields and spears. The *Purplecoat*s reckoned they had recruited plenty of willing volunteers so all was looking good for the following day.

The usual star of Tuesday night's cabaret act was pop singer Ray Starlight but he was still recovering from a throat infection. Jason's previous substitute - Frank Lee Magic - turned out to be Frank Lee Awful so he got a mind reading act instead. Jason hadn't seen the act before but was confident that nothing would go wrong this time as Mandy the mind reader and her assistant Boris had perfected the act over many years.

Jason enthusiastically introduced Mandy the mind reader to the *Seaview* audience as if they were old friends. Mandy didn't seem as friendly when she snatched the microphone off him. Mandy had a severe way of acting and talking, much like TV chef Fanny Craddock. Coincidentally, she treated her assistant Boris much like Fanny berated her husband Johnnie – in a terse and demanding way. Mandy explained in detail every part of her act to the audience, at least every part that she wanted them to understand. While holding up a thick black scarf above her head she said she would be blindfolded while reading the minds of volunteer members of the audience. 'In order to assure you that I cannot see through this scarf, I invite members of the audience to check it out. Please raise your hand if you would like to inspect the scarf.' A half-dozen hands were raised and Mandy continued 'Boris – come up here. When my assistant - Boris – finally gets here, he will bring the scarf to you'. Mandy seemed impatient as she sat down on a chair placed in the middle of the stage while waiting for Boris to take the scarf from her. Boris seemed agitated as took the steps down from the stage. Suddenly, the scarf slipped from his grasp and floated to the floor. He soon recovered it and continued across the ballroom floor so that the unofficial adjudicators could confirm nothing could be seen through it. Boris returned to Mandy with the scarf and she said 'Boris will now wrap the scarf tightly around my head so that it completely covers my eyes. Not that tight, you clumsy oaf – do you want my head to explode?' He raised his eyebrows at the audience which elicited a few laughs and got them on his side. Once he'd tightened the scarf to her satisfaction, she said 'Boris, are you still here in front of me?' He replied 'Yes, I am', then waved and gestured to the audience to make sure they were watching while he playfully swung his fists towards but just missing Mandy's face. She did not flinch in any way, even while the audience were once again laughing with Boris taking advantage of her temporary blindness. This proved that she could not see anything through the scarf so Boris walked away. Mandy said 'Boris, can you please stand at the bottom of the steps leading up to the stage?' He said 'I'm already there, Mandy!' This raised more laughter from the audience, but all the laughs were secretly intentional as far as Mandy and Boris were concerned. It was designed to avoid suspicion that they were in cahoots. Mandy continued 'I now invite any four volunteers from the audience to bring an item of jewellery up to the stage. They just need to concentrate hard, thinking of their jewellery item while clearly showing it to the audience. I will obviously not be able to see the item through the scarf but will read each volunteer's mind and shout out the item that I sense each one has brought up to the stage'.

Unbeknown to the audience, the trick worked as follows: Earlier in the day, Mandy and Boris set up a microphone in the dressing room and connected it to an earpiece via a small cable pinned along the floor from the dressing room to the floor beneath the chair where Mandy would be sitting on the stage. The wires were hidden underneath black tape used for the public address system. Boris intentionally distracted the audience, when he dropped the scarf and bent down to pick it up. This gave Mandy the opportunity to grab the wired earpiece off her chair, push it into her right ear then hide the wire down her back while pretending to get her hair straight. When Boris wrapped the scarf around her head, he would make sure it hid the earpiece. Boris would then line up the four volunteers at the end of the stage, look at their items close up and ask them to present them one by one to the audience, concentrate on them while Mandy read their minds then return to their seats once the items had been identified. Once inside the dressing room, he could peek through a gap in the door and use the hidden microphone to communicate each object to Mandy as each person was presenting it.

That night, the trick was going perfectly - the audience checked the scarf, Mandy got the earpiece in her ear, Boris tied the scarf firmly over it and around her head and Mandy told the audience she was sending her assistant to the dressing room to that he couldn't give her any hints. Unfortunately, she declared this before two of the volunteers had reached the steps leading up to the stage so Boris hadn't seen the items they were going up on stage with close up. He didn't expect this to be a problem as he could still peek through the gap in the door to describe each volunteer's item as they presented it to the audience. Getting sent to the dressing room early must have put Boris out of his usual rhythm as he flicked the microphone switch on before lowering the volume. Mandy winced as she was briefly deafened by the feedback then she heard her accomplice whisper 'Sorry if that was loud, ready for the first volunteer?'

Mandy asked the first volunteer to show their item to the audience while thinking about it. Volunteer number 1 walked to the centre of the stage and waved his large chunky watch to the audience. Boris peeked through the gap in the door and spoke carefully through his secret microphone 'a gentleman's large chunky watch, repeat, a gentleman's large chunky watch.' Mandy said 'I'm sensing something and hope I'm reading your mind clearly - is it a gentleman's large chunky watch?' The audience gasped and applauded. Mandy thanked the volunteer and asked him to go back to his seat.

Mandy asked the next volunteer to show their item to the audience while thinking about it. Volunteer number 2 walked to the centre of the stage, unclasped her pearl necklace and swung it around carefully to the audience. Boris peeked through the gap in the door and spoke through his microphone 'a woman is waving a pearl necklace, repeat, a woman's pearl necklace.' Mandy said 'I have the feeling that this is a woman and believe she is waving some sort of necklace. Wait, it's possibly a pearl necklace - is that correct?' The audience once again applauded to confirm that she was 100% correct.

Volunteer number 3 was next up the steps to the centre of the stage. He took his gold cigarette lighter out of his pocket and showed it to the audience. Boris peeked through the gap in the door and was relieved to just about see what it was. He spoke through his microphone 'a gentleman's gold cigarette lighter, repeat, a gentleman's gold cigarette lighter.' Mandy said 'I'm getting an excellent reading from a gentleman I believe and he is apparently waving a gentleman's gold cigarette lighter - is that correct?' The audience applauded and were now convinced she was actually reading the minds of all of the volunteers.

Mandy asked the final volunteer to show their item to the audience. Volunteer number 4 took her gold wedding ring off her finger and held it firmly as she showed it to the audience. Boris peeked through the gap in the door but a very large man was standing in front of the gap. Boris said through his secret microphone 'I can't see any of the stage because some stupid fat man is blocking my view'. Mandy got hot and bothered underneath the scarf while waiting for her assistant to find a solution. Volunteer 4 was also getting impatient waiting for the mind reader to read her mind. She was visibly concentrating hard on communicating gold wedding ring, gold wedding ring, to the mind reader. For both ladies, seconds seemed like minutes as time passed by without another word being said. Mandy broke the silence by saying 'I'm struggling to get a reading from this gentleman.' The audience laughed loudly which confirmed to Mandy that she had guessed the wrong sex. Mandy blushed and sweated under the scarf as she corrected herself but her excuse still sounded lame 'I'm sorry, this volunteer is of course a woman but sometimes minds are clouded by other thoughts so are very difficult to read. If this volunteer really concentrates on her item, I will again try to read it.' While Volunteer 4 screwed up her face straining to send a message telepathically, Boris spoke to Mandy through the secret microphone 'I'm giving up on this one. You'll have to make an excuse so we can finish the show.' Mandy was in damage limitation mode so would have preferred it if Boris had simply asked the blocker to move - the fat man might have seen through their trick but the majority of the audience would still have believed in her powers. Unfortunately, she couldn't pass on this advice to Boris as the secret communication was only one way, from his microphone to her earphone. Instead, she sounded even lamer when she said 'I'm sorry, it's very unusual but I just haven't been able to read the mind of this volunteer.' Volunteer 4 was disappointed and the fat man must have been her husband as she fell into his arms for comfort before they made their way back to their seats.

Boris dashed up onto the stage, grabbed the stage microphone from Mandy and announced 'Volunteers, please stand up… Ladies and Gentlemen, please applaud all our volunteers for bravely coming up to get their minds read.' While the audience's attention was again distracted by Boris, Mandy quickly but discreetly discarded her scarf making sure the ear-piece and wire was hidden inside it.

Now it was Jason's turn to step up to the stage and take over the microphone. In his usual professional way, he said 'Ladies and Gentlemen, I'm sure you'll all agree that reading 3 out of 4 minds is really something very special, so let's hear your appreciation for Mandy the mind reader … and her assistant Boris.' They both took a bow and sheepishly walked off the stage to the sanctuary of the dressing room. They hid there until Callum knocked on the door to tell them that the only remaining holidaymakers were too busy drinking to see them, implying it was safe to come out.

Wednesday was Callum's day off but Jason used the incident with Mrs Burren to persuade him to come up the hill that morning to help get all the volunteer guests made up and on the float. Lenny took the guests that were not interested in the carnival on a ramble to Warm Park - Jason told him to look out for their rival's float and report back on his opinion of it. Dale went off on a fishing trip with Baz that morning as they knew the seas away from Brixham harbour would be especially quiet while the carnival was taking place.

More than a hundred guests turned up in front of the *Seaview's* float, willing and excited at the thought of taking part in a unique public and historic spectacle. Mike was in charge of getting them made up and dressed to suit the theme of the float. Mike announced that he had appointed himself as jungle king and Jeannette as jungle queen then, of course, chose two of the prettiest girls to pretend to be handmaidens waiting on them.

Mike explained the whole transformation process to the volunteers and stressed that it was important all volunteers obeyed his orders throughout the day, starting immediately. They all had to be willing to go through what looked like a weird initiation ceremony in order to be transformed into jungle tribesmen and women. Firstly, they had to undress down to their swimwear. Some of the volunteers were so excited at participating and keen to be the first on the float that they lost all their inhibitions and flung off their clothes right where they stood. The next part of the preparation process was getting them tanned up. Volunteers had to queue up to a *Purplecoat* armed with a sponge and stand bare feet in a washing bowl full of black liquid. Each volunteer then had to allow the *Purplecoat* to sponge them from head to toe with the black dye until they looked the part.

The idea was that Mike, Callum, and Bill would sponge the men while Tricia, Yvonne and Jeannette would sponge the ladies. Unfortunately, the ladies queue moved a lot slower than the men's due to the spongers needing to be more delicate. This caused some of the more impatient women to jump across to the shorter queues for men. A pretty and voluptuous lady in a skimpy bikini jumped in front of Callum's queue. Without waiting to be told, she stepped into Callum's bowl and urged him to start sponging. He panicked and looked to see if one of the female *Purplecoats* should take his place but they were busier than he was. He started splashing the dye over her body, desperate to avoid touching her more personal areas. Once he'd sponged all the safe areas, he told the beauty that he was going to carefully run the sponge across her neck and shoulders. The woman raised her arms and held her long hair back with both hands to avoid it getting painted. This action caused her ample bosom to bulge out of her bikini top toward Callum. His hands were shaking as he sponged her neck and some black dye dribbled down to the top of her breasts. Ever the gentleman, Callum handed her the sponge and suggested that she might want to finish the more personal areas herself. She looked disappointed and smiled naughtily as she whispered that he should just finish the job. Luckily, Callum looked over her shoulder and noticed the man behind her was looking daggers at him. He quietly asked her if her boyfriend was waiting in the queue. As soon as she confessed that it was her husband, Callum handed him the sponge and said 'You two can paint each other while I give my arms a rest'. Bloodshed avoided; disaster averted.

As soon as volunteers were blacked up, they went for the fancy-dress items. Loin cloths were the first to be grabbed and put on over their swimwear. It didn't take long for the stock to run out. Mike had to think fast and persuaded the men who missed out to hide behind a shield. When the shields ran out, Mike took the shields off the men that already had spears and reallocated them to the skirt-less men. Once all fancy-dress stocks ran out, Mike persuaded the remaining volunteers to simply splash black dye over their swimwear or cover any embarrassment with plastic *Funtime Holidays* buckets intended to throw donations into.

The procession was a two-mile journey beginning at Furzeham Green – a large field in Higher Brixham overlooking the outer harbour and the wide sweep of the bay. The route descended down winding hills to and along the quayside in Fish Town harbour, through the centre of Brixham, then up yet more hills to the grounds of the Rugby Club in Cow Town. A temporary VIP stand had been erected half way along the route as a vantage point for invited celebrities and dignitaries to see the procession and rate each float as it passed. Points would be awarded based on strict criteria, including originality of the theme, artistry of float design and authenticity of props and costumes. Once all the floats had made it to the Rugby Club, the points would be totted up and cups awarded for Best Small and Large Children's Float and Best Small and Large Adult's Float plus Best in Show. Certificates would be awarded for runners up.

The *Seaview* set off to join the rest of the carnival floats amassing at Furzeham Green. It would only have been a mile and a half away if the driver could have taken the most direct route. Unfortunately, the low loader would have been too large to negotiate through its narrow roads, so it had to be taken along a circular route that was a mile longer. Mike packed as many volunteers as he dared onto the float. A few more squashed into the cab, much to the consternation of the driver who ended up with black dye on his clothes and passenger seat. The volunteers that missed out on getting a lift were forced to follow behind on foot - it was just as well they were fit and the weather was kind.

As the float and runners departed, Callum and Tricia were left to clear up the mess from the black dye sponging session. They did the best they could but, while carrying the bowls of dye to a drain, an inevitable trail of inky black drops was left behind them. They hoped it would wash away with the next rain shower, if not, they couldn't be held to blame because it was Mike and Jason's idea.

They checked each other out for stains from the dye they'd just plastered on the willing guests. Their legs and arms were splattered with dye but they were more concerned that dye might have sprayed onto their uniform. Callum confirmed that Tricia had miraculously avoided any stains on her uniform but she pretended dye had splashed on Callum's shirt. She kept pointing to different areas, saying 'There … There' which made him keep pulling at it to see for himself and saying 'Where … Where?' Eventually, she burst into giggles and he playfully shoved her saying she was learning from Dale how to make fun of him. She apologised and said she'd be the last person to make fun of anyone but he was such an easy target. Callum knew she was right.

As Tricia walked with Callum down the hill to the purple flat she asked 'Were you okay helping to do the sponging work on your day off?' He said 'It was a penance after Mrs Burren caught me in reception with a jam doughnut in my mouth. Nonetheless, splashing dye over guests was weirdly quite enjoyable. How did you cope with yesterday's zoo excursion?' He only asked because he noticed the coach was jam packed when she went off with the kids. She confessed unnecessarily 'Ahh. Kenny must have told you he had to take the kids into the shed where the snakes were kept because I was frightened of them'. 'The kids?' 'No silly, the snakes!' 'Oh really? Well Kenny hadn't told me anything. When did you know you had a phobia for snakes?' Tricia explained 'When I was a child, my older brother used to frighten me by saying serpents would get me if I misbehaved. I've been afraid of snakes or anything slivering ever since!'

Callum saw the subject had upset her, so, as they reached the flat, he changed the subject 'You know, I'm really looking forward to jumping in the shower and washing off all this dye'. Tricia said 'I had exactly the same thought – bagsy I go first!' Ever the gentleman, Callum let her use the bathroom first to clean up before him. In his bedroom, he carefully unpeeled his uniform, narrowly avoiding the dye stains on his arms and legs. Just as he'd wrapped a towel around his naked body, he heard a loud scream. Without knocking, Tricia burst into his bedroom also only wearing a towel. She was delirious, shouting something about nearly stepping on serpents that were writhing around in the bath. Callum thought she'd lost her mind from some type of flashback or hallucination where she believed snakes were serpents. Whatever they were, what were they doing in the bath? He sat her down on Lenny's bed and said 'Don't worry. I'll go and investigate'. Callum noticed that the door to the bathroom was shut. Did Tricia close it? He started wondering if the bathroom was haunted. He carefully opened the creaking door to the bathroom. He could certainly hear wild splashing noises inside the bathroom but what creatures were causing the din? Suddenly, he felt a nudge in his back which made him jump in the air and stumble into the bathroom. Holding back his own scream and the towel around him he looked back and saw it was Tricia that had nudged him. She apologised but said she was desperate to know what creatures were in the bath. Callum dared to look into the bath and breathed a sigh of relief as he identified the culprits. He was pretty sure they were eels, rather than serpents, but how they got there, and why they were in a bath used by most of the Purplecoats, was a mystery. Having got over their shock Tricia and Callum took it in turns to spread towels on the floor of the kitchen then wash themselves as best they could, using the sink, while the other stood guard in the corridor in case anyone else turned up.

By the time the *Seaview* float finally made it to Furzeham Green, more than twenty floats had already parked up. The marshals directed the *Seaview* float to line up behind them in readiness for the procession to start. While they waited for the off, the *Seaview* volunteers that had got a lift on the float took the opportunity to jump off and stretch their legs, while those that had walked or jogged behind the float were grateful to swap places with them, albeit briefly.

Kenny decided to walk up and down the line to take photos and check out the other floats for comparison. Jeannette got up from her throne to chat with the volunteers but Mike remained on his. He was feeling uncomfortable in his own skin, conscious that his safari suit was way too tight, showing off the additional fat he'd gained since the suit had been made for him a few weeks earlier. Apart from his bulging belly, he was very pleased with himself. He had only seen a few of the opposition creations as they joined the queue but was confident that the *Seaview* float would take the top awards - for the Large Adult's Float and Best in Show. He smiled as he imagined the extra kudos the *Seaview* float would get from *Funtime* executives when they beat local rivals Warm Park. More importantly, he alone would be singled out with special praise for his management of the float and all its volunteers.

Jeannette snapped Mike out of his dreams by suggesting that now would be a good time to provide some sustenance to the volunteers. He agreed and opened a wooden compartment between their thrones. It contained over one hundred packed lunches that had been prepared for them by the *Seaview*'s kitchen. The problem was that there were more than a hundred volunteers, so, when the packed lunches were handed out, there was a lot of pushing and jostling amongst the *Seaview* volunteers. Kenny returned from his recce just in time to see jungle warriors crowding around Jeannette and Mike, desperately ripping apart packed lunches, fighting over whatever they could get their hands on and trying to stop anyone else taking it off them. The dominant ones were scoffing rolls and crisps and guzzling fizzy drinks, throwing to the ground unwanted items and packaging. Kenny managed to pick up a wrapped cheese roll, a scuffed but intact hard-boiled egg and a bottle of lemonade that had been rejected or mislaid after an altercation. He chomped his way through the egg and roll before anyone could grab it off him. He was just about to wash the food down with a sip of lemonade when Mike went up to him, asking how he'd got on with his spying mission. Before Kenny could empty his mouth to respond, Mike boldly said 'I bet there weren't any floats anywhere near as good as ours'. Kenny didn't want to burst his bubble but suggested 'You'd best take a look yourself but be sure to include the Warm Park float'. Mike was a little shaken by Kenny's response so told Jeannette 'Hold the fort, or should that be *hold the float*, while I take a quick look at the opposition.' He never could deliver a funny line.

Mike walked along the line of floats, bulging out of his safari suit front and back. He thought that the other floats were sweet or clever but none had the professional look that the *Seaview* float had. At least none did until he saw the Warm Park float. He was amazed and a little dismayed that their theme was the extremely popular Diddymen. The real-life Ken Dodd himself was in pride of place waving his tickling sticks from a raised platform at the front of the float. He was flanked by two of his loyal Diddymen - Mick the Marmaliser and Hamish McDiddy - and twenty-odd Diddymen, presumably children of Warm Park guests. Mike recognised two Warm Park *Purplecoat*s, despite them being disguised with face make up and goofy teeth. They were appropriately the shortest in their team and were supervising the kids as they ran excitedly up and down the float. Everyone wore authentic-looking Diddy outfits that included a variety of the distinctive tall hats and clothes padded around the belly to emphasise the traditional paunch. Mike was jealous of the costume, especially as he could easily have played a part on this float without needing any padding.

Mike returned to the *Seaview* float, somewhat crestfallen. Jeannette asked how he'd got on but, just as he was about to tell her, he was distracted by noise and movement at the front of the queue. Earlier in the day, Bernard Bresslaw had officially started the carnival proceedings by opening the funfair in the adjoining field. Now, he was walking toward the head of the queue of floats with other celebrities and dignitaries. Even though a crowd of admirers were surrounding them, Mike could just see Mrs Burren amongst the VIPs, talking to someone he half recognised as an actor in the popular soap opera called Crossroads.

Another introduction and speech followed that was indecipherable from where the *Seaview* float was located near the back of the cortege but Mike did see what happened next. Bernard Bresslaw was handed a green motor racing flag and, after a few more indecipherable words, he waved it in a swift downward movement to signify that the procession could begin its journey.

The brass band started playing while Mr Bresslaw was immediately hurried away in a limousine along with the other celebrities and dignitaries. They would soon take their places in the VIP stand so that they could judge the floats as they passed by.

The noise of the brass band signified to the rest of the cortege that the procession had begun. An old Bentley led the way, pulling along a small trailer stacked with straw bales on which were sat the Mayor of Cow Town and his colloquially-named Lady Muck. The car and the trailer were festooned with brightly coloured garlands and the green and white flag of the ceremonial county of Devon, also called St Petroc's Cross. A float carrying the beauty queens was next, followed by a marching band of young girls called Torbay Tigerettes. They trooped and twirled their batons to the beat of the brass band that followed immediately behind them. The Brixham Girl Guides float had an Olympic theme then there were floats from other clubs, schools, churches and local businesses including butchers, bakers and candlestick makers. Adults on horses, children on ponies. Float designs and fancy dress on varying themes and of course the two *Funtime Holidays* floats.

The procession's sudden departure caught some of the cortege off guard. None more so than the Seaview float. Most of the volunteers who had missed out on a packed lunch, or didn't like the meagre offerings, had drifted over to the fair to get something else to eat. Luckily the floats were moving forward at a walking pace and the Seaview float was near the back of the procession so the Seaview volunteers that had gone AWOL managed to catch up with their float before too many bystanders saw them. For those that did, it must have made for a confusing sight to see cannibals running past unrelated floats carrying candy floss or toffee apples in their hands!

Service vehicles were slotted in between floats and they all had their lights flashing and made as much noise as they could. The tribesmen on *Seaview*'s jungle float jumped out of their fake tanned skin when the Fire engine behind them started ringing and hooting. Elsewhere in the procession, ambulance sirens and police bells could be heard bleeping and ringing. The cacophony added to the excitement as the procession slowly negotiated the steep and narrow streets down toward the harbour. Kenny jumped on and off the float as best he could to take photos of the tribespeople on board, the volunteers and the onlookers enjoying the day. He expected bumper sales once his photos were developed and displayed in the photo shop in a few days' time.

The *Seaview* float was certainly a unique and impressive sight. As jungle king and queen, Mike and Jeannette sat proudly on their thrones, surrounded by the handmaidens. The more impressive looking tribespeople were sat on the edges of the float like guards. The rest of the volunteers marched or jogged alongside or behind the float, waving their Funtime Holidays buckets to collect donations from the ever-growing crowd of onlookers.

The cortege passed through the harbour quayside and continued through the centre of Brixham. The whole area was buzzing with people enjoying the spectacle, all brightly illuminated under the blazing sun. The participants in the procession waved to the excited crowd on both sides of the road. The bystanders applauded, waved back and threw or dropped plenty of money into the charity buckets.

Huge cheers went out when onlookers recognised Ken Dodd at the helm of Warm Park's float, waving his tickling sticks toward his Diddymen and the crowd like an Arthurian wizard. He danced and mimed to the Diddymen songs being played from a cassette in the cab. 'We Are The Diddymen' and 'Doddy's Diddy Party' were repeatedly played as well as 'Diddicombe Fair' - Ken Dodd's parody of the Devon folk song 'Widdicombe Fair' that featured a chorus by the Diddymen and refrain naming 'Old dodgy Doddy and all' instead of 'Uncle Tom Cobbleigh and all.'

The themes of some other floats were also based on TV programs such as Doctor Who and Sale of the Century. In addition to the *Seaview*'s take on Carry on Up the Jungle, other popular film themes included Seven Brides for Seven Brothers and The Railway Children.

Other floats presented fashion trends through the ages including hippy clothes, miniskirts and hot pants. A Guide Dogs for The Blind float carefully followed courageous beneficiaries with white-sticks as they were helped along the way by their obedient pooches and staff members. The Beatles song 'Octopus' Garden' was being played from a float full of papier-mâché underwater creatures. Another float depicting a Teddy Bears Picnic had a sign above the rear number plate with the words 'Have You Seen My Bear Behind?!'

Midway along the main thoroughfare called Bolton Street, Jeannette saw ahead of them the stand where their float would be ranked by the VIPs. She warned Mike and the two of them quickly stirred up their volunteers by shouting out mock commands to encourage them to raise their energy levels and put on an exciting show for the judges. It was the hottest day of the year thus far so all of the stripy black tribespeople were glad to be scantily clad while dancing wildly on and around the float, like they might imagine jungle tribespeople would do.

As key donator and business Guest of Honour, Mrs Burren sat in the front row of the VIP stand. Bernard Bresslaw - looking twice her size - was sat one side of her along with the Mayor of Cow Town. Warm Park's Business Manager was the other side of her.

Mike dreamed that one day he might be important enough to be in a VIP stand. He watched the judges intently, as they marked the *Seaview* presentation. They seemed impressed and wrote comments on their clipboards as they privately awarded their points. Plenty of thoughts were going through Mike's mind regarding the points they might be inclined to give. Surely Bernard Bresslaw would recognise and acknowledge the float's homage to the film he starred in and give it a high score. He then wondered if the points Mrs Burren gave for either or both Funtime Holidays floats would be allowed to be included in the final tot up. More importantly, would Warm Park's Business Manager be allowed to give points for his own float? Surely not, as it wouldn't be fair, especially as he would be looking for every opportunity to show Warm Park as the most professional holiday centre in the Torbay area, to the detriment of the *Seaview* - its nearest rival.

The procession took hours to snake through the narrow streets, trying to keep a reasonable walking pace and only stopping when encountering vehicles trying to get past them from the opposite direction. Most drivers saw sense and turned back on themselves but a few inconsiderate ones tried to carry on against the tide. They ended up being stuck for more than an hour while the whole procession marched past them. A substantial delay ensued when an old and unsteady driver took ages to reverse her car around a sharp corner. She dented the side of a van parked there and words, as well as details, were exchanged while the procession squeezed past the scene. Another delay was when a horse did a poo in the centre of town. The bystanders gave out an ironic cheer until they choked as the smell hit them. All the vehicles, floats and entertainers that followed the pony had to take evasive action to avoid the mess.

Back at the purple flat, Callum had the rest of the day off so took the opportunity for an afternoon siesta rather than go down to see the procession. A number of times he vaguely heard more noises coming from the bathroom but assumed the eels he'd seen in the bath were getting frisky or dying. He didn't want to check either possibility so ignored the continuing swishes and bangs and fell back asleep each time.

The cacophony that had been exciting for the float volunteers at the start of the journey became a real headache by the end of it and most of them were flagging by the time the procession reached the Rugby Club. While the *Seaview* float waited for the marshals to get them parked up, Mike was still mulling over the unfair advantage of Warm Park's Business Manager on awarding points for the best floats – he would naturally choose his own and Mrs Burren might then be persuaded to follow suit.

It took another hour for the rest of the cortege to squeeze into the available space, by which time the sun had started to set. Finally, the loudspeaker crackled with static before Bernard Bresslaw was yet again introduced and applauded by the large crowd of participants. He took to the microphone, thanking the mayor and organisers for a fantastic day, then tantalised his audience by mentioning that the judges were completing their deliberations and about to announce the winners of each of the float categories. Mike pushed his way to the front of the crowd, hoping to be called up to accept an award, but less confident than he'd been before he'd seen Warm Park's float, the famous celebrity starring on it and the potential for bias from Warm Park's manager and Funtime's executive staying as his VIP guest.

Mike was not at all surprised when Warm Park won the top awards for the Large Adult's Float plus the Best in Show. Some consolation for Mike was that the *Seaview* holiday centre was awarded second place in both cases. As Mike went up to collect his Best in Show certificate, the announcer pointed out that second place was quite an achievement when considering this was the first year the *Seaview* had entered. Knowing that Mrs Burren would hear it, Mike grabbed hold of the microphone, pretended to be respectful rather than resentful when he congratulated Warm Park then pretended to be appreciative when thanking everyone that had worked on the *Seaview* float, especially his jungle volunteers.

Kenny stood alongside the local newspaper reporters, taking photos of the winners holding their cups in front of their floats with the VIPs somewhat blocking the view. Mrs Burren was smiling which was unusual and disconcerting but she was clearly delighted that the two *Funtime* floats had been placed first and second in the top categories.

Once the sun had disappeared from view, the temperature dropped quickly and many of the scantily clad jungle tribesmen were feeling the cold. They asked Mike if they could use the showers at the Rugby Club to warm up under the hot water and wash off the dye that remained in random blotches over their skin. Mike sent Jeannette off to check but she confirmed that the club's changing rooms were out of bounds. Mike realised they needed to be taken back to the *Seaview* quickly before hypothermia set in. Unfortunately, their float happened to be trapped in the middle of other floats whose owners had disappeared. The only thing that could make this predicament worse was if Mrs Burren found out how badly he had failed to plan this part of the day. Thankfully, she was busy socializing with the other VIPs but how long would his luck last for? Mike had no idea what to do and could just imagine the headline: 'A hundred holidaymakers freeze to death on a *Funtime* carnival float!'

Kenny came up with a solution. He happened to see Dale and Baz in the crowd and asked them if they could ferry volunteers back to the Seaview. They said they were too busy doing something else but he persuaded them to drop him off there so that he could get other drivers to help.

Kenny was glad Baz drove at breakneck speed to the *Seaview* because his van was even smellier than usual after his fishing trip with Dale. He went straight to reception and, after Jill choked on the smell, got his girlfriend to help him recruit drivers.

For the shivering tribespeople marooned at the Rugby Club, it must have seemed like an eternity but within 20 minutes Kenny and Jill managed to get the *Seaview*'s minibus, staff vehicles and a dozen more cars to pick up the coldest volunteers in the spirit of Dunkirk. The drivers brought with them blankets from the laundry to wrap around the tribespeople to warm them up and avoid getting black dye on the upholstery of the vehicles returning them to the *Seaview*. Mike and Jeannette allocated vehicles and blankets to those who needed them most and, in scenes reminiscent of the sinking of the Titanic, it was women and children first to get driven back to the *Seaview*.

It took around a dozen round trips by all the rescue vehicles for the coldest volunteers to be shuttled up to the *Seaview*, by which time Mike and Jeannette had managed to get the jungle float manoeuvred out of the jam. The more macho or hot-blooded volunteers were happy to go back on the float. After dropping off Mike and Jeannette at the purple flat, all of the tribe got safely back to the *Seaview* to wash and change then regroup in the dining room to eat whatever food was left.

That evening, Tricia and Lenny were helping Jason at the Empire Cigarettes Olympics evening when Mike and Jeannette turned up, apologising for being late but said they had to take it in turns to shower and wash off the dye before grabbing some food in the dining room. Tricia said 'Didn't you see the serpents in the bath?' Like Jason, they had no idea what she was talking about and wondered if she was making a silly joke. Mike did admit that he noticed dirty green and greasy slime along the base of the bath when he stepped in to shower and, when he tried to wipe it off with a towel it had a horrible fishy smell. Jason assumed that one of the girls had used too much bath oil or spilled make up and made a point of looking at them as he said 'Dale and I always make sure the upstairs bathroom we share is spotless after we use it. You lot should all do the same with the downstairs bathroom'.

[*Playlist* Track: *"The Carnival Is Over"* – The Seekers]

During breakfast the morning after the Carnival, Jill Tully went up to Jason and Mike while they were still eating to tell them that they'd been summoned to Eric Arden's office to review the previous day's events. They thought they were going to get congratulated by their business manager for being awarded second best float, but, instead of praising them, Eric said he'd heard that the day was a disaster that could have ended up as a catastrophe: A hundred guests nearly froze to death on the carnival float; the kitchen staff and waitresses had to work extra hours because all the float volunteers were late returning after being stranded at the Rugby Club; and; the cleaning ladies had to clear up black dye in dozens of chalets. Eric had been forced to dip into the *Seaview*'s working capital to fund urgent replacements for bedding and blankets that were so badly stained that they had to be thrown away.

Jason wasn't taking criticism lying down. He responded with a long speech, putting a positive spin on how well the day had gone; praising Mike for doing a sterling job managing the float and a hundred volunteers; getting them all back safely after being faced with an unfortunate predicament following a number of factors that could not have been foreseen, including an error by the marshals at the Rugby Club in directing the float into an area that blocked it in. Jason ended his spiel by emphasising that none of the guests required hospital treatment and most, if not all of them, thoroughly enjoyed themselves. Crucially, Mrs Burren no less, was very impressed that *Seaview*'s first float just missed out on being awarded the best float. The reasons why the Warm Park float won was because their manager was one of the judges and he spent more than the Seaview to get a much-loved star on their float. Eric sensed that the last point was directed at himself for cutting corners. He rolled his eyes in submission and let Jason and Mike go after insisting that they write up a list of lessons learnt - the first one being never use black dye again!

That afternoon, Kenny was approaching the security hut when he caught a strong fishy aroma that he recognised. It was similar to the whiff he smelled when Baz gave him a lift in his van the previous night. Peering into the hut, he saw Baz sat with a large bowl on his lap spooning something gooey up to his lips. When Camp Fuzz saw him, he picked up a metal mug from the wooden shelf and said 'Yo Kenny, want a cupful of freshly caught jellied eels?' Kenny declined the offer after seeing the state of the cup in addition to the half-sucked bones and jelly dripping down through Baz's moustache back into his bowl. After spitting out a particularly large bone, Baz apologised that he couldn't help out with the ferrying of float volunteers the previous night. Kenny cheekily said 'Tell me I'm being nosey if you like but what did you have to do that was more important?' Baz said 'I'll tell you if you promise to keep it a secret'. Ken said 'Okay. Fire away.' Baz naively believed him and explained: 'Dale and me went fishing for eels that morning and filled a damp sack with our catch. We took the eels to the fishmonger's shop but the owner – who we always call *Mister Fish* - was out driving his van on the carnival procession. Dale suggested we take the eels to the purple flat and immerse 'em in the kitchen sink temporary-like until we could get *Mister Fish* to pick 'em up. He had a bath fitted in the back of his van to drop 'em into. Trouble was, the sinks in the kitchen and bathroom were too small so we decided to leave the eels in the bath then catch up with *Mister Fish* at the rugby club. We found him and he agreed to follow us back in 'is van. We were just about to leave when you turned up asking for a lift. Dale didn't want any of the *Purplecoats* to know we'd used their bath so *Mister Fish* had to follow behind us while we dropped you off then return down the hill to the purple flat. *Mister Fish* helped us move the eels from the bath into his van then got 'em cooked and jellified overnight. Let me know if you want a bowl for yourself'. Kenny said 'How many bowls did *Mister Fish* manage to fill?' 'Seven! Me and Dale are eating a bowl each today while they're fresh, then Dale bribed one of the chefs with a bowl of eels to get him to store our remaining four bowls in the camp fridge'.

Some *Purplecoat* tasks were exciting or good fun but many were tedious. Since Dale found out that Lenny, not Callum, was the Jack the lad in Biddy's profile, he looked for ways to get at him. One surefire way was to order him to umpire the Junior Tennis tournament matches. Lenny hated this task. There was no umpire's chair so he'd be stood alongside the net leaning against the court fence for hours - this left him with a mesh tattoo on his back. Then there would be arguments over whether the ball landed in or out of the court. The complaints were not so much from the players, more from their parents who were overzealous at pushing for their kids to win at any cost. Lenny had no help so had to bite his lip and politely ask the complainers if they'd like to be line judges. They always declined. After a particularly fractious game under the blazing sun, Lenny moved on to another tedious task - supervising an adult's trampoline session. He had been sweltering all afternoon and the sweat made his eyes sting as he squinted at two middle-aged couples acting like kids on the trampoline. They giggled and goaded each other to bounce higher and higher then made silly gestures while they floated in the air. Guests were allowed to bounce off their hands and knees on the trampoline as well as their feet, but, if they tried to do something more dangerous like a somersault, Lenny had to tell them to stop.

Callum turned up to keep Lenny company but his mate was still feeling depressed about Connie. Lenny made this obvious when, at one point, he suggested the movements of the trampoline jumpers were a metaphor for the ups and downs of his love life!

The middle-aged couples soon ran out of steam, got off the trampoline and put their shoes back on. A gang of excited teenagers had been waiting at the gate and they ran in to take over, almost knocking over the oldens as they were leaving the enclosure. Lenny stopped them from jumping onto the trampoline until they'd all taken their shoes off. When he turned around to resume his conversation, Callum was nowhere to be seen. Lenny assumed even Callum couldn't stand his company. He was proved wrong however when, just a few minutes later, he saw his mate returning with a smile on his face and concealing something in both of his hands. In an act of kindness, Callum had gone to the café and purchased two midnight mint choc ices to share with his pal in an attempt to brighten his mood. The choc ices were freezing his hands so he jogged back to the trampoline area, expecting to see Lenny's face light up when he realised what a generous friend he was. Callum joyfully handed one of the choc ices over and said 'Here you are LE – this'll cheer you up!' Lenny looked at the generous and thoughtful treat and, instead of being thankful, bluntly said 'I don't like midnight mint' before handing it back. Callum had finally had enough of Lenny's self-pity and instinctively jammed the still-wrapped choc ice into his pal's gaping mouth. The teenagers on the trampoline and other guests who saw this happen laughed hysterically. They all thought this was another of those scenes that *Purplecoat*s were prone to act out to entertain their guests.

Lenny knew he'd gone too far and, once he'd pulled the squashed choc ice out of his mouth, apologised to Callum for not appreciating his kindness. As he ate the melting misshaped choc ice, he added that the silliest part of his bad reaction was that he really liked midnight mint and they both said *Oomballah*!

The choc ice incident finally persuaded Lenny to move on after Connie. He recalled the many times he took a corner too fast on his motorbike and fell off after sliding into the kerb. He simply dusted himself down and got straight back on the bike to continue his journey. The main benefit from being a free man now was that he could make the most of the rest of the season and recommence with renewed vigour his mission to bed as many girls as possible. He could also test out the tips about erogenous zones that the Irish girls had told him about. As Mick Jagger of the Rolling Stones once sang 'You can't always get what you want. But if you try sometime. You'll find. You get what you need.'

Dale developed a deep bronze sun tan that was the envy of holidaymakers and colleagues, especially the kitchen lads who were cooped up in front of hot and smelly ovens and washers for most of the day. One afternoon, Terry - a kitchen porter and one of Tommy's gang - saw Dale talking to Lenny while he was sunbathing on a relatively private lawn behind the TV room. Terry took the initiative and went up to Dale, asking him how he got such a good tan. Dale couldn't resist the opportunity to have a laugh at someone else's expense and said that his family had passed down the secret of developing a fantastic tan. Terry asked what the secret was. Dale repeated that it was a secret but he'd be willing to divulge what it was for just a pound. Lenny was too wily to fall for Dale's story but Terry was hooked and handed over the only note he had left from his meagre wages. It meant that he wouldn't be able to afford his usual scrumpy treat that night but it would be worth it to get a nice tan and attract a girl he desperately wanted to go with … or any girl really. Dale slowly scrutinised and folded the note to continue teasing his victim before placing it in his pocket and putting on a poker face. Terry couldn't stand the suspense any longer and blurted out 'So what's the secret?' Dale pretended he'd forgot that Terry was waiting for the answer but he'd had enough fun by now so slowly spilled the beans. He said that the secret passed down through the family was a surprising ingredient mixed in to the sun tan lotion. Dale could see that Terry was now getting annoyed with his stalling tactics so put him out of his misery by whispering in his ear that the secret ingredient was Salad Cream. Terry looked shocked until Dale added 'I told you it was surprising.' Lenny pretended not to hear and hid his disbelief but Terry fell for the whole story.

Terry stole a couple of bottles of salad cream from the kitchen stores and mixed it in a bowl with what was left of an old bottle of sun tan lotion. His next day off was a scorcher so he splashed the concoction all over his face and as much of his body as he could lawfully expose. After about four hours of intense heat under the sun, his shoulders were burning red. He assumed this was just part of the tanning process and the pain would be worth it once his skin turned chocolate brown. Tommy and his gang turned up after their shift and laughed at him mercilessly because he looked as red as a lobster. His room-mate warned him that he should watch he doesn't get sunburnt. Terry ignored all the signs and warnings, smirking to himself as he thought 'they just don't understand the secret ingredient.' That evening, he had a splitting headache and felt dizzy and nauseous, his skin was burning yet he felt ice cold. He took himself to bed but continued shivering and shaking all through the night. By the next morning, his throat was desert dry and voice croaking. He struggled to get out of bed and drag himself to the toilet. After being sick, he couldn't physically get dressed, let alone make it to work. His room-mate fetched the nurse who checked his temperature and confirmed he had second degree burns and sunstroke. She gave him some skin cream and muscle relaxant tablets and told him to keep as cool as possible, drink plenty of cold water and stay away from alcohol and the sun for at least a week.

Terry was really angry that Dale had clearly tricked him but was more annoyed with his own stupidity for believing Dale's story. When he told his gang how he felt, Tommy vowed that he would make one of these *Purplecoats* pay for making a fool of him. It sounded like he was saying this in sympathy for his most loyal follower but it was really because he enjoyed bearing a grudge and was always up for a fight.

Callum was nearing the end if his Saturday shift at Paignton station. He'd met plenty of guests as they arrived and ensured they got on the connecting train to Churston, where a minibus was waiting to transport them on the final leg of their journey to the *Seaview*. When both trains had departed, the station became eerily quiet. It would be at least another 20 minutes before the next trainload of holidaymakers would arrive so Callum sat on a platform bench under the late morning sun and made the most of the relative peace. He closed his eyes and thought about how his love interests had ended so suddenly: Hazel had been transferred to a *Funtime* holiday centre in Somerset when she was promoted, then, last night his relationship with Anne ended when they both admitted they could not commit to anything formal.

Callum's thoughts once again returned to Pauline and he dozed off, dreaming about finally bedding her. Just as the dream started to get steamy, he was rudely interrupted by a familiar voice echoing from the entrance to the platform 'Wake up, sleepyhead - you're supposed to be on duty!' Frustrated by the untimely interruption, he slowly opened his eyes and said 'Oh, hi Jackie!' by which time she had already plonked herself down alongside him.

While waiting for the next train to arrive, they got into a light-hearted conversation about the weather, life at the *Seaview* and general gossip. Jackie mentioned that she was thinking of escaping the dining room and becoming a children's nanny. Callum didn't read the signals that she was waiting for his reaction or opinion. He also barely noticed that she was smiling and keeping her eyes fixed on him even when she wasn't talking. A train arrived from London so Callum jumped off the bench and met the guests as they stepped off the train. Jackie sat patiently watching Callum direct them to the platform for the connecting train. She seemed happy just to hang around with Callum but she didn't give any reason why she was there and he didn't think to ask.

Eventually, the last scheduled train of his shift arrived. No guests got off so Callum's work was done. He and Jackie walked round to the platform for the connecting train to Churston but the station porter came up to them with bad news. He advised that there would likely be a long delay because the maintenance engineers had uncovered a mechanical fault on the steam engine scheduled to take them on the Kingswear line. Worse still, an alternative diesel engine would not be available to take over that service for some hours. He suggested they would be better off catching a bus back to Brixham.

As they reached the corner of the main road on their way to the bus stop, the traffic lights turned to red and an estate car stopped. The driver wound down his window and shouted out 'Hey Callum!' Callum was thinking that this seemed to be a day of coincidences as he recognised the driver as being Tony Garner - the leader of the big band at the *Seaview*. Tony said: 'Need a lift back?' Ever the gentleman, Callum answered 'Yes, please if you can take us both' and opened the door for Jackie to jump into the front passenger seat while he got in the back seat, just as the lights turned green.

On the journey around the bay, Tony mentioned he just happened to be driving through Paignton on his way back to the *Seaview* after meeting Tricia's boyfriend - Geoff – at the hotel he worked in. He divulged that he'd asked Geoff if he wanted to join his big band to be nearer to Tricia, but Geoff said he didn't want to let his bandmates down. Tony speculated that Geoff was probably on a contract earning far more than Funtime could afford to pay him. Tony continued chatting with Jackie and forgot that Callum was in the back seat. Callum didn't mind as he once again closed his eyes and caught up with the dream of Pauline that he'd been deprived of earlier. Jackie's laughter woke him up as the car started ascending the hills through Brixham. It was just in time to ask Tony if he'd mind dropping him off at the purple flat. Callum was still a bit groggy as he got out of the car and meekly waved toward Jackie as the car sped off and through the *Seaview*'s entrance gates.

Lenny was flat out on his bed reading the liner notes on one of his albums when Callum walked in to their shared bedroom. Callum told him about Jackie visiting him at the station, the train breakdown, Tony giving them a lift back in double quick time, dropping him off at the flat and continuing up the hill with Jackie. Lenny put the album down and shook his head at Callum. He said he couldn't believe what he was hearing and told Callum in no uncertain terms that he was naïve, stupid or both. Didn't he realise Jackie had gone out of her way to get to know him? Lenny doused petrol on the flames by adding that, if a girl had shown that type of interest in him, he would have immediately taken the initiative by suggesting they go straight back to her chalet or his flat, and kick out any roommates, if necessary, just to see how far things would go. By failing to respond to Jackie's interest, he'd treated her like any other work colleague instead of a potential girlfriend and probably ruined any chances of taking it further. Callum made up the excuse that he thought she would be worried about being late for her next shift - that's why he didn't invite her back to the purple flat. Nonetheless, he took on board what Lenny said and decided to show more interest in Jackie and give her the respect she was due.

That evening in the ballroom, all the *Purplecoat*s were getting ready to be introduced in front of a new batch of holidaymakers, at least all but one of the team. Lenny hadn't been seen for almost half an hour and Jason was getting concerned that he'd turn up too late for the line-up. He would be livid if any of his team missed their introduction and he had to make up a story as to why they were indisposed. Callum remembered seeing Lenny leave the building with a new arrival so decided to go search for him in that direction. His sixth sense led him to the private lawn behind the TV room where Dale sunbathed and, sure enough, Lenny was there, lying on the ground with a half-dressed girl. He shouted 'LE, you better stop what you're doing and get back to the ballroom cos Jason is about to do the introductions!' After giving a quick peck on the cheek to the embarrassed girl, Lenny ran back with Callum and they made it to the ballroom just in time to join the rest of the team and march onto the stage. When Jason asked where he'd been, Lenny said he'd lost track of time while giving directions to a demanding guest. That was true, but not in the way he put it across! Callum's intervention had once again saved Lenny's life, or at least his job this time.

Later that evening, Lenny noticed Callum looking a little sad and deep in thought so suggested they get away from the loud music for a minute and have a smoke break outside the stage door. It was dark and quiet enough for a heart-to-heart chat. As they lit up, Callum said Lenny was dead right about him screwing up his chances of romance. For starters, Callum admitted that he must have upset Jackie's feelings as she practically ignored him when he just tried to talk to her at the bar. Pauline was nearby so he asked her if Jackie was okay. Pauline told him Jackie was more than fine. In fact, she had just started dating Eric Arden's nephew, Samuel, after he had persuaded his uncle and auntie to take her on as a nanny to their baby boy. Muriel had been their trusted family nanny for a few years but one day they returned home to find their new baby crying its head off while Nanny Muriel was taking her dog for a walk. They decided to replace her for the younger, fitter and certainly more reliable Jackie. They told Muriel they were releasing her from family responsibilities simply to allow her to spend more time in her other roles looking after the children of *Seaview* guests. Jackie would no longer be a waitress but would now be mixing in higher circles.

Callum admitted that his feelings for Pauline had stopped him committing to meaningful relationships elsewhere. Callum was sure that Pauline coveted his friendship, but she had consistently stated she wasn't interested in taking it further as she wouldn't cheat on her boyfriend, even though he worked at another holiday centre. She laughed but didn't comment when Callum said that, if he had been her boyfriend, he would never have let her out of his sight for one minute, let alone sign up for a whole summer season hundreds of miles away from her.

As far as Lenny was concerned, Callum's infatuation with Pauline was like a worn-out record with the needle stuck so he swiftly changed the subject: 'Thanks for coming to get me when I went AWOL. You risked your own skin to get me back in time for the introductions'. Callum said 'We certainly cut it fine there, LE. I was nearly giving up the search when I found you with that girl. I don't remember seeing her before.' Lenny replied 'Neither had I. She'd only just arrived but she was insistent we get to know each other straight away!'

Lenny kept the mood light by telling Callum what a great time he was having now that he had started playing the field again without any commitments. 'The uniform seems to have magic powers as if we're pop stars and the love cycle of courtship found in the outside world is speeded up here. Guests are only here for a week or two so what have they got to lose but their inhibitions! Just think about how many different types of reasons there are to *Pull a Purplecoat.'* They took it in turns to list some: 'Girls simply wanting to have sex with a *Purplecoat'.* 'Girls wanting to brag about *Pulling a Purplecoat'.* 'Girls on their first holiday without their parents'. 'Girls wanting a three way with their girlfriends'. 'Single women looking for a younger man'. 'Married women looking for a secret fling'. 'Married women looking for a fling in front of their husbands'. 'Men wanting *Purplecoats* to have sex with their partners in private'. 'Men wanting *Purplecoats* to have sex with their partners while they watch'. 'Men wanting *Purplecoats* to have sex with their partners *and* themselves in a three way'. As Lenny and Callum were laughing about the possible scenarios, a gang of kitchen lads walked up. Kitchen staff often came to this door to peek in at the revelry and curse at the good time the *Purplecoats* were having. Even though it was dark, one of the gang was unmistakably Terry. He still shone bright red like a hazard warning beacon after falling for Dale's salad cream quick tan story. Tommy was, as ever, the leader and he had a larger than usual chip on his shoulder since Judy had left him and gone back to Ivybridge with Connie's brother Nick. He was clearly on the lookout to bully anyone who crossed his path and, after Dale had fooled Terry into getting sunburnt, a *Purplecoat* would be ideal.

Tommy said to Callum 'Were you taking the piss out of us when you were laughing?' Callum thought it probably wasn't a good idea to say exactly what they were laughing about so meekly said 'No. Not at all.' Tommy noticed the cigarette packet in Callum's hand and said 'Give me those.' Tommy went to take the cigarette packet but Lenny grabbed it first and said 'Callum can't hand the packet over as it belongs to our boss and he's got to give it back with no fags missing.' Callum knew Lenny had made the story up but Tommy wasn't so sure and snarled 'You two are *the fags*. Are you looking for a fight, purple pussies?' Before they could respond, he continued: 'You *Purplecoats* are so full of it. You look down on us kitchen lads and you're not content with screwing holidaymakers so you screw around with *our* waitresses.' By saying '*our* waitresses' Tommy revealed that he thought kitchen lads should have free reign of all the waitresses while Purplecoats limit their relationships to guests only.

Lenny also wondered if Tommy had heard rumours that he had dumped Ruby and Connie after having his wicked way with both of them. That rumour was only partly true but only Lenny and Connie knew this. Lenny stayed calm and remembered Connie telling him Tommy had been in a fight with Nick so he was probably already on a warning from management. With this in mind, Lenny said 'Hang on Tommy, I know you'd like to hit us and you'd probably beat us in a fight but what good would it do you? Actions have consequences so, if the management find out you've hit a *Purplecoat* you'll probably be sacked, especially if they couldn't do their job. That wouldn't achieve anything, would it?' Lenny decided not to mention Nick's name in case it hit a nerve but Tommy must have been thinking about that fight when Lenny continued, trying to sound as sincere as he could: 'Instead of hating Purplecoats, why don't you apply to be one? I'm sure that, with your looks and a positive approach, you'd get a role where you can enjoy the benefits you think we take for granted.' Tommy was momentarily confused and persuaded in equal measure. Before he could think about a reply, Lenny stubbed what was left of his cigarette on the path between them and said 'We've got to get back to work now but have a good think about applying.' Callum followed Lenny's lead as he opened the stage door and returned to the ballroom. After he closed the stage door on the gang, Callum said 'LE, I'm amazed at what just happened and what you said – do you seriously think Tommy would get a Purplecoat job?' Lenny replied 'No frigging way, CC!' Callum concluded 'Then that was a great escape and you're a master bullshitter LE. Zezeze!'

The last few weeks of July flew by. Callum was still looking for love but the sexual exploits of his mates were taking up all of their spare time. Kenny's relationship with Jill Tully was blowing hot and cold so, even though he was still courting her, he couldn't resist having his wicked way with his bunny girls whenever the opportunities arrived. It was sometimes Di sometimes Vi and sometimes Di and Vi together. As far as Lenny was concerned, the 'Pull a *Purplecoat*' virus was reaching epidemic proportions. He couldn't believe the effect the uniform seemed to be having on Funtime guests - they treated him like a pop star and he was getting plenty of invitations to stay awhile at different chalets. He was happy to comply, finding sexual magnetism and a great deal of satisfaction in every case. If an ice breaker was needed, Lenny adapted the astrological chart approach that he'd first heard when Lady Knightsbridge seduced him. He simply asked what star sign the girl was then pretended to be surprised that it *happened to be compatible* with his. He was actually born under the star sign of Aries so references to *the ram* raised the innuendo level straight away. Once the target was in or on a bed or anywhere reasonably flat, Lenny wasted no time. He honed his skills at finding and exciting the previously elusive erogenous zones, or the nearest things to it, using a variety of techniques including tickling, fondling, kissing and licking.

The regularity of Lenny's liaisons often led to subsequent demands and awkward situations, much like a French farce. Most of the girls he went with expected to go beyond his intended one-night stand. As he spoke to his next target, he needed to look over her shoulder in case a previous conquest was after him. He didn't know which way he was coming and going, literally. The complications continued after the girls went home. Many of them would write a letter to him as soon as they got home, expecting some sort of ongoing dialogue and some future reunion. When Lenny first started getting this type of fan-mail he was pleasantly surprised but became totally overwhelmed when the volumes increased.

One morning after Lenny led his Keep Fit class, Jill handed him the latest batch of letters that had arrived for him. When he got back to his bedroom at the purple flat, he opened the envelopes and briefly read the contents before spreading them across his bed like a blackjack croupier dealing cards. He was just pondering what to do with them when his room-mate walked in.

Callum saw Lenny's puzzled expression as he looked at the letters on his bed. 'You okay, LE?' 'I've got more fan-mail CC.' 'So, what's the problem?' Lenny explained his predicament: 'I know I sound really shallow but most of the girls in these letters are a mystery to me. I can't quite identify or recall anything about the sender. What she looked like, what we did together, whether I want to be pen friends or see her again, etc. etc'. Callum came up with a solution: 'Okay LE. How's this for an idea: You simply draw up and maintain a chart containing key information regarding each girl you go with. That way, if you subsequently get a letter from them, you'll know if you want to take it further or politely reply with a fob off.' 'Fob off?' 'Yea, maybe say you enjoyed her company and will see how things stand when the season is over or bluntly say you're now seeing someone else'. Lenny agreed that it was a great idea and started writing up a draft straight away. It was no surprise to Callum that Lenny went further than was decent. To begin with, he made the title of the form *LE's Conquest Chart*. Then, his criteria for different factors included scores for the most personal of topics. Much like a personal diary, Lenny kept the existence of *LE's Conquest Chart* secret, except of course, from his room-mate.

Callum was also drawing up a chart, but on a completely different subject. He was fed up of being close to broke for most of the time and Kenny was always looking to generate extra cash so they got their heads together to think of the best way to accomplish this. They came up with the idea of organising a private ticket-only barbecue party in a secret location on the beach for *Seaview* staff only. Callum listed the who, what and when on his chart and they soon worked out that they would need a few helpers. Kenny of course nominated his girlfriend - Jill - and Callum of course nominated Lenny. The four of them got together and Kenny went through the basics of his plan. They would each sell a batch of tickets and all profits would be shared equally between them. Each partygoer would be sold three tickets - one for entry, one for their first drink and one for a burger or a hot dog from the barbeque. Callum somehow estimated that they would need to sell around forty sets of tickets to break-even so Kenny suggested that each of the four of them should have twenty sets and try to sell at least a dozen so that they would be sure to be in profit.

Kenny emphasised four rules they had to strictly abide by:
1. The coastguards had to be formally advised exactly where and when the private beach party was going to take place and likely numbers invited
2. Only those who paid for tickets must gain entry, otherwise supplies would run out and profits hit
3. Tickets should not be sold to holidaymakers or there would be too many to cater for and manage
4. Tickets should not be sold to kitchen porters as they couldn't be trusted to behave sensibly and the party would get out of hand.

On their next day off, Callum and Kenny ventured out on a scouting mission along the beach to find a suitable location for the party. After walking up and down the beach they decided on a sheltered cove where a few small boats had run aground and broken up. The sand in that area was relatively firm so would be ideal for dancing on and they could use the wood from the broken boats for a fire to provide light and warmth for the party.

The following Saturday afternoon, Kenny, as chief organiser, got the four of them back together around a table in a hidden corner of the empty ballroom for an update to the plan. Firstly, Kenny advised that he had checked the weather forecast and it looked good for the next five days so decided the Beach BBQ party should take place that Thursday night starting around 11:30pm. It was Continental night so all the *Purplecoats* would be wearing smart casual clothes instead of their usual evening uniform in order to emphasise the international theme. Callum and Lenny should therefore be able to slip out as needed during the evening without it being as noticeable as if they'd had their uniform on. Once their shift ended at 11pm they'd be dressed ready to guide ticket holders down to the secret location on the beach and take with them any last-minute extras that were needed.

Now the date was set, they had just five days to sell the tickets and get everything prepared. Kenny wrote a letter that he would deliver to the coastguard's office to formally advise them of the exact location and time when the private beach party was going to take place. The letter also included Kenny's estimate that the number of party goers would be between thirty and forty. This was based on getting most of the *Seaview* waitresses and other female members of staff to buy tickets.

Kenny appointed Callum as the treasurer so that all of the money from sales would be kept in one place. Callum took the treasurer's role very seriously. He presented a pack of raffle tickets that he'd found in the *Purplecoat* dressing room and explained that they could sell the numbered tickets for admission to the party then the markings on the stubs would confirm the numbers of partygoers they needed to cater for. He carefully double counted twenty sets of tickets as he tore them off his ticket book, wrote the initials of each seller - LE, JT, KT or CC - on each stub, then placed each batch in front of Lenny, Jill, Kenny and kept a pack for himself.

Lenny hadn't been paying too much attention to the arrangements and rules. He was simply excited at the prospect of inviting girls to a beach party so shot off as soon as he got his batch of tickets. The three remaining discussed and finalised the plans for food and drink, including hiding places where supplies could be stored, how they would be carried down to the beach and all related timings.

Less than an hour later the meeting finished and Callum walked through the buffet lounge on the way back to the purple flat. A pretty teenage guest he'd not yet spoken to smiled at him as she saw his *Purplecoat* uniform and said 'See you at the beach party.' Callum smiled back and thought 'God, LE is a fast worker but he wasn't supposed to sell tickets to guests.' He continued into reception and a group of girls asked him if he knew where they meet Lenny to be taken to the beach party and what time do they need to be there?

When Callum finally caught up with Lenny down at the purple flat, he congratulated him on spreading the word about the beach party so quickly then asked how many tickets he'd sold. Lenny casually admitted 'I've told loads of girls about the party but haven't actually sold any tickets yet - Zezeze!' Callum was exasperated and explained that they needed the cash up front to pay for the food and drink and be sure of making a profit. He also reminded him that they were only supposed to sell tickets to staff. Lenny replied 'Oh yes, sorry, but I just thought it would be better to run out of food and drink than run out of girls! I'll go back to the ones I spoke to and get the tickets sold'. Unfortunately, all of the girls Lenny invited gossiped to other female and male holidaymakers who then gossiped to their waitresses who then gossiped to male and kitchen lads, not only in the Seaview but also the neighbouring holiday centre, all without a single ticket being sold.

In the days and hours leading up to the Thursday night, the gang of four - Kenny, Jill, Callum and Lenny - spent most of their spare time purchasing food and drinks based on the number of tickets sold. This included a couple of 5-gallon containers of scrumpy that they got from Big Al. They hid the supplies in an unused room at the back of the *Seaview*'s main building, behind a stack of fold-up tables and buried underneath tablecloths borrowed from the dining room to stop anyone uncovering the treasure beneath.

The haul was nearly found out when Kenny came out of the room and almost bumped into Tommy as he was walking by. The bully said that the waitresses were bragging about going to a beach barbeque and he wanted four tickets for his gang. He added that he and his gang didn't have to pay anything because they would act as security. Kenny mumbled an excuse along the lines of 'all the tickets have already been sold unfortunately' and got away sharpish before another word could be said. Tommy was left seething. He was determined to hatch a plan to get his own back on being excluded.

At the start of Thursday evening's entertainment, Kenny was taking photographs of holidaymakers sat at candle lit tables in the ballroom. He realised that the candles would look good lighting up the area around their beach party so, after each photograph, he blew out the candle and snaffled it away into the dressing room. The guests were surprised that the photographer had suddenly taken their romantic lights away but assumed it was due to *Funtime's* safety rules.

When Kenny had finished going around the tables, he gathered all the candles from the dressing room and sneaked out the back door. Once in the kitchen, he placed the candles in a metal crate that he planned to use as a grill to cook the meat on. He then filled the rest of the crate with armfuls of bread rolls before carrying it all away to the secret supply stash. He swore at himself as he realised that they had no charcoal for the barbeque. It was much too late to go out and buy any but he remembered that a bag of coal stood by the fireplace in the centre of the buffet lounge. He found Lenny in the ballroom talking to some girls but dragged him away to help him. They each grabbed a corner of the bag of coal and carried it out of the buffet lounge nonchalantly, continuing down the stairs to the back room where the secret supplies were stashed. Yet again, they managed to avoid suspicion from onlooking holidaymakers but didn't dare think what *Seaview* security or management would have said if they'd caught the two of them carrying stolen goods out of the building.

Lenny had to return to the ballroom to continue working alongside Callum until they could sneak away later. In the meantime, Kenny was alone in the back room organising the supplies into priority order for carrying down to the secret cove. Kenny was just thinking about Tommy's face as he'd left him standing there wanting tickets and wondered if there'd be any repercussions. Suddenly, the door swung open with a bang. Kenny jumped out of his skin thinking it was Tommy then he saw that it was Jill. She had kicked the door open while struggling to carry in bottles of lemonade. The two of them did a final check on the stash of supplies to ensure everything was in order, but it still had to be moved down to the secret cove. Jill guarded the room while Kenny jogged down to the beach with fold-up tables plus as many items as he could carry. This was no mean feat as it was a quarter-mile walk down the field at the back of the site to the clifftop, then a hundred and fifteen steep and uneven stone steps down to the beach then hundreds of yards along the shore to the secret cove. When Kenny returned from his second delivery, Lenny and Callum had just made it to the supply room. They had managed to sneak away from their official duties in the ballroom for a short while and offered to carry the heaviest items down to the secret cove. The evening dew made the ground slippery and they nearly dropped the containers of scrumpy as they struggled down the stone steps.

It took Lenny and Callum much longer than expected to get the scrumpy down to the party venue and thought it best to return to the ballroom before Jason or Mike came looking for them. Kenny and Jill were left to carry the remaining food and drinks down to the secret cove on their own. After many exhausting journeys, they finally had everything in place. Kenny got a fire going with newspapers and shards of wood from the wrecks of the boats that had been beached there. As Jill set up the tables, she commented that it was just as well that the promising weather forecast was accurate - the evening was bone dry with only a slight sea breeze in the sheltered cove.

At around the same time, Tommy led his kitchen porter cronies to another bay where a number of pleasure boats were tied up for the night. He had hatched a plan to get his own back for being excluded from the beach party. His idea was to steal a boat, sail it around Berry Head Point and make a grand entrance into the cove where the party was to be held. He would then offer the four best-looking girls a ride. His dirty mind went into overdrive as he imagined how grateful the girls would be to be rescued from a boring party for a private and intimate session with just him and his mates.

The moonlight illuminated the bay just enough for them to spot that all the boats were tied together with thick rope but the furthest one out was only tied with one rope. They climbed over the security fence and clambered along the rocking boats to reach the furthest one. Tommy had stolen a long sharp bread knife from the kitchen and gave it to Terry to cut the rope that tethered the boat to the rest of the fleet. Having embarrassed himself by being the fall guy for Dale's sun tan joke, Terry needed to restore some credibility in the gang. He thrust the knife back and forth over the rope with all his strength but struggled to cut through the thick strands. Minutes passed that seemed like hours as Terry's already bright red face looked like it would explode, especially as his exertions didn't seem to be making any progress. The other gang members were getting increasingly concerned that they might get caught. They kept looking back at the shore and fidgeting or jumping with every noise they heard or thought they heard. Tommy eventually lost patience and took over from Terry. With great gusto, he quickly tore through the threads of the rope and finally released the boat from its tether.

The boat's propulsion was enabled by bicycle-like foot pedals in the hollow of the boat whereas the steering was directed by a tiller at the back of the boat that was linked to an underwater rudder. They each took turns on each device while the others looked back in case the owner or the police were following them.

The boat travelled out of the bay along the coast toward Berry Head Point. Tommy was delirious with excitement at the prospect of floating up to the beach where the party was being held. They should get there while the party was in full swing to make the grand entrance. None of the gang had anticipated any problems getting the boat around the point but they were unaware of the dangers of this area. Despite their best efforts to avoid them, the waves were so strong that they buffeted the boat against one after another of the jagged rocks under the sheer cliff face of Berry Head Point. Excitement soon turned to panic as the boat started to take in water but there was no way back.

When the regular entertainment finished in the ballroom, Callum jogged down to the beach to help Kenny and Jill prepare for their first customers. Lenny gathered together the girls he'd sold tickets to and led them down the back of the Seaview toward the cliff top. News of the beach party must have spread like jungle drums and, by the time Lenny got to the top of the stone steps, more than forty teenagers and twenty-somethings were following close behind him. He couldn't work out who had tickets and who hadn't so he had no choice but to let all of them follow him down the 115 stone steps and along the beach. As they arrived at the no longer secret cove, a roaring fire lit up the party area on the beach. The whole scene looked even more continental than the ballroom, especially with the candles stolen from there now flickering under the evening sky.

Callum was busy chopping up wood from the wrecks of the old boats and throwing the fragments on the fire to keep it going. The stolen coals were burning nicely on the makeshift barbecue and Kenny was cooking burgers and sausages on the stolen grill. Jill was placing the food and drinks on fold-up tables.

Lenny was feeling guilty at informally inviting too many people rather than selling tickets and forgetting to tell them to keep the party quiet. He joined Jill to try to ensure only ticket holders got near the food and drinks but they were soon swamped, not only with genuine ticket holders, but also non-ticket holders pretending they'd already thrown their tickets onto the table. Everyone grabbed as much food and drink as they could carry.

Callum and Kenny counted more than 50 partygoers and estimated that more than twenty waitresses and kitchen lads had turned up without tickets and were taking advantage of the chaos. They hoped that there wouldn't be any fights once the drink had been consumed but relieved that trouble maker Tommy and his gang were not amongst the party-crashers.

In the waters around Berry Head Point, Tommy had somehow managed to steer the holed boat toward a small sandy section of the shore. As the boat came to a shuddering halt, the gang jumped off and dragged it out of the water. Once the shock of their near disaster had dissipated and their nerves and breathing returned to normal, they turned the boat onto its side and drained most of the water out of it. The underside of the boat was too badly damaged to risk putting it back into the water so Tommy had to give up on his grand plan to float the boat up to the party. Instead, he persuaded his cohorts to lift the soggy boat over their heads and attempt to carry it there. It was just as well that they had some protection over their heads because a large colony of bats flew out of the nearby caves and swooped around and into them. Carrying an upturned boat along a shore packed with sharp-edged rocks while being attacked by bats was like a freaky army obstacle course but the gang continued as there was no alternative. Once they'd rounded a huge boulder, the bats left them alone and they had their first sight of the bonfire blazing at the beach party along the coast.

The weight of the boat was getting to be too much for them but Terry was the first to buckle. His hands already had blisters from helping Tommy cut the rope to free the boat and now the salty seawater was seeping into the cuts. He tried not to react to the searing pain but his grip slipped. This caused the boat to suddenly twist and fall to the beach floor, taking all the gang members with it. After cursing Terry and kicking the boat, they brushed the damp sand off their clothes as best they could.

Tommy had run out of patience again. With a snarl he told his cohorts to smash up the boat where it lay and use the pieces to make a bonfire while he checked out the party.

Tommy sneaked into the party and immersed himself within the hubbub, grabbing someone's cup of scrumpy that they'd left on a table while dancing. He looked at the partygoers and was surprised to recognise plenty of colleagues from the dining room and the kitchen. He went up to them thinking the worst and asked how come they had managed to get tickets when he hadn't. Once he realised that most of his colleagues were party-crashers like himself he tried to get some of the girls to go off with him to what he promised would be a much better private party. He succeeded through a combination of persuasion, inebriation and desperation.

Unfortunately, there was no roaring fire to greet Tommy and his girls when they got to the so-called private party. Tommy's gang had smashed up the boat and built a bonfire stack but were finding it impossible to get a fire going with matches and cigarette lighters because the wood had got so damp.

The girls were bored and discussed returning to the beach party but Tommy insisted they hang on to give him time to go back and get something. He left them sitting on boulders talking to Terry in the dark while he went back to the main party with the rest of his gang. They stuffed themselves with scraps of leftover food and drink, then sneaked around the back of the roaring bonfire to pull out some of the larger sticks that were half alight. They carried the still burning sticks back to their smashed-up boat and plunged them into the damp bonfire stack. This immediately caused clouds of smoke to smother them, but after coughing and choking for a while they somehow got their own fire going.

A few other partygoers copied Tommy's actions and sneaked away with burning sticks for their own private parties further along the beach.

Luckily, around fifty ticket holders remained at the official party and didn't mind that the food ran out quickly - there was still some scrumpy left and DJ Sub was blasting out a good mix of party music from his portable cassette tape player. The DJ had been promised free food and drink in exchange for recording a half dozen cassette tapes and playing the right tracks.

DJ Sub certainly delivered on his choice of music and everyone was enjoying themselves. They happened to be dancing, jumping around and singing along to 'Hi Ho Silver Lining' when the cassette tape ran out before the end of the song. Some of the dancers were so far into the party spirit that they continued to jump around, laugh and sing the rest of the song unaccompanied while DJ Sub shuffled through his tapes to select the best one to play next.

Lenny had been dancing with a brown-haired beauty called Tina and cajoled Callum into dancing with her friend Vicky. When the music stopped, he walked Tina down to the water's edge. They were attracted by the flickering bioluminescent lights that were sparkling like gemstones from plankton floating in the waves under the sea mist. Sparkling plankton shouldn't be appearing in this area but somehow it was. They marvelled at the magical sight then noticed that the water was getting more turbulent. Waves splashed onto the beach much more vigorously than before, as if a tsunami was imminent. Suddenly, through the sea mist, a large boat emerged heading straight towards them like a huge blue whale. They jumped back in surprise as the boat skimmed and thudded to a halt against the sandy shore. Two burly men dressed in shiny orange and yellow overalls and white crash helmets jumped out of the boat straight into the shallow water and swiftly waded ashore. The startled partygoers thought it was a scene from a James Bond film. All but Kenny who realised that the red and yellow stripes above the blue hull and letters on the front of the vessel identified it as belonging to the Royal National Lifeboat Institution. He was the first to walk up to the RNLI men in their waterproof suits and they immediately demanded to know what was going on along the beach. Kenny explained that this was a private beach party and definitely legal because he'd dropped a letter off at the Brixham Coastguards office to formally advise them where and when it was taking place. The RNLI captain admitted that the coastguards had notified him of one private party but when they saw a number of fires along this stretch of the beach they were forced to investigate. As a number of illegal gatherings were taking place, the laws had clearly been flaunted, so he ordered that all parties along this beach had to finish straight away and any mess cleared up.

The RNLI men left Kenny standing there and walked off and along the beach to shock the other groups of people and disappoint them with the news that their parties were also over, much like beach attendants closing up deck chairs at the end of the day.

As everyone from the legal party reluctantly started walking back to the *Seaview*, Vicky looked out for Callum but he was busy folding up tables and picking up rubbish with Kenny and Jill. Lenny was giving Tina a long goodnight kiss when Kenny spoiled the fun by shouting to him 'Oi, LE. Get your arse over here and help us clear up the mess.'

The gang of four let the fire slowly burn itself out to give them enough light to pick up all the rubbish they could find. They gathered as much as their arms could carry back to the

Seaview but getting it up the 115 stone steps to the cliff top then along the path to bins at the back of the *Funtime* holiday centre was laborious and exhausting. Lenny suggested 'We should have asked everyone to carry something up'. Kenny had had enough and said 'Stone the crows, LE. Perhaps you would have got more involved in organising the party if your brain wasn't trapped between your legs!' Rather than escalate the argument, Lenny smiled as he replied 'Fair enough KT but I must have been born that way' and they all burst out laughing.

The dawn light was coming over the horizon by the time Lenny and Callum finally got back to their flat. They only managed a few hours of sleep before it was time to rise and get their day uniform on for another full working day. As they walked as fast as they could up the hill, they shared the same feeling about the party - there must be easier ways of making money.

After breakfast, Kenny and Callum returned to the beach to see if anything else needed sorting out. The fire had gone out but the bright morning light illuminated the whole area. They could see they had done a thorough job throughout the night clearing up all the rubbish within the area of their party but found lots of rubbish nearby where the kitchen lads and others had made their own parties. There were empty beer cans, bottles and cider containers dumped or hidden in the rocks and roaches from spliffs thrown everywhere. They gagged when they also spotted a used condom. Curiously, along with fragments of boats still smouldering in their makeshift fires there also seemed to be the remains of long wooden posts still showing traces of white paint. Kenny and Callum didn't have the will or energy to clear up someone else's rubbish so they trudged back up to the *Seaview*, hopeful that enough kitchen lads or their cronies would have the collective conscience to eventually clear up their own mess, especially the guy who'd filled the condom.

Back at the *Seaview*, Lenny had made the rounds of talking to most of the people he'd sold tickets to. He eventually found Tina - the girl he took to the water's edge when the RNLI boat arrived - and her roommate Vicky. He apologised for the sudden ending to the beach party. They giggled and said they really didn't mind as they had a fab time while it lasted and they had amazing story to tell their friends when they get home. Even though Lenny was dog-tired, he couldn't miss an opportunity and mentioned that he still had some scrumpy and great records back at his flat so they could have their own private party there anytime. Both Tina and Vicky smiled and said they'd like to go there straight away. Lenny was happy to oblige and, as he walked them down the hill, wondered if Vicky was hoping that Callum would be in their room when they get there or turn up to make up a foursome. If not, Lenny thought he just might have to entertain the girls on his own - he was happy with any eventuality.

Callum was indeed in the room he shared with Lenny at the purple flat, but so was Kenny. They were busy counting up all the takings from the beach party. After laying the cash out on Lenny's bed they started to divide the profit amongst the four ticket sellers. When Lenny suddenly opened the bedroom door, he saw his mates hovering over a lot of cash spread out on his bed. Kenny and Callum heard girls giggling in the corridor right behind Lenny so they quickly threw a blanket over the money and sat on it to prevent the girls from seeing it. Lenny instinctively stopped abruptly which caused the girls to bump into the back of him. The three of them almost fell into the room and the girls were surprised to see Kenny and Callum just sitting on a single bed looking guilty. Lenny told the girls that he'd forgotten he had a meeting with his mates to plan the next party. Both Tina and Vicky sensed Lenny was trying to cover something up but didn't complain as he practically bundled them out the front door.

Lenny soon returned to the purple flat and Kenny immediately chided him for nearly giving the game away. Lenny apologised for surprising them but added 'Don't worry - Tina and Vicky simply assumed you two were lovers as you looked so guilty at being interrupted while sat together on a single bed - Zezeze!'. After more laughter, Callum split the profits into four equal shares, handed one to Lenny, kept one for himself and gave Kenny the remainder for him to share with Jill.

When Kenny met up with Jill to hand over her share of the profits, she said there were more serious matters to talk about. The police had visited the *Seaview* that morning and spoken to Eric Arden. She overheard them talking about a number of disturbances reported in the area the previous night. The police were called to the neighbouring *Funtime* holiday centre, where a chalet door had been ripped off its hinges and stolen and a football goal post was also missing. The Brixham harbour master reported that a half-dozen hire-boats belonging to a local beach vendor had been set adrift overnight. The coastguards found and returned five of them the next morning but one boat is still missing and the owner is hopping mad. The policeman believed that all these disturbances were related to illegal parties that took place on the beach that night and asked Eric if he had any idea who the culprits might be. Eric truthfully said that he didn't know anything about illegal parties on the beach but it seemed unlikely that any culprits were from the *Seaview* as no disturbances were reported here. The policeman accepted Eric's reasoning and left without any further investigation.

The gang of four were relieved to have escaped any trouble and they decided there and then not to plan any more parties.

During the peak season, the Seaview was so popular that some of the waitresses had to move out of their chalets on site and share staff accommodation in the neighbouring holiday centre. To get there, they had to climb over stiles, walk across fields and clamber along an unlit coastal footpath. Kenny offered to escort them when it got dark as a "safety precaution" but they usually thanked him with more than just a peck on the cheek. If the waitresses were extra grateful, Kenny would end up walking back to his own chalet well into the early hours. One particularly late night he heard a noise in the Wendy house opposite the Seaview's reception entrance. The clouds parted and, in the moonlight, Kenny was pretty sure that he could see a naked man inside it. This wasn't that surprising because, in addition to children innocently playing in the Wendy house during the daylight hours, it was a regular late-night venue for adults indulging in kinky sex. Then again, it was usually couples using it overnight rather than males on their own. Just as Kenny was about to leave what he assumed was a pervert to his entertainment he heard the occupant say 'Kenny zat eeuu?' He realised it was Big Al, although when he stepped out naked from the Wendy house he was not as big as usual in the cool of the evening! Trying not to look or wake up the local residents, Kenny whispered 'How come you're naked and alone?' Alan was clearly inebriated but had the self-respect to finally put his hands over his private parts as he tried to explain what had happened in part Devon accent, part drunken gibberish. Either way, Kenny somehow managed to get the gist of the story:

Big Al had delivered the latest scrumpy order to the Gaff that evening and the kitchen lads invited him in to drink some of it with them. Some girls joined them for an impromptu scrumpy tasting party. When he woke up some hours later, he was in a bed in a chalet that he didn't recognise, naked and next to a girl he vaguely recognised. The evening had been a blur but the pounding in his head told him he'd got *proper shamfered up* on the *Pixie Juice* he'd delivered. Before he could say a word, the girl got out of their bed and went to the toilet. When Alan heard her peeing, he realised he urgently needed to *go* as well. The toilet was unlikely to be available in time so, in a desperate panic, he staggered out of her chalet and searched for the nearest bushes to pee in. He was 'Pixie Led', in other words, his feet were going backwards when he wanted to go forwards, so it took a while to find an appropriate location where a naked man would not be disturbed and he would not disturb anyone else. Once he'd emptied his bladder, he looked around to return to the chalet he'd come from but he had got so disorientated that he couldn't remember which chalet it was. He couldn't go home to his parent's house in the nude and drunk as a lord but then he saw the Wendy house. He reasoned that he could use it as a sanctuary, get a few hours' sleep inside it and clear his head, by which time there would be just enough light to hopefully find the chalet where the girl, and more importantly his clothes, were waiting inside for him.

Kenny could hear Alan's teeth chattering with the cold so he kindly put his coat around him and helped him stagger and sway down to his own chalet without anyone seeing them. Once inside, Kenny picked out some clothes that Al could borrow to send him on his way. The shoes were no problem once the laces were undone but Al was taller and plumper than Kenny so, even after leaving buttons undone, Alan's bare wrists and ankles stuck out like *The Incredible Hulk* magazine character. Nonetheless, Alan had enough flesh covered for him to make it home without getting arrested. He returned the borrowed clothes a day later but Kenny would have preferred it if he'd washed them first. It took Al two days to find the girl he'd been with but, when they went back to her chalet to pick up his clothes, they finished what they thought they'd only started when they were drunk.

That same week, a group of six teenage girls arrived from South London. One of them was called Carly and, as soon as she met Lenny, she made it abundantly clear that she fancied him. Unfortunately, Betty – her best friend and chalet room-mate - wanted to retain full control of her and wouldn't risk anything or anyone spoiling that. At every opportunity, Betty tried to put Carly off Lenny in any way she could.

One afternoon, Carly asked Lenny to have a drink with her and the rest of the girls in the bar at the *Inn Paradise*. Lenny couldn't afford to buy even one round of drinks for six teenage girls so came up with an alternative plan. An older woman that Lenny had satisfied the previous week had given him a bottle of rum as a thank you gift on the last day of her holiday. He offered to share it with his mates but Kenny didn't like any spirits and Callum felt seasick after any mention of the word - he said it gave him flashbacks to the Trawler Race when Captain Hogg, egged on by Dale's girlfriend Sue, had obliged him to knock back more tots of rum than his metabolism could handle. So it was that Lenny came up with an idea of making the most of the gift, though not in the way the woman who gave it to him would have appreciated. He told the girls that it was a local custom for a group of like-minded people to knock back a whole bottle of rum between them as a sign of friendship. The officious bar manager Warren was on duty that afternoon so Lenny arranged to meet the girls in a quiet area of the ballroom next door to the *Inn Paradise*. He smuggled in the contraband bottle inside a sports bag then carefully opened it under the table away from Warren's prying eyes. Lenny kept ducking down mid-conversation to top up everyone's glasses from the bottle's hiding place under the table. All the girls laughed at Lenny's deception except for Betty. She continued to keep watch over Carly like a mother hen would do to her chick and got angrier the more Lenny and Carly chuckled together. When Betty thought Lenny was out of earshot, she told Carly that she didn't trust him, correctly assuming that he was only after one thing. Lenny overheard the conversation but saw Betty's interference as a challenge.

By the time the bottle of rum had been emptied, everyone was well intoxicated. Lenny chose the moment to make a play for Carly, asking if the two of them could sneak back to her chalet for a cuddle *or whatever*. She giggled in agreement and they staggered away from the table, leaving the others busy rambling incoherently from the aftereffects of the alcohol.

As soon as Carly let Lenny in to the chalet she shared with Betty, they kissed and caressed on her bed. Lenny could tell Carly was very keen and he was more than ready to progress to the next stage. Their levels of passion were doubtless raised by the booze they'd just consumed. They were already half undressed when they suddenly heard the other girls returning and Betty's voice shouting the loudest. If her intentions were to surprise Lenny and rescue Carly then her timing couldn't have been better. Carly urgently pulled her blouse and skirt back on and fumbled to do up the buttons as her friends reached the chalet door. Lenny was used to quick changes so managed to get his day uniform back on but his level of excitement could clearly be seen bulging out of his flimsy shorts. He was in a panic as Betty pushed her key into the lock of the chalet door - his erection was as hard as rock and would not go down. He had to hide somewhere in the next few seconds but, being trapped in this small chalet, the only private room he had a chance of reaching in time was the smallest room. As the key turned in the lock, Lenny ran to the toilet and made it inside just before the door swung open.

The girls walked in and sniggered amongst themselves as they stared in a sarcastic way at Carly. They could see her cheeks were flushed bright red after embarrassment had taken over from passion and they could hear her breathing heavily as she tried to pull her clothes straight and flatten out the tell-tale creases on the bed. Betty milked the situation of course. She looked around and asked where Lenny was. Carly explained that he'd just gone to the loo. Her friends pretended to be surprised and held back from giggling, especially when Betty asked why his plimsolls were on the floor by the door. After a brief but telling pause, Carly made up the excuse that he'd left them there in case there was mud on the soles. Mother hen knew that her chick was lying.

Funtime chalets were made of the cheapest building materials and all the walls were paper thin so Lenny knew that he would have to take a pee while shut in the loo or the silence would give the game away. This presented Lenny with a physical dilemma - how could he pee when his penis was rigidly perpendicular? It reminded him of his explanation of stalactites and stalagmites to those language students in Torquay. Thinking of those girls in their miniskirts just made his predicament impossible to resolve by bending. There was only one way he could aim downward into the porcelain and that was to do some sort of a handstand in the cramped space. He moved his legs and knees to climb up the wall like a spider, then tried to bend his body around like a clumsy Houdini. After much uncomfortable manoeuvring, he managed to wedge his body around until he was almost upside-down. Unfortunately, this meant he had to place both his hands on the floor in order to hold himself up as he tried to aim hands-free as best he could.

Just outside the loo, the girls could hear scuffling and banging from inside the loo then the noise of pee water splashing everywhere except for its intended receptacle. The sound of spray and dribbles was followed by a crunch then the sound of toilet paper being torn and dabbed on clothes and around the floor. Eventually, Lenny emerged sheepishly from the toilet to face the gaze of six girls. He leaned on the front door to slip his plimsolls back on but failed to hide what was left of his erection and the pee stains down his shirt and shorts. Defeated and embarrassed, he quickly blurted out 'Fanks for the use of the loo Carly - gotta go' then rapidly escaped out of the chalet to run down to the purple flat, wash his clothes and try to sober up for the evening shift.

It was Callum's day off but he wasn't relaxing at the purple flat. Jason had once again persuaded him to put on his *Purplecoat* evening uniform and represent the *Seaview*. He had been taken by taxi to the poshest hotel in Torquay for a VIP charity event. Jason assured him that it would be a pleasant afternoon - he just needed to look smart, talk sensibly and act appropriately. Sir Albert Burren had sponsored the event and would be the guest of honour. As Sir Albert was head honcho of the *Funtime* organisation, Jason said it would be a feather in Callum's cap. Jason added that it would also be an opportunity to make up for his misdemeanour with Sir Albert's second in command - Mrs Burren - when she caught him eating a doughnut on duty. Jason told Callum to always bear in mind that these executives demand and expect respect wherever they go, especially from their employees.

When Callum got to the hotel reception, he was directed to the ballroom on the top floor. As he went to take the lift some American tourists looked at his purple uniform and thought he was a bell-hop so they gruffly told him to carry their luggage. They looked very confused when he said 'Carry it yourself, I'm a *Purplecoat*' then jumped into the lift, leaving them to stand there aghast with their bags unmoved.

The conference ballroom was very plush with huge picture windows looking over the seaside road out to a huge sweep of the bay. Torbay's most popular comedian - Charlie Farley - introduced the sponsor and guest of honour. Sir Albert Burren took the applause and recalled his impressive achievements; starting in the entertainment business as an all-round entertainer he had taken over his first *Funtime* holiday centre nearby and quickly grew the organisation to become a nationwide favourite. After the applause, the VIPs and business executives enjoyed the free canapes, champagne and Charlie Farley delivering his best jokes:

'I'm lucky to be here with you tonight. I've only just got over a Hokey Cokey addiction. It was really difficult but I turned myself around … and that's what it's all about!

I haven't always been a comedian you know. What do you mean I'm not one now – behave yourselves! No, I used to be a door-to-door salesman. I did. One evening, a lady opened the door in her nightie - I thought to myself, that's a funny place for a door!

I then tried my hand at selling window blinds door-to-door. I rang the bell of this one house and a lady inside shouted out asking who I was and what I wanted. I shouted through the letterbox that I was a blind salesman. She shouted back "Ah, bless you. The front door isn't locked but I'm just getting out of the bath so come in, shut the door behind you and I'll be right with you". I did as she asked and waited for her in the hallway. Next minute, she comes down the stairs with everything showing and said "Where's your white stick?!"

Blimey, you're a tough audience tonight, smiling, instead of laughing. It makes me wonder if you're enjoying yourselves or you've just got trapped wind!

One of my cousins lives in a big house in Scotland and it has a large apple tree in the garden. One day, his Granddaughter wanted him to pick some apples from the tree but it was late in the season and the only apples left were high up. He got a ladder and climbed up the tree while his Granddaughter waited below him with a basket. Like all true Scotsmen, he didn't wear anything underneath his kilt so when Granddaughter looked up, she noticed something hanging that wasn't apples. She said 'Grandad, what are these for?' He said 'Four?!'

Callum had heard the jokes so many times he could almost do the act himself. The waiters also thought he was hotel staff and passed by him with their trays of goodies. He just managed to catch up with one of them to grab a sandwich and a glass of bubbly. The sandwich was so small that he managed to swallow it in one mouthful. He'd only had a couple of sips of the champagne when he heard a loud crash. One of the executives nearby may have already had a few too many drinks because he'd dropped his glass, smashing it on the ballroom floor. Callum offered to hold onto a tray of champagne while a waiter cleaned up the mess. Just then, Sir Albert walked through the crowd and saw Callum standing still with the tray of champagne. He went up to him and said abruptly 'Don't just stand there boy - serve the drinks out to the guests.' Callum felt like telling him it was actually his day off and he was just holding the tray until the real waiter could continue but he thought it better to bite his tongue and button his lip. He handed out what was left on the tray before dumping it on the bar, sneaking out of the ballroom and hiding from Sir Albert and any American tourists in a quiet corner of the lounge. He kept looking at his watch until it was time to get his taxi back to the purple flat.

Behind the bar at the *Inn Paradise*, Warren was looking forward to finishing his afternoon shift and having a rare night off. He pushed a large tumbler under one optic and whisky drained into the glass. Before he'd even put the glass to his lips, he followed up with vodka, then gin. Satisfied that it would have the desired effect he swigged the potent mixture down and said to himself 'that takes the edge off another boring day *in paradise*' alluding to the name of the bar he was in charge of.

Being able to pour himself free drinks was one of the perks of Warren's position as bar manager at the *Inn Paradise*. Another perk he made the most of was using his position to take liberties with his staff. He'd had this in mind when he promoted Rachel - his most attractive barmaid - to become his shift assistant to replace one that transferred to another resort. He'd assumed that the promoted girl would show her appreciation beyond a thank you but, so far, like her predecessor, she'd refused to comply and politely but firmly rebuffed his advances. There was no doubt that his latest protégé looked good but she had turned out to be a lousy assistant. The lack of any personal benefits, work-wise or relationship-wise, made Warren wish he'd instead promoted George - one of the guys in his team who was much more deserving and proficient. George was so upset at the snub that he was now talking about leaving.

Despite the perks of free alcohol and distant possibility of flesh, Warren's satisfaction was inevitably limited and fleeting. The initial buzz from the free booze usually led to a hangover and the sexual relationships he *had* managed to negotiate never seemed to develop into mutual respect, let alone what he thought might be the mythical holy grail called true love. He therefore felt lonely and hollow inside. He would have felt even worse had he been aware that his lewd approaches to staff members had led to complaints from his victims and he was now under scrutiny from upper management.

The relief bar manager arrived to take over the evening shift and Warren gave him a quick review of the day so far - consumption, takings and items that needed ordering soon. He also mentioned that he thought *Purplecoat* Lenny had smuggled in some booze as he, and a gang of girls he was sat with in the ballroom, got rowdy despite buying no drinks from his bar. As Warren handed over the till keys, he put on some sort of a smile and shouted 'Adios' to the rest of the bar staff. He made a point of looking at George when he said it, hoping to elicit a friendly or at least friendly response but none was forthcoming. Even though his colleagues weren't particularly respectful, he'd already cheered up, safe in the knowledge that he didn't have to answer to anyone or anything for the rest of the evening.

Warren walked through the *Seaview*'s reception to the car park. He smiled in admiration at his baby - a shiny blue Triumph Bonneville motorbike. It proudly stood out against the comparatively insipid two- and four-wheel alternatives parked alongside it. One thing he did get genuinely excited about was riding this classic feat of engineering. He recalled the barmaids he'd taken out on this beast of the road. The exhilarating ride, helped by a few drinks, sometimes led to something sexual but he didn't realise that most of the girls who gave in to him were only doing so because he was their boss and they needed to keep in his good books.

He slung a leg over the frame and placed his feet on the pedals before kicking the lever to start it up. The beast roared powerfully and responded the instant he clicked it into gear and let the clutch out. Warren felt the full gravitational force as he accelerated away from the car park, down the hill through the gates toward the town centre.

Once onto the main road, he opened up the throttle until the wind was rushing through his hair and body - he thought to himself: this is as good as sex. Warren always had a sense of euphoria when riding his pride and joy but the drink he'd consumed made him feel like a hero in an epic movie - a king of the road, like Dennis Hopper in the *Easy Rider* film. Unfortunately, as in the film, the story didn't end well.

The day seemed like every other day for Lucy. She gulped down the dregs of her regular third scrumpy of the day and inadvertently slammed her tankard down onto the bar at *The Three Elms Inn*. The barman approached, assuming she wanted another drink but she ignored him and flopped down from the barstool. On reaching the door, she looked back and returned to the bar to scoop up her tobacco pouch, pack of skins and, most importantly, her skull and crossbones cigarette lighter. In her gravelly voice, she mumbled something, perhaps some sort of farewell to the barman or, more likely, an admonishment to herself for not picking up her belongings first time. A late afternoon gloom had descended as she stepped out to take the short walk to her tiny cottage a few blocks down on the other side of the street. Halfway there, she went to cross the road but had to wait on the pavement while an oil truck drove past followed by a convoy of cars. Lucy allowed herself the hint of a sardonic smile as she noticed the car drivers showing their frustration at being held back. While waiting, she took the cigarette lighter out of her pocket and thought about the person who had given it to her. It had been many years ago - decades in fact - when she had been thrilled to accept it from the only love of her life. He was a pirate, not a real one, but one of the guides dressed up as pirates that showed grockles around the Golden Hind, moored in Fishtown Harbour. The only thing he plundered was her heart. She wasn't even sure if his love was real or fake. He seemed genuine when he held her hands and gave her his lighter but it could simply have been a ruse to get her into his bed. The gift worked but she didn't get any chance to find out his true feelings as he suffered a heart attack the next day on a fishing trip. The loss was too much for her own heart and she didn't dare or want to try again with anyone else who showed her any affection. Halfway across the road the cigarette lighter slipped from her grasp. She strained to bend down to pick it up and heard a motorbike stutter around the bend, a brief screech and the fast-increasing sound of metal sliding along oil toward her …

Warren woke up in a hospital bed many hours later. A doctor and a policeman stood before him with solemn faces. The doctor carefully explained that Warren's motorcycle had hit and killed an elderly woman who had been crossing the road in front of him. Warren had been thrown off his bike as it slid along the road into the old lady. He was knocked out when he followed a different trajectory into a lamppost. He was still unconscious when the ambulancemen took him to Brixham hospital, but the doctor confirmed he'd only suffered minor cuts and bruises - his crash helmet and leathers undoubtedly saved his life.

While the hospital staff were patching him up, a police officer investigating the crash asked to see the results of his blood test. It confirmed that his blood alcohol ratio was three times higher than the maximum legal drink driving limit. The policeman formally advised Warren that he was arresting him. He had already committed a crime by being on the road in charge of a motor vehicle while in a drunken condition but the accident increased the level of his offence to the much more serious charge of causing death by careless driving while under the influence of drink or drugs.

The landlord of the Three Elms arranged and paid for Lucy's funeral at Cow Town's Parish church nearby. It was a Saturday so, as this was Kenny's day off, he attended, along with a few other colleagues from the *Seaview* who had or could get the time off. Miraculously, one of the pub's regulars found Lucy's skull and crossbones lighter quite a distance from where she had been struck. It was placed in her coffin to help reunite her with the only love of her life.

Lucy's wake of course took place at the Three Elms Inn and all those present raised a glass of scrumpy in memory of her. One of the other regulars at the pub was a carpenter and, with the landlord's permission, he etched 'Lucy' on the bar counter where she always sat. The etching remained as a sign of respect to the pub's most eccentric but fondly remembered customer.

When Warren was finally able to return to the *Seaview*, he was scarred physically and mentally. His face was scarred and he had constant flashbacks about the crash. Another significant change was that he had been demoted from bar manager to assistant. He was now working for George - the guy in his team who he had snubbed when he made Rachel his assistant. She was nowhere to be seen so Warren dared to ask if she was on holiday. George couldn't hide his delight at telling him that Rachel had been given her marching orders when it became clear that she couldn't cope with the position *he* had given her.

Warren was well aware that everyone at the *Seaview* had heard about his culpability from either the gossip grapevine or because news of the tragic accident and funeral had made the front page of the local newspaper. He could no longer leverage his position as power and his colleagues treated him like a leper - none of them wanted to be near him or speak to him.

At the formal hearing, Warren showed remorse and managed to escape with a suspended prison sentence but came face to face with Lucy's supporters as he left the court. The look they gave him would no doubt haunt him for the rest of his life.

Warren decided that the only thing he could do to diminish the torture and try to put this dark chapter behind him was to return to his family home in Cheshire. As soon as he got back to the Seaview, he went into Eric Arden's office and tendered his resignation. He agreed to tie up any loose ends with his colleagues and left the same day.

Eric Arden reflected on the season so far and wondered how good a job he had been doing as the Seaview's business manager. Filled with melancholy from Warren's accident and departure he also recalled Jason's inference that they'd lost the carnival float competition because he'd cut corners. He was wondering if there was something positive that he could do to brighten everyone's mood. As luck would have it, the answer came during his weekly meeting with the catering manager, Margot Medway. She wanted to introduce a weekly feature that some staff could provide to the guests for a bit of harmless fun. Eric listened to her idea and thought it was a good one so agreed to support it with the appropriate funding. There and then, he ordered all the items needed.

[Playlist Track: *"Going to the zoo"* - Julie Felix]

Every Tuesday morning Uncle Dale and Auntie Tricia were scheduled to supervise a coach excursion to Paignton Zoo for the *Seaview* kids. The day before this particular week, Tricia went up to Dale to tell him that she couldn't go on the excursion because she had particularly severe women's problems. He put his hand out quickly as if he didn't want to hear another word. He wasn't sure how to respond: 'I hope it will soon clear up' didn't seem at all appropriate so he just said 'Okay. I'll get Nanny Muriel to cover if you can help Uncle Bill on the magic show'. Tricia agreed and Dale left her standing there while he stomped off to find the children's nanny.

Dale knew Muriel's eccentricity had increased of late but thought the requirements were pretty straightforward: Help gather together about forty kids, get them onto a coach to take them to Paignton Zoo, supervise them for just a few hours as they look at the animals then get them safely back onto the coach back to the *Seaview* where their parents collect them outside reception in plenty of time before lunch.

Kenny was as usual covering the excursion to take photos of the kids enjoying themselves with the animals. He was surprised to see Nanny Muriel helping Dale shuffle the kids onto the coach instead of Tricia. He asked Dale 'Where's Tricia?' Dale simply said 'Women's problems.' Kenny whispered in Dale's ear 'Are you sure Nanny will be okay looking after these kids? She's been acting weirder than usual lately.' Dale said 'What do you mean?' Kenny explained: 'Well, the other day I was walking along the cliff path taking coastal photos when I saw Nanny Muriel in her white overall standing dangerously close to the edge. She had a perplexed look on her face so I carefully called out and asked her if she was okay. She replied in a frail voice "I've lost my knitting - have you seen it?" I didn't understand why she would be looking over a cliff edge for knitting but suggested it was more likely that she left it in the buffet or ballroom. I don't know if she heard me but she didn't respond, she just continued along the path mumbling to herself'. Talking of being unresponsive, Dale hadn't been listening to Kenny either - he had been distracted by loud shouting at the back of the coach. Dale jumped up the steps and ran down the aisle to speak to two gangs of kids fighting over who sat on the back seats of the coach. He sorted out the squabble by making both gangs share the seats without further argument.

When the coach got to the zoo's car park it parked alongside coaches from the other *Funtime holiday centres* in the area. The *Purplecoats* took their groups through the entrance to the zoo and escorted them around the various enclosures. The kids marvelled at the wild cats, tropical birds, reptiles and so many different monkey species. The day was going well without any hitches – the kids even got past the usually unruly woolly monkey and full-grown chimpanzee without getting urinated on or worse.

Back in the car park, the coach drivers got together for a chat. Some drank a hot beverage from their thermos flasks, others ate sandwiches or lit cigarettes. After an hour or so, rain clouds darkened the sky and the drivers returned to their coaches.

Groups of kids and their temporary guardians started running out of the zoo back to the car park just as the rain started pelting down. Nanny had been having a crafty smoke so was annoyed when Dale told her to get a move on and help get the kids onto the coach before they all got soaking wet. She quickly threw her burning cigarette on the pavement and stubbed it out, then helped Dale push the brats that were crowded outside the coach door up the steps, just escaping a sudden deluge. The coach driver started the engine and flicked on the wipers for the journey back to the *Seaview*. As the large wipers swished and squeaked against the front windscreen, Nanny looked out of the side window. The driving rain was pelting down so hard that it was merging with the splashes coming up and along the window as the coach hit puddles along the road. She was relieved that they'd all boarded before the heavens opened up. Dale was relieved that the little brats didn't get soaked enough to risk any complaints from their overprotective parents. A few boys started running up and down the aisle but they soon did as they were told when he shouted 'Sit down and stay where you are until I tell you to get up'.

The rain had eased by the time the coach ascended the hill to the *Seaview*. Dale shouted out 'Hey, kids - have you all had a good time at the zoo?' A generally positive 'Yes' came back. Dale quipped 'Well, don't forget to tell your parents you've had a *triffic* time even if you didn't!' The kids who didn't look confused were starting to understand Dale's humour. The coach stopped outside the *Seaview*'s reception and the driver opened the door. The kids were still over excited and making a commotion as they started pushing each other down the aisle. Dale shouted out 'Oy, brats - be quiet.' When the noise had subsided, he said: 'I told you to stay where you are until I tell you to get up – we need to wait for Nanny Muriel to make sure there's no traffic around when you get off'. Nanny stepped down the stairs and put a thumb up to tell Dale the coast was clear. Dale shouted out 'Okay, brats - be careful as you get off the coach, look out for your parents and, if they're not there, don't wander off. Just tell me - I'll be waiting at the bottom of the coach steps.'

The kids disembarked to be reunited with their parents and tell them they had a *triffic* time, as instructed by Dale. Kenny and Nanny Muriel headed straight for the staff canteen for lunch. The level of noise and excitement dwindled quickly until only one kid was left standing on his own. He was crying so Dale went up to him and said 'Haven't your parents arrived yet?' The boy whimpered as he said 'Naah - where's Uncle Roy?' Dale knew that the *Funtime* resort of *Warm Park* had a Kiddies Uncle called Roy. He suddenly realised that this kid had come back on the wrong coach. As the boy fought through his tears, he explained what had happened: He'd been talking to some other boys alongside the coaches when the rain started pouring. Before he could get his bearings, the woman in the white overall pushed him with the other boys up the steps of Dale's coach. Every time he tried to ask where Uncle Roy was, Dale shouted back that he should sit down. He ended up sitting in the nearest available seat.

An embarrassed Dale phoned up the Warm Park resort and got a message to Uncle Roy and the kid's parents. He said that the boy had mistakenly jumped on the wrong coach but he was now bringing him over in the minibus. When Jason and Eric found out about the mix up, Dale put all the blame on Nanny as she was an easy target.

Kenny had missed the mix-up with the kid and made sure he sat far away from Nanny Muriel in the staff canteen. He had just finished eating the latest muck on his plate when Ian - the organist in the trio that regularly worked at the *Seaview* – came up and sat opposite him. Ian was unusually chatty and friendly which made Kenny noticed that Ian was after something. Soon enough, the reason became clear when Ian came out with it. 'Kenny - would you be best man at my forthcoming wedding?' Kenny was surprised and shocked in equal measure. He had chatted with Ian on many occasions but he was never a best buddy like Callum and

Lenny were to him so he was initially taken aback. Still, he supposed that it was an honour to be chosen for something that important so said 'Sure. When is the special day happening?' 'This Saturday'. 'You're joking, aren't you? That's only four days away! What's the rush?' 'Well as you're going to be my best man I guess I should confess that I've made her pregnant and she's insisting on us getting married before it becomes obvious. Don't worry. I'll do all the driving and it won't be a long-drawn-out affair. Just a quick ceremony then I'll bring her back with us straight after as I'm booked to play organ at the Barnacle Bar that evening.

Before Friday's dinner, the guests walked into the dining room for what would be the last night of their one-week holiday. They went up to their usual table and sat down on their usual seat but the atmosphere was definitely not usual. It was eerily quiet because the waitresses were nowhere to be seen. The guests looked over to the Purplecoats table for some explanation or reassurance. All the Purplecoats were there, apart from Uncle Mike, and they looked very serious and avoided eye contact. This made the guests even more anxious. Eventually, Jason took to the microphone and said 'I'm sorry to announce this but I have some bad news, but also some good news'. The guests all murmured amongst themselves as to what the news might be or bragged that they knew something was wrong, as if nobody else had noticed the missing waitresses. After an interminable pause, Jason continued 'The bad news is that all of your waitresses went out on a coach trip this afternoon and we've heard that the coach broke down. They're all fine but, unfortunately, they won't be able to make it back in time to serve your dinner tonight'. Sounds of dismay filled the dining room so Jason waited until the noise died down to say 'Quiet please, if you don't mind. The good news is that we've been able to arrange for last-minute replacements tonight from a local agency. They're just getting ready, although you may notice that the uniforms they are wearing are not the same as you've become accustomed to and they may not match the high standards your waitresses set throughout the week. Nonetheless, I hope you'll allow them to do the best they can. Will you?' Some acceptable responses were heard from the diners, along with more murmuring. Most were upset at losing their favourite food server, some wondered how bad the replacements could be and a few mean ones thought that the tip they planned to hand over to the waitress would now stay firmly in their pocket. Mike emerged from the kitchen and whispered something in Jason's ear. Jason smiled and flicked on the microphone, announcing 'OK, ladies and gentleman, Uncle Mike has just informed me that the girls are ready to come in so please give them a welcome to encourage them to do a good job.' Suddenly, the kitchen doors burst open and the joke became obvious to all the guests. Their usual waitresses were there after all, but dressed up as provocative Saint Trinian's sirens with red and white bows in their hair, a tight black overall as short as it could be, dark stockings with holes in them and bandages here and there. They all sang a song as they marched around the dining room clanging saucepans with wooden spoons: 'We are the Funtime girls, we wear our hair in curls, we wear our o-ver-alls way up above our knees, we never smoke or drink, that's what our parents think, and when it comes to boys, we treat them just like toys, dada dadaa da daa, dada dadaa da daa, dada da da, da da da, dada dada daa, dada dadaa da daa, dada dadaa da daa, dada da daa da da da, dada dada daa'. The surprise show helped the waitresses give their guests a good send off and, by and large, the guests reciprocated with a better tip.

At first light on Saturday morning, Kenny put on the same clothes he'd worn for Lucy's funeral and met Ian in the car park. His black blazer and tie didn't match Ian's navy-blue suit, but it was the only formal wear he had so *needs must*. Ian anticipated that the journey would take an hour and a half to complete but they got stuck in multiple road works around Exeter. More than three hours had passed by the time they finally reached their destination - a tiny church in the girl's hometown of Sidmouth. The delay meant that the usual protocol was reversed - the bride to be was waiting for the groom at the aisle, along with her disgruntled parents and a few friends. Kenny was introduced to the ensemble but noted that there wasn't anyone from Ian's side, apart from himself of course. As Ian had suggested, the ceremony was a brief affair, probably like the newlyweds' courtship. The reception followed the short and sweet theme - one drink and a slice of wedding cake at the run-down pub next door. Once the feast had been consumed, the bride changed out of her ironically white wedding dress and handed it to the friend she'd borrowed it from. Everyone waved off Ian's car as he drove his new bride west to begin their married life together. Best man, Kenny, was of course relegated to the back seat as the newly-weds bickered about the late start.

Ian managed to avoid the road works around Exeter and shaved half hour off the journey back to the Seaview. Kenny helped Ian carry the bride's luggage down to the chalet they would be sharing. Just as the groom was preparing to carry his new bride over the threshold, a very flustered Seaview waitress turned up. Eyes firmly fixed on Ian, she loudly claimed that he had made her pregnant! Kenny left Ian and the two pregnant girls to work things out amongst themselves.

On one of his nights off, Kenny visited the neighbouring Warm Park holiday centre for a change of scenery. That evening's entertainment happened to be a horse racing event run by the resident *Purplecoats*. Guests could watch a cine film showing riders and horses as they were walked around the ring of an unnamed and unknown American racecourse. The film was then paused so that bets could be taken. Cash was paid out for winning horses with reducing payments for those coming in second and third. The *Seaview Purplecoats* ran their horse racing event the following evening and Kenny watched it to see how it compared. He noticed that the same batch of films were used at both holiday centres but the *Seaview Purplecoats* made sure each film was paused just before the race number was shown. Warm Park didn't pause the film until the horses were at the starting post. Crucially, this was just after the race number had been displayed on the screen. Kenny also noticed that the same race number was marked on the outside casing of the tape reels when they were handed over to the *Seaview Purplecoats*. His money-making brain soon worked out a way of beating the system.

The next week, Kenny revisited Warm Park and sneakily made a note of the race numbers shown in each race, along with the numbers of the winning horses. The next evening at the *Seaview*, he just needed to spot which reel was going to be used to guarantee which horse would win.

Armed with his list of race numbers and winning horses he needed a willing guest to place a bet, share the winnings and keep everything secret or they would both be in trouble. Anyone working at a *Funtime* resort was banned from betting or making money from events. This scam was therefore a very risky venture but, with his regular interaction with holidaymakers, he soon worked out who he could safely share the illegal profits with. He kept the winnings relatively low so that nobody suspected anything. Nonetheless, this scam made him more money each week than the beach party did for a fraction of the effort. As the weeks went by, he also noticed that Dale's friends seemed to be on a winning streak too. Kenny recalled that Dale's cousin played in a band at Warm Park so perhaps he'd also shared inside information!

The summer season was nearing the end and so was everyone's patience, especially the cabaret acts.

Veteran husband and wife singing act Danny and Dee had a big argument – the latest of many - before going on. Halfway through the romantic duet that closed their set of songs Danny decided to make a protest. He walked off the stage, sat with the audience and joined them in clapping along to the song, leaving Dee to sing on her own. She managed to retain her composure and save the act by singing the male parts in a deep voice as well as the female parts in her usual voice. The audience thought it was a hilarious part of the act, much like Esther Ofarim did in the 1960's parody duet *Cinderella Rockefella* singing with her husband Abi Ofarim. Danny returned to the stage to raise Dee's arm like a boxing champion and the audience gave Dee a standing ovation. They decided to keep this trick in all their shows going forward.

As well as being a true professional, Jason could be quite philosophical. When Callum and Lenny were laughing about another elderly performer, Jason reprimanded them. He explained that all critics, especially those working in the entertainment industry, should be considerate to the people they meet on their way up as they will surely be meeting them again when they are on their way down.

One of the acts that was definitely on their way down was a four-piece pop band ironically called The Four Highs. They had written a catchy ballad in the mid-1960's that made them famous, albeit briefly. The ballad helped them win a talent contest, earned them a recording contract, then, when the record was released, it went all the way up to number one in the singles charts. The band mimed to the song on the television pop music show called Top of The Pops. The Four Highs then went on a nationwide tour of concert halls but bad reviews and even worse behaviour from the lead singer damaged their reputation and led to dates being cancelled.

As the years passed, new and better bands came through the ranks and the manager of The Four Highs couldn't get any profitable gigs. He was just about to terminate their contract when he happened to speak to one of the senior managers in the *Funtime* organisation at a charity do. Mrs Burren, of all people, remembered hearing the ballad and assumed the band would have other songs as catchy so, not realising how desperate their manager was, signed a lucrative contract for them to tour all the *Funtime* centres.

Tonight, The Four Highs would be playing at the *Seaview*. Even though they had only the one-hit from many years earlier, the lead singer still thought he was a god and even called himself Comet because it's Greek for long-haired star. Kenny happened to be carrying his camera kit into the ballroom while the band were setting up on the stage. Comet saw Kenny and yelled out to him 'Oi you'. Kenny was the last person to accept arrogance from anyone, especially a pompous 'has been' but he politely asked the self-made god if he was yelling at him. Comet simply said 'Yeh, take my picture.' There were no pleasantries like 'please', 'would you mind' or 'thank you' so Kenny couldn't help responding with both barrels: 'No can do, buddy. The problem is that my equipment is not insured and I reckon your face would damage the lens!'

Kenny walked on and Comet was dumbfounded. His bandmates did their best to hide their sniggering but were delighted that someone had finally got one over their egotistical leader. That night, they all played with greater enthusiasm than usual while Comet used his ego to maintain his confidence through the handful of songs they had to get through before finishing with the only song that any of their audience would remember.

After a few hours and a few drinks, Kenny felt a little bit guilty at ridiculing the lead singer so he waited for the band to turn up in the buffet lounge after all the holidaymakers had gone back to their chalets. The buffet lounge girls had also finished for the night but Kenny knew where everything was behind the counter so offered to get all four of the band a cup of coffee or tea. Comet hadn't learned his lesson and tried to be smart by demanding a hot chocolate.

One of the band members went up to help Kenny and took the opportunity to thank him for making a fool of their singer and giving the rest of the band a gem of a quote to laugh about. He went on to disclose that their lead singer had been a diva from the start. He'd tried to call the band name *Comet and his Constellation* but the manager and the rest of the band suggested it was too high-brow. Instead, they named it after the street where they first started playing, hence The Four Highs. The most annoying thing that Comet did was claim that their number one ballad was all down to him even though he'd only written a few words and the rest of the band had turned it into the big hit it became. Nonetheless, he pocketed more than his fair share of royalties so the only way the other band members could recoup any money was to perform with him on this tour of *Funtime* resorts.

Kenny happened to see a bottle of laxative tablets under the counter and thought Comet deserved some sort of punishment for his arrogance. He crushed a couple of the tablets and stirred the powder into the singer's hot chocolate until it dissolved. When Kenny handed it to Comet, the pop god swigged it down without a thank you. Soon after, the band left the lounge to get back to the chalets they'd been put in overnight.

The next day, Jill told Kenny that the cleaners at the *Seaview* had complained to Eric Arden that one member of The Four Highs had really messed his bed. Kenny pretended to be shocked.

Another band that crossed Kenny was a harmony singing group that had got into the charts several times covering easy listening classics. They lived locally and were friends of Eric Arden. They used their fame and abused his friendship by sponging drinks, food and anything else they could get for free. One day, Eric asked if they'd like to hand out awards to the winners of a swimming gala. Their lead singer insisted on some sort of cash payment so Eric paid the band out of his own pocket. The next day, they turned up at Kenny's shop and selected about fifteen photos from the previous day's event. When Kenny told them the price they refused to pay and asked Kenny if he knew who they were. Without hesitation, Kenny said 'Yes I know who you are but you still have to pay like everyone else.' They stormed off without any photos or dignity.

One day, Lenny was lying on his bed at the purple flat, contemplating what details to put into the next page of a large writing pad when Callum walked into the room. He said 'You okay, LE?' 'Yea, CC. I'm just updating my chart.' 'I'm sure you had a smaller writing pad when you started *LE's Conquest Chart*. 'I did, but I had to get a larger pad for the extra comments!' As if teasing Callum, Lenny put his pad down on his bed and went to the bathroom. Callum's curiosity got the better of him and he sneakily opened the pad. Most of the chart made sense but, while he was trying to work out what the columns titled BPBR and SU meant, Lenny came back into the room. He said 'So you couldn't resist a sneaky peak, ehh CC?!' 'OK LE, you caught me. I just wondered what BPBR and SU meant.' 'OK, as it's you, I'll tell you. BPBR stands for Body Parts Best Reaction.' '*Best Reaction* to what?' 'Blimey CC. Use your imagination. Its *Best Reaction* to touching, stroking, tickling or whatever stimulus you can fink of'. Lenny took the pad and scanned his finger over some examples in the chart: Paula's ears, Lyndsay's hair, Nicola's buttocks, Amy's wrists, Michelle's neck, Vicky's shoulders, etc. Callum said 'OK, so what does the column titled SU mean?' 'It stands for Special Unique' Callum looked confused again so Lenny explained 'It's girls with special or unique attributes.' 'Okay. So, Michelle has DblJnt in the Special Unique column – what's that mean?' 'I don't suppose either of us will see Michelle again so I'll tell you that DblJnt means she was double-jointed. I found out that she could bend herself every which way in positions I didn't fink were possible'. 'And InvNip?' 'InvNip was a girl with inverted nipples. They went in rather than out'. Callum said 'Didn't that put you off?' 'No, quite the opposite. They were fascinating because they popped out when she got excited as my tongue found out'. As Lenny put the pad back in its hiding place, Callum laughed and said 'LE, you've definitely become the camp stud that Dale thought I was going to be!' Lenny replied '*You* could have been the camp stud if you hadn't been holding yourself back for your perfect girl, or Pauline.'

On the last week of August, two particularly stunning holidaymakers arrived at the *Seaview*. Chrissie was a buxom brunette with a soft voice and sweet old-fashioned smile while Val had a cheeky infectious laugh and straight black hair over a slim figure. Chrissie got ten out of ten for looks and sexual attraction on Lenny's ranking. Contrary to his usual tactics of going for the most likely lay, he was determined to go all out for this star prize and he spent most of his available time wooing her throughout the week. If Lenny was going to be able to add Chrissie's name to his conquest chart, he would have to persuade her to open up to him on the last night of her holiday. On Friday evening, Lenny found both girls sat on a table at the far side of the ballroom. He kept popping by their table when he could but had been unable to speak to them until all the usual Friday night activities had finished. He sat next to them and asked them why they didn't step up for the "Battle of the Planets" games. He was privately hoping to see Chrissie throw some of her clothes into the line for the last game. The girls said they were too shy to participate but they really enjoyed watching the *Purplecoat Show*. Lenny said 'What even the *Mother I Die* sketch?' They admitted they didn't understand the point of it until they saw the vertical stick of rock being measured. Chrissie then giggled at their unintentional pun but it was drowned out by Val's cheeky infectious laugh. Once she'd calmed down, Val confessed that she thought Callum looked good in doctor's uniform, even when he was sliding across the stage. Lenny sensed her keenness and said he'd ask Callum to join the three of them for a chat. Chrissie said 'That's a good idea' and both girls smiled at one another. Callum didn't take any persuading when asked and the conversation flowed from the moment the four of them were sat together at the table.

Lenny's shift ended a half-hour before Callum's so, while his mate was busy chatting to Val, Lenny asked Chrissie if he could walk her back to her chalet. She accepted the offer with a knowing smile. Soon after, she was undressed and in bed waiting for Lenny to join her. He pulled back the sheets and gazed at her body before lying against her. He was amazed how voluptuous she was - her breasts were the largest of any of the girls he'd been with. The feel of them pressing against his chest added a new dimension to any love making he'd previously experienced. After they finished, Lenny said 'Callum seemed to be getting on well with Val tonight'. Chrissie said 'I'm not at all surprised. Val told me she really fancied Callum, especially after seeing him in that doctor's uniform. If he felt the same about her, he'll have a night he'll never forget'. 'Why?' 'Because Val is a nymphomaniac!' Lenny once again felt the pleasure of Chrissie's breasts vibrating against his chest in rhythm with her laughter.

Lenny and Chrissie stopped laughing when they heard male and female noises from outside the chalet. They lay dead still and pretended to be asleep as the door opened and Val invited a man in. Val didn't put a light on but she could just about see that her roommate was in bed with someone. They weren't moving so Val assumed they were fast asleep after doing the deed. She tried to close the door quietly so as to not awaken them but it squeaked as she did so. Stifled giggles were followed by the shuffling of clothes being taken off in the dark. Lenny recognised Callum's laugh and was desperate to say 'Wotcher CC, Zezeze!' but didn't want to put him off so he and Chrissie stayed silent while the sounds of grunting and groaning built up and continued for what seemed like an hour or more. Lenny was highly impressed by the stamina of his friend and Val certainly lived up to the reputation that Chrissie had divulged to him.

The next morning, the couples looked across at one another as they awoke but there was no time for embarrassment or further activity. Callum and Lenny had to get dressed and run down the hill to the purple flat to quickly change out of their uniform. About half way down the hill, a familiar looking car was driving up towards them. As it drove past, Eric Arden looked out of the open window, recognised Lenny and Callum and visibly tutted while shaking his head. He'd noticed that the two so-called *rookie Purplecoat*s were still in their evening gear from the night before thus revealing that they had been entertaining overnight. He probably wouldn't have envisaged that they'd been entertaining in the same chalet!

Lenny and Callum wouldn't have missed that night of passion for anything but they were nonetheless concerned that Eric might reprimand them for their actions. Never mind - there was no time to worry about what might be - they were too busy changing out of their evening uniform and getting back up to the dining room for the breakfast send off for guests leaving that day. They spotted Chrissie and Val and, as soon as they'd all had breakfast, the two couples met up in a quiet corner to privately kiss, whisper and laugh about their memorable night together. Such was the affection that Lenny and Callum felt for these girls that they offered to carry their bags to the station and see them off on their train home.

Big Al was driving the minibus to and from Churston station. Lenny and Callum knew that Chrissie and Val's train was scheduled to leave at 11am so worked out that, even if it was running a little late, there should still be plenty of time for Al to get them back to the purple flat to change into their day uniform then run up to reception to start their shift at 1pm.

Big Al got everyone to Churston station by 10:45 but there was quite a crowd on both platforms. Callum asked the porter what the big occasion was and was told it was the first time the local railway had laid on a classic steam special that would continue all the way to Paddington station. When Lenny heard this, he was in dreamland - his favourite transport vehicle and him and his mate saying farewell to beautiful girls that they'd spent the previous night with. He smiled and said to Callum 'Wow, CC - life couldn't get better, could it?'

There was just enough time for Big Al to take photos of the four of them on the station before the puff, puff, puff of the train was heard and all other cameras were pointed toward it. The engine was a classic LNER A3 - the same class as the famous 'Flying Scotsman.' The train was resplendent with authentic 50's carriages but this meant there were fewer doors than on modern carriages. When the old carriage doors were opened there was a mad rush to board the train. Train enthusiasts had less baggage than the holidaymakers so they jumped into the first seats that were empty. Callum and Lenny followed Chrissie and Val through the doors and along the central aisle while carrying their luggage. There were no seats left and very little space for luggage. They had to climb over bags that had been plonked in the aisle in order to put the girls' luggage down in the middle of the carriage. They kissed the girls to say farewell before turning back toward the exit doors, just as the sound of a whistle could be heard. Unfortunately, more baggage and holidaymakers were now blocking their exit and, by the time they got back to the doors, the train had already chugged out of the station. The girls had caught the train but the train had caught the boys! Callum grimaced with shock and said 'LE, we're in big trouble!' Lenny grinned back and said 'Zezeze CC - what do we do now?!' They returned to the girls and the four of them laughed at their predicament. The steam engine chugged its smoke over the beaches of Broadsands and Goodrington Sands but didn't stop at either station. For the second time that day, the boys were concerned that they might end up being sacked for their actions. Every second felt like an embarrassing minute as the train continued to speed through stations and they felt everyone's eyes on them and their hot red faces. If this train wasn't due to stop until Paddington station, they would still be trapped on it when they were due to start their shift on reception at 1pm. They toyed with the idea of pulling the emergency cord but thought they would be in even more trouble if they resorted to the desperate measure of stopping a train in full flow, especially a heavy classic steam train with a hundred or more enthusiasts and holidaymakers on board.

Thankfully, the train's next stop turned out to be Paignton station and not Paddington station. As it slowed down, Lenny and Callum made sure their exit route was clear before kissing the girls for their final goodbye and getting off the train before even more passengers on the platform waiting to board could push them back.

Callum went up to Paignton's stationmaster to sort out the return journey. The stationmaster recognised Callum, even out of uniform, as he had worked so many shifts at the station, welcoming Funtime guests throughout the season. Callum explained what had happened and, after everyone had a good laugh, the station master allowed them to jump on the next train back without tickets.

Mike and Tricia were standing on the platform at Churston station displaying signs saying 'Welcome to *Funtime Seaview* Guests.' They were there to greet any guests that had arrived on the early train so were shocked to see Lenny and Callum get off out of uniform. Callum explained half the story - they'd been carrying bags onto the London bound train for departing guests and unfortunately got stuck on the train. Lenny chipped in 'We did well to get back as quickly as we did!' Tricia laughed and Mike grunted, half believing their story before he walked off to board the next train to Paignton and meet new guests arriving there.

Big Al was in the car park waiting in the minibus and was relieved to see them. He said 'I didn' zay anythin to anyone but was tizzicky with worry - I waz zertin you'd be zo many miles away traipsin yer way to Landin n getting a good thraiping if you ever returned!' They explained what had happened as Al sped them back to the purple flat. Al kindly waited while they changed into their day uniform then took them up the hill to drop them off at reception in the nick of time for the official start of their shift.

Eric didn't make a fuss about seeing Lenny and Callum sneaking back to the purple flat in the previous night's uniform and Mike didn't make a fuss about them getting stuck on the train, even though he probably spoke to Paignton's station master and got the full story. They were all probably thankful that the *rookies* hadn't run off with the guests and had the wherewithal to make their own way back quickly.

Once August had passed by, the number of visitors dropped dramatically as Wrinkly Weeks 3 and 4 bookended Weeks 1 and 2 from the start of the season.

Pensioners took over from families occupying *Seaview* chalets and the attention of the *Purplecoats* changed to accommodate this. Lenny and Callum hoped there wouldn't be a repeat of the type of incident encountered in the first week of the season - a fatality like poor Mr Gordon. The chances of this happening were perhaps lessened by the fact that the bunny girls were no longer around. Kenny had said *Goodbye* to Di and Vi when they left for a more lucrative contract as Bunnies at London's Playboy Club. They would soon be serving food and drinks to high roller members and their guests. Di and Vi also told their new employers that they were willing and eager to be featured in a future Playboy magazine, separately or in the same photo shoot. Jill was pleased to see the back of Di and Vi as it meant Kenny would no longer have them as a tempting distraction. She wasn't sure if he'd already been tempted but was willing to give him a second or maybe third chance to get their relationship back to how well it had been before the girls arrived.

Some of the more energetic competitions and sports activities were cancelled. This meant that Lenny had more time on his hands to chase his prey but was forced to return to a familiar hunting ground to go after his next conquest – his female colleagues. Lenny had no intention of getting back with Connie – there was too much water under the bridge and the love boat they'd boarded and jumped off sailed elsewhere long ago never to return. He was therefore happy to hear that she was now going out with the chef who took over from her brother. Lenny had spoken to him a few times and he seemed a nice enough guy so he was pleased for them both. He was also relieved that she would unlikely be hitching back up with Damien when the season ended. Fate seemed to be working satisfactorily: two people had grown more closely together and he himself had certainly had a good time doing what Damien had told Connie he was doing the night everything changed - playing the field.

Lenny was attracted to a sexy blonde barmaid called Lily as soon as he spotted her working at the *Inn Paradise*. One evening she noticed him ogling her. After serving drinks to punters of all ages over two years, she was used to getting plenty of attention. Ignoring his roving eyes she said 'Where's your mate tonight?' Lenny said 'My mate?' 'Yeah, the other Purplecoat you usually hang around with.' 'Oh. You mean Callum.' 'I guess. So where is he?' 'He's in London staying with his parents overnight.' Lily said 'My. That's a lot of traveling for one night back home?' She ended the sentence with the hint of a question, attempting to provoke an answer. It had the desired effect as Lenny divulged 'Callum's been summoned to appear in court tomorrow morning but he'll be back by the end of tomorrow night … unless he gets locked up of course!' She played along with Lenny's joke by asking 'Has he murdered an unruly guest?!' Lenny completed the explanation with 'No guests were involved, ha ha. Callum had to attend court to answer to some sort of speeding infringement from before the season started'.

Lily was clearly up for a laugh and the two of them enjoyed chatting over the bar about things they had in common, including spending some of their childhood in North London. When her bar colleagues weren't looking, Lily sneaked a few drinks to Lenny without charging him for them. He was delighted to accept free drinks, especially from someone as desirable as Lily. Encouraged by the alcohol, Lenny flirted with her and posed a hypothetical question: 'If you could have any booze in the world what would it be?' Lily thought long and hard about it and said 'I'd love to try a new Italian fizzy drink I've heard of. It's called Asti Spumante but they didn't stock it here. Never one to miss an opportunity, Lenny found out that they were both free the following afternoon so offered to take her into town and buy her a bottle that they could taste privately at his room in the purple flat. She realised Lenny had an ulterior motive but he persuaded her to go along with his proposal by saying it was the least he could do after she had sneaked free drinks to him.

Lily met Lenny outside the purple flat at the start of their afternoon off. They ambled into Brixham for what they laughingly called *the Asti huntie* and elbowed each other when they spotted a bottle at the first establishment they ventured in to. Lenny could only just about afford the one bottle but noted that it was way cheaper than the champagne bottles displayed alongside it. He'd dodged a bullet there. Once back in Lenny's flat, she sat on his bed while he got some plastic cups from the kitchen. While Lenny was trying to work out how to open the bottle, she pointed at the single bed opposite and asked him if he shared his room with anyone. He confessed that he shared it with Callum and, for some reason, added that they get along really well – like best friends. After unwrapping the foil, he twisted and pulled at the cork until it exploded out of his hand and hit the ceiling. Despite the shock, he managed to keep hold of the bottle and pour the fizzy liquid into the cups Lily had placed in front of him without too much spillage. Their first taste of Asti Spumante was bliss and they lay on the bed together chatting and laughing. The drink was so relaxing that they eventually ignored the cups and simply swigged the nectar from the bottle. By the time the bottle had been emptied, they were well sozzled.

Lily looked at Lenny with twinkling eyes that confirmed she was ready to move on from social chit chat to something more carnal. She asked Lenny if he was sure they wouldn't be disturbed. He understood why she asked and tried to contain his excitement when he assured her that all the *Purplecoat*s who stayed in the other rooms were busy working up at the *Seaview*. 'What about your roommate?' Lenny reminded her 'Relax. Don't forget, Callum's in London for his day in court and won't be back until late this evening'. Unbeknownst to the two of them, Callum was not in London. He was currently speeding through Brixham! His court case finished much earlier than expected, so he managed to catch an earlier non-stop express train to Paignton then, because his speeding fine was less than he'd expected, treated himself to a taxi ride for the last leg of his journey.

When Callum got back to the purple flat, all seemed quiet, so he opened the door to the bedroom without knocking. He was greeted by the sight of Lily's slender and naked back with her long hair shaking from side to side and her bottom bouncing up and down on top of Lenny like a cowgirl riding a stallion. As they turned to see what the noise was, Callum chuckled and said 'It's good to be back, LE - Zezeze!' Without pausing, he dropped his bag on his bed and thoughtfully left the two of them to finish what they were doing while he went into the kitchen to put a pot of tea on. Lily looked confused more than embarrassed and asked why Callum had just called her *Ellie Zezeze* when her name is *Lily Cicily*. Luckily, it didn't put either of them off their rhythm, even when Lenny repeated the word Zezeze!

Dale wanted to do something nice for his girlfriend Sue's upcoming birthday but it had to fit in with everyone's busy work schedule. Sue loved Indian food but spicy food, especially curries, were not the forte of the *Seaview*'s team of chefs and it was quite a trek to get to the nearest decent authentic restaurant. In any case, Dale had bragged that he could make a better curry himself. Sue reminded him of this on several occasions until he finally offered to make one in the downstairs kitchen of the purple flat to celebrate her birthday with their friends. Sue insisted that he also share it with the rest of the *Purplecoat* team as they would feel left out if they weren't included, especially as they would undoubtedly hear and smell it being made.

Dale had used his favourite recipe a few times for up to four people but now had to multiply all the quantities in his recipe to allow for twenty or more diners. The kitchen would be too small for all the diners to eat together so he had to allow for a maximum of four or five people at a time eating in separate shifts. Each group could help themselves to a portion of rice and a portion of curry. After they'd eaten, they would have to wash up their used plates and utensils so that the next group could follow on and do the same.

To prepare for the day, Dale borrowed the minibus and took Sue into Torquay to purchase all the ingredients needed plus large stirrers and serving utensils as well as two of the biggest saucepans they could find.

The night before the big day, Dale slaved away in the kitchen preparing the ingredients, marinating the meat and letting it cook slowly overnight in the biggest pot that just about perched on the hob. The aroma of curry permeated every room in the flat and the *Purplecoat*s were tempted to help themselves to a cheeky taste. They resisted the urge as they didn't dare upset Dale. The next morning, Dale continued cooking the curry while the other *Purplecoat*s went off to work for the day, no doubt smelling of Indian spices. He stirred the big pot, prepared selected vegetables and mixed them in with the curry, then started boiling the rice. He and Sue had the whole day off so that they could be together while he finished cooking the curry. They would be the first to try it with their chosen best friends early that evening while Dale's colleagues were having a spice free dinner in the dining room then working in the ballroom.

Later on, Dale, Sue and their friends ventured up to the *Inn Paradise* to walk off the food and quench their thirst. Dale told Mike that there was plenty of food to go round so the rest of the *Purplecoat* team could help themselves so long as they give the pots a stir and clear up their mess when they finish.

Jason and the *Purplecoat* girls went into the kitchen first then Mike, Callum and Lenny took their turn. When Lenny saw what was left in the pots, he said Dale wasn't kidding when he told Mike there was plenty of food to go round. Even after they'd had their share there was still enough remaining at the bottom of the saucepans to feed a half dozen more.

The three of them were full but Mike saw how much Lenny enjoyed the food and told him he might as well eat what was left otherwise it would only be thrown away. Lenny was always up for a dare but this was almost too much of a challenge as he forced mouthful after mouthful down. Lenny had the feeling he would explode if he swallowed one more grain of rice so he left that in its pan and emptied the remainder of the curry onto his plate. It took a lot of effort but he stuffed the last spoonful of curry into his mouth and chewed and chewed at it trying to get it down. Just at that moment, Dale and Sue walked into the kitchen with two men Lenny recognised instantly. Dale had been bragging about his curry to his table tennis buddies and promised them that they could finish it off. Unfortunately, all Dale could now see was a layer of half dried rice in one pot, a few dregs of his curry in the other pot and a red-faced Lenny with his cheeks bulging.

Lenny tried to but couldn't hold back a burp as he apologised after admitting that he'd just eaten what was left of the curry. Dale couldn't have been more furious with Lenny but Mike didn't help matters by keeping quiet instead of explaining that he had actually told Lenny to finish the food. Mike may have misunderstood what Dale had suggested to him at the *Inn Paradise*. Alternatively, he may have intended to set Lenny up and annoy Dale at the same time. If that was the case, his plan worked.

It was nearing the end of the summer season and all the staff had got used to all of the different personalities, quirks and accents of their colleagues. Some even craved their company for their last few days working together. They all wondered how much they would miss them and this life when back in civvy street. Conversations were based on the realisation that they would all have to go back to the world they lived in outside the camp. Some looked forward to seeing family and friends, others were dreading the drudgery of finding and getting an ordinary job.

Callum Lenny and Kenny had a last *Lemon Top* scrumpy together at the Three Elms and recalled all the highlights and lowlights of the season. Callum said that the three of them had been through so much together that they were now much more than just friends - they were *Number One* mates. They vowed to always call themselves *Number One*s whenever they got together thereafter, as well as their initials CC, LE and KT. LE asked his *Number One* mates if they would want to return to the Seaview or any other Funtime holiday centre year after year. KT said he'll go wherever he can make the most money and still have a good time. CC said he'd maybe do one or two more seasons but definitely wouldn't carry on into old age like Bill or even middle aged like Mike.

The *Purplecoat*s 'slush fund' built up over the season from bingo and other fiddles had raised enough money to cover the cost of an end of season treat: Evening meals at a posh local restaurant for all the team. They were late booking a table and the restaurant could only accommodate them all on what would be the last Tuesday night of the summer season. The senior *Purplecoat*s knew that the only problem was that someone would have to miss the night out and look after all of that evening's entertainment in the ballroom, including hosting the cabaret acts. Jason craftily didn't mention this when he lined up his team and asked if any of them would rather have their share of the money than go out for a meal. Lenny quickly put his hand up for the cash, not realising the implications of staying behind.

Jason asked Mike and Dale to hang around while the others went off to carry out their duties. Once out of earshot he told them he was concerned that Lenny might not have sufficient skills to look after things while they were away and wondered if one of them should stay behind as well. They looked at each other and agreed that it wasn't necessary for one of them to stay behind. Dale said 'Lenny should surely be okay as a host for one night, after all, he's seen these acts introduced almost twenty times.' In reality, they secretly thought Lenny might be a bit flaky but put any concerns to one side for different reasons. Dale saw it as a way of getting Lenny back for the curry incident and Mike was desperate to enjoy a well-deserved all expenses night out. Jason accepted their advice but suggested they all get back from the night out as soon as possible in case they were needed.

The last Tuesday night of the season soon arrived. Lenny and Callum were deep in their own thoughts as they got dressed alongside each other for their very different evenings. Lenny got into his *Purplecoat* evening uniform while Callum got dressed in his smartest night out clothes, including the purple round collar shirt that Lenny had given him. Unlike his senior colleagues, Callum felt guilty about going out with the rest of the *Purplecoat* team and leaving Lenny to host the evening's entertainment on his own. He knew Lenny wasn't a confident host which was why he'd taken over those types of roles from him early into the season. He was genuinely concerned and asked Lenny if he wanted him to stay behind and help on the night. Lenny said 'Thanks for the offer CC but you go ahead and enjoy yourself – I'll be fine.' In reality, Lenny was only just starting to get nervous about running the show on his own but didn't want to spoil anyone else's night out so kept his feelings to himself, after all, what could possibly go wrong?

The evening started off well when the artistes for the first cabaret - an acrobatic act - arrived in good time. They had only recently been added to the cabaret schedule so were dismayed that only a rookie *Purplecoat* like Lenny was there to meet them. Lenny explained that the rest of the team were having their one night out of the season so he was running things on his own. They grunted as if they felt worthy of better treatment but insisted on a couple of things from Lenny: He should wait for their signal from the dressing room door to confirm they were dressed and ready then be sure to introduce them as Alex and Anthea. Lenny recalled that they had called themselves The *Acrobatic A's* the previous week. They changed their name from one week to the next on purpose. It was to prevent guests who were staying for more than one week from complaining that they'd seen the same act twice even though that was exactly what they would be doing, albeit under a different name.

Lenny listened to Tony Garner's big band play a waltz for the audience to dance to but there was no way he could simply do his usual job of chatting and dancing with *Seaview*'s guests - tonight he was in sole charge and the nerves were starting to kick in.

The shout of 'Hey, Boy' from the dressing room door snapped him out of his thoughts. The acrobats gave him the nod that confirmed they were ready in got up on the stage so he stepped up on the stage and tried to compose himself by slightly swaying from side to side along with the big band's rhythms. All too soon, the music finished and now it was Lenny's turn to address the audience. 'Hello ladies and gentlemen. We now have for your entertainment the first cabaret act of the evening. Please give a big hand for …" the audience thought he was pausing for effect when in actual fact he was having a panic attack as he couldn't remember the name of the act. He repeated "Give a big hand for …" as if something would come to him but it didn't so, as they ran up to the stage, he simply raised an arm to them and shouted "… and here they are!" The acrobats gave him a look of utter contempt so it was just as well they weren't a knife throwing act, otherwise he would have been the first target. He sneaked back to the sanctuary of the dressing room and peered through the slightly opened door as the acrobats went through their routine, seething but without any accidents. As the acrobats bowed to the audience and started to leave the stage they shouted their names as an aside to Lenny so that he could announce 'Let's hear it for … Alex and Anthea - a fabulous acrobatic act.'

Lenny tried to drum up sustained applause from the audience to encourage Alex and Anthea to come back for an encore but, with their egos deflated, they left Lenny to stew a while. Once he realised that they wouldn't be doing any encore, he managed to recover some self-respect by announcing 'There will now be a short break to allow you to top up your drinks before the start of the next cabaret act - the fantastic Rosa Lee – then the amazing voice of Ray Starlight will top off the evening'.

Lenny knocked at the door of the dressing rooms to apologise for his less than professional hosting but Alex and Anthea were still getting dressed and more like *Angry A's* than *Acrobatic A's* as they curtly told him to come back in five minutes, only they used much cruder words to say the same thing. Lenny used the break to go to the buffet lounge and meet Rosa Lee. She was a small, tubby woman who generally sat drinking a pint glass of milk with her legs wide apart under a thankfully long dress. This eccentric appearance belied a long career in the entertainment business. She started off as a *Purplecoat* then moved on to become an exuberant and accomplished comedienne and singer who was now well known for playing a witch on a popular kid's television show. She could rightfully be called a seasoned professional but she would be a real star for Lenny this evening.

Lenny went to shake the hand off Rosa Lee by way of introduction but she instead kept hold of her glass of milk in her hand and swallowed the lot before plonking the empty glass on the table, wiping her mouth and extending her sticky hand out for Lenny to shake it. As their hands stuck together, she asked him to get her another pint of milk and carry it to the dressing room with her stage clothes.

Thirty miles away, headlining cabaret singer Ray Starlight was going down a storm at the prestigious Beaumont Hall holiday centre. It had rightfully earned a reputation as the poshest of all the *Funtime holiday centres* and its high paying guests expected the highest levels of service and attention. They demanded encore after encore and the *Purplecoat* host forced Ray Starlight to perform three additional songs before he'd exhausted his repertoire. Finally, he returned to the stage and simply bowed in acknowledgement to signify that he appreciated their enthusiasm but he hadn't any more songs to give them.

Once back in the dressing room, Ray changed out of his black dinner jacket and tuxedo stage outfit into his equally smart Italian three-piece suit. Once dressed, he felt for the hidden ledge in the dressing room and scooped up his belongings. His small change seemed out of place alongside his soft leather wallet embossed with the name Ray and a luxury designer watch. As he glanced at the hands of the watch, he realised he'd gone twenty minutes past his agreed time.

Ray called the *Purplecoat* host into the dressing room. The host saw the coins in the star's hand and thought he was getting a tip. Instead, Ray asked him why he kept bringing him back on stage. The host hid his disappointment and said 'Beaumont Hall guests are the crème de la crème so it's a matter of quid pro quo.' He didn't realise he was mixing French and Latin phrases but Ray Starlight looked blank as he didn't understand either phrase. The host simplified his point by saying 'We gotta give these people their money's worth.' Ray Starlight replied 'That's just as well but now I'm gonna be late for my next gig at the *Seaview* holiday centre.' The host didn't have any concerns about a rival holiday centre but promised to phone them straight away to let them know he had been delayed.

As the host went to phone the *Seaview*, Ray Starlight put the change in his waistcoat, picked up his stage outfit and walked the short distance to the car park.

Ray Starlight's chauffeur was looking under the bonnet of his limousine with a concerned look on his face. The chauffeur had always been instructed to start the engine when Ray Starlight had finished his encore - this would ensure that the temperature in the car was not too hot or cold by the time his very important passenger was ready to travel. The chauffeur could just about hear the show from his reserved space in the car park so turned the ignition off each time he heard Ray Starlight come back on stage to perform another encore. As the driver flicked the ignition on for a third time, a dull click was heard instead of the sound of a roaring engine. The extra flicking on and off of the ignition and heating may have overloaded the system or run the battery down but, whatever the reason, the car would not start. Ray Starlight sat in the back of the limousine frustrated at the passing minutes while the chauffeur went to get help. Beaumont Hall staff members and interested guests took a look at the problem but no amount of re-clipping or fiddling would get the car started. Eventually, the chauffeur got the holiday centre's receptionist to phone the RAC. The breakdown and recovery company estimated that they should get a patrol mechanic there within ten minutes. The receptionist also had the good sense to phone her counterpart at the *Seaview* to give an update on the delay.

Jill called out to Lenny in the coffee lounge, while he was carrying out a pint of milk for Rosa Lee and a coffee fix for himself. She felt sad for him as she told him the bad news that Ray Starlight had a problem with his car and would be at least an hour late getting to the *Seaview* for the final cabaret act of the night.

Lenny had a quick sip of his coffee before leaving the remains at the table where Rosa Lee was sat. He needed both hands free to carry her pint of milk and stage clothes as he escorted her to the dressing room.

Lenny was cursing his misfortune that tonight of all nights there was a major problem with the star of the show but was relieved to see that the dressing room was empty - he wouldn't have been able to take any more grief from the acrobatic act over his inability to remember their stage names. He closed the door of the dressing room behind him and stood in front of Rosa Lee with her stage clothes hanging over his left arm and her glass of milk in his right hand. Before he could place either of them down, Rosa Lee started taking her clothes off. With no sense of embarrassment, she undressed down to the largest bra and knickers that Lenny had ever seen on flesh. After scooping up her stage clothes from Lenny's left arm and putting them on, she grabbed for the glass of milk and took a few large glugs - she loved her milk.

Lenny thought it wise to mention that the next act was running late but didn't know how long the delay would be. Ever the trooper, Rosa Lee assured Lenny that she had plenty of material and would just keep going until he tells her to stop by chopping his hand across the front of his neck as if he was slitting his throat.

To play for time in case he ran out of it later, Lenny waited as long as he could before giving the thumbs up to Tony Garner to confirm that Rosa Lee was ready to come on stage. As soon as the band's dance number ended, Lenny took the sheets for Rosa Lee's musical numbers up onto the stage and handed them to the bandleader to hand out to his bandmembers. Once he was sure everyone was ready, he grabbed the microphone and turned to address the audience. 'And now ladies and gentlemen I'm delighted to introduce your second act of the evening and what a treat it is. She's an exuberant and accomplished comedienne, singer and star of the popular kid's TV show 'Willow the witch'. It's none other than Miss .. Rosa .. Lee!' Rosa Lee walked up to the stage to wild applause and got straight into her act with some quips and anecdotes before cueing the band and launching into her first singing number. Rosa Lee gave Lenny some respite but, after performing for an hour and a half, there was still no sign of or word from the top of the bill.

Ray Starlight was sweating in the back of the limousine. Thankfully, the RAC patrol mechanic had turned up within the ten minutes promised and managed to get the limousine going with a temporary fix. The chauffeur was now speeding him toward the *Seaview* and estimated that they would get there almost two hours late. Under the circumstances, and to avoid any more delays, Ray Starlight decided to go straight on stage in his three-piece suit without changing into his black dinner jacket and tuxedo stage outfit.

Rosa Lee and Lenny were also sweating. Rosa Lee was sweating while performing a mammoth session that was twice as long as any other show she'd given. Lenny was sweating in fear of what to do if she ran out of ideas before the top of the bill turned up. They were both relieved to see Ray Starlight stride in with his music sheets but no stage outfit. He mopped his brow with his handkerchief as Lenny introduced himself, shook his clammy hand and offered to get him a quick drink of water while he got his breath back in the dressing room. Ray said he needed a whisky before he went on so Lenny ran up to the bar and got one for each of them. They both swigged the drink down in one go then Lenny gave Rosa Lee the sign to say her performance could end as soon as she wanted.

The audience were getting a bit weary of Rosa Lee's show but heartily applauded her after Lenny pointed out that she had gone above and beyond after the star act was delayed by more than an hour. Needless to say, Lenny didn't push for an encore and handed out Ray Starlight's music sheets to the band before swiftly introducing him.

Ray Starlight started with a masterful rendition of *It Had to Be You* that segued into *I Got Rhythm*. He wasn't wearing the usual crooner's black dinner jacket and tuxedo stage outfit but could certainly belt out a tune.

Lenny went back into the dressing room to see if Rosa Lee needed anything. He found her slumped exhausted on a chair in the dressing room with her legs even wider apart than usual. He tried to ignore the view as he thanked her for being a real star and saving the evening from becoming a disaster. She modestly said 'that's showbusiness' then insisted Lenny get her another pint of milk with a large brandy chaser. Lenny brought both drinks back, along with a large brandy for himself - he thought he deserved it after such a fraught night, especially after seeing Rosa Lee's body and her underwear soaking wet from her superhuman efforts while helping her change back out of her stage clothes into her day clothes.

Rosa Lee finished her drinks then pecked Lenny on the cheek before leaving him to watch Ray Starlight belt out more singalong favourites from the Great American Song Book, including *Fly Me to The Moon*, *The Lady Is A Tramp*, *That Old Black Magic*, *One For My Baby*, *Cheek To Cheek* and *I Get A Kick Out Of You*.

Big Al drove the *Seaview*'s minibus up to the reception area and dropped off the *Purplecoat* team. They were all merry after enjoying a good meal and night out together. Secretly, they also harboured guilt and bad feelings about leaving Lenny to host the evening on his own. As they got out of the minibus, they could hear that the headline act was still singing. It was well past the deadline when cabaret acts should have finished so they wondered why Lenny had allowed the show to go on so late.

On stage, Ray Starlight got all the audience to sing along to his big classic final number: *You'll Never Walk Alone*. As soon as the song ended, Lenny jumped up onto the stage and said 'Let's all show our appreciation for Ray Starlight - an amazing singer and performer.' Some of the audience had already left their seats to get back to their chalets but those that remained heartily applauded.

Unfortunately, a night of misfortunes still had a sting in the tail. Ray Starlight had forgotten that he had a lot of loose change in his waistcoat so when he bowed forward to thank the audience for their applause, all the coins fell out onto the floor of the stage and rolled off in all directions. Lenny tried to help Ray Starlight recover as much money as they could.

The rest of the *Purplecoat* team happened to walk into the ballroom from their night out only to see a sight they never expected to see in their worst nightmares. The star act and the *Purplecoat* host were crawling around the floor while the audience were laughing hysterically at their rear ends. In bending down quickly, Ray Starlight had ripped the seam going up the back of his trousers and the audience could see his underwear through the gap - thank God he hadn't gone commando. Jason audibly gasped at the sight. Mike said 'What on earth has Lenny done?' Dale snarled 'What a prize cock up', the *Purplecoat* girls laughed nervously under the effects of their drink but Callum shook his head and said to himself 'LE, LE!' as he felt very sorry for his embarrassed pal.

Kenny was always looking for opportunities to make money but his resolve was never keener than in the last week of the season. The visitor numbers had dropped significantly so he was bound to get less commission on sales of his photos and merchandise plus the racing fiddle he'd perfected. He therefore needed a quick alternative and came up with a devious plan. On the last Friday afternoon of the season, he deliberately sat right next to the slot machine in the buffet lounge just as the regular man – Vernon - arrived to collect the weekly takings. The man said 'Hi, Kenny' but got a gruff mumbled reply. This wasn't the usual response he received from the normally cheerful photographer so he asked ''Why the glum face? 'Are you okay?' Kenny slightly nodded his head from side to side. Vernon persisted: What's the matter, mate?' Kenny lied 'Well if you must know, I'm pissed off because I've lost way too much money on your bloody slot machine this season!' The man fell for Kenny's story and felt sorry for him. He'd had a very lucrative twenty-odd weeks so thought he'd do Kenny a big favour. Instead of emptying the machine and turning it off for the season, Vernon scooped only half of the takings into his money bag. He then fiddled with a few settings inside the machine. As he went to leave, he gave Kenny a few spare coins and whispered in his ear 'Go play the machine as soon as I've gone but before anyone else has a go!' Kenny did as he was directed and immediately hit the jackpot.

Another *Funtime* summer season had ended and the 'Seaview Class of 72' were preparing to leave the holiday centre they'd lived in for five months or more and the friends they'd got to know, love or hate to return to life outside this bubble.

Lenny and Callum were packing their bags alongside each other in their bedroom at the purple flat. They both laughed when Lenny showed Callum the large box of condoms he'd purchased before the season started. As he placed the unopened box into his case, he wondered when he would finally break the seal on the cellophane packaging! He then opened the pad and skimmed through his *Conquest Chart*. It reminded him of the mind-blowing volume and variety of sexual partners he'd been with. He was a naive boy when he first arrived at the *Seaview*. Now he was leaving the holiday centre with more experiences than any red-blooded male could dream of. He thought back to the start of the season and the way Ruby started his journey to sexual awakening. His time with Connie was bittersweet due to the way their relationship ended but he understood and agreed with the saying - *It's better to have loved and lost than never to have loved at all*. He spent the rest of the season enjoying himself with no boundaries or consequences. What an eventful season it had been - it was going to be very boring going back to the outside world. He silently thanked Sir Albert for creating these wonderful Funtime pleasure palaces, Birdy for having pretty much blind faith in him and sending him to work at the picturesque Seaview holiday centre, Jason and his colleagues for helping him find his way in the Purplecoat team and the Number Ones for being his new best mates. As he went to put the pad containing the *Conquest Chart* into his case, he suddenly felt ashamed of it. He realised that it was demeaning to all the girls who'd given themselves to him, so, he tore the relevant pages out of the pad, ripped them up and placed them on a heap in the back garden and burned them to ashes. He felt as if he was cremating their secrets in honour of the love or generosity that they gave to him or whoever they thought the guy in his purple uniform was.

Callum was deep in his own thoughts. He still hung on to the hope that he could persuade Pauline to dump her unworthy boyfriend so that he could become something more than her reliable and supportive friend. Perhaps Jackie could help him accomplish this when they all spend time together on the long journey back to London.

Big Al filled the *Funtime* minibus with *Seaview* staff and took them to Paignton station to drop them off with their luggage. Lenny, Callum and Tricia were the only *Purplecoat*s in the group along with Seaview waitresses, bar staff and kitchen lads – none of Tommy's gang thankfully. Tricia's boyfriend, Geoff, was there waiting to take Tricia back to his hotel. He still had a week to run on his band's contract so, while Tricia's colleagues were preparing to travel back to their homes, she would be moving down the road to the hotel Geoff and his band were working in. Tricia recalled the night they first stayed at the hotel when they first came to work on the English Riveria, more than twenty weeks ago. Their relationship survived the summer season, despite sleeping 10 miles away from each other most nights. She hoped the hotel would once again let them use the matrimonial room. The champagne bucket had remained empty then but she wondered if returning to the romantic surroundings might persuade Geoff to put a bottle of fizz in the bucket this time and maybe make a proposal?

Everyone was sad as Big Al said goodbye to each male and female with a hug, kiss or both. They all waved as he drove off then looked at each other and wondered if they would be returning next year or if they would be even asked back for another season. They had all got to know each other in so many different ways, plus the thousands of holidaymakers that had visited the *Seaview* over the summer season, that they could undoubtedly have written their own books about their experience.

Tricia and Callum had worked plenty of holidaymaker meet and greet shifts at Paignton station and were on friendly terms with the station master. He offered to take a group photo of all the gang. It took him a while to take photos from all of the cameras that were handed to him but it was nice to know that a memento of the day and the gang's friendship would be captured on camera films traveling up and down the country. In days, weeks, months and years to come, the printed photographs from these films could well be brought out to be reminisced over or laughed at amongst old and new friends and families. The station master even allowed the gang to leave all their luggage in his office so that they could go into town for a final drink together and maybe some lunch before they needed to come back to catch their respective trains home.

After drinks at a few town centre pubs, the gang were hungry and someone had the bright idea of getting a trendy Chinese meal. The Golden Rickshaw was the first Chinese restaurant they found on the way back toward the station so they all piled in and asked the tiny waitress if they could look at the menu. As they surveyed the options, the drinks consumed at the pubs had got through many of them. Their bladders were bursting so they asked where the toilets were. The waitress pointed to the corridor at the back of the restaurant and a half dozen lads slipped away to relieve themselves. This made everyone else want to go, but there were only two single toilets at the back so a queue soon developed. By the time everyone had visited the toilets, the majority of the gang had decided the prices were too steep for them so handed the menus back to the waitress and started walking out of the door. The waitress was furious that they were all leaving without spending any money and said in a high-pitched voice 'You cheeky bruddy monkeys - you think this is a bruddy public convenience?!' After going for a cheaper option at the fish and chip shop, all of the gang made their way back to Paignton station.

Callum was yet again looking for Pauline so asked Jackie if she'd seen her. Jackie sighed and pointed to the station's phone box. Pauline was clearly shouting at someone down the telephone line. Callum's thoughts took over once again.

> Callum imagined Pauline was once again arguing with her boyfriend but this time he was giving her a hard time about them both getting back together after working so many weeks apart at different holiday camps. She would be upset and run up to Callum. He would put his arms around her while she was telling him what had upset her. He would console her as he had done many times during the season. This time, she would hold him tight and ask him to be her saviour then they would be happy together forever thereafter.

A dig in the rib from Lenny shook Callum back into the real world. Lenny had been telling him a joke and realised Callum had stopped listening when he didn't respond to the punch-line, ironically. Pauline rejoined the group just as their train arrived. Everyone picked up their bags to board the London-bound train. Callum tried to shuffle over to be near Pauline, but, whenever he got close, she seemed to turn away and talk to someone else. She even chose to sit in a separate compartment so he made do by sitting with Lenny and Jackie.

On the train journey from Paignton, A variety of emotions were cursing through all of the *Seaview* gang. Some were looking forward to getting back to their friends and family. Others were feeling sad that the season had ended and wondered if they would lose touch with these colleagues that had become friends. Would they be offered a contract for next season and would they want to or be in a position to take it? Depending on how good a time they'd had this season, would next season be better or worse?

Lenny and Jackie were doing their best to keep Callum amused as they sped through the countryside but he was still hoping to have a romantic heart to heart with Pauline, otherwise this could be their last journey together. He pretended he needed to go to the toilet, just so that he could visit her compartment. Kenny and Jill were entertaining themselves in the corridor, playing cards while sat on piled up cases. Callum passed them, just as Kenny slapped his cards down with a jubilant cry of 'Full House – I win'. Pauline was sat in a compartment full of kitchen lads and bar staff but she seemed aloof in their company. Callum made small talk to the group she'd chosen to sit with and tried to bring her into the conversation, but he once again failed to get her attention. She certainly wasn't her usual bubbly self, with him or anyone else in the group. It was as if she was falling deeper and deeper into her own anxious thoughts the nearer that they got to London.

The train finally came to a screeching halt at Paddington station late in the afternoon. All of the *Seaview* gang congregated in front of the Departures Board on the concourse to check their ongoing trains and say their goodbyes. They hugged and kissed with various levels of intensity as they wondered if this would be the last moment that they would ever see each other. One by one they departed in different directions to start the next phase of their life.

Callum went to hug and kiss Pauline to show how much he cared for her but she was ignoring him and looking across the concourse for something or someone. Her face changed when she spotted a man waving at her and she dashed away from the *Seaview* gang without saying Goodbye to anyone. Callum saw her walking off hand in hand with the stranger without even looking back. Whether she left so suddenly because she thought she might burst into tears Callum would never know but he couldn't hide how upset he was feeling. Jackie saw Callum looking tearful and said 'You can say goodbye to me if you want - I'm off to get the next train from platform five.'

Callum looked at Jackie and remembered how kind she had been to him throughout the season. He also realised how beautiful she was. It was the first time he had noticed this since she'd introduced herself to him and Lenny way back on that first night at the *Inn Paradise*. Somehow, his head had been turned away from Jackie by the more glamourous Pauline. Now, at last, Callum realised that Lenny had been right all along when he told him it was folly to chase after Pauline and miss out opportunities with other girls. Could the girl he should have gone for been the one right in front of him now? He told Lenny to hang around with the group and wait for him while he helped Jackie carry her bags onto her train. He even managed to sneak onto the platform by holding her hand and pretending to be her boyfriend. It felt good. Now that Pauline was definitely out of the picture, Jackie revealed some home truths. 'You saw how Pauline didn't give you a second thought as soon as she was back in her own neck of the woods? Well, I kept telling her it was cruel to string you along'. Callum said 'Why did she do it?' Jackie explained 'She said she enjoyed the attention even though it would never amount to anything. I knew Pauline was stringing you along and teasing you but I couldn't break your heart by telling you the truth, even though I desperately wanted to.' Jackie paused as if uncertain if she should be totally honest about her feelings. They stopped outside the first open carriage door and put their bags down before she added

'I think Pauline enjoyed keeping you on a leash because she knew how I felt about you'. Callum was a little shocked and said 'How *did* you feel about me?' Jackie confessed 'God, Callum - how do you think I felt about you. How I still feel about you.' They embraced and kissed. Jackie was crying as she said 'Do you remember the day I turned up at Paignton station to sit with you while you waited for guests to arrive?' 'Yes, that's when we got a lift back from Tony Garner.' 'Well, Eric Arden's nephew, Samuel, kept asking me to go out with him but I kept turning him down as I wanted to be with you. When he persuaded Eric to take me on as a nanny, I felt I owed him something but thought I'd give you one last chance when I took the bus to Paignton station to get you on your own. I fantasised that you would ask me out then I'd take you back to my chalet for our first cuddle or whatever. Unfortunately, my fantasy went up in smoke when you kept saying *Pauline this* and *Pauline that*, fell asleep when we got a lift back then you asked to be let off at the purple flat without any recognition that I'd come all that way to sit with you. It made it easier for me to agree to go out with Samuel, but I found him to be too arrogant to be with so the relationship didn't go anywhere.' Callum realised he'd been just as cruel to Jackie as Pauline had been to him. Not only had he wasted time and energy going on about his dream girl and chasing what turned out to be an impossible dream. He had cruelly asked the one person who cared deeply for him to help chase that dream.

The guard interrupted further thoughts or conversation when he shouted 'All aboard' all too soon. Jackie stepped on to the train and Callum lifted her bags on board before clicking the door shut. She opened the carriage window and reached out her hands towards him. The guard's whistle went as Callum walked up to the window and they held hands sensitively as the train tooted and slowly moved forward. Jackie continued to hold onto Callum's hands firmly and what seemed to be a charming goodbye was becoming a bit of a challenge for his legs. Jackie seemed so deep in her thoughts that she didn't realise the train had started to speed up faster than Callum could run. He was concerned that he would soon fall over or into the train. Mercifully, Jackie let go before an accident could occur. She waved with tears in her eyes as the train click clacked away from the station. Callum waved back, now also fantasising about what sort of relationship he would have had with Jackie had Pauline not diverted all of his attention.

When Callum returned to the spot in front of the Departures Board where the rest of the gang had been, only Lenny remained, waiting for him. He said 'How did you get on saying goodbye to Jackie?' Callum said 'I think I missed out big time wasting my time with the wrong girl, LE. Chasing Pauline when I should have been with Jackie' Lenny said 'Well, CC. At least you can call Jackie to arrange to see each other soon.' Callum said 'Oomballah - I forgot to get her telephone number!' Lenny saw his Number One mate was upset and put an arm around him. He tried to lighten the mood by quipping 'Don't worry, there's always next season!' Callum, ever the pessimist, said 'We might not get invited back, LE'. Lenny reassured him by saying 'I've got a really strong feeling we *will* return to the Seaview and have many more adventures.' Both Lenny and Callum had screwed up their relationships with the opposite sex but at least they'd bonded with each other as true best friends.

Perhaps our lives are not driven by some god who guides us through but pure luck - the toss of a coin - as to how we encounter obstacles or narrowly avoid them. All we have any control over is what we do with whatever we're dealt. In many ways, the holiday centre was a microcosm of the outside world, an enclosed bubble of opportunities and mishaps, love and hate, lust and envy, life and death, faith and uncertainty but fate always plays a part.

Acknowledgements

Artwork: Ken Smith

Memory Joggers/Content Suggesters: Ken Smith, Keith Strong, Kath Kaveney and Patricia Cox

Devon Dialect Expert: John Germon

Proofreaders: All of the above, plus trusted friends

Printed in Dunstable, United Kingdom

75126820R00127